YOU'D BE HOME NOW

"As beautiful as it is raw, *You'd Be Home Now* is an unflinching tale of addiction. Vivid with fear and resplendent with truth, Kathleen Glasgow's stories will always break your heart, but so too will they give you the hope to rebuild it."

Amy Beashel, author of *The Sky is Mine*

"I absolutely loved it. An insightful and powerful story about the impact of addiction on young people and their families, filled with gut-wrenching emotion and hope."

Anna Day, author of *The Fandom*

"Raw, honest, and overflowing with feelings… Emory and her devotion to her brother, Joey, will stick with me for a very long time."

Erin Hahn, author of *You'd Be Mine*

"A love story like you've never seen. In her gripping tale of an addict-adjacent teen and the fragile ecosystem she inhabits, Kathleen Glasgow expands our hearts and invites in a little more humanity."

Val Emmich, author of *Dear Evan Hansen: The Novel*

"With heartbreaking honesty and breathtaking beauty, Kathleen Glasgow renders the invisible faces of addiction with rare humanity, giving a voice to the often-forgotten constellation of struggles reflected in the lives and love of those impacted by another's addiction."

Amber Smith, author of *The Way I Used to Be*

"Kathleen Glasgow not only nails what it's like to love someone with an addiction but humanizes the struggle of a teenage drug addict. Emory and Joey's story as devoted sister and brother will tear you apart and put you back together again."

Hayley Krischer, author of *Something Happened to Ali Greenleaf*

"Stunningly written, this is a sad and real and beautiful story. I couldn't put it down."

Perdita Cargill, author of *Take Two*

BOOKS BY KATHLEEN GLASGOW

YOU'D
BE
HOME
NOW

KATHLEEN GLASGOW

ROCK THE BOAT

This book contains material which some readers may find distressing, including discussions of a car accident, PTSD, substance abuse, addiction, and rehab.

A Rock the Boat Book

First published in Great Britain and Ireland
by Rock the Boat, an imprint of Oneworld Publications, 2021
Reprinted twice in 2021, three times in 2022, and once in 2023

Published by arrangement with Random House Children's Books,
a division of Penguin Random House LLC

ISBN 978-1-78607-969-5
ISBN 978-1-78607-970-1 (ebook)

Printed and bound in Great Britain by Clays Ltd, Elcograf S.p.A.

Oneworld Publications
10 Bloomsbury Street
London WC1B 3SR
England

To all the Emmys and Joeys:
Love remains

You'd Be Home Now

W E ARE FLYING IN the blue-black night, rain slashing the car. Trees become hands, become fingers, become teeth reaching out for us. I don't know if we make sounds, because my heart is in my ears, drowning me. The car is weightless and heavy at the same time as it smacks against the earth, bounces, rolls and rolls, and Luther Leonard is half in, half out of the splintered windshield in front of me, his sneakered feet dangling at strange angles.

I say my brother's name, but there isn't any answer.

My hands feel around the seat for the belt lock, but they quiver so badly they can't settle down. There is something I feel, but I can't tell what it is. Something in my body that is not right. Something out of place.

In the lopsided rearview mirror, my brother, Joey, is a useless thing in the backseat, splayed over Candy MontClair, blood in his hair.

I say her name.

The sounds that come from her are not words. They're raspy and wet, full and thin all at once.

I have to get out of this car. I have to tell someone. I have to get help. I have to leave this place of shattered glass and crunched metal and Luther Leonard's dangling feet, but I can't move. I can't get out.

Through the broken window comes a howling in Wolf Creek Woods. There's howling, and maybe it's me, and then I realize it isn't. It's the howl of sirens, and beams begin to fill our broken car with light.

ONE

———

Tell me, what is it you plan to do
With your one wild and precious life?

——MARY OLIVER

1

M Y SISTER, MADDIE, IS crying, her pretty face damp and
frightened. One of my legs is heavier than the other and
I don't understand and I want to ask her why, but I can't form
words, because there's an ocean inside me, warm and sweet,
and I'm bobbing along the waves, just like the ones that car-
ried me and Joey all those years ago in San Diego, when everything was perfect or as close to it as we could get. That was a
nice time, when I was twelve and Joey was thirteen, letting the
waves carry us, Maddie stretched out on the beach in her purple bikini and floppy-brimmed hat. Far away from Mill Haven,
we were in a different world, where no one knew who we were.

I try to ask Maddie where Joey is, but she can't understand
me. She thinks I'm saying something else, because she leans
forward and says, "Do you need more? Do you need me to press
the button?"

And her finger presses a button on the side of the bed and
the largest wave I've ever known billows over me, like the para-
chute game we played in the gymnasium in kindergarten, all
of us laughing as the fabric gently overtook us and blocked out
the world.

My mother's voice is trembling. "This is not normal. This is not
something that happens to people like us."

My father sounds weary. He has been weary for years now. Joey makes people weary.

He says, "There is no normal, Abigail. Nothing has ever been normal. Why can't you see that? He has a problem."

My finger stretches out for the button to make the waves come again. My parents make me tired, years and years of fighting about Joey.

My mother's hand touches my head. Like a kitten, I respond, leaning into it. I can't remember the last time she touched me, stroked my hair. Everything has always been about Joey.

"There was *heroin* in his system, Abigail. How did we miss that?"

The word floats in the air before me, something eerie and frightening.

There was vomit spattered on his hoodie at the party. When we found him in the bedroom. He was woozy and floppy and strange and made no sense and I thought . . .

I thought he was just drunk. Stoned, maybe.

"I will fix this," she says to my father. "He'll go to rehab, he'll get better, he'll come home."

She says rehab in a clipped way, like it hurts to have the word in her mouth.

"That's not a magic wand you can wave and make it all go away, Abigail. He could have died. Emory could have died. A girl *did* die."

The ocean inside me, the one that was warm and wavy, freezes.

"What did you say?" I whisper. My voice feels thick. Can they understand me? I speak louder. "What did you just say?"

"Emory," my father says. "Oh, Emory."

My mother's eyes are wet blue pools. She curls her fingers in my hair.

"You're alive," she tells me. "I'm so grateful you're alive."

Her face is blurry from the waves carrying me. I'm struggling inside them, struggling to understand.

"But she just had a headache," I say. "Candy just had a headache. She can't be dead."

My father frowns. "You aren't making any sense, Emmy."

She had a headache. That's why she was in the car. She had a headache at the party, and she wanted a ride home and it can't be right that a person has a headache and gets in a car and dies and everyone else lives. It can't be right.

"Joey," I say, crying now, the tears warm and salty on my face. "I want Joey. Please, get me Joey."

2

WHEN I OPEN MY eyes, he's there.

I've seen my brother cry only once before, the afternoon he and Luther Leonard decided to dive from the roof of our house into the pool. Luther made it; Joey didn't, and the sound of his sobs as he writhed on the brick patio echoed in my head for days.

But his crying is quieter now.

"I'm so sorry," he says. His voice is croaky, and he looks sick, pale and shaky. There are stitches above his left eye. His right arm is in a sling.

"I thought you were drunk," I say. "I thought you were just drunk."

Joey's dark eyes search my face.

"I messed up. I messed up so bad, Emmy."

Girls swoon over those dark eyes. Or they did. Before he became trouble.

Joey Ward used to be cool, a girl said in the bathroom at Heywood High last year. She didn't know I was in the stall. Sometimes I stayed in there longer than I needed to, just for some peace. It's hard all the time. Pretending.

Not anymore, another girl answered. *Just another druggie loser.*

I cried in the stall, because I knew Joey was more than that. Joey was the one who taught me to ride a bike, because our parents worked all the time. Joey was the one who let me read aloud to him for hours in a bedsheet fort in my father's den, long after he probably should have been ignoring me in favor of his friends, like most older siblings do. He taught me how to make scrambled eggs and let me stay with him in his attic bedroom while he drew.

Until he didn't. Until the day I knocked and he told me to go away.

He stands up, wiping his face with his good hand. His beautiful dark hair is in tangles, hanging over his eyes.

"I have to go," he says. "Mom's waiting."

Rehab. It floats back to me from when Mom said it. Was that yesterday? Or this morning? It's hard to tell. I don't know how long I've been here. Things are bleeding together.

"Joey, why did you do . . . it?"

I wish I could get out of this bed. I wish my leg wasn't hanging from some damn pulley in the air and that my body wasn't heavy with the ocean of drugs inside me.

At the door to my hospital room, Joey turns back, but he doesn't look at me. He looks at the floor.

"I love you, Emmy, but you have no idea what it's like to be me."

And then he's gone.

3

I'M IN THE DOWNSTAIRS bedroom off the kitchen that my mother remodeled for Nana, hoping she'd come live with us, but Nana is stubborn and says she wants to stay in her own house until the day she dies.

The walls are painted pale gray. The sheets and blankets are white and crisp and perfect and I'm imagining how the sweat dripping off my forehead is going to stain the pillowcases. My mother doesn't like messes.

At my feet, my dog Fuzzy nuzzles closer to my good leg, whines softly. I rub her with my toe. Her fur is coarse; no one's been brushing her. Westies need brushing.

My bad leg is in a blue brace, propped on more white pillows. My knee is throbbing, sparks of white heat that make me breathe hard. Make me sweat.

I can hear them in the kitchen, my sister Maddie and my mother, arguing.

"Mom, she's in pain," Maddie's saying. "Just let her have a pill."

"She can have ibuprofen. She was on so much medication in the hospital. I don't want her . . ."

My mom's voice trails off.

"Mom," Maddie says forcefully. "She fractured her *kneecap*. And she's not *Joey*."

"That's right," my mother answers, in a suddenly hard voice that makes me shiver. "And I want it to stay that way."

4

MADDIE SLEEPS NEXT TO me in the gray room, her eyelids growing heavy as she clicks the television remote from one show to another: *Keeping Up with the Kardashians, My Lottery Dream Home, Friends.* When the remote finally slips from her fingers, I turn the television off and just listen, Fuzzy tucked next to me, soft and sleeping.

Maddie snuck me a pill after my mother went to bed, fed me crackers and juice, and I'm not sweating anymore.

I'm listening to the quiet of the house.

Some things haven't changed since I came home. My dad still gets back late from his shifts at the hospital, peeking into the room at us to say hello and ask about my knee before he eats whatever Goldie has left for him in the refrigerator before going to the den and settling down with his drink to watch his own shows. He'll fall asleep in the recliner, glasses slipping down his nose, while my mother is asleep upstairs. That's the way they've been for what seems like years now, my mother up, my father down. I thought that might change, with everything that's happened. That they'd get closer, somehow, after the accident.

I thought they might stay home with me, too, at least for the first few days, but they didn't. They went right back to work. Maybe because Maddie is here now and can take care of me. And Goldie, too, if it's one of her days with us.

Sometimes I feel like I don't exist in this house because I'm not beautiful and loud, like Maddie, or a problem, like Joey. I'm just me. The good one.

The one thing that's changed is the sound of our house.

It's quiet.

It was never quiet with Joey, especially last year, when things got bad. So much yelling and fighting with my mom about his grades. His attitude. Slammed doors. Joey burying himself deep into his hoodie when my dad would try to talk to him. I did whatever I could to make things better. Woke him up for school, even if I had to pour cold water on his face to do it. Did his homework, just enough to get his grades up, make it look like he was trying, but not enough to raise suspicion. I just wanted the noise to stop.

Next to me, Maddie rolls over, her knee knocking into mine. Little flares heat my knee, but not too much, because of the pill. I bite back a little gasp. Maybe I need another one? But I don't want to wake her up. I don't want any more fights about taking pills. I don't want noise anymore.

Because this quiet? Even though I love Joey, he's my brother, how could I not love him?—this quiet is *peaceful*.

It's finally peaceful now that my wild and troubled brother is gone.

And I feel guilty about loving this peace.

5

"IT'S A MESS UP there," Maddie says. "But I think I got most of it cleaned up." She drops a milk crate on the living room floor and flops down on the couch next to me. Her hair is in a ponytail and her neck gleams with sweat. The stairs to the attic are steep.

Even sweaty and with no makeup, my sister is beautiful. I shouldn't feel jealous, but I do.

"Mom really tore Joey's room apart. I don't know if I told you. Maybe you don't remember. You were so out of it in the hospital. But we came back here a couple of days after the accident to shower and change clothes and went up there. You know? To see what he'd been hiding, and she just . . . kind of lost it."

She leans forward and shuffles through the milk crate. "I don't think she found much. Maybe a bong and some weed. But look what *I* found."

She hands me a stack of papers. Joey's art. Gold-winged dragons with orange fire spilling from their jaws. Hulking creatures with sharp talons and red eyes. A whole world he created in the attic when our parents let him move up there when he was thirteen. He could sit for hours at his drafting table, immersed. My mother turned his old bedroom into her exercise space.

"I don't think he draws anymore," I tell her. "Maybe he will now. When he comes back. When he's better."

Maddie looks at me carefully. "Emmy, I'm not sure there's going to be a 'better.' He took *heroin*. That's some serious stuff. That's not something you can just . . . brush off. I mean, I had no idea. Did *you*?"

I arrange the papers into a neat pile on my lap, avoiding her eyes. "I thought . . . I don't know. It was hard. I was just trying to take care of him. I thought it was just . . . being stoned and stuff. You don't know what it was like, last year. You were *gone*."

I start to cry, tears spilling onto my T-shirt. I haven't taken a shower in days and I'm wearing the same clothes I came home from the hospital in, the crutches are giving me sores under my arms, and I feel awful and rank sitting next to my beautiful sister with her hair up in a messily perfect ponytail.

And I feel guilty about Joey, like part of this is my fault, for keeping his secrets for so long.

And then there's Candy.

It's too much, everything bubbling inside me at once.

"Oh, Emmy," Maddie says, wrapping her arms around me. "It's okay. Don't cry. It's not your fault. I swear, it's not your fault."

But somewhere, deep down, I think it is.

Because if I hadn't tried to hide Joey's secrets, maybe Candy MontClair wouldn't have died.

6

WHEN I LIMP INTO the kitchen, my mother flips over the newspaper she was reading and sets her coffee cup on it.

"Well, hello," she says brightly, turning to the stove. She slides scrambled eggs onto a plate for me. "It's a big day. You need to eat. You haven't been eating much. I'm getting a bit worried."

She sniffs the air delicately. "Did you shower?" She pulls her hair back and weaves it into a stylish, casual bun. She's wearing a lovely cream blouse, dark gray jacket, pants that flare elegantly over her crisp black shoes. Her work clothes.

"You're going to work?" I ask, my heart sinking. I thought she'd want to come with me when I finally got my leg brace off. It's been five weeks. I don't know why I got my hopes up.

She frowns. "Of course. I can't miss today. We've got a deposition. Maddie's here. She'll take you to your appointment."

I take a few bites of egg and then push the rest around on the plate while she busies herself with wallet, keys, purse. My mother is a lawyer and my dad is a doctor in the ER, which means they're both always pretty much working, but I thought at least one of them would want to be there the day I got my leg brace off.

"Don't pout, Emory. Blue Spruce isn't covered by insurance and Daddy and I can't take the time away." Blue Spruce is the place in Colorado where they sent Joey.

I look back at my plate. Once in the third grade when my mother dropped me and Joey at school, one of the mothers on the sidewalk whispered, "That family is richer than sin, I'm surprised they don't have a chauffeur for their precious babies."

When she realized I'd heard what she said, she gave me a big, fake smile and waved to my mother as she drove away. I was eight, but I understood her just fine.

My mother's family money could pay for Joey's rehab a million times over and we'd still be fine. She doesn't have to work, but she does.

Maddie wanders into the kitchen, holding Fuzzy. "Where's my breakfast?" she says sleepily.

"You're in college," my mother answers. "You can make your own breakfast. And get a move on. Emmy's appointment is at ten."

I push my plate in Maddie's direction. "You can have the rest of mine."

"I almost forgot," my mother says. "Here."

She hands me a pink phone.

"The other one," she says softly, her eyebrows creasing ever so slightly. "It was . . . smashed."

I bite my lip. Smashed. In the accident. I was holding it tightly, in my lap, as Luther Leonard laughed and drove faster and faster.

"Same number," she says quietly, taking a sip of coffee. "They transferred everything over." She puts her cup down and turns, taking the egg pan off the stove and rinsing it in the sink.

"Ha," Maddie says, setting Fuzzy down and popping some of my scrambled eggs into her mouth with her fingers. "They always say that, but I never believe them. Stuff is always missing."

She reaches for the newspaper my mother was reading. "Is this today's?"

My mother whirls around. "No!" She tries to snatch the paper from Maddie's hand.

"Mom!" Maddie arches away, opening the paper. Her face drains of color and she quickly folds the paper up, tucking it under her arm.

"What?" I say. "What is the big deal?"

My mother and Maddie look at each other. I pull the paper away from Maddie.

There, on the front page of the *Mill Haven Ledger,* is a photograph of Candy MontClair. Even in black-and-white, you can see the freckles dusting her face. Her hair is strawberry blond, curling over her shoulders. One hand tucked under her chin. Junior year photo.

Community Mourns Local Girl

"Put it down," my mother says gently. "You don't need to read that, Emory."

Summer belongs to teenagers in Mill Haven. Swim parties and bonfires. Friday night drives up and down Main Street. Candy MontClair was headed to theater camp in upstate New York, just as she had every summer since she was twelve. Tragically . . .

I feel like I've been punched in the stomach. Sentences swim before my eyes. *How could this have happened in Mill Haven . . . failing our teenagers . . . prevalence of drug and alcohol use in our community . . . who is to blame . . .*

"Emmy," Maddie says, drawing the paper from my fingers. "Emmy, breathe."

Tragically.

The way her breath sounded in the backseat of the car, pinned under Joey. Like she was drowning.

Dying.

I close my eyes, the sound of her broken breath swirling in my head.

"Mom," Maddie says sharply. "How about getting her one of those pills now, or I don't think she's going to make it to her damn appointment."

"It's no one's fault," my sister says as she drives. "They did a tox screen on Luther. He had no drugs or alcohol in his system. It was pouring rain. He lost control of the car."

Candy was crying and Joey was passed out and I was shouting at Luther, rain smearing the windshield, because he wanted to turn left off Wolf Creek Road, not right, which was the way home. Luther was laughing. *Just one little stop. Five minutes. You girls are such babies. I'm doing you a favor.*

I just want Maddie to shut up. I just want this pill to start working. I haven't had one since my first week home.

"Shit happens," Maddie says. "People die for no reason. I know that sounds callous, but this was an accident in the purest form. Jesus, what's going on at Frost Bridge? How many people are *down* there?"

I look out the window. Frost Bridge is the exit from town, right by the ever-cheery Mill Haven sign: LEAVING SO SOON? IF YOU LIVED HERE, YOU'D BE HOME NOW! Down on the rocky river

18

beach, there are tents and tarps, ratty blankets and sleeping bags. People are in tiny clusters. Sitting, smoking.

"The city," I say. "The city started doing that stuff. You know, uncomfortable benches. Fines. To drive them out. I think they're coming here instead. To be safe."

Please kick in, pill. Kick in, kick in.

Is this how Joey felt? Desperate to feel better, get numb, lose himself?

Maddie says, "Huh. I can't see our esteemed town council, of which our esteemed mother is a member, taking this well."

I feel the warmth then, spreading through me, loosening everything. Milder than the ocean that poured through my veins in the hospital, but still soothing.

I look out the window, Mill Haven passing by in a humid, blurry haze. Red, white, and blue banners hang across Main Street. In the distance, the Mill looms at the edge of the town. Our family's legacy, the thing that built this town long, long ago.

The Fourth of July is in a few days. If Joey was here, we'd be in Kingston Park, giggling while Simon Stanley led the Mill Haven Gleefuls in a spirited rendition of "R.O.C.K. in the USA" and then watching the fireworks explode across the sky. Sucking the juice from cold lemons through peppermint sticks. Making fun of the parade.

No, that's not right. I shake my head. My brain is getting fuzzy from the pill. Joey stopped going to the fireworks with me a few years ago. He hung out with his friends instead. Came home late and drowsy, sneaking in quietly after my parents had gone to bed. I watched the fireworks split the sky by myself in the backyard. I always waited up for him, even though I was tired.

Maddie is still talking, her words dissolving as soon as they leave her mouth.

Maybe that's what Joey liked about drugs. The way they re-arranged things, shifted memories, erased what he didn't want to deal with. Make uncomfortable things fade away.

"Emmy."

Maddie's sharp voice shatters my thoughts.

"What's the matter with you? Is it the Vicodin? You have to eat before you take it. Jesus."

Dr. Cooper's office is cold. Even though my insides are warm from the pill, I shiver.

"It's like an icebox in here," Maddie murmurs, wrapping her arms around herself.

The door opens. "Ah, the famous Ward girls, gracing me with their presence!" Dr. Cooper closes the door to the exam room and grins at us, exposing expensively whitened teeth.

Maddie side-eyes me and I try to hide my smile. I know she's thinking of what Mom calls him. *Doctor Vampire.* "You can see those teeth from miles away," our mom said once.

He busies himself washing his hands. "Madeline, your studies are going well? Dartmouth, is it?"

"Brown," Maddie answers.

He dries his hands and gazes at her. "And what will be your field, eh? You're a Ward, the world is your oyster."

"I'm joining the circus," Maddie says.

Dr. Cooper chuckles. "Is that so?"

"Seriously. I'm headed back next week to take a summer circus course. My life's dream is to be shot from a cannon."

"Always so spirited, Madeline," he murmurs, turning to me. "And this one."

His smile wobbles as he struggles for something to say.

Because he and I both know that I'm not spirited, or exceptional, or anything much. Dr. Cooper literally has no small talk to offer me.

I'm just "this one."

"Emory," he says finally. "Let's take a look at that knee, shall we?"

He hooks a hand under my armpit and hoists me onto the table. The tissue paper rips underneath me as I slide back.

He pats the blue brace gently.

"Are we ready?" he asks. His breath smells minty and there are little hairs springing from his ears. I feel like someone who takes such good care of their teeth might also want to trim their ear hair, but what do I know?

I look at the ceiling. "Sure," I say.

He starts unsnapping the buckles on the brace, moving slowly. "Tell me at any time if you feel pain, Emory."

"I can't feel anything. I took a pill before I came in."

He eases his hand beneath the brace and slides it out from under my leg.

It feels weird without the brace on. My leg feels lighter than it has in weeks.

"Yikes." Maddie prods my thigh. "You lost a lot of muscle tone. Well, you can build that back up before dance team in the fall."

Dr. Cooper presses his fingers all around my knee. "Oh, she won't be dancing for quite some time."

"Wait," I say, trying to keep the excitement out of my voice. "I can't be on dance team?"

"Oh, goodness, no," Dr. Cooper says. "You've got a good bit of physical therapy ahead of you before you can even attempt that."

"Mom is going to freak. Dance team is Mom's jam," Maddie says. "Maybe you can still dress, Emmy, but just sit out."

"I don't care," I say. I'm pretty sure I only made the team because Mom made a call, to be honest. "I never liked dance team anyway. That was just Mom trying to make me Maddie 2.0."

I don't know if I would have said that if Vicodin wasn't buzzing through my body.

"Emmy," Maddie says, but not harshly, because she knows it's true.

"I'm an alternate, Maddie. I suck. I sit out most of the time anyway and when I am in, I'm in the back."

I'll have to act disappointed when I tell my mom, but really, I'm relieved. No more pulling and tugging at the itchy royal-blue skirted shorts and gluing sparkles on my eyelids. Pasting a fake smile on my face.

Dr. Cooper is looking at me.

"What?" I say. "Are we done?"

"There's a bit of swelling," he says, "but it all looks good. It's healing nicely. I just need you to bend it. Very slowly, just a bit at first."

Suddenly I'm panicked. I look down at my pale, thin leg, the skin wrinkled from the brace. I think of the car, the accident, how I felt sitting in the passenger seat, feeling like something was missing from my body, that something wasn't right. My kneecap had smashed against the dashboard as we flew through the air and then again when we landed. I think I remember it, some sort of cracking sound maybe. The sound of something splintering.

I don't want to hear that sound again.

I feel sick.

"No," I say. "I don't want to."

"Very common," Dr. Cooper says. "You're afraid it will break again? Very understandable. But I assure you, it won't."

"You can do it, Emmy," Maddie says softly. She puts her hand on my shoulder. "You can."

"I can't," I say. "I'm too afraid. I'm . . ."

Dr. Cooper slides his hand under the back of my knee. "A very awful thing happened to you, Emory, something much larger than you can possibly articulate right now. But the first step for you to move forward and heal is bending this knee. Making yourself healthy."

I close my eyes.

It's so stupid. Joey is somewhere in the wilds of Colorado hiking and talking and doing god knows what so he comes back better, Joey 2.0, and Candy is never coming back again and here I am, afraid to bend my damn knee. The simplest thing in the world.

"Just a little bit. You may feel some discomfort."

Dr. Cooper's fingers press the underside of my knee, pushing up gently. His hands feel overly cold and creepy.

"Emmy," Maddie whispers.

My leg is everything that happened in that car and I will carry it around forever, literally and figuratively. I should feel lucky to be alive. I didn't overdose, like Joey. Or go through the windshield, like Luther.

Or die, like Candy.

I jerk my knee up. My knee feels like fire and I groan.

"You did it!" Maddie claps her hands.

"Pain level," Dr. Cooper says. "A scale of one to ten."

"I don't know," I say, breathing hard. The pill is tapering off. "Maybe five. I don't know."

"All right. I'll write you a prescription for more Vic—"

Maddie shakes her head, cutting him off. "Thanks, Dr. Cooper, but our mom wouldn't like that."

"I'm sorry?"

Maddie sighs. "You know, our *brother*. He's in rehab. She's already guarding the prescription from the hospital with a tight fist."

I watch Dr. Cooper's face shift from confusion to understanding. Mill Haven is small. Of course he's heard.

"Yes, that's right. Well, I'm glad he's getting the help he needs, but Emory's pain is her own. Certainly, her medication usage can be monitored, but she shouldn't go without just because—"

"You don't know our mother," Maddie says. "Or maybe you do."

They stare at each other.

"Well." Dr. Cooper clears his throat. "Let's try again, Emory. A few more times before you go. I see from your chart that your mother's arranged for in-home physical therapy starting next week, and I'll give you some instructions on knee care and strength exercises. And if you change your mind, I'll send you home with a scrip, just in case."

I watch from a chaise lounge in the backyard as Maddie does somersaults off the diving board, bouncing into the air and then curling into a tight ball, barely splashing as she enters the water. It's sticky outside and I flap my T-shirt to get some air on my body.

As Maddie slithers and sidles through the pool like an eel, I sneak a look over the brick wall separating our yard from the Galt's yard. Let my eyes travel up the ivy snaking the siding to the corner window, the one that's right across from my own bedroom window, a room I haven't been in for weeks, because of my knee. Sixteen stairs from the first floor to the second.

The blind is still drawn. He's not home from pitching camp yet.

I thought he might visit me in the hospital. Break our rule. Just that once. But he didn't.

I check my new pink phone. I start to open my texts and then, before I can stop myself, I'm switching to Instagram to check his feed. I can't help it. I want to see his face. He's like my drug.

There he is, smiling, in sunglasses and his ball cap, the picture of glossy, perfect health.

Feelin great, he posted.

And then, beneath that, a tornado of messages from girls. Triple hearts, smiley faces, fire. *Ur so hot, Gage. Gage you're the best. Miss you. You are fire. DM meeee.*

My body fills with heat.

I wonder what those girls would say if they knew I'd kissed that perfect mouth. A lot. Not very far from this chaise lounge, in fact. Just over there in our pool house.

You are perfect, CuteCathy commented.

Scrumptious, said PristTine.

I look at Gage's plump mouth again.

It's nice this way, he said the last time, his fingers tracing my neck. *Just you and me, this way. Private. Our own thing.*

An ache runs through me.

"You are bright red. Whatcha looking at there?"

Maddie's voice startles me. She's standing above me,

squeezing water from her thick hair, the droplets landing on my bare legs.

"Nothing." I press the phone against my thigh.

"Ah, secrets." She winks. "I get it. Well, you deserve some fun. But I'll get it out of you. I have my ways." She starts tickling me and the pink phone slides off my thigh and onto the damp patio. She snatches it up and starts tapping.

"Maddie!" I make a swipe to take the phone back, but I'm not quick enough.

"Oh," she says quietly. Her smiles dies. "Oh."

"It's not anything," I say quickly. "It's stupid, really—"

Maddie looks at me and she doesn't look mad, like I thought she might. Instead, she looks sad. But why would she look sad about Gage Galt and his Instagram feed?

I grab the phone from her.

My heart drops.

She wasn't looking at Gage Galt. She was reading my messages.

Tasha. I blink, scrolling down.

The first texts were just a day after the accident.

OMG are u ok? Please call me
What happened???
I can't believe this
Call me

And then a few days later.

Hey Emory, call me if you get a chance
There's a lot happening, rumors and stuff

Why were you in a car with Luther Leonard
I can't believe Candy's dead God I'm so sad
I went by your house and no one's there

I take a deep breath. There are others, from the girls on the dance team. Mary, Madison, Jesse. Candy was on the dance team with us freshman year. She was nice, bubbly and friendly and laughed at herself when she'd mess up a move. Then she moved on to Drama Club.

Everyone loved Candy MontClair.

Listen I'm really sorry, Tasha texted a week ago.

Leaving for dance camp tomorrow sorry we can't talk
But there's a lot going on
I'm really sorry, Emory. I hate this but
I think maybe in the fall
When school starts
You should lay low, ok? Some of the girls
Well, they're just, I mean, we're all sad
And there's just so much to deal with
Did you know that Luther guy had drugs in the car?
I mean, that's awful and kind of scary and we all talked
I mean, they just feel really uncomfortable with all this
So it's better I think if you kind of back off a little bit
Until everybody is feeling more comfortable

My heart's thudding. I can't look at my sister.

"You've been dropped," Maddie says. "I was worried that might happen. Kind of wondered why no one's come around to see you since you've been home."

I heard about your knee, that really sucks
You probably can't do dance team anyway
And let's be honest, you didn't really like it
I'm really sorry

"Emmy," Maddie says, touching my shoulder.

I turn the phone facedown on my stomach. Shake my head. "Doesn't matter," I say. "No big deal. We weren't friend-friends, really, anyway. I was just on the team."

And it's the truth. I wasn't close with any of them, but I was on the team, and that meant built-ins like eating lunch together, hanging out when I wasn't worrying about Joey. Being on the team meant a kind of protection at school. People to be *with,* so you didn't appear to be completely alone. Some kind of social umbrella, by proxy, since I am not like Maddie, outgoing, beautiful, chatty, popular. All the things I should be, according to the family I come from, the house I live in. My mother.

And now I don't have even that.

And the person I most want to talk to about it, who would list each and every thing wrong with each and every one of those girls, even if he didn't really believe it, would be Joey. *Screw them,* he'd say. *Snooty bunch of hags. Who needs that? You're better off.*

But he's not here. And I can't even call him, because Blue Spruce doesn't allow phone calls. Something in the family handbook they sent us about *building a base of inner strength before reentering the outside world.*

"Let's get you inside," Maddie says gently. "Take a shower, maybe eat something. We can talk about this. I can help you."

I nudge her hand off my shoulder and stand up, wobbly on my weak leg. My knee is starting to hurt again, more than I admitted at the doctor's office, and I'll have to ask Maddie for a pill, and my mother will wonder why I need it, and my brother is an addict, and now I don't even have what little friends I thought I had, and I just want to disappear.

"Hey, be careful, Em, what are you doing?"

Just . . . disappear.

I hobble away from Maddie and her concerned face, ignoring the pain vibrating in my knee, and stand at the edge of our ridiculously large, too blue, achingly beautiful pool in our achingly beautiful and carefully landscaped backyard.

Then I let myself fall in.

My shirt and shorts billow out across me and I swim beneath the surface, with just my arms and one good leg, encasing myself in silence, away from an accident, a dead girl, and my broken brother, and I decide, then and there, my lungs bursting, that I will spend the rest of the summer underwater, weightless and unharmed and silent and safe.

7

A *STAR IS MIGHTY GOOD company.*

Those are the words from a play we read last year in American Stories. They float up in me as I bobble on my back in the pool, arms out, water lapping my cheeks, the sky a dark, speckled tapestry above me. The story of a small town, small lives.

All summer I have been looking at this sky.

I don't know any constellations, I don't know what happens up there, I don't know what it means, I don't know anything but the calm that floating at night gives me. The way my body moves gently in the water, protected, the eerie sound of water drifting in and out of my ears every so often. The peculiar quiet of Mill Haven late at night, all our secrets gone to sleep. The water takes my pain away.

I have been floating in the water for two and a half months. Making myself invisible.

We're supposed to seek solace in the stars, right? That's what poets and painters and movies and books tell us. The great unknown. The mystery of life tantalizing us from galaxies far away. Look up, and revel in the wonder. Consider your little spot in the vastness of it all, I guess.

Invisibility does that to you. Strips away fancy layers, leaves just the bones and blood. Just enough to get around.

I butterfly my legs a bit to adjust my position. My right knee suddenly tingles with pain, causing me to suck in my breath, which causes me to choke on water.

And then the stars disappear.

At first, I wonder if I'm starting to drown, everything getting dark.

But it's just my mother, hovering above me, blocking the last of the night stars and my sky as she reels me toward her with the pool skimmer. She's annoyed with me, but what else is new?

"Emory," she says. "Get out. I leave for the airport in an hour."

My body bumps against the side of the pool. She drops the skimmer on the brick patio, where it makes a wet, thwacking sound.

"I don't need," she says, gesturing vaguely to the pool, to the lightening sky, "*this* nonsense today, do you understand?"

She's already expertly made up, hair pulled back against her neck in a tidy turquoise barrette, dressed in her traveling clothes: burgundy leggings, black flats, expensive but casual-looking cream-colored cotton shirt, and a long, open-stitch cream-colored J. Jill cardigan.

"I just want you out of the water, showered, and ready for your appointment with Sue. All right? Can you do that for me? Can you do that *one thing*?"

Water streams down my face as I drop my legs and stand in the pool.

Her eyes meet mine. I nod. She goes back into the house, sliding the patio doors shut behind her. Lights glow from every window, like our house has a thousand eyes.

Of course I can do that *one thing*. I've never *not* done that *one thing*.

Today is the day my mother is getting on a plane to fetch Joey from the wilds of Colorado, where they've been hiking and counseling and tough-loving the drugs and bad thoughts out of his body for two and half months. She's going to bring him back and dress him up and send him off to senior year at Heywood High like nothing ever happened. That's how we do it in our house.

Like Joey's chipped-paint, torn-seat, dented and busted-up old Toyota Corolla didn't fly off Wolf Creek Road one night this past June, Candy MontClair screaming, Luther Leonard laughing like a maniac as his head splintered the windshield in front of me and Joey's body flung against Candy in the backseat, crushing her, because he was dead weight, because he was so high he was no longer even conscious, he was on a whole other plane. He was like one of those fading stars hovering above me right now as I climb out of the pool and limp toward the house: so beautiful to look at, so full of secrets, but too far away to reach.

In my bathroom, I massage my knee while the shower warms up. Run a finger gently down the scar.

When I was in the hospital, they had a chart on the wall with six round faces, and the expression on each face got worse and worse until the last face was all scrunched up and crying. Each face had a number. The last, crying face was a ten and meant your pain was at "Hurts Worst." That was the most you could hurt. That was the one I always wanted to choose, because it really felt that way, my knee and lots of other things. But my parents were down the hall with my brother most of the time and they didn't need to worry about me, too. And I didn't want Maddie to cry any longer. I said I was a four most days, the face that was mostly just a grim line for a mouth, neither here nor there. "Hurts A Little More."

I bend over, grabbing the sides of the claw-foot tub with both hands, stepping my good foot in first and then carefully, painfully, sliding my bad leg over the side. There are four bathrooms in our house, three with claw-foots, restored originals. This is what it means when you grow up with a certain type of mother in a house built in 1884: you might have Sub-Zero and Wolf in the kitchen, but the rest of the house stays "true to history." My mother is a fan of the past, except when it's inconvenient.

I try to measure the throbbing in my knee. Is it a four? A six? Hurts a little more? Hurts a lot? I think about the scrip Dr. Cooper gave me back when Maddie was home, the one I never told my mother about. When Maddie left, she hid my pain medication.

That's what happens when your brother is addicted to drugs: your mom gets so paranoid you might turn out the same way, she restricts your pain meds. She keeps them in a locked cabinet in the garage, along with every other possible medication in the house: aspirin, ibuprofen, Tylenol, Midol, whatever she takes to fall into her zombie sleep at night.

When I asked her where she was going with the Tupperware full of painkillers, she said, "I just want your brother to come home and have no temptations."

When I asked her why she was putting all her jewelry in the safe in my father's den, she said, "To be careful."

"Joey never stole from you," I said. "He wouldn't do *that*."

My mother stared at me in a way that unnerved me.

Would he? Would Joey steal?

"Well, did he?" I finally asked, exasperated by her silence.

"No, not that I know for sure." She blew a strand of hair from her cheek. "But I just want the best for all of us, Emory. Check off all the boxes."

She's hired a puffy-haired woman with a name tag that says SUE S., CARE ANGEL to come to our house and help me exercise my leg, but that lady just ends up watching television when I give up, flat on my back on the blue mat in the living room, tears streaming down the sides of my face, silently crying from the pain, but really crying from so many other things, too.

Sue S. makes nine dollars an hour; how much should she be expected to care about me, some rich girl who lives in a big Victorian on a hill in Mill Haven?

The thing about being invisible is, you'd think it would feel light and airy and easy, no pressure, but it doesn't.

It's the heaviest thing I've ever known.

After I dry off and get dressed and join her in the kitchen, my mother nudges a plate of eggs, strawberries, and toast across the kitchen island.

She slides a piece of paper after that. *The List.*

I skim it, noting the usual: feed Fuzzy, give Sue her check, make sure Goldie's left food for Daddy for when he gets home, and then I see it.

"Mom," I say, wishing my voice wouldn't shake. "This one. I don't . . . I don't think I can do this one. You can take Joey shopping when you get back."

My mother's voice is smooth as silk. "Nonsense, Emory. You

34

need school clothes, too. It will do you good to get out. Walk around the mall a bit. Look, I've listed his sizes and exactly what you should get. Use the Uber account to get there."

The mall in the city. I don't want to go there. See kids from school. *Uncomfortable. Rumors.* That's what Tasha texted.

Kids who miss Candy MontClair.

"Mom," I say again. "I'm not ready. I don't . . . I might see kids from school."

She gives me what Maddie and Joey and I call the Look: a thing where her face somehow morphs into something blank and impenetrable, as though she's waiting for you to react so she can summon up the proper expression: disapproval, resignation, slow burn. It's a warning and a challenge at the same time.

Through the kitchen window behind her, the sun is rising, orange and gold backgrounding my mother like a gleaming crown.

"Toughen up, my dear." My mother smiles. "People have been talking about *me* my whole life. You'll come out of this stronger than before. We all will."

She slips her phone into her purse.

"I'm counting on you," she says, checking her watch.

"I still don't understand why we can't all go get Joey together," I say.

"I don't want to overwhelm him. This is going to be difficult. He'll need a little time to adjust. I'll pick him up, we'll have dinner, stay a night in the hotel, and fly back."

I'm not sure what would be overwhelming about having your whole family there when you get out of rehab. Wouldn't it just mean they loved you?

She rubs Fuzzy's head and leaves through the door to the

garage. In a few minutes, her car starts, the garage door rolls up and then down, and then she is gone.

I look at the plate of bright yellow eggs, glistening strawberries, buttered toast. I stand as still as possible, listening or feeling for any sign of hunger in my body.

There is none, so I scrape the food into the trash and limp back upstairs and put on a fresh swimsuit. The sun is fully up now, the neighborhood is quiet; I can get at least two more good hours of floating in before Sue arrives.

8

"**B**ROTHER COMES HOME TOMORROW, then?" Sue says. She's stretched out on the honey-colored leather sectional with her bare feet propped on my mother's favorite accent pillow. A color called Bungalow Rose that's a cross between Pepto-Bismol pink and the strawberries from my breakfast, now crushed and bleeding in the trash.

"Yes," I pant from the mat, slowly bending my knee in infinitesimal degrees. Sometimes Sue helps, one warm hand on the front of my knee, the other under the back. Mostly, we seem to have silently agreed that she will watch television while I lie on the mat and halfheartedly do my exercises.

Sue might possibly be my only friend now, and she doesn't even know it.

"Bet you'll be sorry not to have this big old house to yourself anymore, huh? Noisy older brothers, am I right?" Sue clicks from *Forensic Files* to *SpongeBob SquarePants.* The unhappy face of Squidward fills the giant television hung above our fireplace.

My eyes drift to the ceiling as I lower my leg. Carefully.

There are lots of rooms in this house, but Joey asked for the attic space when he turned thirteen. The highest point. Slanted ceilings, a perfect triangle, his drawing table perched right under the window between the slopes. You can see everything in the valley that is Mill Haven from that window, even the Mill, which my family built all those years ago, and which

37

ran this town for so long. It's been closed for years, since long before even Maddie and me and Joey were born. It sits on the edge of Mill Haven at the far end of Wolf Creek, nestled at the base of the mountains, surrounded by barbed wire fencing and KEEP OUT signs. The small buildings the workers used to live in plunked like worn-out Monopoly houses on the land surrounding the mill.

Joey tacked his drawings everywhere. The edges fluttered when he cracked the window for a breeze. If I was walking Fuzzy and Joey was home, I could look up from Aster Avenue and see him there, head bent over his table, shoulders at his ears, drawing. Sometimes he would glance down, noticing me on the street.

Pot smoke drizzled from his mouth as he smiled at me, a finger to his lips.

Shhhh.

It was just pot. Lots of kids smoked pot. Even my dad said so once. "A little rebellion, a little experimentation. That's a teenager. It's to be expected."

"Actually," I say to Sue, "he was always pretty quiet."

Except when he wasn't.

Only all that's done now. Things will be different, right? That's the plan. Like the Blue Spruce handbook says, *Family should be prepared to provide a stable, consistent environment.*

But Sue isn't paying attention. She's watching SpongeBob argue with Squidward. "I wish I lived in a pineapple under the sea, I tell you *what,*" she chuckles. "Be better under the water. Like you and that pool."

*   *   *

38

Before Sue leaves, I give her twenty dollars to go up the attic stairs for me and bring down Joey's clothes and art supplies. Maddie took care of cleaning it up when she was here, but she didn't bring down everything. I'm hoping when he sees his pencils and sketchbooks that maybe, just maybe, he'll want to draw again. That it might help him.

Sue shrugs. "You really need to see Cooper about that leg. I don't think your progress is progressing if you can't even make some stairs, yeah?"

"I'm tired."

She goes up twice and comes back down with milk crates full of his stuff. She plunks the crates on the bed in Maddie's room, which will now be Joey's room.

"That's a real nice space up there. Lot of light," she says.

I could probably have gone up the stairs myself, slowly, *maybe,* since I can now make it up to the second floor and sleep in my own room, but the truth is, I didn't want to. The attic room was Joey's disappearing place and I don't want to go up there.

Sue pauses by Maddie's desk, looking at the pile of Joey's drawings Maddie brought down from the attic. "Nice stuff. I was always happy drawing, when I was a kid." She looks through the papers, touches the edge of one of Joey's dragon illustrations. "That kinda got lost in life, you know?" She seems like she might say something more, but she shakes her head. "You got my check? I have another appointment over on Jefferson."

I hand her the check. Listen to her thump down the stairs and out the front door, past Goldie puttering around in the den.

I'm transferring Maddie's clothes from her dresser drawers to a giant plastic tub when she texts.

You okay?

Sure, I type back.

I sit down on the bed, relieved to be off my knee. It's hard to imagine Joey in this room, sleeping in this explosion of weirdness that was Maddie before she left for Brown last year: tie-dyed bedspread. Batik-covered pillows. A hanging hammock chair in the corner. My mother hates Maddie's room. She prefers solid colors and things that match.

If only we could match what my mother wants.

I don't believe you, Maddie writes.

I didn't think you would

**Mom texted me. She's on
her way to Blue Spruce now.**

She left a list of stuff for me to do.

**Her lists! Well, you don't have
to do everything in one day, ok?**

Yeah

Does anything involve leaving the house?

Yeah. School clothes. The mall.

It'll be good for you to get out.

I guess

You have to face people sometime

Right

Emmy

What

Everything that happened, it's not your fault

My chest squeezes. I don't want to cry.

It's NOT your fault, ok?

Have to go

I turn the phone facedown on the bed. Ignore the buzzing, go back to emptying my sister's drawers.

It's past nine o'clock when my father comes home. He seems surprised to see me in the kitchen, or maybe he's just surprised to see anyone at all. My mother is always asleep by now, zonked on sleep meds in their room upstairs, surrounded by her notepads and pens and laptop, preparing for her cases. I'm normally in my room down the hall, on my side in my bed in the dark, watching the window across from mine in the house next door, waiting for a flicker of life.

If Joey's attic was where he kept his secrets, mine live next door, just a window away.

"Hey," my dad says, setting his bag on the island. This sort of thing makes Mom wince. She doesn't like clutter.

"I have hooks for a reason," she likes to say, pointing to the row of nickel-plated hooks by the door in the mudroom.

"When do they get back?" he asks. "Mommy's sent me so many texts, but I can hardly make sense of them all."

"I think tomorrow afternoon."

He sighs and looks at his phone. "She says he looks good."

He smells like cigarettes. That's when my dad smokes: in

the car, on the way home from the hospital. He keeps packs in the glove box. I imagine him reaching for them right away, in the parking garage, grimacing at his aching fingers, stiff from a night of pumping stomachs, suturing, stapling, staving off pools of blood. It's what he does: tries to save the messes that get wheeled into his ER. Sew people back into versions of themselves. And then he gets in the car and fills his own lungs with smoke.

Parents don't make any sense. My dad works to save people, but he can't even stop smoking. My parents send Joey to rehab, but my mother can't sleep without a pill.

"What did Goldie leave for dinner?" He slides onto a stool.

Last spring, my dad's hair was still thick and dark and wavy. Only a few threads of gray.

In June, after the accident, I swear it turned white overnight.

I hand him a fork and a warmed Tupperware of cauliflower and lentils.

"Maybe I'll watch a little television and turn in," he says, like this is a novel idea and not what he does every night when he comes home.

He'll take his dinner to the den, fix a large tumbler of something that will make him fall asleep before it's even finished, the television still running the British baking show, all airy pastels and fusty judges.

I wait, like I always wait, like I've waited for years maybe:

Hey, you, let's go roller-skating?

Hey, you, how about a movie?

Hey, you, how's about we head out for some cupcakes?

Hey, you, how you doing?

Or even, *The weight of that girl dying must be heavy in you and I am sorry.*

I wish people would ask about that. How it makes me feel, Candy dying.

Or even how it feels about Joey, which feels like a different kind of death.

But all my dad says is "Bad night in the pit, kiddo." That's what he calls the ER, the pit. It makes me think of piles of bodies and blood and my father picking his way through them, which I guess is really kind of what it must seem like.

He must see something in my face then, because he suddenly says, "Things are going to be *better* now, Emmy. It's been so hard on all of us, but it's really up to Joe now. All we can do is love him."

It's out of my mouth before I can stop it. "But we always loved him and still—"

"Emmy." He takes my hand. "It's all we can ever do. It's the one thing we cannot stop doing."

I turn away, to the sink, pretend to move some dishes around.

"Emmy, you will be okay, too. I promise."

I don't want my dad to see me cry.

When I turn back, he's gone, the Tupperware still on the counter, untouched.

I should be sleeping, but I'm floating again instead. Night is my favorite time to float and soon, when fall comes, it will be too cold.

I should be in bed, resting, getting ready for Joey to come back tomorrow. I miss him. It feels like forever. Once Maddie left for her summer session, the house became eerie. We've been three ghosts floating inside the whole summer.

In two weeks, school starts.

My heart begins to pound, that flippy feeling where it feels like you can't breathe.

I don't want to go back to school. See Candy's friends.

I will never forget the rain that night, heavy and cold. The way it kept pouring through the broken window and washing away the blood that streaked down Candy's face. The way the blood just kept coming back. The way she panted in the backseat, her body twisted, her eyes staring back at me in the cracked rearview, Joey across her lap, trapping her. The world was upside down and smashed in a billion pieces.

I'm sixteen. According to the apps on my phone, all the kids in Mill Haven are out doing the last of summer partying, red Solo cups and beer bottles lifted high, music pounding. Crackling bonfires and beer pong. Bongs and whatever else. That's what kids do, right? This is the best time of our lives, or so everyone keeps telling us.

And for one rainy night in June, I tried to be one of them. I really did.

9

I WAKE UP EARLY, LIKE I always do these days, and get in a good float before I take another awkward, slow shower and make my way carefully down the sixteen steps to the kitchen, where I look at my mother's list again.

1. Empty the dishwasher
2. Fold the laundry
3. Clean out Maddie's drawers; bring J's clothes down
4. Give Sue her check/therapy 9–11 am
5. Feed Fuzzy
6. Daddy's meal is in Tupperware labeled *Daddy*
7. Clean your room
8. Clean your bathroom
9. J needs school clothes; sizes and styles attached; credit card in file cabinet; the key hanging inside spice cabinet
10. Clothes for you; sizes and styles attached
11. Thank you!

I guess my mother is hiding everything now, including the key to the file cabinet, where she keeps the clothing credit card. We hide pain medication, jewelry, and credit cards now, as though Joey is a black-masked thief and not some messed-up kid.

I fold the list up and slide it into my purse.

I am less my mother's daughter than her staff member, somewhere between Goldie the housekeeper and the silent guy in the wide-brimmed hat who comes to trim our hedges and mow our lawns every few weeks, or the stone-faced father and son who show up every Friday at nine a.m. to tend our pool.

At the end of our driveway, I allow myself one quick look at the Galt's house. At Gage's house.

The blind is still drawn in his window. He's been gone the whole summer, pitching camp and traveling with his buddies. But he'll be back. Soon. And I need him back, because maybe, just maybe, a little part of me is like Joey.

I need my fix. I need to lose myself, too.

I take the bus to the mall in the city instead of an Uber, because you can never tell which driver will be chatty. The bus stop isn't far, and the air is filled with the cherry-ish scent of heliotrope. Mill Haven is filled with them. People take expensive pride in their lawns in our neighborhood: yards are landscaped lushly, each mound of clean gray rock and tumultuous spray of lavender arranged just so.

The mall isn't too crowded so early on a Monday morning, which makes me and my knee grateful. Maybe a few kids here and there, but none from Mill Haven. I feel relieved.

I head to the Gap. The things on my mother's list are not what Joey wears. He's usually in dirty hoodies and saggy jeans and anime T-shirts. I finger some clothes on the racks, picturing him in this soft chocolate T-shirt, that pair of artfully faded jeans. Joey's jeans have holes in them because he wears the same pair forever, unwashed, until they die. These jeans *come* with holes. It's almost like my mother is trying to re-create him, turning him into someone else, a popular, clean boy, like . . . Gage.

Gage Galt has lived next door to us forever. He's lean and handsome and has shining white teeth, the right amount of tousle in his hair, unlike Joey's permanently messy and tangled hair, and he has a million-dollar pitching arm. At least, that's what the papers say. He couldn't be more destined for greatness if he literally had SUCCESS! tattooed on his forehead. He lives, sleeps, and breathes baseball.

His is the bedroom window I gaze at from my room. Sometimes, during the school year, I can see him, slumped late at night over his homework, forehead creased in concentration. Smarts don't come as easy for Gage as flinging a ball; he has to work at it, because as much as scouts lick their lips every time he sets foot on the mound, his father wants him to get a college degree and do something that doesn't destroy his body. And if he doesn't keep up his grades, he can't play ball. And if Gage can't play ball, Gage won't be Gage.

My mother loves Gage. Or, perhaps, the idea of him: strong, uncomplicated, local boy making good.

I know I shouldn't, it just makes me nervous and jumpy and jealous, but I take out my phone and look at his feed.

Back to my hometown soon can't wait to see you miss you all

You are delicious, says CharleeZ.

So fine, says Aimee443.

I look at each and every word, trying to find something, but I'm not sure what. Is *you* code for *me*? Does he think of me when he's away? Does he miss me?

I'm not sure I miss Gage the person, since we don't actually talk very much when we're together. He's more like a series of sensations I crave: deliciousness, a secret, one that I want to stretch out as long as possible, something that is only *mine*. Away from everything, like my family and Joey. And it can't be bad if it feels good, right? I mean, it's not *drugs*.

I look around the store. The salespeople are folding clothes, chatting behind the counter, looking at their phones.

Look at me, I want to say. *Notice me.*

No one does.

That's the thing about Gage. At least, in those moments with him, I feel like someone sees me. I'm not the plain girl in the big house on the hill.

I sigh, shoving my phone back in my purse. And then I see it.

It's pretty. A caramel-colored bracelet, soft and sweet in the bright lights of the store. I haven't done this in so long, but I can't resist.

There's just a thin tag, papery, nothing like a bulky security tag that has to be detached at the register.

The salespeople are still bustling around, chatting.

I lift my shirt slightly, like I'm scratching an itch, which maybe I sort of *am*, and then I carefully tuck the bracelet between the waistband of my leggings and my hip. I slide my purse around my stomach.

Better. I feel better.

And then take a deep breath to clear my head. I'm on a mission for my mother and I can't fail.

In just four stores, I buy Joey a whole new life.

I keep my secrets in my closet where no one can find them. Innocently hidden in the open, in my great-grandmother's black velvet hatbox on the top shelf.

My mother has never had to tear my room apart in anger, searching for reasons, for evidence, about why I don't match, because I try my best to match. I don't have room to not match. Someone has to be the good one.

I stand on tiptoe, ignoring the flare of pain in my knee, and bring the box down. Peel back the creamy red satin cloth inside.

Pearly costume jewelry from the thrift store on Rose Street: pins and brooches, necklaces with tangled chains. Crumpled ones, tens, twenties from my father's pants pockets left in the basket in the laundry room, clothes that Goldie will dump in the washing machine twice a week and then artfully iron and hang in his closet. A watch left in the library from freshman year. It was beautiful, shiny and expensive, and who would leave such a thing? They didn't love it, so I made it mine. Hair ties left on benches in the humid locker room at Heywood High. An expensive pen abandoned on a side table at a dinner party in the city my parents took me to. It glittered in the soft light of the foyer. It was so easy to tip it off the table with a finger, slide it into my purse. The adults were wearing exquisite clothes and drinking. They weren't paying attention to a teenage girl.

Looking at my box of things makes me happy. *I* did this. *I* have secrets.

I'm running a finger over my things when I hear the car. My mother's car, pulling into the garage, the door rising up, and then down.

Joey is home.

10

THE FIRST THING I notice is his hair.

It's gone. Before he left for Blue Spruce, it hung down to his shoulders, full and dark, unusually beautiful for a boy.

Now, in our bright white and stainless-steel kitchen, my brother Joey's hair is barely two inches long. I don't think I've ever noticed how big his ears are and suddenly I wonder if that's why he grew his hair long, once he knew he could: to cover them.

Fuzzy yips and swirls around Joey's legs. He nudges her playfully. "Dumb dog," he says, but he's smiling.

The second thing I notice is more subtle. A difference to the way Joey inhabits his space.

He used to hunch, his chin almost to his chest, hands deep in his pockets, like he was afraid for anyone to look at him too closely, and maybe he was. He had a lot to hide, after all.

But he's standing straight now, his jacket unzipped, his hands on his hips and no longer balled inside the pockets of a dirty hoodie, and he's looking right at me, his brown eyes alert and clear.

His eyes were always so murky last year.

My mother makes an impatient clucking sound.

"Don't stand there *gaping,* Emory. He's *home.*" She hangs her purse on one of the nickel-plated hooks.

"Hey," I say.

Then I rush at him and wrap my arms around him. For a brief moment, I'm afraid he'll push me away. He doesn't. He folds his arms around me tightly and I sigh with relief. "I'm so glad you're back."

"Me too," he whispers. "How's your . . . how's your leg?"

"It's okay." I let go of him. "It's fine."

"Everything is always fine with you, Em."

Is there a note of sadness in his voice? I can't tell.

I smile. "The hair?"

"I know, right?" His eyes shine with the absurdity of it.

Madison and Joey are both dark-eyed and dark-haired, but I'm light as a feather. Light blue eyes, light brown hair. *Mały kwiatek,* our nana would coo at me when I was tiny. Little flower, in Polish.

My mother says, "It's a condition of Blue Spruce. They shave your head. You could hide drugs in your hair."

Joey says, "There were a lot of rules in that place."

"Rules exist for a reason, Joe," my mother says. "You did well and I'm proud of you. We're going to beat this."

She's gazing at her phone. "Can you bring our things in, Emory? I'm going to call out for dinner. Golden Dragon okay with everyone? Has your father texted what time he'll be home?"

"Not yet," I say.

Under his breath, Joey says, "Of course he's not home." His eyes flicker. Is that disappointment? I wish my dad had stayed home, just for once.

Mom's voice is sharp. "He has to work, Joe. Blue Spruce wasn't entirely covered by our insurance."

Joey and I are silent, pretending my father is dedicated to his job, and not to hiding.

In the garage, Joey takes his duffel bag from the trunk.

"Mom left for two days. She took three suitcases for two days?"

He smiles. "She went shopping before she checked me out of Blue Spruce. And bought new suitcases to bring it home in. You know Mom."

It's out before I can stop it. "Are you mad? At me? If I hadn't let Luther drive—"

"Emmy." He drops the duffel bag at his feet. "I'm not mad. I promise. I don't even really remember what happened. It is what it is. In the end, *I* screwed up."

It is what it is.

A girl died and my brother overdosed but lived.

I change the subject. "Who puts drugs in their hair, like, is that even possible?"

Joey sighs. "You'd be surprised where a person can hide drugs. Can we just not talk about it right now? I'm tired. I think I hiked a billion stupid miles. They even taught us how to make fires and cook meals in the forest and, like, shovel a hole for your poop."

"Oh my god. Like, you had to squat in nature?"

"I know. Shit got real. Like, literally."

We laugh, but it doesn't feel good to me; it feels hollow. Not like it used to be.

"I want things to be okay," I say softly. "Are we going to be okay?"

"I don't know." Joey heaves his duffel bag over his shoulder. "But maybe we can get somewhere close to it."

* * *

Upstairs, Joey looks around Maddie's room. "So, I'm going to be living in Woodstock, basically. That's my punishment?"

I look at the hanging hammock chair, the stars and half-moons and weird things Maddie stenciled over the deep, dark blue she painted during her sophomore year at Heywood High. The seashell chimes. The fairy lights strung along the walls.

Right on cue, my phone buzzes. It's Maddie, video calling. Her hair is pulled back in a tight bun and she has gold-and-purple glitter on her eyelids. "Put him on," she tells me.

"What's on your face?"

"Shut up. I just came from circus class. Did you think I was joking about that?"

I hand Joey the phone. He takes it, jumping on her bed and settling back against her batik pillows. "Hello, weird one. You fixing to run away to the circus now? That'll really piss Mom off."

"It's a summer class. I get *credit*. It's done wonders for my self-esteem and fear of heights. And I really might just join the circus. Wouldn't that just make Mom ballistic? Now, how are you, baby boy? Clean as a whistle? How do you like my room?"

"Your room is like living inside *My Little Pony*. If anything is going to make me relapse, it's this room."

I wince. *Relapse.* The Blue Spruce website said forty to sixty percent of people with substance addictions relapse during the first year of recovery.

I don't want that to be Joey. I have to make sure that isn't Joey.

"Joe." Her voice is soft. "I miss you. I was worried about you. I'm here for you. You're my *brother*. Everything doesn't have to be sarcastic."

Joey doesn't say anything.

I can tell she's crying now. "I'm just so glad you're *alive.*"

"Okay." He closes his eyes. "Okay. I'm going to try. I am. I learned stuff. Okay? Talk later."

He gets off the bed and hands the phone to me and goes into her bathroom and shuts the door.

Maddie wipes her eyes. "Sorry. I'm very emotional right now. You'll tell me how he's doing, yes? I won't be back until Thanksgiving."

"Of course," I tell her.

"You two are so close. You know I've always been jealous about that, right?" She breathes deeply. "I have to go. Call me, okay? Or text. Is Mom getting him another phone?"

"Probably. She's *Mom.*"

"I love you, Emmy-bear."

"Love you, too."

Her face disappears.

I help my mother put out the cartons of lo mein, orange chicken, egg rolls, plates, utensils. She pours a glass of wine. I wonder if that's a good idea now. Like, shouldn't she—well, she and Dad—both not drink, if we're trying to keep Joey safe? I looked at the Blue Spruce website. I read the advice on *bringing the patient home* and how to create a *supportive and sober environment.*

Tentatively, I open my mouth.

Without looking up from her phone, my mother murmurs, "Alcohol was not his issue, Emory. Go tell your brother it's time for dinner."

When I go upstairs to Maddie's room to get Joey, he's lying facedown on the bed, perfectly still.

Out of habit, I panic. What if he took something in the

bathroom? Mom swept the place of all painkillers, aspirins, everything except alcohol, but maybe she missed something. A fallen pill, a bottle of cough syrup pushed way back in the cabinet beneath the sink—

My heart starts to pound, thinking of those mornings last year when I had to throw cold water on Joey's face in the attic to get him up for school before my mother could see how wasted he was. Sometimes I had to slap his cheeks so hard I left red marks. Wait up for him to come home, watching endless re-runs of *Friends* in the living room with the volume turned low, and help him up the stairs, worried the entire time we might wake up our mom and dad.

I do not want to go back to those exhausting and lie-filled months.

"I'm not high," Joey mumbles. "Just tired. Not hungry."

In a minute, he starts snoring.

Mom's forehead creases in annoyance when I tell her he's asleep. "Well, I'm not really hungry, anyway. I'm going to check my email. I've lost a lot of work time. Eat, Emory. I don't want you getting too thin."

And there I am, in the kitchen, surrounded by food again, with only Fuzzy staring hopefully up at me.

I'm woken up by the sound of grunting and drilling. I get out of bed and go into the hallway.

My dad is taking the door off Maddie's room. Joey leans against the wall, still in his clothes from yesterday, frowning.

"No, Neil, I think you can just use a screwdriver, I don't—"

My dad holds the drill out to my mother. "Be my guest, Abigail."

"What's going on?" I say.

Everyone looks at me.

"I don't get to have a door," Joey says angrily. "I don't get to have privacy. Do I have that right, Mom?"

My mother says, "No, Joe. You don't. We gave you an attic and you did god knows what up there. This is part of your recovery. You can earn back your door when we see good grades, good behavior, a real effort on your part. I don't want any more locked doors. I don't want you *hiding* anymore."

"I'm not allowed a place to think, at least? Do my homework so I can concentrate?"

My mother gives him the Look.

"Joey," I say. "Just . . . let it go."

My dad starts drilling again, raising his voice over the sound of the drill. "You can do your homework downstairs, with Emory. You can do it together. Do you think I like doing this? Do you think this makes me—"

I close my eyes, listening to them all argue, back and forth, back and forth.

It's like last year all over again and Joey's only been home a day.

Last year: Mom rattling the attic door after he'd lock himself away. Grounding him. Taking his phone. Long lectures about his attitude. Joey kicking a wall. My father slamming his fist on the kitchen island, glasses slipping down his nose, still in his stained scrubs. Joey one long litany of *Okay okay okay okay okay get off my back okay okay okay just leave me alone.*

I thought that would be over now. I hoped it would be over now.

My mother shouts, "A girl died!"

My heart squeezes, a terrible fist punching me from the inside.

At the exact moment that I scream *Stop it,* the door falls off the hinges, pinning my dad to the doorframe. My mother pulls the door away with a groan. Leans it against the wall in the hallway, stumbling a little under the weight of it.

"Now you've upset your sister," she tells Joey.

"Just *stop,*" I say.

Dad adjusts his glasses. "Take the door downstairs, Joe, and put it in the basement. I have to take off the bathroom door, too. These are the conditions of living here. Do you want to be here?"

"Dad," I say. "He needs a *bathroom* door. It's only been a day. Give him a *chance.*"

"Emory," my mother warns. "Don't."

"Mom, this is ridic—"

"I want to be here," Joey cuts in. "Whatever you say. It's fine."

Finefinefinefinefine.

I start to say more, but Joey cuts me a look, his jaw tight.

"Good," my father says. "Then follow the rules, Joe. Because I spend more than half my job dealing with overdoses and I don't want to go to work and see my own son wheeled in on a gurney again."

He picks up the drill and starts on Maddie's bathroom door.

"Do as your father says, Joey," my mother says quietly. "And I'll make breakfast and we'll talk about the rules."

She looks at me. "Emory, go shower. I bought you a special shampoo and treatment. All that time in the pool has really done a number on your hair."

In the shower, I think about what my mother left out.

Candy MontClair died, yes.

But Joey almost did, too, and my mother never seems bothered by that.

We learn the Rules for Joey at the dining table, uneaten plates of fruit and eggs surrounding us.

—You will abide by the rules or you will no longer be
  able to live in this house.
—All doors removed until further notice.
—A phone will be reissued with limited data and will
  be handed back each night. Texts will be checked.
—A tracker will be installed on the phone.
—Outside time is limited to school hours and
  outpatient therapy until a part-time job has been
  secured.
—Paychecks from the job will be handed over and kept
  in a fund for future college.
—A car will be purchased for school transportation
  and job. Mileage will be checked. You may not use
  the car without permission.
—Outpatient recovery appointments must be kept.
  You will text a parent when you arrive and when
  you leave.
—You may have friends over if they are sober and all
  visits take place on the first floor of the home, when
  a parent or your sister is present.
—You may not drink, do drugs, or smoke cigarettes,
  and this includes vaping.

—You will submit to unannounced drug and alcohol tests.
—You will eat dinner with your family each night.
—You will meet with your outpatient counselor once a week.
—You will maintain at least a B-minus in each class.
—You will have no contact with Luther Leonard.

My brother swallows hard after reading the list.

My mother blinks at him from across the dining room table. Her hands are folded tightly.

"Okay," he says finally. "Okay."

It seems like a lot. I mean, how is he supposed to feel better, get better, or *whatever*, if he's basically a prisoner in his own house?

But I stay quiet, because I already pushed it with Mom upstairs. You have to tread carefully with our mother.

Okay okay okay okay, just like last year, but now his voice is soft, and not scratched and hard, like it would have been last year.

When he came home yesterday, his head was high. A different Joey. Now he's slumping, his head low, his eyes down.

He signs the paper.

My mother rises from the table and walks into the kitchen, placing the contract under a magnet on the refrigerator.

Joey eats two strawberries and three bites of toast and goes upstairs to Maddie's room. I follow him, limping behind him on the stairs.

He flops down on the bed, staring at the ceiling.

"She's just trying to help," I say. "She'll relax things. Eventually."

"You don't have to explain Mom to me. I get it."

He folds his hands on his chest.

"Hey, you know what Maddie found? In the attic? Your drawings." I point to the milk crate by her dresser. "I almost forgot how good they are. Maybe you can start drawing again."

"Emmy, I was stoned when I did those. I don't even remember what I was thinking."

"Maybe, but if you just tried, I'm sure—"

Joey rolls over and looks at me. "I know you want to be helpful, Em, but can you . . . not? Not right now. I just . . . I just need to be alone, okay? Sorry."

"Oh, okay," I say. "Sure."

"Sorry," he says. "Wait, I'm not sorry. I'm not supposed to apologize for needing space."

He takes a deep breath. "I just need some space, okay?"

I know I shouldn't feel hurt by that, but I do, just a little. "Yeah," I say. "I get it."

In the hallway, I lean against the wall outside his room.

I knew when he came back he might be different. I knew that. I mean, he's *supposed* to be different, because of the sober thing. Maybe I thought he'd come back the version of Joey I like to remember best, the one when we were younger. Like that part of him would be allowed to rise to the surface again.

I didn't expect to have to get to know a whole new brother.

When my mother is asleep that night, I go down to the pool. I'm slipping in when Ryleigh, Gage's little sister, peeks up over the brick wall separating our yards. She's got a ladder on her side. It used to drive Maddie crazy when she'd be out in the pool with her friends and suddenly this little kid would pop over the wall.

"Hi, Emmy," she chirps.

"Hello, Ryleigh. Back from camp?"

"Yep. And I think I got Zika from all the mosquitoes. I was like their pincushion."

"I don't think you can get Zika from a summer camp in New Hampshire."

"Then I definitely got something from all the mosquito repellant they sprayed on us. All organic, my butt. Anything that repels those suckers has to be toxic. I'll probably be dead by morning."

"Probably."

She waits.

"Well, if you're in your suit, come on over," I say. "Where's your mom? It's late."

She hoists a leg over the wall, slides down. Her swimsuit is pink and green. "Asleep, like always. Like yours. Do all moms go to bed early?"

"Yes. It's to get away from rotten kids like us." I walk around inside the pool, testing my knee.

Ryleigh stands by the pool steps, the lights from under the water casting a milky glow over her body.

"You got really tan," I tell her.

"All that sunscreen is probably toxic, too. I stopped wearing it and then I thought about skin cancer, but by that time it was too late and here I am. Brown as a nut, my dad said. He's working late at the paper again, in case you were wondering where *he* was."

"Well, the news never stops, I guess."

She looks around the pool. "What happened to the swan floatie? I liked that one."

"I don't know. But it was some sort of plastic, so it was probably toxic, too, and you're better off."

She plops into the water. "I was watching earlier. Joey's home?"

"Yeah."

"That's good. I like him. I was worried. Did you know that nearly twenty-one million people in the country struggle with drug addiction? That's more than the number of people with cancers combi—"

I hold up a hand. "Stop."

"Okay." She dips under the water. Her body swivels past the underwater pool light, like a skinny mermaid. She pops back up in the deep end. "I'm going to be in sixth grade."

"I know! Very exciting. Did you get your school clothes?"

"Yes. I did my research and had Mom order ethically made clothes, but then I thought about the environmental cost of shipping and was that really ethical or just more environmental damage and maybe I didn't do the right thing. Maybe I should make my own clothes. Maybe that would be better, like in olden times. The air was better then." She sniffs the humid evening air. "Heliotrope smells nice."

"It's a hard choice to make. That might be fun, to learn to sew. Probably come in handy for the future apocalypse," I say, letting water drizzle through my fingertips. Ryleigh dives back down and shimmies up next to me.

"Look." She uses her fingers to spread her mouth wide.

"Oh my gosh! No more braces! Cool you! Someone will definitely fall in love with you this year, for sure. Sixth grade is middle school. You'll have dances now."

She takes her fingers out of her mouth.

"No," she says. "That won't happen. I'm too difficult. That's what Mom says, anyway. She says I talk too much and tire people out and I should probably see a doctor. I don't know why I need to see a doctor for *talking*."

When I was in the sixth grade, I asked my mother if she thought I was pretty and she put down her phone and took off her glasses and said, "That's not something you need to worry about, Emory. There are far more important things to be worried about than looks."

I still think about how she just didn't say *Yes*. How it shouldn't be hard for a mom to just say *Yes, you're pretty*. They tell us plenty of critical things, how hard is it to throw some positives in there? A B is always "Well, if you'd applied yourself" and never "That was a hard class for you, good job." It's like they're constantly paring us down, whittling us away so the only part that remains is the one they think is most acceptable.

"Well, Ryleigh, you know what?"

She bounces up and down. "What?"

"There's somebody out there in this big old world who's very quiet, and you know what?"

"What?"

"You're going to meet them, and they are going to love every single thing you have to say."

She smiles and does a handstand. I tickle her water-wrinkled feet.

Upstairs, the light in Maddie's room switches on and then off again.

Ryleigh has gone home, pushing a lounge chair to the wall to climb back over. I hoisted her as best I could, made sure to listen to the click of her back door, that she got in safe.

I float for a little bit longer, staring at my stars, before I decide to get out. I'm toweling off when my phone flashes.

Hey

My heart starts pounding so hard my ears swim. Maybe if I'd listened closer in Biology and Anatomy last spring I'd know what this particular sensation is called.

My fingers tremble a little as I type back, *Hey.*

I'm about to pull up in the drive. You outside?

Yes

See you in 15

Ok

I wait in the pool house. It's like a tiny house, with a simple shower and some long built-in benches with cushions. Extra towels, sunscreen. Silly signs like BEACH THIS WAY with an arrow pointing outside, toward the pool. I shake out my hair.

The door opens. Moonlight floods the small room.

"Hey, you," says Gage.

He closes the door, encasing us in darkness. It takes a few minutes for my eyes to adjust, but then there he is, finally home, here in front of me.

"Hey," I say lightly. I can't act too excited to see him; he gets weirded out by that. I did that in the spring once and he didn't text me back for a week.

"Stand up," he says.

Gage is so much taller than me, I barely clear his chest. Standing so close to him feels electrical, bolts of heat and light that erase the pain in my knee, my thoughts about Joey, everything, because I know in a few minutes I am going to feel *better*.

"I missed you," he says. He snaps the strap on my swimsuit. "I like this. Did you miss me, too?"

But he doesn't wait for me to answer.

11

I T STARTED WITH ANNE Sexton. Or maybe Arthur Miller. Possibly Henry James. All I know is, three dead writers led to me hooking up with the boy next door. Not the most romantic start, but as Joey would say, it is what it is.

I was waiting up for Joey last spring, in my room, reading at my desk in front of the window, when the light in Gage's bedroom suddenly came on and startled me. It was late; I thought he'd be asleep. He's always training and then sleeping and then getting up early to run. In a weird way, he's like an extremely hot-looking hamster stuck inside a wheel.

I looked up, blinking.

There he was, staring at me. He gave me a little wave and then sat down at his own desk. Pulled out some notebooks, his iPad, lowered his head. Frowned. Chewed on a pencil. Sighed. Fiddled with his phone.

My phone vibrated on the desk. I picked it up. I didn't recognize the number, but I looked at the message anyway.

U should be sleeping

How did you get my number? I typed back.

I have my ways what are u doing

I was afraid to look up. Would he be staring at me through his window? Could he tell my face was bright red? Could he see my hands shaking? Stupid stuff like that.

Reading a book for class

Me too, I dont get this book at all haha

What is it?

Death of a Salesman

That's not a book, it's a play

Well it's IN a book so it's a book it has pages!
The dad is too sad everybody is sad

I would say that's a very true
statement of life in general

That's funny!

I guess

I still remember that party your mom gave. 8th grade,
remember? She had you recite that poem.

I remembered. We had to memorize a poem for English. It could be anything we wanted, as long as we learned it by heart. "The Black Art," by Anne Sexton. I found the collection in Maddic's room. My teacher said it was advanced, possibly because the word *erections* shows up. To be honest, I wasn't exactly clear on that at the time and there was a lot of giggling when I recited it for our class. My parents had a cocktail party and my mother made me put on a nice dress and stand in front of everyone and read it aloud, this time from the book. This time, *erections* seemed to create a hush in the roomful of adults, but no one was going to question my mother. I remember that my voice shook, and the party guests stood awkwardly in lovely clothes.

People clapped politely when it was over.

Gage texted, *She thinks she can warn the stars*

It's a line from the poem. The one that really made me love the poem, in fact, when the rest of the poem is a little weird. But I think there's something interesting about warning the stars, when in most poetry, the stars would be warning *you*.

. . .

**I never forgot that line. I don't know
what it means, but I liked it, I guess.**

Me too

I decided to sneak a glance at his window and there he was, a half smile on his face, looking directly at me.

I'd known Gage my whole life. Our parents lumped us together to play when we were little, there were neighborhood barbecues, elementary school with soggy snow boots and runny noses, and through most of it, Gage was just a blur, really. Always with a glove in hand, the thwack of the baseball on his side of our backyard wall as he practiced. If the ball landed in the pool and I was outside, I fished it out with the skimmer and tossed it back over the wall and waited for the thwacking to resume.

You can be around people every day of your life and not really see them, you know? They're just a collection of things, like baseball gloves and tousled hair and wide grins, and you don't paw around any deeper because you think you have them all figured out already, just by what you can see on the outside.

But something in Gage's eyes was different.

> How can you remember a line from
> a poem I read years ago?

**I don't know, I just do. Stuck with me. How can we live
next door to each other and we never talk, you know?**

I glanced at him again. He didn't have the half smile anymore. His face was softer. Sadder, somehow.

He looked back down at his phone.

**Give me some words I have to go to sleep Something
interesting, like the stars thing**

I looked down at my phone, thinking.

Then I typed: *If you look for grand examples of anything from me, I
shall disappoint you.*

Isabel Archer. From *The Portrait of a Lady*. I was reading it right
then, for my class. I liked that line, too, because it's kind of how
I felt when I thought about my mother.

It took a long time for Gage to answer.

...

**I'm not sure it's possible for you
to be disappointing, Emory**

> Tell that to my mom, ha

Funny. You can never win with parents, tho

> Def not

Night, Emory

> Night

He pulled his blind down. I didn't know what to think,
really. I thought he was just being weird, texting me out of

the blue. Gage had his own crowd, and baseball, and we didn't intersect all that much. But then, after the texting, he'd sort of lift his chin at me in the cafeteria during lunch, or glance at me in the hallway, maybe a beat too long, and every once in a while after that night he'd text again, after everyone had gone to bed. About baseball. Or his homework, or nothing at all really. A smiley face. A frown. The tiny-person-sleeping-in-bed emoji.

I guess I thought, for all his popularity, that maybe he was kind of lonely, too.

It's nice talking like this, he texted once. *Easy.*

Yes, I answered.

And then, *Want to hang out? I could come over.*

It's late.

Just for a bit. I can come over the wall.
We could hang out in your yard. It's nice tonight.

My parents are asleep.

We'll be quiet. You have that pool house.

It was late. It was Friday night and I was tired. I'd waited for Joey to come home for hours and when he did, my mother intercepted him in the hallway on the way to his attic room and there was a fight, and I was exhausted from all that. I was tired and lonely. And if I'm being honest, I wanted to be kissed. Because I knew the moment he said "pool house" that he was going to kiss me, because no one asks to go into a pool house late at night just to recite poetry from memory or discuss the plays of Arthur Miller, and I'd been thinking about Gage and his mouth for a very long time.

Ok, I finally typed back.

That's how it started.

And after that night, I felt alive in a way I never had before.

Gage and I do everything but have sex-sex. He doesn't want to mess anything up, he told me. He doesn't want to get somebody pregnant. "Condoms break," he said. He doesn't want to date anyone. "Too complicated," he said. "People would get up in our business. It would be a *thing*. I need to concentrate on my game." I don't know if what he does to me is spectacular or anything, because how would I know? He's the only person I've ever done these things with. But it makes me feel better.

"We've known each other forever," he said once, kissing my neck. "It could be destiny, but it has to be secret. My mother would freak out." I didn't mind that secret, like I don't mind the secrets in my box of stolen things. Something that's *mine*. Like I've stolen him from all the girls who sidle up to him in the hallways of Heywood High, who text him photos of their bodies in bras and bikinis and who can't figure out why he doesn't pick one of them. Because he could pick one of them. He could pick any one of them to do the things he does with me, in secret. They could be his secret, but instead it's *me*. And when you live in a house where all the energy is directed toward one person, and that person is your troubled brother, well, you get kind of hungry to be seen.

I think about this in bed, after Gage has gone and I'm up-stairs, still warm and electric, my hand on my stomach, the whole house quiet. Maddie is the pretty one, Joey is the bad one, and I'm the good one, and that's where I have to stay.

Last spring Gage said, "I don't want to fall in love with anyone and I don't want anyone to fall in love with me, not right now."

Too late, I think as I fall asleep.

Too late.

12

JOEY AND I ARE on the sectional, watching television, Fuzzy curled in my lap. I'm trying to be quiet with Joey, slow. He's mostly been in his room, sleeping, for the few days he's been back and I just felt so grateful when he came downstairs and sat on the couch with me. I don't want to ruin it.

The doorbell rings, making us both jump. Fuzzy goes crazy, leaping off me and running to the foyer, yipping all the way. The doorbell rings again. Joey and I look at each other.

"Don't look at me," he says. "You get it." He nudges me with his foot.

When I open the door, Max deVos is standing there, hands in the pockets of his jeans.

"Hey, Emory," he says. "Joey home?"

Max deVos once got so messed up at school his head dropped into the mashed potatoes on his lunch tray. All his friends laughed and kept eating. Only Joey lifted him up and cleaned him off. Slapped his face until he came to and told the cafeteria monitor, Ms. Richards, that Max was just tired from studying, which I'm sure she didn't believe for a second, because, well, it's *Max deVos.* His brain is only wired for two things: pot and skateboarding.

"I don't know, Max," I say tentatively. I'm thinking about what our mom said about Joey's friends coming over. You don't want to get on my mother's bad side.

"I just want to say hi. I don't have anything." He takes his hands from his pockets, holds them out, empty.

From behind me, Joey says, "Hey, man." His voice sounds hesitant.

Max's eyes brighten. "Dude, hey. Wow, your hair. That's intense. How you been?"

"How do you think?" Joey says.

Max's smile dies. "Sorry, man. I just thought I'd come over, maybe play some *Assassin's Creed*. Hang out."

Next to me, Joey shifts in an uncomfortable way.

"You high?" he asks Max softly.

"What? No! I mean, not right now, anyway. I swear, I just want to hang out."

"I can't," my brother says slowly. "I can't hang out with anyone who's using. I'll get kicked out of the house."

Max's face falls. "Are you kidding me? I can't even play a video game with you?"

Joey swallows hard. "No."

"Dude. I'm your *friend.*" Max's voice cracks. "This is stupid."

"I can't. I just can't. It is the way it is. I gotta go, Max." Joey walks away.

Max looks at me. "I mean, for real?"

"For real," I answer.

"Like for how long?"

"I'm not really sure? I mean, he has to try to be sober forever, Max."

"Shit." Max shoves his hands back in his pockets, shakes his head. He turns and walks down the steps, back to his skateboard, rides away. I shut the door.

Joey's pacing in the living room.

"You'll make other friends," I tell him. But I'm not sure

I believe it. The kids Joey hangs out with all get high, for the most part. And like me, he's probably not going to get the best reception when school starts, because of Candy MontClair.

"No, I won't." He stops pacing. "Can I borrow your phone? Mom hasn't bought me another one yet."

"I don't know . . ." My fingers tighten around my phone. What if he calls someone, maybe Max, and he disappears, and they get high?

"I just want to call Shadow, okay? He was my Blue Spruce counselor. I need to talk to someone. You can check the damn number if you want. I can put it on speakerphone! Jesus!" He's yelling.

"Okay," I say, my voice shaking. "Calm down." I hand my phone to him.

He grabs it from me. Takes a few deep breaths. "Sorry."

Then he says, "No, I'm not sorry. I need to do this. I should have just said thank you."

"It's okay," I tell him, but is it? It's good that he's calling his counselor, right? My mom can't get mad about *that*. Calling your counselor is definitely something that spells *reaching out* and *asking for help*. The Blue Spruce handbook says that's a good thing.

Joey goes into the kitchen. I stand outside the doorway.

In a few minutes, he starts talking. "It's me. Joe Ward. You said I could call anytime."

Came to my house

Just wanted to play video games

How am I supposed to

I don't know anyone who doesn't use

Outpatient and school start next week it's overwhelming

You didn't tell me they'd take my doors

Well, they did

I'm like a prisoner here

Shit

Can't calm down

My sister

Okay

Joey calls my name. I step into the kitchen. The tile is cold under my bare feet.

"He wants to talk to you."

"What? Me? Why? No." I shake my head. What am I supposed to say to his counselor? "Hi, tell me how to keep my brother from dying?"

"Please." Joey holds the phone out, his hand shaking. I take it.

"Hey, Emory," the voice says. "This is Shadow, Joe's leader from Blue Spruce. I heard a lot about you over the summer. I need your help right now, okay?"

My voice is only a whisper. "Okay."

I'm trying to picture what he looks like. He sounds young-ish, but how young could he be to have a job like this?

"Joe's in a bad place right now. You know the situation?"

"Yes. Max came over."

"Yes. It's really, really hard when old friends come by when you're trying to maintain recovery. Your desire for friendship and connection is huge, but you have to say no to people who aren't sober, and that can be an extremely hard and lonely thing to do. You know?"

"Yeah."

"So, I'm really proud of Joe for telling his friend he couldn't come in, but I need you to do something for me, okay? It's going to seem really small, but it's actually pretty big.

"I want you to take Joe for a walk, a hike, anything to clear his head. Sometimes being active, getting our blood flowing, is a way to calm down and refocus. Be outside. Breathe the air."

Joey is holding Fuzzy tight, nuzzling her fur. I can't see his face.

"I can't . . . I can't hike or walk for a long time. I have a bad knee."

There's a pause. "That's right. You were in the car. I'm sorry. I shouldn't have forgotten that."

"We have a pool, though. It's a nice day. We could swim. Can we swim?"

"Oh, for sure! That's excellent. I love that. Thank you. These are just things that we need to do to help Joey, okay? Keep him safe, keep him feeling like he has a support system. I'll give your mom a call, let her know what—"

"Oh, no, not our mom." My voice rises in an embarrassing squeak. Joey looks up, shaking his head. "No, you can't . . . don't do that. She'll get . . . that just wouldn't be a good idea."

Shadow pauses. "I see. Okay. I get it. I'm not a fan of omission, but I get it. Can you save my number in your phone? In case you need it sometime? I'll save yours, too, okay? I'm a big fan of yours, Joey talked about you a lot. You sound like a good sister. Joey said you taught him to read. That's amazing."

I don't say anything.

We used to read for hours in the fort in my dad's den. My parents were always frustrated with him. They thought he wasn't working hard enough, that he was lazy. I read a lot of books to Joey, just the two of us, until he got the hang of it.

"Can you let me talk to Joey again, for a minute? And then you guys can swim. Tell Joey to do a cannonball for me, okay?"

"Okay."

Joey and I trade the dog and the phone.

I hear Shadow say, "You're amazing, brother. You reached out when you needed to and that was exactly the right thing to do."

Joey angles his head, mumbles something, and then hands my phone back to me.

"I think I left my suit in Colorado. I remember swimming in a lake and hanging it in a tree to dry and that's the last I saw of it. I don't think I have another one," he says.

We both turn at the sound of a tap on the patio door. Ryleigh is standing there in her pink-and-green swimsuit. She holds up an inner tube.

"I think I have an idea," I say, smiling.

Gage's swimsuit is a little droopy around Joey's skinny waist, even though he tied it as tight as he could. He was always pretty thin, but it looks like he got skinnier in rehab. It must have been all the hiking. The suit has surfboards and sunsets on it. "I hope this doesn't fall down," he mutters.

"He said to do cannonballs," I say, lowering myself into the water.

Ryleigh shouts, "Cannonball contest!" And jumps in the water, splashing Joey.

"All right, now, that's war," he says when she bobs to the surface. "Prepare to be drenched." He takes a run, lifts, and tucks himself tight. Ryleigh squeals as she's pulled and pushed in the waves.

When Joey comes up, he's got a grin on his face. "I bet I can do fifty. How many can you do?"

"One thousand. Do you know this one guy once did eighty-nine cannonballs in twenty minutes? He was wearing a Speedo."

Joey treads water. "This is a lot better than the lakes we swam in this summer. I could never see the bottom. That kind of freaked me out. I like to know where the bottom is, you know?" He smiles at me, ducks back under.

Each wave bumps more and more water against me, which feels nice, like being in the ocean when we went on vacation to San Diego. Joey and I spent whole days in the sea, going farther and farther out, holding each other and screaming as the waves tried to knock us down. At night, my parents would go to dinner in the fancy hotel restaurant and give us money to walk the boardwalk in Mission Beach and get hamburgers at Woody's. We ate on the beach as the sun went down, our hair still crunchy with salt, Maddie digging her toes in the sand. Sometimes Joey would give me one of his earbuds and we'd listen to music together. Sometimes he'd light a joint if no one was around. I don't know where he got it or if he was stupid enough to bring it on the plane. The beach seemed like you could probably get it anywhere, from somebody.

It didn't seem like a problem then. And it was nice being with Joey, looking at the sea as the sky changed colors, watching the waves as they went from blue to black, music in our ears. I felt like I could live beside the ocean forever.

I wish we could be back there. I wish we could go back, way back, to before all this ever happened.

"Ryleigh!"

Gage is leaning over the wall. His eyes slide to me and then back to Ryleigh.

Ryleigh yells back, "What!"

"Mom wants you to come in. You've got a hair appointment."

"No!" She scrunches up her face.

Gage holds out his hands. "Sorry, kid. Clarissa at Curl Up and Dye waits for no one."

He looks at Joey standing at the edge of the pool.

"Hey, Joe."

"Hey."

"You all right?"

"Yeah."

"Cool." Gage squints. "Are those my trunks?"

"Uh, yeah."

"I let him borrow them," Ryleigh says, getting out and wrapping herself in a towel. "You have like fifty million."

"I do?"

"Yeah."

"Then I'm coming in." He disappears.

I can feel myself flush, so I duck under the water really quick. Joey's sitting on the pool steps when I come up. "Thanks," he says. "I feel better. That was one thing about Blue Spruce, they kept you really active, so whenever you'd start to feel crazy, it was hike time or gym time or time to make dinner. I still feel like shit, because I have no friends now, but whatever, right?"

"You'll make friends," I say. "Different ones."

"Says the sister who has no friends." His face reddens. "Sorry. Maddie told me. Screw them, though, right?"

"Yeah," I say, grateful. "Screw them."

Gage drops over the wall.

I try to keep my cool as he dives into the pool. I've seen parts of Gage without clothes, but not in the daylight, and I'm not sure how I feel about keeping it together while he's wet and in a swimsuit in my pool. He used to swim here all the time when

80

we were little, before Joey tried to fly off the roof, but his parents didn't let them come over after that. It was Maddie who convinced Mrs. Galt last summer to let Ryleigh come over. "It's *hot,* Beth, let the girl swim. Let's move *on.*" I was shocked how easily Maddie let Mrs. Galt's first name roll off her tongue, but that's just Maddie, I guess, and Ryleigh has been a mermaid in our pool ever since.

Gage flips his wet hair out of his eyes. "God, this feels good. You guys ready for another year of Heywood High Hell?" He's not serious; he makes that jerking-off gesture that guys like, which is gross.

"Not particularly," Joey says.

"You'll be okay, Joe. Gotta have a goal, is all. Work toward it. You don't have to get screwed up."

"Everybody's screwed up at Heywood," Joey says. "Half your teammates sell their pain meds on the side."

Gage shrugs. "Maybe. But not me. Never touch the stuff."

And then his eyes are on me. Like we're just normal neighbors, enjoying an afternoon in the pool. "What about you, Em? Ready for dance team again? Shimmy-shimmy." He wiggles his hips. Joey laughs.

"I can't because of my knee," I say.

Gage grimaces. "Ah, no. I guess I didn't realize it was that bad."

Suddenly I realize there weren't any texts from Gage when I checked my new phone. Hazy as I was in the hospital, I sort of got why he didn't visit me. It would look weird, to suddenly have Gage-from-next-door there.

But he didn't text, either. And no one would have seen those.

He could have texted. Just once.

Maybe he was just too busy getting ready for his pitching camp. Maybe . . . a thousand things run through my mind.

"You okay? You look weird," Joey says.

Gage and Joey are both looking at me.

"I . . . it's no big deal," I say. "I wasn't any good, anyway. I was just an alternate."

"You looked pretty good to me."

I splash water on him, trying to be playful, but mostly so some gets on me, too, and washes away the awful feeling in my stomach.

He could have sent one text. Just one. That wouldn't have been breaking the rules.

From the corner of my eye, I see Joey frown and I think Gage notices, too, because he quickly says, "Hey, Joe, you still got all those games, man?"

"What?"

"You know." Gage makes a motion with his thumbs, like he's using a controller. "I might be down for *Fortnite* right about now."

Joey looks at me and then back at Gage. "Um, okay?"

I nod, because I guess I'm supposed to, now that I'm Joey's keeper. Of course Gage is safe. Like he said, he never touches the stuff. In the universe my mother would like us to live in, Gage would be the perfect friend for Joey.

"Cool. Let's get to it," Gage says. "I got a whole free afternoon."

They get out of the pool and wrap themselves in towels.

"You better put some dry towels down. You know how much Mom hates pool water on the floor! And put some towels on the couch!" I call.

Gage turns around and gives me the thumbs-up. At first,

I'm hopeful he'll say, "Come in and play with us, Em," but he doesn't.

Instead, he turns his head ever so slightly to the pool house and mouths, *Later.*

13

THERE'S A TEAR IN the shoulder of her blouse, like someone yanked it suddenly. Or took it between their fingers and she pulled away quickly, the thread separating the fabric. Her eyeliner is smudged. The strobe lights in the basement flash across her face redblueredblueredblue. Is she crying? I don't want to be at this party, either, but my mother told Joey he had to take me if he wanted to go. She thought it would keep him from getting high. *You need to take care of your sister.* That was actually code to me for *You need to watch Joey.* So we got in his Toyota, Nana's old car. The seat belts in the back didn't work. She gave it to him when she gave up driving. Now she takes the bus everywhere. There are too many kids in this basement and it's too hot. I don't know where Joey went. Not knowing where Joey went is bad because it means I haven't done my job. Now the girl is crying. Her name comes slowly, like a drop of water down window glass. That's right. *Candy.* From dance team freshman year. I don't like any of this music. Or maybe I would if I was like other kids. I text Joey. The girl has her head in her hands. I text Joey again. *I want to leave.* The girl's eyes meet mine. I slide in and out of kids dancing. *Candy, are you okay?* Can she even hear me? Her eyes drift away from mine, to a boy in the corner. He's staring at us. I don't like his eyes. *Do you have a car? I just want to go home. Please take me home. I have a really bad headache and that guy grabbed me.*

And then her mouth opens, and blood drains out. I catch it in my hands.

I wake up slicked with sweat, my heart racing.

Why am I dreaming about Candy MontClair? I don't want to dream about her. I have her, in my head, when I'm awake. I don't want her when I sleep.

Fuzzy shifts her tiny body at the end of my bed, lets out a sigh. I rub my feet against her. I have to go back to sleep. Tomorrow is the first day of school. The first day of everything. I don't want to be tired like I was last year, because I was up late waiting for Joey or helping him with homework. Sometimes I'd start to fall asleep in class and catch myself at the last minute, before my head hit the desk.

I walk down the hall to Joey's new room. Peer around the doorway. He's splayed across the bed, in the pink-and-yellow glow of Maddie's unicorn night-light. I climb into her hanging hammock. Maybe the swaying will make me sleepy.

Joey stirs. "Em?"

"Sorry," I say. "I couldn't sleep."

He leans on an elbow. "You can come in, if you want."

He scoots over in the bed. I slide in.

"Joey?"

"Mmm."

I have to tread carefully. I don't want to upset him.

"Do you ever think about her?"

"Who?"

I hesitate. "Candy." Her name feels off in my mouth, like the first bite of a food gone sour.

A rustling on his side of the bed. "Sometimes. It's sad."

"I had a dream about her. A bad one."

"Emmy," he says, looping his arm around me. "It's probably because of school tomorrow. You're worried about seeing everyone. Having them see you. Us."

"I can't believe Tasha dropped me," I say.

He sighs. "I guess we'll be friendless together then, huh?"

"I guess so," I say.

"Well, at least we have each other, right?" he says.

Before I can answer I hear soft snores.

When I was little and had nightmares, my dad would always come for me. He was usually up, because of his late shifts. He'd climb into bed with me, tuck me against him.

I didn't even know what song he was singing to me for the longest time, until I was older and heard it over the loudspeaker once at the Mill Haven county fair. I thought maybe he'd made it up, this song about a guy who wanted to give a girl numbers, like actual numbers: a giant three, a giant nine. Maybe he took them and wanted to give them back. My mom used to make fun of my dad for singing that song.

Jenny I got your number
867-5309

Maybe it was his soft voice back then that lulled me to sleep. Maybe it was the cadence of the song. But I try it now anyway. Murmur it over and over to wash away Candy MontClair and the dream blood pooling in my hands, Candy Mont-Clair and her ripped blouse and her simple headache that changed everything.

Jenny I got your number. 867-5309. 867-5309.
86753098675309 . . .

Mis_Educated

Hey, hey, Heywood High!
Here we are again
Are you ready
For another year
Of useless tests
Books by dead white men
Trigonometry triggers me
How about you?
Let's see who'll be back this year
Who got sent away for being
Sad, mad, drunk, gay, drugged out, just
Being a problem Mom and Dad can't handle?
What MEDS are you on this year
Besides the fun ones
I hear you can get some good ones
At the house where the shoe
Hangs in the trees
Let's see who's back to teach us the
finer parts of humanity
Will it be Grabby Hands McGregor
(watch out kids)
How about Helen Hoover from Hell
Ready to fuck up American history for us
I wonder how Mistuh Brody's summer was
(don't you dare forget to call him mister, you ingrates)
And let's remember who isn't here
You know who I'm talking about
And I miss her too
We are too young
To have had so many deaths
(oh and all you vegans your petition
for better lunches was DE-NIED)

11 likes

#heywoodhigh #heywoodhaulers #schoolsin #backtoschool
#millhaven #nightmare

Lzysusan so much for keeping school kidz healthy

87

FrancesP44 what is this account who are you

MandyMandy I miss her, too

NatetheGreat those kids shoulda gone to jail after Candy

TupacLives @NatetheGreat That Luther guy went to juvie

Stewie13 I hate school

PristTine party at the bridge 9 tonite

HelenOfJoy Did you see that reading list for Watson's class? Lolita omg

GiGi oh god Grabby Hands not again I can't take another year of over the shoulder boulder holders for god's sake man just teach me molecular something and stop feeling me up already

14

JOEY WALKS INTO THE kitchen with a disgusted look on his face. "I can't wear this stuff," he says. "I want my old clothes back."

He's dressed in a charcoal-gray hoodie, a chocolate-colored T-shirt, and a pair of the holey jeans I got him at the Gap.

"You look good." I give him a granola bar. "Handsome."

He tugs at the neck of the T-shirt. "I feel like I'm suffocating."

My mother comes into the kitchen. "You look wonderful. Emory did a nice job picking out these clothes." She brushes his shoulders with her fingers, though there is nothing there that I can see.

"I'm glad I know who to blame," Joey says, unwrapping the granola bar.

"First day of the rest of your life, so to speak, Joe." My mother pours a cup of coffee and takes a sip. "Emory, you look very nice, too. Lunches are in the fridge. Joe, you're clear on the rules?"

He pulls at the pockets of his hoodie. "Sure thing."

"It's going to be a big year for you, Joe. I know you can do this."

Joey grabs our backpacks. I get the lunches out of the refrigerator. My mother hands him the car keys and his new phone.

"You'll be responsible for getting your sister home after

school every day," she says. "She can study while you have your tutoring sessions."

Joey salutes her and walks quickly out the door before she can react.

In the garage, I hesitate before getting into the car.

I wasn't worried when Maddie drove me, why would I worry about Joey driving me? I feel guilty for even thinking about it. But it's making me think of that night. The last time I was in a car with him.

Joey touches my arm, like he knows.

"I'll drive slow," he says.

I open the door, slide in, my heart beating nervously.

I start talking quickly so I don't have to hear the sound of my heart. "I can't believe Mom got you such a nice car."

Joey runs a hand over the seat leather. "I wish she hadn't. I don't think this is going to make a good impression, if you know what I mean. I liked Nana's junky old car." He backs down the driveway. "We should go see her soon."

Joey revs the engine. I jump.

Luther was driving too fast, no seat belt, and I was shotgun and Candy and Joey were in the back and Candy kept saying she was scared and what was wrong with Joey and—

"Sorry," he says sheepishly. "I had to. I mean, this car . . ."

Concentrate, Emory, I tell myself. Fixed point on the horizon. Keep talking.

"Nana's been upstate visiting Aunt Dory all summer. Dory had that hip replacement," I say. "We don't have the same lunch period, you know."

"You don't have to hold my hand for lunch."

"I just—"

"I know." He looks at me. "But I have to suck it up. You can't do everything for me."

I'm quiet, watching the rows of shops on Main Street pass by. Hank's Hoagies, Kaminski's Hardware, Betty's Café with the potted flowers by the door and the painting hanging in the window of a black cat, with one white ear, lapping a milk shake. Mill Haven is neat and tidy, nothing out of place. The public library, stoic and brick, built by people in my family who died long ago. Everything in this town has a connection to me and I've still never felt at home here.

My stomach feels hot. Finally, I say, "Everyone is going to be, like, mad at us, I think. That's what Tasha said."

Joey bites his lip. "Maybe."

"Mom wanted to send me to boarding school," I say. "Did you know that? After it happened. She wanted to send you to military school. Maybe she was right. Maybe it would be better to be someplace nobody knows about us, or what happened."

"No *way* am I getting shipped off to military school. I'd rather die than do that."

Joey slows the car down. "Is that Liza?"

I look where he's pointing. Liza Hernandez, my former best friend, is walking down the sidewalk, backpack jiggling, her hair almost as short as Joey's. She's in overalls. She's been wearing them for two years straight.

Last year in PE, I heard her tell Mandy Hinkle, "I'm removing my body from the male gaze."

Mandy said, "Okay, *fine,* but *everybody* can still see you, you know that, don't you? They're just *imagining* what's underneath."

Every time I see Liza, my heart hurts. Even though it's been four years, it still hurts.

Joey pulls the car over.

"What are you doing?" I whisper. "Don't!"

"Hey, Liza!" Joey rolls the window down. "You want a ride?"

Liza stops. She bends down to see into the car and deliberately looks past me, to Joey. I stare at my hands, my face burning.

"I did miss my bus," she says, considering. "Fancy new ride, Joseph."

"You know our mom."

"I do. I remember her quite well. Her high standards."

She lets that hang in the air.

It was my mom who severed my friendship with Liza, because of Liza's parents. I don't like thinking about that time.

But I wonder, now, if my mother might have more sympathy for what happened with Liza's parents because of what happened with Joey.

"Yeah," Liza says finally. "I'll take a ride." She opens the back passenger-side door and slides in.

Joey says, "You two going to acknowledge each other, or what?"

"Hello, Emory," Liza says in a monotone voice.

"Hello, Liza," I say back, in the very same way.

That's the most we've spoken in four years.

Joey whistles. "All righty, then."

When we pull into the parking lot, Liza says, "Thanks for the scintillating conversation and the sweet ride, Joseph. Stay out of trouble." She pops out of the car and takes off.

That's Liza for you. No one said anything the entire ride and she has to be snarky about it.

Joey and I stay in the car.

Eventually, I say, "We can leave. We've got this car. We can drive away, start a whole new life in the woods. Build a cabin with our bare hands. Live off the land."

"Kind of did that all summer. Not as good as it sounds."

My brother takes a deep breath. Pulls the hood of his jacket up.

"Let's go."

We walk through the parking lot. It only takes a few minutes for the stares and whispers to start. Joey keeps his head down.

We go through the metal detector. In the middle of the front hall, Joey stops abruptly, and I bump into his back. One guy walking past us suddenly looks over his shoulder. "Hey, man. Look at you, back from the dead."

Joey says, "Hey, Noah."

"You got Stetler this year for first period?"

Joey nods.

"Me too. Dude sucks. See you in a few?"

"Sure."

"Rock on." The lanky guy drifts down the hall.

"Friend?" I say. "Or foe?"

"That guy smokes a bowl just to wake up. Not a friend candidate," Joey says, hiking his backpack higher on his shoulders. "If I don't see you, meet at the car after?"

"Sure."

We squeeze hands. He whispers, "Whatever happens, don't react. Stay cool. Remember the ocean, Emmy."

Then he lets go, turning left, while I turn right.

On my first day of freshman year, Joey pulled me aside in this very same hallway of Heywood High and leaned down, breath warm in my ear. I felt protected by the very heat of it.

I'd spent most of the morning in the bathroom, my stomach in knots.

Listen, he said. *The way you have to think of it is this: high school is like the ocean, like when we went to Mission Beach. There's a lot of it and sometimes it seems scary, like if you go too far out, you'll never get back. You'll lose sight of land. And remember all the times we went under and came back up and how great it felt, the sun on our heads, like we beat something? Everybody here is just a different kind of sea creature. Some of them suck, literally and figuratively. Some of them are so beautiful you can't believe they even exist. And some have scary teeth and weird floppy things, but they're beautiful, too. And some want to eat you, because that's just the way it is. I'm sorry about that. I didn't make the rules of the ocean. The ocean, like high school, has its own laws. But remember this: sometimes the waves knock you down and it seems like you won't have the strength to push back up, but you do, because whatever the water takes down, it gives back. But you have to adapt or die. Now, go swim.*

Midway down the hall, halfway to the counselors' office, heads whip around. Kids peer at me.

I try to keep my eyes focused on the end of the hallway, on the glossy brown door to the counselors' suite.

Girl who was in the car

Candy MontClair.

Brother OD'ed in the backseat.

Is that her?

Oh my god, is it?

Didn't think she'd be back

Don't react, I tell myself.

Remember the ocean, like Joey said. There's Mandy Hinkle, the Heywood High newspaper editor. She's extremely talkative and kind of clenchy, like always touching your arm and leaning

94

close to you when she talks. She's probably a barnacle. There's a kid with a lot of teeth in his mouth. Maybe he's an anglerfish. There's Suki Rappaport and her band of worshippers. She's so petite and pretty and in her own world. Maybe she's a seahorse, lovely and perfect. There's Nick Rabinowitz. I've heard girl stories about him. He could be a shark, always on the hunt for prey. There's a speckled crab, there's a ray, there's a jellyfish, there's . . .

The walls of Ms. Diaz's corner office are loaded with aspiration.

AIM HIGH! EVERYONE HAS A CHANCE TO MAKE A DIFFERENCE! YOUR ATTITUDE WILL DETERMINE YOUR ALTITUDE!

I wish she had more honest posters, like GOOD JOB FOR GETTING OUT OF BED! YAY, YOU BRUSHED YOUR HAIR! HOORAY, YOU GOT A C! YOUR BROTHER DIDN'T DIE OF AN OVERDOSE, GO YOU!

Ms. Diaz looks at me over her glasses. She started last year, when I was a sophomore, and I don't think she's even thirty yet, so I'm assuming the over-the-glasses gesture is her way of seeming older and more in charge. I don't know why she has to do that, though. I mean, of *course* she's in charge. It's her *job* to be in charge, but who is she trying to fool? She went to high school and college and then . . . here, so what life has she lived that means she can tell us the right way to live ours? She's always *been* in school.

I grit my teeth. Adults never tell you the truth about anything, anyway.

"Hello, Emory. How are you feeling?"

"Fine."

She tilts her head. "I'm not going to ask how your summer was. I think I have a pretty good idea. I'm here if you want to talk, and Mrs. Kim is also available. We have resources for you."

"Fine."

"Fine to talking to me? To Mrs. Kim?"

Hi, Mrs. Kim. Last night I had a dream about Candy MontClair, the girl who died, and a boy went through the windshield and then they sent my brother away to get sober. My parents haven't hugged in years. My dad sleeps in the den. My leg hurts. I steal things. And let me tell you about Gage Galt.

Probably Mrs. Kim would choke on her Earl Grey tea.

"I'll think about it."

She glances at her computer. "You'll need to register for the PSAT. Remember, there are only two test dates this fall and you'll want to be prepared in case you need to redo the study course."

"I will." I bite my lip. "I promise." The other night I thumbed through Maddie's old prep book, but everything just swam before my eyes, because I was listening for Joey down the hall. What was he doing? Was he okay? I thought I would feel relief when he got home, but I don't. It's as though I'm waiting for a sign that rehab didn't take, some small tell that he's just biding his time, and this makes me feel guilty as hell, because if I don't believe in Joey, who will?

Ms. Diaz is murmuring. I snap back to attention.

"Obviously, because of your injury, you can't do dance team anymore," she says.

I wonder if she can see the relief on my face.

"We need to make sure you've got some extracurriculars for applications next year, not just pure academics." She starts tapping away. "What about ceramics? Not too physical, not hard on the knee, some out-of-school exhibits, the art festival in the spring at the community center?"

Joey did ceramics last year. He said he found clay in areas of his body he didn't even know existed. *I hate the wheel. If you mess up, everything flies off and goes everywhere. Not a fan of getting slapped in the face by hard, wet things.*

"Not a fan of getting slapped in the face by hard, wet things," I blurt out.

Ms. Diaz laughs. "Inappropriate, but funny. You're usually so quiet. I'd like to get you out of your shell a bit. How about Drama Club?"

"Like acting? I can't do that. I can't get up in front of people. They're already . . ."

"Already what?"

Whispering about me.

"Nothing," I say.

She frowns. "Emory, we have to put you somewhere. If you don't want to act, there are other things you can do. Scenery, costumes. Might help you make some different connections here."

"Okay," I say, "but my brother . . . my mother said he's supposed to take me home every day after school. I kind of have to watch out for him, so I don't know if that will wo—"

She taps again at her computer. "Joseph will be in tutoring after school, on the days he isn't in outpatient. I've got his schedule here. He needs the tutoring to stay focused and catch up. I can certainly call your mother and explain."

The last thing I need is my mother getting a phone call from school.

"All right. Fine."

My fine is just like Joey's okayokayokay.

She starts to print out my schedule, but the paper jams halfway through the cycle. She clicks her teeth. "I hate this printer. I'll print it on Mrs. Tisby's in the front office. Wait here."

I hold my backpack against my chest. Ms. Diaz has dishes

of candy on her desk. Butterscotches, Smarties. A collection of shells, like the ones I bought on the boardwalk in San Diego.

I listen to Mrs. Tisby murmuring to Ms. Diaz.

I palm a shell. It fits perfectly in my hand. I put it in the front pocket of my backpack.

Better.

Ms. Diaz comes back in and hands me my schedule and sits back down.

She looks at me over her glasses again. "Your grades dipped last year."

Dipped means all As to A-minuses and some Bs. It's hard to get all As when you're doing your brother's homework, too.

"I don't see what's wrong with some Bs."

"Nothing, if you're a B student. But when you're an A student and suddenly become a B student, colleges will notice that."

Then it's just her mouth moving and me watching her mouth move.

I know things are hard.

Because of your brother.

Because of Candy.

That's such a difficult thing.

But we don't want you to lose sight of your grades.

Your work.

You've worked so hard.

Such a bright future.

Promising.

I nod, nod, nod. Like I'm a bobblehead, incessantly and stupidly agreeing.

Because everything is *finefinefine.*

*   *   *

I've made it through three classes so far, keeping my head down mostly, but there were still whispers. Madison and Jesse from dance team were in Chem, but when they saw me come into the lab, they angled their heads away and pretended to be busy.

Lunchtime is a very particular beast, though.

The cafeteria is kind of like the hallway ocean: you have to identify the different species and their specific habitats. One species cannot encroach on another's habitat without fear of reprisal or death. Dance team there, baseball team there, footballers there, artsy kids over there, and so on.

I scan for an open seat without trying to land on anyone's face, skimming bodies for potential threat points. Then I see a seat, in the back.

There are certain species in the ocean that have yet to be discovered, and in cafeteria-land, those unidentifiable, mysterious creatures live in the back, in the semidarkness, beneath the wall with no windows, and that's where I go.

The open seat is by Jeremy Leonard, Luther's brother. Unkempt hair, head bent low over the table, reading a comic book, fingers moving along the paper. His black-rimmed glasses are sliding down his nose. Sack of Doritos and a Gatorade.

I walk along the wall so I can avoid the center aisles between tables, but I still hear them.

There she is

Oh damn is she limping, she get hurt

Saw her bro in GovPol dude looked freaked out

"Can I sit here?"

Jeremy Leonard looks up, pushes his glasses up his nose. "Emory. Yeah, sure."

I slide onto the bench across from him.

Jeremy goes back to his comic book. I make the mistake of looking around and meet Tasha's eyes.

She's sitting with the dance team across the cafeteria, wearing a red sleeveless top that shows off her broad shoulders. The corners of her mouth turn down slightly, but not in a mean way. More of a resigned way. She was always nice to me, even when the other girls on the team got frustrated. Madison and Mary and Jesse avoid my eyes.

Tasha shrugs, ever so slightly, so the other girls don't notice. I think about what Joey said. *It is what it is.*

I pull the Tupperware of carrots and hummus from my backpack, moving the carrots around with my finger. I used to really like playing Lincoln Logs when I was little; I could do that for hours, stacking and restacking them into wobbly little houses. I start making a tiny carrot log cabin. My phone buzzes. Joey.

This sucks, he texts.

Agreed, I text back.

Jeremy glances up at me.

A carrot on top of my house teeters and falls on the table. Jeremy restacks it for me. His nails are dirty. I remember, suddenly, my mother and father talking in the den after she'd dropped Luther back at home when he'd stayed the night at our house one time. "That boy comes from hard people," she murmured.

"It's bad," Jeremy says quietly. "This stuff. You know?"

"Yes," I say. "Very much so."

We look at each other.

When we were thirteen, our brothers got hauled in to the police station for getting high down at Frost River. Not the part where the people are living now, which is under the bridge, but closer to town, where there are picnic benches and grills for happy families on Sundays. My mom and dad took me with them to the Leonards' house and Jeremy and I sat in his basement, which had a Ping-Pong table and beanbag chairs and a big TV with an old plaid sofa in front of it. We played *Minecraft* and ate Cheetos and drank Sprite for hours while our parents drank wine and bourbon upstairs and complained about how awful our brothers were and how it would do them good to stay at the station until morning. "Scare the pants off them, that's for sure," Mr. Leonard bellowed. I didn't like him much. He seemed loud and cruel and I could understand why Luther preferred our house to his. Jeremy and I even fell asleep on the couch together, watching some movie about a mermaid who washes up in Manhattan. I'd never really hung out with him before, even though we were the same age and went to school together. After my mom came downstairs to tell me it was time to go, Jeremy said, "Sorry if I drooled on you. When we were sleeping." He looked embarrassed.

What I remember most is how comfortable it felt, gradually falling asleep on the couch, Jeremy's head falling on my shoulder. I wonder if he remembers that.

"Do you still have that Ping-Pong table?" I ask.

Jeremy shakes his head. "My parents sold it. A long time ago."

"We never had anything fun like that in my house. My mom was always afraid we'd break something. I was jealous."

"Really?"

"Yeah."

I can feel them, between us, uncomfortable and unmoving.

Our brothers.

A hand slaps flat on the table in front of Jeremy, startling us both.

Lucy Kerr and two of her friends are standing next to Jeremy. Lucy's arms are crossed, her hair a straight brown helmet cupping her ears.

Any fight I had left for this day drains away, because I know what's coming. It always comes, in some shape or form. In books and movies, the richest girl in town is always the most popular and sought after, and sometimes quite mean, but in real life, or at least mine, most of that narrative isn't true.

"Isn't it nice," Lucy Kerr says, her voice dripping with fury, "that in your family, when you get in a car accident and kill someone, you get a brand-new car."

Joey was right; the shiny new car is a problem. It probably seems callous and uncaring.

Lucy Kerr's eyes are shining, as though she's about to cry. Her friends are on either side of her and they each put a hand on her arms.

"She was my best *friend*," she says hoarsely. "And now she's gone because she got in a car with you and your druggie brothers. I was at that party. *I* was supposed to give her a ride home."

Please take me home, Candy had said to me in the basement, her eyes glossy with tears.

Kids are staring.

Jeremy says softly, "I'm sorry, Lucy." He keeps his eyes on the bright orange table.

"Go to hell," Lucy says. "And if I ever run into your brother, watch out."

She looks back at me. "Is it great, living in that house? All your money? Jesus Christ, *look* at you. Who *dresses* you?"

"I'm sorry, Lucy. It wasn't my—"

"Hey, can I sit here? Yeah? Cool."

Liza Hernandez thunks her backpack on the table and plops down next to Jeremy. She pulls a sandwich wrapped in wax paper out of her backpack and starts peeling it open. Peanut butter and jelly. Like always. She's been eating peanut butter and jelly sandwiches since first grade.

She looks at Lucy. "Wait, did I interrupt some classic high school bullying? Goodness, it's certainly started early this year. The first day! A-plus for effort, Lucy."

"You shut your—"

Liza holds up a hand. "Listen, Lucy. I know you're effin heartbroken. I *know* that. But it isn't Emory's fault. She wasn't drunk or driving. It was a rainy night. A wet road. Driving too fast. It's all shit. It all sucks."

I wish Liza would stop talking. I don't want to think about this at school. In front of Lucy Kerr, of all people. But here it comes.

Rainy night. Slick road. Luther laughing and then getting angry when we kept asking him to drive slower. Candy crying for us to let her out. There was so much rain it was hard to see where we even were. Luther's hands on the wheel, jerking hard. So much screaming, but not from Joey, because he was passed out, dead to the world.

Luther, stop, I kept saying.

And then we were flying, the world slowing down as it turned and turned and turned and finally stopped.

I squeeze my hands together, hard, under the table, where Liza and Lucy can't see.

"Dumping on Emory and Jeremy isn't going to make you feel better," Liza says. "You think they don't feel terrible? Emory was in the car, too. How do you think she feels? You're just adding pain onto pain here. It's a useless circle of shit. If you want to do something, get Candy's photo up in the memorial cabinet. It's not there yet, and it should be. Candy was a cool person, and this isn't any way she'd want you to act, you know?"

Lucy Kerr's mouth trembles.

"Stay out of my way," she tells me, her voice shaking. "Or I cannot be responsible for my actions."

As soon as she's gone, Jeremy lets out a tremendous breath.

"Thanks," I say softly to Liza. "You didn't have to do that."

She shakes her head angrily. "For god's sake, Emmy. I stuck up for you our whole childhoods, remember that? But back then, it was kind of cute, this meek mouse thing. It's not anymore. I would tell you to grow a pair of balls, but that's too patriarchal. I would tell you to grow some tits, but that seems antiwoman.

"So I'll just tell you this: grow a *spine*. Grow a goddamn spine or this whole next year is going to suck ass."

We stare at each other, her face unsmiling and flat and mine flaming red. Liza has always been good at nailing a person or situation down. Maybe because she had to deal with her parents for so long. There isn't really time for nuance when your parents are constantly high.

And even though I want to hate her right now, she's right. It's only the first day and it's already sucked, and I'm going to have to figure out how to deal with it. If they can make handbooks for bringing addicts home, they should have one for surviving high school life.

Liza turns to Jeremy. "I got the new issue," she says, in a nice, normal voice now, tugging a comic from her backpack. They spread the pages on the table between them, leaning their heads close, and I'm on the outside, looking in. Liza might have just saved me, but she didn't make room for me.

I don't want to look at them looking at the comic and I'm not hungry anymore, so I raise my head, just a little, to see where he is.

And I catch him, out of the corner of my eye, at the baseball table by the wall. They're all laughing about something.

Did they see what happened with me and Lucy Kerr? A couple of girls are there, too. One girl puts her hand on Gage's arm. He moves smoothly, almost imperceptibly, so that her hand falls away.

If Gage was my boyfriend, I would be sitting there. Lucy Kerr would never say things to me. Gage and his shiny perfection would protect me from everyone.

I will him to glance over, look at me, anything. Acknowledge me.

He doesn't.

But I notice someone else, over by the exit doors.

Daniel Wankel. Leaning against the wall in his black sport coat, the same jacket he wears even in the coldest of months, fingerless gloves, black-and-gray scarf wound around his neck, even though it's September and still warm.

He missed most of fall and spring semester last year. There were whispers about why he went away. *Got drunk, fell in the river, sent to rehab. I heard pray the gay away. I heard he bit the shop teacher. I heard he went nuts.*

Daniel Wankel's face is steady, watching me. And then he smiles. But it isn't a happy *Hey how ya doin* smile.

It's more like *Sucks to be you.*

15

I N MR. WATSON'S LIT class, I take a seat in the back, by the window. I like being by the windows. The flowers are nice outside and if there's a breeze, I like to look at the leaves in the trees weaving back and forth. I wonder how Joey is doing. I checked for him in the hallways after lunch but didn't see him. I send him a quick text while Watson is fussing about at the whiteboard.

Hope you're good

I still feel a little shaky after what happened with Lucy Kerr in the cafeteria. Maybe I should eat lunch in the library from now on.

"Good afternoon, gentle people," Mr. Watson says, writing his name on the whiteboard at the front of the room. "Welcome to American Classics, where we'll delve deep into works that define our culture. The reading list went up on the student portal two weeks ago, so I hope—"

Liza Hernandez raises her hand.

He pauses. "Yes, Liza. Lovely to see you again."

Watson is kind of a crusty old guy. Navy-blue tie, white button-up shirt. Black shoes. Why do men's eyebrows get so bushy and wild when they grow old? It's like he's got two crazy caterpillars crawling across his forehead.

"Why did you assign a book about a pedophile?" Liza's voice is clipped and strong. She's sitting a few rows in front of me on the right.

Someone snickers. A couple of kids shuffle in their seats. I'm glad she said it, though. I know what that book's about and it sounds gross and I've been avoiding reading it since it doesn't come until further in the semester.

"Excuse me?" Watson's caterpillars crease together.

"*Lolita.* By Nabokov. Am I pronouncing that right?"

"You are." He writes it on the board. Says it out loud, slowly, for all of us.

"It's a book about a man who sexually assaults a girl."

"Oh, shit," someone says. "Here we go."

Watson blinks rapidly. You can tell he's really working to get some words out. Finally, he says, "Well, I hesitate to use those words or to say that's the *subject* of the book, as a whole."

Mandy Hinkle's sitting next to Liza. She clears her throat. "It is actually the whole subject of the book. He preys on her and her mom, who's like totally loopy and out of it, for the entire book. And then, like, another old guy comes along and basically does the same thing to her."

"I think that guy kidnapped her, didn't he?" says Amani McKinney. "I couldn't tell. This book is weird and creepy and the writer made it seem like maybe she liked it? But technically, you can't consent under the age of eighteen and besides, isn't she, like, *twelve* when everything starts?"

"My point is," Liza says, "this is a really problematic book about the assault of a child by an adult, some hellacious gaslighting, and there could be, you never know, some people in this very room who may be sexual assault survivors. Did you ever think of that?"

"It would be different," Mandy Hinkle adds, "if the book was about a survivor's experience. But this is not that, at all."

The room gets very quiet. I wait. You can never tell how some teachers are going to react to pushback. The old "my way or the highway" thing. We have a bunch of yellers at Heywood, but I haven't had a class with Watson yet, so I don't know what he'll do. I would rather not have any yelling, but I also don't want to read this book, either, and I'm glad Liza said something.

Mr. Watson lays down his Magic Marker. He taps his desktop once, twice, three times, before speaking.

"Firstly," he says. "Let me commend those of you who have read the book already—"

"I watched the movie," Max deVos says. "There was a sexy chick. Does watching the movie count?"

Mandy Hinkle says, "There were two movies and *no*."

"Secondly," Mr. Watson says, louder.

I wince. This might be the start of the yelling.

"The book is an important introduction to literary technique, structure, allusion, the unreliable narrator. There are many ways to discuss this book and perhaps your ideas are ones we can explore."

A girl in the seat next to me raises her hand. "If I get a note from my mom, can I read something else? This makes me really uncomfortable."

"Well, we don't always look for comfort when we read. Sometimes we have to read uncomfortable, difficult books. Sometimes those books are the very ones that inform our intellectual and emotional growth." Mr. Watson's eyes scan the room.

He stops. "Yes. You have a question."

Tasha puts her hand down. "There are two Black kids in this

room, including me, one Mexican American, and one Asian American. But there are no books on this list telling Black stories. Or Asian American stories. Or any stories that feature people of color as the main characters. If we are there, we're side pieces. Slaves. Serving food. Stuff like that."

"Jesus, you guys, what do you *want*? You wanna read *Charlotte's Web* for the rest of your life?"

Everyone turns to see who spoke. The kid in the back row, opposite corner from me. He's chewing on a pencil, his jaw working hard. Tom Kidder. He never talks much.

Max deVos slides down in his seat.

Tasha turns toward Tom. "Actually, that's a great book about empathy, friendship, and sacrifice. Although, again, no people of color that I can recall, but I can get behind a pig and a spider, for sure."

Everyone starts talking at once.

"Did you ever notice that Wilbur got all the credit for the writing in the spiderwebs? Some pig! Terrific! And, like, Charlotte did all the work! Guys are always taking credit for women's work."

"Her name is in *the title*. That's the credit. It's not called *Wilbur's Web.*"

"Did you ever notice how supportive Fern's dad was? Like, he even kind of believed her when she said the animals were talking. Her mom thought she was crazy and called the doctor!"

"And then the doctor was all, 'Well, she'll start thinking about boys soon and that will take care of it.' "

Next to me, Daniel Wankel says, "Actually, I think Fern *did* ditch Wilbur for Henry Fussy."

I can't help it. I giggle. She totally did.

Mandy Hinkle ignores Daniel. "I don't think I should have to read a book that makes me feel sick in order to further my intellectual growth. What kind of nonsense is that? And also, *The Scarlet Letter* is on here and that book has been assigned every single year since eighth grade and I simply cannot with Hester Prynne anymore, thank you very much."

A couple of people clap. But a lot of kids, like me, stay quiet, too. I'm not really one for outspoken rebellion. The outspoken part, not the rebellion part.

Janey Foster says, "Can we just redo this list? And why can't we ever read books that actually have teenagers as the characters? Why are we always reading about adults? I'm so *sick* of adults."

"Why are all these authors men? I'm just noticing this."

"Do you not read women authors, Mr. Watson?"

"Please don't make me read *The Great Gatsby* again. I had that last year and it is *insufferable.*"

"West Egg, East Egg. Why so many Eggs? Really putting all your eggs into one basket, Fitzgerald," Daniel murmurs.

I giggle again. This might be the first time all day I've felt okay.

Daniel smiles at me.

Mr. Watson sits down at his desk. "Well, we have reached an interesting place. I'm going to have to take some time with this."

I can tell by the way Liza leans back in her chair that she's pleased.

"Take all the time you need," she tells Mr. Watson. "We're here for you."

*   *   *

I text Joey after last period.

> Have to take Drama Club now instead of dance.
> What about your outpatient meeting today?
> Isn't it at 4? I won't be done until 5.

There's a meeting at 4 and one at 6. We can
do the one at 6. Just have to text Mom.
I don't really want to go alone, okay?

> Okay

I'll meet you in the auditorium when you're done

> Okay. Looked for you in the
> hallways but didn't see you

I'm FINE

The auditorium is dark, except for the stage, where kids are sitting cross-legged or with legs stretched out. Liza is here. And Lucy Kerr, which makes my heart drop. I'll have to stay out of her way.

Jeremy Leonard is here, too. He seems like a safe bet, so I slide next to him on the stage and dangle my legs over the side. I don't think I can do cross-legged yet, and my knee hurts after walking and sitting all day, and I definitely don't want to be anywhere near Lucy Kerr.

"You again," Jeremy murmurs.

"It was involuntary, to say the least. I don't really want to get up in front of people and emote," I say.

"It gets easier. Simon's pretty cool." He pulls at a fingernail. "That was pretty bad in the cafeteria. But I get it. You know?"

I nod.

"Your leg okay?" he asks.

111

"It hurts a little."

He looks at me carefully, as though he's debating whether or not to say something.

"What?" I ask, prodding him. "Just say it."

"Luther lost an eye."

"What?" I blurt, flustered, then lower my voice. "I'm sorry . . . I didn't know that."

I think of Luther's legs hanging over the steering wheel, the dirty bottoms of his sneakers. I don't remember much between when the police and ambulance showed up and when I woke up in the hospital, so I wasn't really sure what happened to him at the time.

"Yeah," he says. "Messed up his face and neck, too. The glass from the windshield. He's in juvie. Because of the other stuff."

That's right. Long after I'd gone home from the hospital, I overheard my mother and father talking about Luther. That he'd been carrying a lot of drugs in his backpack. Too much for one person, which meant he was going to sell them. That's why he wanted to turn instead of driving Candy home, to go to the shoe-in-the-tree house, I think. To drop off the drugs.

"He gets out in October, because he turns eighteen," Jeremy says. "I haven't seen him in a while, to tell you the truth. My parents don't want to visit him and it's hard to get out there without a car. It's like they want to pretend he doesn't exist."

I think of my mom and her Rules for Joey and how my dad just walks through the house like a ghost at night. How my mom seems to think a list of rules will fix everything and my dad doesn't even seem to want to deal.

"I guess we both know a little something about difficult brothers," I say softly.

"I used to feel like I didn't exist in the house, because everything was all about Luther," Jeremy says, "but now that he's gone, I'm still invisible. I thought that would be different. Does that make sense?"

A huge swell of relief floods through me. "Yes. Yes, I get that. So much."

We smile at each other, but it's not entirely out of happiness. More like something sad and resigned.

"My people! My thespians! Arise and greet the day!" Simon Stanley's voice pulls everyone's attention to the wings of the stage where he's walking from, waving a small baton, wearing slippers.

"Are we really supposed to stand up?" I whisper to Jeremy.

"Yeah," he says. "We do some exercises to get loose. Here." He holds his hand out and pulls me up.

Simon Stanley closes his eyes and takes a giant breath. He spreads his arms out and raises them above his head. "Up!" he shouts.

Everyone goes quiet and raises their hands, so I do it, too. But I keep my eyes open.

"And down, shake it out," Simon says, breathing out.

Everyone bends over, flapping their arms. The stage floor is scratchy and dusty. The dust tickles my nose. I did not expect exercise, arm-flapping, and dusty floors, to be honest.

"Aaaaannd, up."

We all rise.

Mr. Stanley smiles at all of us. "If you're new, my name is Simon Stanley. You can call me Mr. Stanley. You can call me Simon. You can call me Si. If you're nervous because you've never done this, good! If you're scared to be here, good! If you feel brave, bold, and ready to take on the world, go home! You scare me! Just kidding. All are welcome here. Understood?"

Everyone nods, but I'm kind of wishing I'd joined ceramics club after all. I definitely do not feel bold, brave, and ready to take on the world, whatever that means.

Simon Stanley's face turns serious. "Now, before we really get to the nitty-gritty, I do want to take a moment of silence for our fellow troupe member Candace MontClair. Lucy, dear, is this too much? Should we stop?" He takes one of her hands. A couple of kids look over at me and Jeremy.

Oh, god. Jeremy and I both stiffen at the mention of Candy MontClair.

I never should have agreed to Drama Club. This is a whole *group* of her people.

In unison, Jeremy and I both look at our feet.

"Lucy?" Simon says.

"Yes," she says. "I want to."

Simon Stanley bows his head.

The stage gets so quiet that I'm sure people can hear how loud my heart is beating. I want to run off this stage and I would, if I could make it on my bad knee, but I'm stuck.

The longer it's quiet, the deeper the quiet seems to get, making the stage seem like a spooky, weirdly special place.

I'm looking at the dusty stage floor and all I can think about is Candy and how pretty she looked the night of the party, even tearstained and with a ripped blouse. I liked her, too, and I was the last one to hear her breathing. Last spring she was walking on this very same stage.

I feel crushed and heavy inside and then I see wetness on the stage floor, dotting the dust.

Oh, god, I'm crying. I don't want anyone to notice, because in some ways, I feel like I'm not allowed to cry. I wasn't close to her, but I am the reason she was in the car.

Like, if I hadn't said I'd give her a ride home, and if I hadn't had two beers and let Luther drive, she might be here, right now, doing silly warm-up exercises.

I bite my lip, but I can't stop the tears from falling.

Next to me, Jeremy touches my hand with his finger.

"It's okay," he whispers. His eyes are shiny behind his black horn-rims.

Finally, I hear shuffling. I wipe my face quickly and look up.

Simon Stanley starts walking around our circle on the stage, hands behind his back, wiggling the baton. Looking at each of us in turn, like he has something very, very important to say. He's wearing a loose, tunic-like shirt, no buttons, and I don't think I've ever realized how small and wiry he is. I had him freshman year, for advisory period, and we mostly watched clips from movie musicals, which meant "Seventy-Six Trombones" played on a loop in my head for months afterward.

When he gets to me, he pauses.

And touches the baton lightly on my shoulder.

You can do this, he mouths.

I'm not so sure, but I nod anyway.

Simon whirls away, to the center of the stage.

"Now, let's talk about the *thea-tuh,*" he says.

Joey has a big grin on his face as I walk down the auditorium aisle toward him when we're done.

"That was brutal," he says. "When you guys started howling, I thought you might actually bail."

Simon Stanley asked us to imagine being animals: first a horse, then a cat (we tiptoed around the stage, hands curled like paws at our chests, mewing), then a coyote (heads thrown back, keening at the moon). I felt awkward and silly doing this, but a part of me also kind of liked it. At least I wasn't sweating through my dance clothes and missing beats and getting frustrated looks from Tavi Dean, the dance coach.

"Shut up," I tell him. "At least it wasn't ceramics. Hard, wet things, remember?"

Joey's smile dies as he stands up. Jeremy has come up to us. He looks sheepish.

"Hey, Joe."

"Hey, Jeremy. Man, you look different. You grew."

"I had a growth spurt this summer, I guess. My mom's mad because she had to buy me new clothes."

"Moms."

"Yeah."

A giant, sad silence seems to wrap around all of us.

Finally, Jeremy says, "I don't really know what to say."

"Me neither." Joey's voice is quiet.

Luther Leonard spent more time than not at our house for years. Swimming in the pool with Joey. Playing video games with Joey. In the attic with Joey. They were inseparable. Like me and Liza were for years.

Jeremy says, "Well, see you tomorrow, Emory. You did really good today. I swear it will get less weird. Later, Joe."

"Later."

We watch him leave the auditorium, hiking his frayed backpack over his shoulders.

"At least today is over, right?" Joey sighs.

"Let me see," I say. "I have no friends, I got yelled at in the cafeteria, there was a rebellion in lit, everywhere I went people were whispering about me, and I had to howl like a wolf. This semester is going to last forever."

Joey grimaces. "All my teachers made me sit in the front row, Noah and Chris tried to get me to smoke pot by the ball field, and I had a small lecture from the principal about pulling up my bootstraps and putting in the work."

"Wait, someone asked you to get high?"

He shrugs. "Gonna happen. Don't worry, I can handle it."

He pulls his hood over his head and I can't help feeling a spark of fear, like he's trying to hide red-rimmed eyes. Joey catches my look.

"I didn't," he says sharply. "You have to trust me."

I take a deep breath. "Okay."

There's an awkward space between us that I don't like.

Finally, he says, "One day at a time, right? At least, that's what they told us in Blue Spruce."

"One day at a time," I say back and then in my head, over and over. One day at a time.

Mis_Educated

Hey, hey, Heywood High!
How was your first day
Every year I think this is the year
That things will be different.
That we'll all be nicer to each other.
No more jocks over here, geeks over there,
Stoners by the ball field, losers at the back
Of the cafeteria. But it never changes.
Every year, I hope that somebody
Won't make fun of my clothes
Or a teacher will actually listen
When I have something to say.
I always hope we'll be kinder to each other
Even when we're feeling lost
And angry. And you know what else?
I really missed Candy today.
And Wilder Wicks.
And Shannon Roe.
They should have been with us today.
Cancer happens
Suicide happens
Accidents happen
And I just couldn't shake it
How heartbreaking it is to be us sometimes
How heartbreaking it is to be young sometimes
I don't think adults get that
I don't think they see that
I think they've forgotten that

#heywoodhigh #heywoodhaulers #candymontclair
#wilderwicks #shannonroe #heywoodhypocrisy #millhaven

LzySusan Daaaammmn

TupacLives i miss wilder every day

MandyMandy I might write a story for the Heywood Hauler about
Candy

GentleBen seeing their photos in the memorial case makes me
pretty sad, tbh

HelenOfJoy Everybody says kids are resilient but I beg to differ

LucyK My friend is gone you guys don't really understand

Sharon99 did you see LL's brother came back kid's gonna get his ass kicked

Sharon99 JW and his nerdy sister 2

Frank4 I'm actually glad we don't use lockers anymore because I was tired of getting stuffed inside them

BethanyRules Storm brewing in Watson's lit class

FrancesP44 Sometimes I'm so lonely at this school I don't think I'm gonna make it Kids can be so cruel

16

JOEY'S OUTPATIENT CLINIC IS a brick building just outside of town, sandwiched between Nina's Nail Salon and the Salvation Army thrift store.

"Are you nervous?" I ask as he parks the car.

"Not really. I did a lot of group talk at Blue Spruce." He takes out his phone. I watch as he texts Mom to let her know we're here, just like the Rules for Joey dictate.

"Did you . . . I mean, did you like it there?"

He slides his phone into his pocket and just sits there.

"I'm sorry," I say quickly. "If you don't want to talk about it, that's fine."

"It's not that," he says. "It's complicated. I don't want to hurt you."

"What does *that* mean?" I say.

He slides his hood off and runs a hand over his short hair. "It's not that I liked it or didn't like it, but I felt safe there. I felt like I was in a little cocoon, almost. No more Mom, no more Dad. No more disappointing them and you. I felt safe. Like all the noise was gone."

All the noise was gone. Just like me, Joey was tired of the noise. But for me, Joey *was* the noise. I never really thought *we* were noise for him, too, and that makes me sad.

"And everybody there, you know . . . they were like me. I wasn't *wrong*."

"Joey, you're not wrong," I say, touching his arm. "Please don't think that."

He swipes at his eyes. "Sorry, I'm tired. Let's just go in. This is the last meeting tonight and they don't let you into meetings late. You have to follow the rules and my life is all about the rules now."

The waiting room is hot and crowded and there are no more seats, so I squeeze into an empty space against the wall while Joey goes to the front desk to check in. There's a clear barrier protecting the woman behind the desk and just a little hole to speak through and a slot in the bottom. Joey slides his insurance card and driver's license through the slot. The security guard in the corner looks bored.

The boy next to me has a lot of marks up and down his forearms. They look like round, faded scars. His fingernails are rough and yellowy. The lady on my other side holds her purse really close to her blouse, like she's afraid somebody will steal it. There are some kids here, too, a couple I recognize from school, though I don't know their names. Last year a few kids overdosed in class and soon after, posters for drug abuse and Narcan appeared in the school halls and in the nurse's office. I don't think the kids came back to school. I wonder if these are the same ones. If Joey knows them.

I didn't know there would be so many people here. For every person who looks kind of rough, though, there are two or three who just look . . . regular. Clean clothes. Combed hair. I guess I thought everybody here would look like they do in the movies: dirty, desperate addicts.

Suddenly the Blue Spruce handbook flashes in my brain.

The way you aren't supposed to call someone an addict, because it makes them feel shame, labels them, like I just did, *dirty addict*. Like the person is seen as a problem and not a real person anymore.

There are two people doubled over, rocking back and forth, grimacing. I can't tell if they're nervous or sick and to tell the truth, I'm a little freaked out.

The boy next to me, the one with the yellowy nails, murmurs, "They're waiting for their fix."

"What?" His face is very tan and rough, like he's spent a lot of time outdoors.

"Suboxone. It's a little strip you take while you withdraw from Oxy or H. They have to come here to get it."

"I don't know what Oxy is, really." *H . . .* that must be heroin.

"Good," he says. "Don't ever learn. It's only through the grace of God that I'm alive and here. I prayed to him at my lowest hour and he answered me. My parents disowned me, but God took me in. God answered me."

The woman next to me leans across me and tells the boy, "Don't start that with her."

"I'm just passing on my story."

"God didn't save you. God doesn't care. If he cared, if he *existed,* I would hope he'd send all the pharmaceutical companies straight to hell. Give a pill for pain, get them hooked, then sell them another drug to get off it. They should burn for what they've done to this country."

I think of Dr. Cooper trying to write me another prescription, and Maddie telling him no, and him giving it to me anyway, and me hiding it in my dresser drawer. All the morphine they gave me in the hospital that worried my mother. Would she have been worried about that if it wasn't for Joey? If he hadn't OD'ed, would she have let me take the Vicodin whenever I wanted, just because a doctor said it was fine?

"Ma'am," the boy says. "Please——"

She cuts him off. "This is my daughter's ninth time withdrawing. She is twenty-one years old. There's no saving this. There's only waiting until it's over."

I wince. Nine times?

A young woman comes out of a door by the front desk. Her face looks pasty, like dough, like you could just press your fingers to her skin and shape it anyway you wanted. She's thin and wearing flip-flops and jean shorts.

Purse-woman pushes herself off the wall. She gives the boy a hard look. "I'm working two jobs just to pay for this. I should be in Cancún. I should be drinking Bloody Marys with my girlfriends after work down at Jasper's, but instead I'm here, every day, and I go home and have soup from a can, because that's what I can afford now, and put my daughter to bed and hope that when I wake up, she's still there. God's just another addiction, son."

The thin girl says, *"Mom,"* like she's embarrassed.

The purse-woman says, "All right, Margaret, let's go, then."

I watch them squeeze their way to the door. What did her mom mean, that it's only waiting until it's over? I don't ever want to feel that way about Joey. But this is his first time, not his ninth, and I want to make sure it's his last, no matter what.

More people have come in and we are packed two and three deep.

The boy lets out a breath and says, "We are weak because we have holes in our souls and the drugs fill them. When we're ready to let the Lord fill us, our holes go away."

I find it hard to look at his searching eyes, so I look down at the floor. Holes. Is that how Joey feels? Like he's empty inside? *Wrong,* like he said in the car? I feel empty, too, and I took Vicodin after the accident, but I never took it all, or tried to steal it, to fill myself up, make myself feel better.

My face gets red. But I do . . . steal. And there's Gage.

Maybe people just use different things to fill up the emptiness. Until it becomes less about feeling empty and more about feeding something *else.*

Joey comes over to me. "The meeting is starting. You'll be okay?"

I nod. "Yeah. Sure."

A man in a blue T-shirt comes out from behind the desk. He's got a clipboard and pen. "Six p.m. support group, it's time." A bunch of people get up from the chairs and push away from the wall and Joey follows them through the door. The boy with the yellowy nails goes, too. I feel relieved when he walks away. Someone from the front desk calls out some names and the two people who were doubled over get up and go through a different door than Joey went through.

I think about where to sit, now that a lot of people are gone, but as soon as I move, more people flood in the door and jostle for the seats. I hang back. It seems like some of them probably need to sit down more than I do, even though my knee is throbbing after a full day of walking around school.

The security guard catches my eye. "It's like this all the time, day in, day out." He shakes his head. "Damn shame. Damn junkies."

"They're *people,*" I say. "With *problems.*"

He shrugs.

I look at the door Joey went through, wonder what's going on inside, what they talk about. How everyone is going to fill up their holes and with what. If my brother will find something else to fill himself up before it's too late.

On the way home, Joey drives by Frost Bridge. From the window, I glimpse them. The people down there. Some people in town call them ghosties. I don't know why people started calling them that. Maybe like they are ghosts of their former selves or something. There are even more of them now than when I drove by here with Maddie. And it isn't just adults. There are kids, too, like our age. Some of the adults I can recognize, like Jim Tolford, who used to mow our lawn for years before we hired the man with the wide-brimmed hat, because Jim started showing up late, and then not at all, and finally was found one day on the Galt's lawn, the mower running, his face in the grass. Then my mom hired the man with the wide-brimmed hat and we didn't see Jim anymore.

There are tons of them, spread out on the rocky river beach. Blankets, tarps, backpacks. Grocery carts. Somebody's made a small fire. Some of them seem shaky, like the people at the clinic.

"Joey." I think of the boy with the yellowy nails. "Did you ever take Oxy?"

He's quiet. "That's a hell of a thing to ask me."

"Sorry. I mean, I know . . . I know you were on heroin."

It feels weird to even say that word in connection with Joey. *Heroin.* Maybe that's what upsets my mom the most about what happened. That things like heroin happen to *other* types of people, not us.

"I mean, at the party. I mean, I know now. I didn't then. I just thought you were drunk. But that boy at outpatient, he was talking about Oxy. Did you do that, too?"

I think about that night.

Joey's head rolls around the seat in the back of the car. His arms are splayed. Luther says, Your brother is messed up, Em. Daaaaammmmnnn. Candy is crying, pinching Joey's arm. He doesn't wake up. He can't be drunk because I know what that smells like, because of our dad. Candy says, We should go to the hospital, I think.

Candy is crying. Joey, wake up.

Luther says he has a stop to make, that Joey will be fine. We argue. The rain is coming down hard. Candy wants us to let her out.

Joey pulls over into the parking lot of Kingston Park. People are walking their dogs, sitting on benches, talking on phones. There are kids in the play area, hanging from monkey bars. The sun is almost down. The park will close soon.

"Remember when I got hurt from jumping off the roof?" he says. "They gave me these pain pills. I don't even remember what they were, probably Percocet, but they felt so good. I felt so calm. Different. That was probably the beginning. And then I ran out, but I wanted more."

He runs his hands along the steering wheel.

Back when Joey jumped off the roof and landed on the brick patio, it was a wet, sickening smack and his cries could be heard all over our neighborhood. He broke some ribs and his arm and lost a few teeth and spent the next few weeks in a haze on the downstairs couch, where I read to him out loud for hours, secretly pleased he was all mine, and not with Luther Leonard. I gave him his pill every four hours with crackers and an icy Sprite in a glass with a straw. My mother was worried, but I also remember she said, "At least he's quiet."

I haven't thought about that in a long time. I thought the pain pill was like aspirin, only a little stronger, and I felt important, because it was me helping my brother feel better.

And now I feel sick thinking about that, like somehow I'm to blame, giving him those pills every four hours. But what else are you supposed to do when somebody is in pain?

An ice cream truck pulls up by the park. Kids run, clumsy as puppies, parents lagging behind, digging for money in pockets and purses.

Joey sighs.

"I told Luther how good it felt to take them, like time stopped, like inside you felt calm and like nothing mattered. He wanted to try it, so he started stealing his mom's pain pills— you know, she has that back condition, so it was real Oxy and not . . . not like the Percocet—and we'd split them and hang in the attic and play games till we fell asleep. He found somebody who hooked us up with weed, too, so we had something for when we didn't have pills. Eventually, his mom caught on, but it wasn't hard to find more. That's one thing I think about all the time now. There's always *more* somewhere. All those athletes at Heywood? When they get injured, they get pills. They're stoked to sell them. There's a place out on Wolf Creek Road, a house. You can buy there. Or when we went to a party at someone's house, we'd go upstairs and raid their parents' medicine cabinet."

Wolf Creek Road. The house with the shoe in the tree.

"Joey." His words are falling over me, heavy and sad, a secret life of raiding medicine cabinets and then sitting down to roasted chicken and green beans with us.

"Doing it just made things easier. I could tune out Mom and Dad always telling me what a loser I was. *Joey, you're lazy.*

Joey, try harder. Joey, why aren't you listening? Joey, why can't you be more like Maddie? Joey, what's wrong with you? Stuff didn't matter much anymore, and I liked it. I could coast."

"But why did you do . . . heroin? At the party? I mean . . . that's *heroin.*"

I don't even like saying the word. It feels sinister in my mouth. Makes me think of people stumbling in the street, sick-faced and desperate, even though I shouldn't, because plenty of the people in the outpatient clinic weren't like that. They looked like they do taxes for a living, or teach school, even.

They looked like Joey.

He's quiet.

"Joey?"

He shrugs. "I don't know, really. I didn't really even think about it. Jake had it one minute and offered it to me the next and then I was snorting it in his pantry. I don't know. Sometimes I do things and I don't know why. Like, some people would say, no way, not me, never doing *that,* but I never think that, I just do it. It's like the receptor inside me that should set off alarm bells is broken.

"And if you want the honest truth, even though I threw up on myself and passed out later, even though I did too much, it made me feel like I was powerful. It made me feel beautiful. It was like wings spreading inside me, the warmest wings you can imagine, holding me close, from the inside."

His eyes are someplace that scares me: dreamy, far away. Needy, which makes me nervous. Maybe we shouldn't be talking like this. Maybe it's going to make him want it again.

"I felt loved, but at the same time, I didn't care if I was loved."

He leans his forehead against the steering wheel.

"But why, Joey? Why? Why would you do that to yourself? I

was right here, whatever you needed, I could have helped you." I'm trying not to cry, but what he's saying is making me so, so sad.

He looks at me, his eyes wet.

"Because for my whole life I've felt wrong, Emmy. Reading was hard, everything floated on the page. I had that special tutor Mom and Dad got, remember that? But I almost felt worse because of it. I got hit in the eye playing baseball because I couldn't focus on anything but the clouds. I couldn't figure out which direction to run in for soccer. Nobody wanted me on class projects because it took me so long to do my part. *Sit down, Joey. Be quiet, Joey. Joey, why do you have to be so wild?* Remember when Mom and Dad made me go see Dr. Tillman? He just gave me different sorts of pills, ones that made me feel dead inside. Remember that?"

I hold my backpack tight against my chest, thinking. I remember some of it. Joey sleeping for long periods of time. The way his mouth was thick and his words garbled. My mother thought maybe he needed a different doctor, but then the roof accident happened.

My brother's voice is thick again, just like all those years ago.

"The only thing I've ever been good at is letting people down, Emmy. My whole life, I just wanted to feel better. Forget about what a loser I was. And then I found a way to do that."

He lifts his head and jams the key in the ignition. "And to tell you the truth, if we hadn't been in that car accident, if Candy hadn't died, I'd be trying to feel better right this fucking minute. You don't know what it's like to feel like you never fit."

"But I do, Joey, I *do.*"

He shakes his head and wipes his eyes.

"Not like me, Emmy. Not like me."

He starts the car, turns on the radio, loud, and peels out of the parking lot.

At home, we do our homework while eating bowls of luke-warm spaghetti. My mom gave us dinner, scrolled her way through Joey's phone to check his texts and searches, and then went upstairs to her room.

Joey works slowly on math, moving his lips. He writes something down, erases it, checks his calculator, redoes it. Over and over. But he doesn't give up. He doesn't ask for my help. Last year, I did just enough for him to get Cs, to maintain, so no one would notice.

I look down at my own homework, check the assignment on the student portal, read about ancient skulls found in Africa, human migration. People have always moved, to find better places, better ways to live. Searching for something. Safety. Food. Love. Survival. It's amazing to think that part of a person could be found, millions of years later. A skull wedged in the crack of a cave. A bone found buried deep in the earth. And then we try to figure out how they got to just that one place. But in the end, that fragment of bone or skull can only tell us how they lived, but not if they were happy.

When I look up, Joey's gone, his things cleared away. No evidence remains.

17

JOEY FOLDS AND REFOLDS the orange Hank's Hoagies T-shirt in his lap. My mother is giving him the Look.

"You start next Saturday," she says, sipping her tea. "Hank was quite nice. I ran into him in the mayor's office. He was making a lunch delivery. Lovely man."

"I just feel like it's too soon," Joey says hesitantly. "I mean, I just started back at school and I have outpatient and stuff."

"Yeah, Mom, he's only been back at school for two weeks. That's . . . too much," I say.

My mother swivels her head to me. "He signed a contract, Emory. He needs to focus. He doesn't need free time."

I drop my head back to the book in my lap. What did the Blue Spruce handbook say? *It's important for some patients in recovery to keep a tight schedule, to know where and when and what they will be doing. Others may need more breathing room and respite. Recovery is not one size fits all, but it is always one step at a time.* The thing is, Joey just got back, and I'm not sure which of these he should do. Fill his days with school and then stuff white bread full of oily deli meats? Or stick to homework and free time, where he can think about getting healthy? It just seems like my mother is throwing all possible Joeys at him at once. It's making even me anxious.

"I'm going to make sandwiches?" Joey says. A flurry of red is creeping up his neck. I feel sorry that he doesn't have his long hair to cover it anymore.

"Yes. And run the counter. All those things." My mother waves her fingers. "It will give you a sense of pride. Everyone needs a first job. I worked in the library during college. I loved it."

Joey's jaw is clenched. I brace myself for his anger, for a fight, but then he just lets out a big sigh, so much air it ripples the leafy arugula on his plate.

"Okay," he says finally.

Okayokayokayokayokay.

"Excellent," my mother says, picking a radish from her plate and crunching it. "Emory can go with you sometimes, if you have to close, perhaps. She can study at a table. Hank was fine with that."

I raise my eyes. "I don't want to hang out at a hoagie shop."

What I'm really thinking is, I need to be *here,* in case Gage texts. Because he's my thing. He's my own personal recovery from the hell of last year and this past summer.

My mother says, "You do need more study time, Emory. Your grades wobbled last year."

"Well, what about Drama Club? I have to do that now. What if I have, like, a performance? And I know at some point we'll have rehearsals and all that stuff." My voice is getting testy, surprising even me.

My mom frowns. "We can cross that bridge when we come to it, Emory, but right now, this is the best solution. Don't you want to help your brother?"

"Mom, she doesn't have to—"

I think of the woman at the outpatient clinic. The nine times she said her daughter has tried to recover. I don't want that to be Joey. I don't. If I can just help him get to a good place, then maybe the Rules can relax a little, and I can ease out of hanging out at Hank's Hoagies.

"No," I say. "Fine. It's fine."

Finefinefinefine. Joey and I are *finefinefinefine* and *okayokayokayokay.*

I hold Candy's hand. It's warm in mine. I want to tell her that her fingers are squeezing me too tightly, but I don't. The music is so loud it's hard to concentrate. My second beer didn't taste as good as the first, but I finished it, anyway, and now I feel woozy. I wish I had it now, because my mouth is so dry. Joey hasn't answered any of my texts. We go upstairs and look in the kitchen. We look in the pantry, in the backyard, we look in the bathroom, where we find Luther Leonard with two girls. *Hey you Emmy baby,* he says. The girls are drunk. *Who's your friend?* Candy keeps her eyes down. No one at school likes Luther, except Joey. I tell Luther we need to go, we need to find Joey because I need the car keys, can he help us find Joey? *Yeah, sure, whatever, he says, but he's not gonna be able to drive you.* He laughs. A long time ago Luther had a sweet laugh and liked to play Angry Birds but he's not like that anymore. His laugh is thinner now, edgier, and he and Joey don't play games anymore. They stay in the attic or lope out of the house with their hoods up, disappearing off the porch and into the night. We go down a long, dark hall, kids kiss each other against walls. A girl is throwing up. In a room at the end of the hall, a Lava Lamp drips drips drips and Joey is on the bed with a girl, lying down, eyes closed. Luther grabs his sneakered feet, shakes them, Joey's eyes flutter open like bird's wings. *Leave me,* he mumbles. Leave me. Luther says *Nah man time to go angel let's get up baby boy* and for such a skinny kid he pulls Joey off the bed in one go, Joey falling against his shoulders. *Keys brother I need the keys baby* and Joey can't get the keys out of his pocket his hand keeps missing so I let go of Candy and dig in and the keys are warm from his body heat and Luther hoists him against his shoulder and Candy grabs my hand again. We walk down the hall, Joey stumbling. He almost falls down the front steps and Luther says *Where is the car* and it's over there, over there and Candy says *I lost my phone* and Luther says *Get it later, girl.* We have to dump Joey in the back and Luther laughs when he realizes the seat belt is broken. Joey mumbles *Oh it's like the ocean* and I say *Is he drunk* and Luther says *Oh honey just don't worry* and I ask Luther *Are you drunk* and he says *Never touch the stuff, Em* and I ask Luther *Are you high* and he says, *No way babe I don't touch the stuff anymore I've moved on to entrepreneurial interests* and Candy says *What?* I say I had two beers and Luther says *Not to worry, I'll drive* and he says, *Buckle up, sis,* to Candy and when he starts the car I can see her eyes in the rearview mirror Luther doesn't put on his seat belt and Candy's eyes are wide and she whispers *I'm scared I'm scared don't kill me*

I wake up, breathing hard, Fuzzy stirring against my feet under the covers. I reach for my phone. I know I'm breaking our rules, but I can't help it.

Can't sleep.

I wait. One, two, three, four, five, six, seven, eight, nine—

2 in the morning

Need

I stop. I almost type *you* but instead I type *something*

                                    Need something

One, two, three, four, five, six, seven—

K

Gage slips through the pool house door, dressed in loose sweat-pants and a T-shirt. His hair is messy. He yawns. "It's late, Em. What's going—"

But I don't give him time, because what would I say? Tell him Candy is in my dreams? That Joey's been places I can never reach?

That your whole life, it seems like no one ever really sees you, they just see what they want to see, what they need to see. They never see the holes inside you.

We kiss and we kiss and we kiss and we bend down to the long bench and his weight on mine feels good and I shift a little to ease my knee and it feels even better. Maybe this is something like Joey felt. This need to get lost in something other than yourself. Lose yourself. Erase yourself. So that none of your awful, wrong self remains, not one blessed thing.

Mis_Educated

"Get over it"
"Move on"
"You'll bounce back"
"These are the best years of your life"
"What I wouldn't give to be your age again"
Did you ever feel that adults never really listen to you?
You say, *I am sad*
And they say, *What for? You're sixteen! What do you have to
be so sad about?*
You say, *I'm afraid*
They say, *Of what! I feed you, clothe you, love you, let me
tell you about being an adult*
You say, *I'm heartbroken*
They say, *Oh, now, now, you'll meet someone else, stop
crying*
You say, *I'm lonely*
They say, *Be more outgoing! Stop staying in your room*
You say, they say, you say, they say
It all runs together, words drifting into unhearing ears
It's like they don't remember what it felt like to be us
To be sad, lonely, heartbroken, afraid, sometimes all at once
They say we should get over it, bounce back, be positive
It's like they don't remember what it's like to be young
They've had a lifetime to paper over their wounds
Ours are still fresh, and bleeding

220 likes

#heywoodhigh #heywoodhaulers #millhaven
#mentalhealthawareness #depression

GiGi I broke up with my girlfriend and my aunt said "that's what
you get for not dating boys"

Stewie13 wtf that's horrible

NutellaAddict honestly I just don't even tell my parents anything
anymore they never listen

LzySusan my dad just tells me suck it up, that it will make me
stronger

JerBear I started to feel out of place in middle school tbh. Mom said it was just hormones and it would pass. Never did

HelenOfJoy I'm crying reading this post. The stuff I could tell you

MrPoppersPenguins My sister has been missing awhile now from Dover. She has an addiction. Was at a party in Mill Haven in May. Name is Carly. Anybody got any leads DM me

18

MR. WATSON HAS US push our desks together in fours for silent reading during class because some kids complained the books were so long they were having trouble reading them with all their other homework. We got a lecture on time management and now I'm in a group with Max DeVos, Tasha, and Daniel Wankel. Mr. Watson changed one or two books from the original list, but people are still unhappy.

Max keeps shifting in his seat, his chair squeaking on the floor. "I just don't get it," he finally says. "I thought we weren't reading a book because it was about rape but this lady seems to get raped."

Tasha says, "She does, but it's a different context. Think about this book in terms of the lasting effects of trauma. And slavery."

"It's *sad*," Max says. "And I thought this was the one that was the movie with Oprah where she suffers but ends up punching the guy and getting her mojo back."

"Max," Daniel Wankel sighs. "That was *The Color Purple* and an entirely different author."

Max shakes his head. "I don't want to read this. This is freaking me out. This is *sad*."

"It is a sad book, Max," I say. "There are a lot of facets to it. To Sethe's experience."

"You have to understand the parts of a person, Max, to

understand the whole," Daniel says. "Emory's right. And some of the parts might be painful."

I can feel him looking at me and it makes me feel weird, because although he's very cute in a bedraggled, slouchy way that I find curiously appealing, there's already Gage, and I don't need any more complications in my life. I busy myself making notes in the margins of my book.

Max's voice rises. "If you guys didn't want to read *Lolita*, I don't want to read this. This is making me feel guilty for being white. Like, this stuff wasn't *my* fault. I'm a nice guy!"

"You gotta face your whiteness, Max," Tasha says carefully. "And everything that comes with it."

Max's face turns red. He raises his hand.

Mr. Watson comes over to our table, holding his mug of coffee. "Yes, Max."

"I don't want to read this book. I mean, this shit is *sad*. And if other people didn't want to read *Lolita* and you changed that, then change *this*."

"What would you read, Max, if you could? There are only so many adjustments I can make. And please, watch your language." Mr. Watson's voice is irritated.

"I don't know. Like, Percy Jackson. I liked those books and they're, like, kind of historical and mythical and stuff."

A couple of kids take out their phones and start filming. People film everything. We're not even human, just a series of ten-second clips and likes/not likes.

Mr. Watson shakes his head. "I don't know those books, and we're well into the semester at this point—"

"Well, damn, man, do you know any books that aren't about *rape*?"

Daniel leans back in his chair. "Fair point."

Mr. Watson's head jerks between Daniel and Max. "I'm not going to have this disrespect in my classroom. I simply won't. You can discuss this with Principal Patterson. Now. Gather your things."

"Are you serious? Ah, my god, man. Really?" Max stands up quickly, knocking his chair to the floor. He slings his backpack over his shoulder, almost hitting Liza, at the next table, in the face, but she ducks just in time. "God, I *hate* this school," he mutters.

Daniel gets his stuff. "Later, people. Come on, Max. I'll buy you a Hershey bar from the vending machine on the way to Patterson's office."

After they leave, Mr. Watson notices all the phones. "Stop that! Put those away! My god, does everything that happens in your world have to be filmed and posted and laughed over?"

Phones slide under desks.

"Any more questions? Changes? Do we remember who is in charge here and who issues grades?"

"Speaking of grades," Liza says, very quietly.

"Yes, Liza." Mr. Watson's totally irritated now. "I'm sure you'll do just fine, as always."

"I don't think I will, actually," she says slowly. "Some of us, we're not going to read the books at all. Or turn in reading logs or take the tests. We told you how we felt and . . . I don't think you took us very seriously. So we're boycotting the list until we have a say in what we read."

The back of her neck is pink. I can tell she's nervous. I look around the room. Other kids are nodding, putting down their pencils. She's not wrong. I mean, if you want me to read, let me read what I want to read and I'll take all the tests and fill out all the reading logs you want.

"That's ridiculous," Mr. Watson says. He looks around the

room. "You're here to learn, I'm here to teach. The rules are mine. And if you're willing to risk a grade—"

"I am," says Liza. She stands up, starts putting her iPad and notebook into her backpack.

"Damn," whispers Mandy Hinkle. "This is getting interesting."

Liza walks to the front of the room and faces the rest of us. "I get it, if you can't risk this, or don't want to. But anybody who wants to can join us."

She looks at Mr. Watson. "Don't worry, I'm on my way to Patterson's office now."

I watch her walk out.

The class is quiet. Then, slowly, kids start getting up, packing their bags. Chairs scrape on the floor. I look down at my desk, my face burning.

Even though I agree with Liza, I can't get in trouble. My mother will freak out. I can't risk piling that on top of the Joey situation.

Half the kids in class have left.

Mr. Watson takes a deep breath. "It seems we have a problem," he says softly. "Please return to your reading."

No one says anything and he goes back to his desk, starts tapping at his laptop furiously.

Tasha and I look at each other. She shakes her head and goes back to her book.

But I can't concentrate on my reading now. Liza told me to grow a spine. I don't want to read some of these books, either, but I don't want to get in trouble with my mother.

Tasha scribbles on a piece of paper and slides it to me.

It's okay to stay and it's okay to go. I have my own reasons for staying. And I'm sorry, about everything.

I write back, *Thank you.*

On my way to the auditorium for Drama Club after my last class, I have to pass the teachers' lounge. There are loud voices coming from inside.

I stop just outside the slightly opened door and listen, pinning myself against the wall.

It's Mr. Watson and Simon Stanley.

"Calm down, Walter." Simon's voice is gentle.

"I mean, it was *ridiculous*. It was like a riot. A boycott, for goodness' sake! They don't want to read *anything* of substance. These are the great books! Reading isn't supposed to be easy. School isn't supposed to be easy. You just do what you're told and learn."

"What's so bad about a little change?" Simon says. "Ease up. Let them feel like they have a voice. Is that so bad? Aren't you tired of teaching the same old thing, day in and day out?"

"They just get worse and worse every year. With their whatsits and hoo-hahs and filming everything. They all just want to be celebrities."

There's a pause.

"And everyone's so *sensitive*. Everyone's so *tender*. In my day, you didn't have a nervous breakdown at the slightest thing. You just dealt with it and moved on. They're like pieces of *china*."

A coffeemaker gurgles. A chair scrapes the floor.

Simon Stanley says, "The world is different now, Walter. Here, do you take cream? It looks like we just have the dry packets. I think the new PE teacher keeps finishing the cartons of cream and not replacing them. So entitled, those athletic types."

"And if I could transfer that deVos kid to another class, I'd do it in a hot minute. That child is dumb as a rock."

"Walter, they're *children*."

"I can't transfer him, anyway. Or give him detention. I play bridge with his grandparents. They'd kill me."

Simon Stanley laughs.

"And that Wankel kid. What a smart-ass. Dresses like he's some sort of beatnik, for goodness' sake. A scarf indoors! Smart as a whip, though. Same with Liza Hernandez. I like her. But her family. What a mess. Did they ever find her parents?"

My face goes red. Liza's parents. Always going out to the car when I would visit. Coming back in the house sniffly and red-eyed.

"No, they didn't."

Simon is quiet before he speaks again. "Walter, Daniel wears the scarf because he had thyroid cancer last fall. Don't you remember? He got very sick around November and had to get surgery and treatment. He did his work at home until he could come back in the spring. He has a scar. That's why he's wearing the scarf. Please, don't make him take it off. Don't make it an issue."

Daniel. Daniel's scarf. Oh. My stomach does little flip-flops. *Cancer.*

"My, my." Mr. Watson sounds sad. "I do recall now. I do. Terrible thing. So young."

"That's what I'm saying," Simon Stanley says. "We were all young once. And we had our nervous breakdowns and our cancers and our heartbreaks and our anger and we hid them and pretended they didn't exist and we moved on because everyone said we should. And we're not one iota better for it. Not one. Let them have this. Just this. Let them be tender, Walter."

Mr. Watson humphs. "I'll take it under consideration. But if I end up reading about hobbits and faeries, I know where you live."

"I'll invite you in for tea. I still have my mother's beautiful set."

I walk slowly to the auditorium. Liza. *Her family. What a mess.*

I don't want her in that house anymore. That's what my mother told my father four years ago. *I went to pick Emory up and I don't know if they were drunk or if they were high or what, but they were passed out in their car, Neil! It's not safe over there.*

My dad was trying to calm her down. *I understand, Abigail. Maybe Liza can just come over here from now on. I'll talk to someone at the hospital. Maybe they can send a social worker out.*

The house is a pigsty all the time. I don't know where her brothers are. Who's taking care of that child?

Have some sympathy.

I am having sympathy! But I have to think of Emory. I've never been comfortable with her over there, but Liza is her only friend, so I let it pass. But it's gone too far.

I didn't really think about her parents. Sometimes when I was there they'd spend a lot of time in their car parked on the curb, and it was just Liza and me, which seemed fun. Sometimes her brothers were around, but they mostly stayed in their rooms playing video games. More often, Liza came to my house. "My house is boring," she'd say. Or "You have the pool," or "You have more toys." Then that day when my mother came to get me, we'd actually been at the library most of the afternoon and were just walking up when my mom's car pulled up behind Liza's parents' car. Liza got very skittish.

"Okay, bye," she said. "See you tomorrow." She moved between me and her parents' car. My mother got out of her car and came around to us. But she was taller than Liza. She saw

Nancy and Lou in the ratty old Chevrolet. I guess I thought they were just sleeping. What was I supposed to think? They went out to their car a lot when I was over there. "Getting some air," they'd say, or "You kids are making too much of a racket."

"Liza," my mother said. I could not figure out her voice, whether it was sad or mad, or both.

My mother leaned down and rapped hard on the car windows.

Liza said, "Please just go, Mrs. Ward. Please. It'll be fine. It's always fine." She was crying.

There was a stirring inside the car. Liza's parents peered at us, confused.

Liza whimpered and looked down at the sidewalk.

My mother told me to get in the car. She didn't talk the whole way home.

That weekend, Liza didn't call me at all. I left messages. I emailed her. I texted. Nothing. I thought maybe she was mad about something, maybe I'd talked too much or made her watch too many of my favorite videos on YouTube.

Then Monday at school, she avoided me all day. She finally came up to me as we were getting ready to leave our classroom, everyone hustling into jackets and zipping backpacks.

"I'm not allowed to be your friend anymore," she said. Her mouth trembled a little. "Your mom said so. She came over to the house and told me. Said it wasn't safe. Said she was calling a social worker. I said if she didn't, that I'd stay away from you. I can fix my parents. I don't need you."

Then my friend walked away, her back straight and proud.

I started to cry. It felt like my body was breaking in half.

It never really fit itself back together. My mother enrolled me in dance classes at Step To It! five days a week. Said piano made me too "interior" and that I needed to develop more social skills. She said Maddie still had her old dance things and I could use those. I think she thought she could make me Maddie 2.0 if she just gave me the right clothes, the right lessons.

And soon after that, Liza's parents left and never came back.

She lasted two whole weeks, taking care of herself and her brothers, before a neighbor called the police, and after that, her grandmother moved in to take care of them.

Mr. Stanley leads us through the cow, the coyote, the Up, the Down, mouth exercises, and then has us all sit down. I keep sneaking looks at Liza. I wonder what happened in Patterson's office.

After we weren't friends anymore, I felt like my heart was broken and I felt guilty, because my mom had made trouble for her.

I really miss Liza. If I had Liza now, I'd have someone to talk to about Joey, about Gage. Things.

I can feel myself tearing up, so I pinch the inside of my wrist until it stops.

"Now, let's talk," Simon announces, pulling me back to the auditorium. "I have thoughts! About our fall show. For those of you who are new, we usually do a little variety show in the fall and a play or musical in the spring. Everyone gets to do something. We're all in this together, so we all take part. Shy birds are encouraged to leave the nest and perform in the fall show, get your feet wet for the spring. Extroverts are encouraged to hang back a tad, especially if you've done this before, as you might have more advanced roles in the spring. But I need all of you. Sets, costumes, direction, running lines, lights, design, all of it. We all have a part to play."

"What if you aren't good at anything?" someone asks. It's a short girl with red hair, the one whose dad owns Kaminski's Hardware. He used to keep a bowl of lemon drops by the register. You didn't even have to be with a parent to go in and have one. You just could. Liza and I would do that on the way to the library.

"Everyone is good at something," Simon answers.

"Not me," she says.

"Maybe you just haven't discovered it yet. People are like onions. Many layers."

"Onions stink," someone says, laughing.

"So do some people," Simon says, wagging a finger. "But we add onions to our food all the time and it really makes a dish, in my opinion." He hands out sheets of paper to everyone.

"Now we're going to choose partners and do a little dialogue practice," he tells us.

Liza immediately chooses Jeremy. Someone chooses the red-haired girl. Everyone is moving around like it's a game of tag. Finally, it's just me and a tall, pretty blond girl. She's usually sitting at the same table as Gage during lunch. I realize she was the one who had her hand on his arm that first day in the cafeteria.

"I'm Priscilla. Have you done this before?" she asks me, smiling. "It's fun."

"No, I'm new. Emory." I feel awkward and short next to her. I think she's on the volleyball team.

She regards me thoughtfully. "Are you Maddie Ward's

sister? I went to your house once. She had a swim party. God, your house is *nice*. Don't you have like six fireplaces or something? That house is like something out of an old movie."

"No," I say. "Just three. Only one works."

"Ha!" Priscilla says. "I don't even have *one* fireplace. Your sister is *beautiful.*" She sighs, waving her fingers.

"Yes," I say. "I know. I live with her."

"Gage Galt lives next door to you."

"What?" I look up from the dialogue sheet Simon gave us.

"Gage Galt lives next to you, right? You guys friends?"

My heartbeat picks up. "I've known him forever, but we don't, uh, hang *out,*" I say. I have to stick to the rules Gage set up, that no one can know. Our secret. I try to keep my face and voice neutral.

"Well," she says, arching an eyebrow. "If you have any inside info, let me know. I'm thinking of asking him to Fall Festival and I need all the help I can get. He's a tough one to crack. Most guys, easy as pie, but not him." She laughs.

My heart spikes again. It's one thing to read the comments from girls on his Instagram, or see them touching his arm in the cafeteria, but to have someone actually say they're interested in him, to my face, is another matter. Especially someone so . . . perfect-looking.

He wouldn't . . . say yes to her, would he? He said he didn't want anything complicated, or public. But what if he changes his mind?

"Is something wrong?" Priscilla asks. "You look a little funny."

"What? No, I'm fine. Fine. Just nervous. I'm not used to, you know, drama," I finally answer.

I look away from her, desperate to see something else, and

land on Liza and Jeremy, who are standing very close to each other, heads bent together, whispering.

They look . . . together.

Oh. Jeremy. Shy, sweet Jeremy Leonard with his comic books and stained hoodie and bags of Doritos. *Oh.* Liza and Jeremy.

"Earth to Emory," Priscilla says, flicking her paper and bringing me back to the moment.

"Yes," I say. "Sorry."

"Cool. You can be Romeo, I'll be Juliet, and then we'll switch. All we have to remember is that we'd literally die to be together."

"Right," I say. "That should be no problem at all."

When Drama Club's over, I head to the library to get Joey. He has tutoring today.

His and his tutor's books and laptops are closed and they're both looking down at their phones, chairs pushed together and faces close.

"Hey," I say loudly.

They look up at me, startled.

The girl says, "Uh-oh, it's the cops," and giggles. She moves away from Joey a little.

Joey smiles. "It's just my sister." He holds up his phone. "We were playing *Fortnite*."

"Weren't you supposed to be studying?" I say, perhaps too sharply, because the ponytailed girl raises her eyebrows and gives me a look like, *What's with you?*

"We did," Joey says. "We finished early. You okay? You look . . . weird."

I'm not sure how I feel about finding Joey sitting so close to his tutor. What if she's not a sober person? *The person in recovery should avoid exposure to high-risk people, those who still use addictive substances.*

"Can we just go? I'm really hungry," I say.

The girl slips her phone into her backpack. "Call me if you need extra help. You have my number?"

Joey nods. "Yup, I got it."

"'K. I'm always happy to help, even outside, like, regular tutoring time." She's stroking the ends of her hair in a cute way, smiling up at him.

"Cool. Thanks," he says.

There's an air between them that feels weighty, like something's happening that I shouldn't be watching, and I feel irritated, though I'm not sure why. Maybe because of Liza and Jeremy, or that girl Priscilla being interested in Gage, and now this. Like everyone gets to hook up in public but me.

I sigh heavily, shift my feet deliberately. *"Joey."*

"Okay," he says tersely. "Well, I gotta go. Take my little sister home."

I bristle. "Little?"

Joey gives me a look like, *Shut up.*

"See you," the girl says.

In the hallway, I whisper, "What, so did you get *any* tutoring done? Or was it all just *Fortnite* and flirting?"

"It was *Fortnite,* flirting, *and* tutoring. And she's super cute. Did you *see* her? Her name's Amber. She's new here this year. From South Dakota."

"I don't think you should be hooking up with anyone right now, do you? What if she's not, you know. Like, sober. She could be high-risk."

"I'm not *hooking up* with anyone, I just met a cute, smart girl. It's nice to talk to somebody who doesn't *know,* you know. And it's not like I want to spring that on her right away. 'Hey, do you use, because if you do, you can't be my tutor.' And to be honest, all of high school is *high-risk,* if you hadn't noticed."

"I guess," I say. I push open the doors of the school and a rush of warm air hits my face. There aren't many cars left in the parking lot at this time of day.

We get into Joey's new car. I think again about Liza and Jeremy. Me and Gage.

"Joey?"

"What?" He puts the key into the ignition. "Are we going to have another deep conversation in the car? We seem to be doing that a lot lately."

"Ha." I pause. "Have you ever . . . you know." My words come out in a rush and I duck my head so he can't see my face flush. I remember our health teacher last year telling us that if you couldn't talk about sex without being embarrassed, you weren't ready to have it. That seems wrong to me, though. I mean, bodies are weird and gooshy, as I've recently learned, and make odd sounds when you put two of them together, and *that* seems like it would be embarrassing no matter how old you are.

"Have I ever what?" He sounds annoyed as he pulls out of the parking lot. The leaves are falling from the trees. Mill Haven looks beautiful this time of year, gold and orange. Crisp, like a landscape painting, each color perfect in its own way. It makes me sad, even though I don't know quite why.

I swallow. Knit my fingers together. "Had sex."

I glance over at him and see his face flush deep red. "Oh my god, this is not the conversation I was expecting to have with my younger sister right now. Or maybe ever."

"Yes or no," I say.

He works his jaw. "Yes."

"Really?" I look over at him, shocked. "With who!"

"You don't know her. It was last spring. She doesn't go to Heywood. I met her at a party."

"Was she your girlfriend, or just, like, a one-time thing?" Joey never brought a girl to the house or mentioned anyone to me. I wonder how much of Joey I don't really know about, even though I thought I did.

"*Why* are you asking me this?" He's frowning.

I look out the window. I could never tell him about Gage. I'm positive he wouldn't get it.

"I don't know. It just seems like everybody knows how to do this stuff. Like it's easy for them. To talk to people. Flirt." I think of Liza and Jeremy leaning their heads together. Priscilla with her hand on Gage's arm in the cafeteria. Romeo and Juliet, pained and desperate and aching. All the kids holding hands in the halls.

He takes a deep breath. "We met up a lot," he says, eyes pinned on the road. "At people's houses. She was there . . . that night. That was the last time we hooked up. Before we got high together. I don't know, we just started talking one time and she was really pretty. But we were also high all the time, so I don't really know what it's like to meet somebody when I'm sober. That's why it was nice to talk to Amber. It felt natural. Nice. I guess that's what it should feel like. Natural. Like you're *meant* to be talking to that person. You shouldn't feel like, I don't know, that you're *trying* to get them to like you. They just should."

He clears his throat. "You should probably talk to Maddie. I mean, she probably has better advice for you. About girl things. Girl parts."

He gets red again. "Don't tell Mom about Amber, okay? It'll just start something, and then she might get me a different tutor, okay?"

"I won't." He's right. That's exactly the sort of thing Mom would put a stop to.

When we pull into the garage at home, he turns to me.

"Listen, Emmy, you're a really nice girl. You're smart, and kind, and really cute. Anybody would be lucky to hang with you, okay? If there's somebody you like, just kind of feel it out. That's really all I think I know."

"You really think somebody would be lucky to be with me?" I ask softly.

"Oh my god, yes. But you have to be careful, because Mom has trained you to go along with people, you know? You're not like Maddie. You have to learn to speak up. You have to learn what *you* want."

It's like he's giving me the spine talk that Liza gave me at lunch, the spine I haven't quite figured out how to use, even though it's sitting right inside my body.

But I wonder if I could. If I could be the kind of person, like Priscilla, who doesn't think anything of asking someone to a dance. It's just something she'd *do*

"But if somebody hurts you, tell me, because I will go all out, and I mean, *all out,* in making them pay," he says.

I'm sitting on the front porch on Saturday afternoon when Max deVos skates down the sidewalk, his thin body weaving effortlessly on the board. He stops at the foot of our porch and kicks his board up, holds it in both hands against his chest like a baby.

"Joey around?"

I shake my head. "He's upstairs getting ready for work. At Hank's Hoagies. It's his first day."

"He got a *job*? You guys, like, have money up the wazoo, what's he need a *job* for?"

"My mom thought it would be good for him. Keep him busy."

Max snorts. "Most people get jobs for money. Your family gets jobs for, like, *character.*"

"Well," I say sharply. "He has a job and he's leaving soon, so he can't hang out."

Max tugs his gray knit hat down his forehead. "Damn, well, what time does he get off? Maybe I can come back and hang with him."

The front door opens and my mother steps out, pulling her cardigan closed. She looks first at me, then at Max.

"Can I help you?" Her voice is pure Mom: chilly, assured.

"Mom," I say. "It's Max. Max deVos. Joey's friend."

"Hey, Mrs. Ward. I just came by to hang with Joe," Max says. He's back to holding the skateboard in front of his chest again, but less like a baby and more like a shield. I wish I had a shield I could use against my mom sometimes.

"Oh. Yes. Meryl's boy." She slides the mail out of the box, sifting through letters and catalogs. "But I'm afraid Joey is busy at the moment."

"I can come back after he gets off work."

My mother straightens her back. "Joey isn't having visitors at the moment, Max. He needs to concentrate on his recovery and if I recall correctly, most of what you and he did revolved around drugs. Am I incorrect?"

My mother's particular brand of chilly enunciation gives

even me the shivers, and I feel sorry for Max, who practically shrinks before us.

His face goes red. "Oh, no, Mrs. Ward, I just came to hang out." Max puts down his skateboard. "I haven't been high in days."

"I don't want Joe to be around temptations, Max," my mom says. "His recovery is very important, do you understand? He could have died."

Max blinks, looks at me. I look at my lap.

"But everybody needs *friends,* Mrs. Ward. I mean, I can hang out with Joey without being high." The neediness in his voice makes me sad. I mean, I get it. Especially now. The friendless thing.

"I'm sorry, Max. It can't be helped. Please tell your mother I say hello."

I hear my mom retreat into the house, the heavy door clicking shut behind her.

"Damn," Max says. "Your mom is harsh."

"Max, I told you when you came by before. I don't know why you came back."

"Because he's my—"

But I look away from him, distracted by the whole reason I'm on this porch anyway.

I *was* reading, but I was also waiting, hoping to get a glimpse of Gage before I have to go to work with Joey.

Here he comes. Jogging down the sidewalk, his face creased with concentration and sweat. He's been out on a run for forty-five minutes, which is about how long I've been on the porch.

He slows at the end of his driveway and stretches. He stands up and catches my eye.

Then his eyes drift to Max.

"Hey," he says.

"Hey?" Max says. He says it hesitantly, because of course, why would Gage Galt be talking to *him*?

"DeVos, right?"

Max blinks. "Yeah."

Gage jogs in place for a minute and regards us. Then he smiles and jogs up his drive, up his steps, and into his house.

I'm not quick enough tearing my eyes away from him, because Max says, "Really? What *is* that? What's up with you girls? You can't have it both ways."

"What are you talking about?" I frown.

"You. That. Big baseball god. You were practically drooling over him, but if *I* did that to a hot chick, like, kept staring at her, you'd call me a pig."

I don't know what to say, really, because . . . he's not wrong?

"And why do you guys always have to go for, like, the most godly-looking dudes? You're always telling us to, like, check out your insides and not concentrate on your boobs and stuff, but you aren't any different. I mean, I'm standing right *here*." He kicks the tail of his skateboard. "Man, this day sucks *hard*."

As he rolls down the sidewalk, he calls back, "And tell your mom she's wrong. Everybody needs friends. You can't have a decent life without friends!"

I'm reading *The Portrait of a Lady* in Hank's Hoagies, even though I should be reading *Beloved* for Watson's class. It's not that I don't like *Beloved,* I do, but it definitely did not feel like hoagie shop reading. I have one eye trained on Joey, who is following Hank around obediently, when Gage texts.

That your boyfriend

Excuse me?

Guy you were talking to earlier. You going out

My fingers hover over my phone, shaking slightly. Why is he asking me this, exactly? I want to type, *Are you jealous?* But I don't.

He was there for Joey

Oh

. . .

I wait. There's that feeling writers describe in books, when they say characters can feel their heart in their throats. I feel that now: this knot of something, of anticipation. Fear, maybe. Or . . . pleasure. That he might actually be jealous.

I miss watching you swim

What?

Swim. In the pool. I could see you sometimes, from my bathroom window. Faces your yard. It's too bad it's too cold now.

. . .

You were watching me?

Sometimes. Not in a bad way! I have to brush my teeth. The window is right there 😊

. . .

So, you want to meet up later? I have a thing, we could meet after

A thing?

Party.

Invite me.

But I don't type that.

Can't stay out long. Have a workout tomorrow. But maybe we could hang out in the pool house.

. . .

Your mom has a meeting with the city council. My dad's on it, that's how I know. They always go for drinks after at Jasper's. You don't have to worry about that.

My fingers are definitely shaking.

Are you there?

Yes

So can I come over?

Scrumptious. That's what PristTine commented on his pitching camp post way back in the summer. A girl with confidence. A girl who wasn't afraid. A girl who said, not in so many words, *Take me. Pick me.*

Okay, I type.

Cool. Around ten. Ok?

Something crashes and I look up. Joey is swearing under his breath, trying to scoop ice off the counter. He spilled a drink container. Hank is standing next to him, apologizing to the customer.

Ok. Gotta go.

I put my phone down. Joey looks over at me, shakes his head, his mouth in a tight line.

Driving home, Joey says, "Well, that wasn't the worst four hours of my life, but it's in the top ten."

"You seemed like you were doing well. Except maybe for when you spilled that drink. And then the ketchup incident."

"I smell like a giant onion." His face is sweaty and his shirt is stained with salad and oil.

I sniff the air. "You kind of do."

When we come in the door, my mother is waiting for us. She frowns. "Are you getting sick, Joe? You look flushed."

She presses the back of her hand to his forehead, but he pushes it away. "It's the sheen of labor, Mom. You should be proud."

My mom bristles. "A little hard work goes a long way, Joe. I just want to help you."

I tense up, waiting for a fight.

But instead, Joey's shoulders sag, and he just says, "I know, Mom. I know."

He heads up the stairs and Mom turns to me, taking a deep breath.

"I mean, you can see that, can't you? I'm doing everything I can to keep him on track." Her voice wavers a little.

"It's just . . ." I look at the floor, at her feet, anywhere but her face, because I don't want to say anything that will make her mad. That's like my whole life, trying not to upset my own mother.

"It's just . . . a lot," I finally say. "He'll get used to it."

She nods. "Well, I'm going out for a bit for drinks with Tom Rigby and some council members. I won't be back until late. These people like to knock it back and I have to play along."

"Oh." I act surprised, like I didn't just learn this from Gage. "Council on a Saturday night? What for?"

She drops her phone into her purse. "It's not a formal meeting. They're feeling me out. Some developers want to buy the Mill. It's falling apart and the council wants me to sell it or raze it and sell the land."

"That's . . . big."

Gage is coming over Gage is coming over Gage is coming over

"Nothing for you to worry about."

"What . . . time will you be back?" I say, trying to keep my voice casual.

"Late. Those people can really drink. I'll be buying, of course." She kind of laughs. "Dinner's warming on the stove, so don't forget about it."

"Okay, sure. Fine."

"Are *you* okay? You seem a little . . . jumpy?"

"Yes," I say. "Absolutely. Tip-top."

"All right, then. I'm off."

It isn't until she's out the door that I realize Joey will be here, and what will I do about Joey?

I'm putting soup into bowls in the kitchen, Fuzzy darting in and out of my legs, when Joey comes in. His hair is wet and he's dressed in a T-shirt and sweats. He slides onto a stool at the island. I push a bowl of soup at him. He grimaces.

"Not hungry. I had to look at food all day."

"It didn't seem so bad," I say.

"Hank is a dick and it was pretty obvious he doesn't really want me there—he wants to get in good with Mom for some reason, but I guess it could have been worse. At least I got to talk to some people there. It was nice to just talk to people, since I can't really talk to anyone at school except Amber."

I think about Max earlier in the day, shouting that everyone needs friends.

I stir the soup in my bowl. "I forgot to tell you Max deVos came by earlier. Mom scared him off."

Joey puts his head in his hands. "Poor Max. He's harmless."

"Yeah." I sneak a look at the clock on the kitchen wall. It's seven o'clock. Three more hours.

Joey's wiping his eyes.

"Joey, what's wrong?" I put my soup spoon down.

"Nothing. It's just . . . Max, I guess. I mean, I don't really have any friends now, you know?" He rubs his face. "Whatever. I'm gonna go to bed early, but you want to watch a movie or something first?"

"Sure." I feel sorry for Joey. I don't have any friends anymore, either, but at least Gage counts for something.

As I'm putting the soup away and rinsing our bowls for the dishwasher, I can hear Joey clicking through movies to watch. I check the clock again. A little less than three hours now. How long a movie will he choose? Will I have time to take a shower after? I want to be clean for later, for Gage. How am I going to get away from Joey and go outside to the pool house? What if—

I slam the dishwasher door shut a little too hard.

I don't want to spend a Saturday night watching my brother. I want to spend a Saturday night kissing a boy. I want to spend Saturday night kissing someone without sneaking around about it. Maybe I should just tell Joey about Gage.

But I can't.

There's an uncomfortable twist in my stomach.

I can't tell Joey about Gage because I think I know how he would react, and that might not be something I can deal with right now. The fact that I'm *me* and Gage Galt is *Gage Galt* and I'm pretty sure Joey's reaction, like the rest of the world, would be Why is *Gage Galt* interested in *you*? Because that type of boy generally doesn't hang out with invisible girls like me, and as much as I would like the world to right itself and make this a normal thing, that godlike boys like Gage could really see invisible girls like me, and could like them, I'm not so sure the world, or Gage, works that way. And in my heart of hearts, I know Joey, if I told him, would think this, too, and that makes the twisting in my stomach even worse. Because underneath it all, it's really me that's wondering why I'm a girl that can only be seen in secret, in the dark. Where all my awfulness and wrongness can be kissed and stroked away.

Joey calls to me that the movie's starting.

I check the clock again, grit my teeth.

I wish I could call Maddie, ask her what to do, who to be, but it would turn into a thing, and I can't handle any more *things*.

I throw the dish towel into the sink.

I have to stay a secret for a little bit longer. It's all I have. The CuteCathys and PristTines of the world have had their share, and even though he's much too large for my velvet hatbox of stolen things, maybe I can keep stealing Gage Galt from them for myself, just for a while longer, until he realizes we don't have to hide, that we can be seen and the world won't end.

Mis_Educated

Hey, Hey, Heywood Haulers!
It's Saturday night in our drop-dead-boring town
What's happening?
Who's got the skinny
On the parties the hookups the broken hearts to be
Who's at home lonely and just wishing for the day
Someone wants you
Invites you
Sees you
Erases all those hours
Of feeling like no one knows you exist
That palpable ache in your throat
When you hear your parents say
These are the best years of your life
And yet it feels like everyone is living it but you?
Aye, screw it
Parents never tell you the truth anyway
But I'm here!
Tell me your truths, you lonely Haulers

#heywoodhaulers #heywoodhigh #lonelyhearts #saturdaynight
#hightimesatheywood #itgetsbetter #millhaven

NatetheGreat party at Stone's house right now it's ripped

Stewie13 Just another fun night blazing it up and playin Apex.
Alone.

HelenOfJoy All my friends are virtual but they're the best people
I know

MandyMandy Killing myself reading The Scarlet Letter for the
millionth time. I hate you, Nathaniel Hawthorne, with every fiber
of my being. Hester did nothing wrong!!

TupacLives stone's party is lit, y'all get here you won't be sorry

FrancesP44 there are like fifty kids at Stone's the jocks are
doing kegstands

LzySusan Jocks are a-holes all muscle and no heart

PaulMall I do wish I had more friends

LaceyZ i can't wait to get out of this hellhole and go to college and meet actual human beings who care about more than partying or hooking up

TupacLives @LaceyZ I have bad news for you about college ?

LaceyZ whatever, i'll find my people. it has to be better than this

ForrestGumpp My dad died last summer and I feel like I'll never be happy again, that's how I'm doing

Stewie13 sorry about that @ForrestGumpp that's really sad

MackAttack I miss Shannon Roe. You guys called her a drama queen and said she was looking for attention and she was cuz she needed help! people don't cut unless they hurt and you were the worst to her and now she's gone you can all go to hell

NatetheGreat anybody think that Tom Kidder guy is one step away from a major meltdown

LucyK I miss Candy

AnnaBanana I feel gray, that's how I feel. I feel gray and cold and I just want to know when I'm going to feel normal because life is really grinding me down does anyone care or understand

LaceyZ @AnnaBanana DM me I'm here, I'll listen

PristTine Damn, GG is at Stone's party and that boy is FINE

TupacLives get it @PristTine

MrPoppersPenguins My sister has been missing awhile now from Dover. She has an addiction. Was at a party in Mill Haven in May. Name is Carly. Anybody got any leads DM me

GiGi Check the bridge. That's where the ghosties are

19

I'M HALF WATCHING THE movie, half checking my phone, Joey stretched out next to me on the couch. It's nine-fifteen. His eyelids are drooping. I nudge him.

"Maybe you should go to bed," I say.

He sits up. "Maybe. I'm wiped."

"I'll turn the lights off and stuff."

"When's Dad back?"

"He doesn't get back until late," I say, clicking off the television.

"I kind of thought he'd be . . . around more," Joey says. "You know, like when I got back."

I sigh. "He's Dad. He's busy saving people. You know how he is."

Joey is quiet. "Yeah, I do. I just thought, is all."

He stands up. "You going to bed, too?"

"Maybe. I might read or something." I try to keep my voice normal so he can't tell I'm lying.

I get up, straightening the coffee table, clicking off lights. Nine-twenty-five. Thirty-five minutes.

Joey goes upstairs. I stand silently, listening to the sounds of his feet in his doorless bathroom, water running, the toilet flushing. Then it gets quiet.

I find my suit, the one Gage said he liked, hanging in the laundry room. I change in the downstairs bathroom, then put

165

my clothes back on, just in case Joey comes back downstairs, or my dad or mom comes home earlier. Maybe Gage will think it's cute I'm wearing the suit. Sexy.

And then I'm just standing alone in the quiet house, waiting, watching the time tick away on my phone.

When it's 9:55, I go into the kitchen and turn off the security lights in the backyard. They pop on with any movement, and the last thing I need is Joey waking up suddenly because a flash of light sprang through his window. Then I slide the patio door open as quietly as possible, my heart thudding in my ears, and wait outside.

Ten o'clock.

Ten oh five.

Why is he late? I look over at the wall.

My phone vibrates, startling me.

Are you in the pool house

Gage.

Not yet

Go in almost there

I'm opening the door to the pool house when I hear a sound from the patio. I whip around, heart in my throat.

Joey is standing outside the patio doors, staring at me. "What the hell are you doing outside, Em?"

His hair is mussed, like he was already asleep and I woke him up.

"I . . ."

Joey frowns.

"I was going to read and the book I wanted . . . I remembered I left it in the pool house. A few weeks ago. I was just going to get it." I try to keep my voice from shaking.

From the corner of my eye, I hear movement on the other side of the wall that separates our house from Gage's.

"Well, hurry up," Joey says sleepily.

Gage is halfway up the wall, starting to hoist his leg over.

Joey is just standing there, hugging himself in the cool air.

"Okay, okay," I say loudly. "Geez. Go inside. You don't have to watch *over* me."

I was too harsh. Joey's face falls. "What's with you," he mutters. He turns around and walks back into the house.

I'm frozen, torn because I've hurt my brother's feelings and because Gage is now over the wall, pinned to it like a butterfly under glass. He heard Joey.

I shake my head quickly and motion for him to go back over. I hold up my hands, like, *Sorry.*

There's a flicker of light in Maddie's room upstairs, then it turns off.

Gage sees it, too, smiles at me.

My heart is thudding. I could go into the house or I could go into the pool house, but what if Joey comes back down? Or did I hurt his feelings so much he won't?

I had to sit in Hank's Hoagies with him for four hours. I should be able to . . . do something for myself.

I look at the pool house and walk straight to it and open the door.

Gage follows me.

Gage's eyes are gleaming. "That was close," he says softly.

Inside the pool house, he steps toward me, strokes my shoulder.

"I will admit, I was a little jealous this afternoon," he says quietly. "When I saw that guy outside your house."

I can feel prickles of pleasure along my spine.

"Really?" I say.

"Yeah. One of the things I like about you is you seem to keep to yourself."

He scoops my hair into his palms, rubs the ends with his thumbs. I want to concentrate on just him, on just this moment, but I'm still tense, thinking of Joey upstairs, worried he'll come back outside, worried I hurt his feelings. I can't relax. If only I didn't have to sneak around.

"But, Gage, sometimes I just . . . I mean, maybe we could try meeting somewhere else, not always here. Like, a mov—"

Then he's kissing me and my words fall away, forgotten.

"Emory."

I slam the patio door shut behind me, startled.

My dad is standing on the other side of the kitchen island, his eyes tired, a drink in front of him.

"Dad. What are you doing here?"

"I live here. And it's past midnight. What on earth were you doing outside this late at night?"

"Nothing. I thought I left a book in the pool house. That I wanted to read. But it wasn't there."

Can he see? Can he tell? Do people look different, once they've been kissed and touched?

"Why aren't the security lights on?" He walks past me, flips the switch.

"I . . . must have turned them off accidentally."

"Well, be careful. There have been a few break-ins in the neighborhood lately and we need to stay safe."

"Oh."

"You look flushed. Are you getting sick?"

Like my mother, he peers at me, puts his hand on my forehead. But unlike her, he uses his palm, not the back of his hand, and I feel an unexpected warmth for him, the way his hand cups my forehead, like when I was little and sick and he wasn't just the man who made other people better, he made *me* better.

He takes his hand away. His eyes look sad and drained.

"Joey's asleep?" he asks.

"Yes. He had his first shift today."

"Did it go well?"

"I think so. I don't know. I mean, it's hoagies." I laugh nervously.

"Your mother says you're in Drama Club this year. I like that. Simon Stanley is a lovely man. Maybe . . ." He pauses. "Maybe you'll make some friends there, eh? I know you miss Liza. And spending a Saturday night with your brother can't be the most fun thing at sixteen, I imagine." If only he knew how true that statement was.

"It's not like he has anyone to hang out with, either," I say. "So it kinda fits."

He picks up his drink from the island. "You have each other."

"We have each other."

It's true; we do have each other. I shouldn't have yelled at Joey. I feel ashamed now. I'm supposed to be helping him, not yelling at him. Whatever my problems are, they aren't nearly as bad as Joey's.

"Good night, Emory. Get to bed, all right?"

"Good night, Dad," I say, and make my way up the stairs to my bedroom.

In bed, I touch a finger to my mouth. My lips feel fuller, swollen almost, and softer. A gentle electric feeling creeps over my body.

My phone pings.

I like what we have

Yes, I type.

Not a thing, but something good, just between us

So he was listening, in the pool house, before we started.

Go slow, I tell myself. Baby steps. Not all at once. One thing at a time.

Okay, I answer. *For now.*

Give me some words

I think, the quietness of my room wrapping around me. If I got up, would I see him in his window, looking back at me? Or is he in bed, too, wondering about his own swollen mouth?

Let the stars, I type, *speak for us.*

20

ONDAY AFTER SCHOOL, WE are all standing on the stage, watching Simon Stanley sitting in a wooden chair. His legs are crossed and he's holding a paperback copy of *Lady Chatterley's Lover.*

"Who am I?" he asks.

No one says anything. I shift from one leg to the other, trying to rest my knee.

"I mean, just by looking at me, do you think you know me? By the way I'm sitting. By the way I'm holding this book."

"Um," says the red-haired girl. "You look relaxed. Your legs are crossed."

"Good," Simon says. "What happens if I do this?" He slouches down in the chair, uncrosses his legs, rolls his head to one side so it almost touches his shoulder. Giggles from the circle.

"I'd say you're stoned, dude," another girl says.

Simon smiles. "Perhaps, yes. What about my book? What does that say about me?"

Liza smirks. "That's a salacious book, Mr. Stanley, so I'd guess you have a lot of saucy stuff on your mind."

Simon laughs. "Indeed. My point is, when we are thinking about our roles in a play, the play gives us direction, and an idea of how to construct our character, but not too much. So, as actors, we have to really think about our characters. The way they sit. The way they speak. *Why* they sit the way they do. What that tells an audience about their whole character, but also about what is happening in the scene in question. No two actors play the same role in the same way. Each approaches their role as a whole, but the character in pieces. They fill in the backstory. The seams of the garment, so to speak. The thread that holds everything together."

"Say what?" someone murmurs.

Simon paces among us. "I'm made up of all my experiences up until this moment, do you understand? Things you will never know have made me who I am, right now, in this moment. Sometimes we have to construct that for characters, even if it is never referenced in the play. Now, let's play."

I shrink back, behind the red-haired girl. I don't want him to pick me. I just want to watch for now.

He gestures to Jeremy. "In the chair, my friend."

Jeremy says, "This isn't my favorite part."

"Bear with me," Simon answers.

Jeremy lumbers over to the chair. Simon hands him the book.

"Jeremy, you are no longer Jeremy, solid, good-guy Jeremy who makes wonderful sets and is always on time. Now you are an angry person. Give me a hint as to why."

Jeremy hesitates.

Simon waits.

I hold my breath. This seems a little scary. I look over at Liza. She's watching Jeremy intently. I wonder how much she knows about him. About Luther. I wonder how much Jeremy knows about her and her parents.

Suddenly I wonder if Liza ever thinks about me now. How my story has changed into something like hers used to be. If it seems ironic to her that the very thing my mother broke up our friendship for is now something that's warped our own family.

And I think of Joey. All his *wrongs* building up into something that made him feel so terrible he wanted to feel . . . nothing.

I feel like Jeremy, all of a sudden. This is not my favorite part, either.

Jeremy clears his throat. He's still for a minute and then leans his elbows on his knees, one fist clenching the book. He jiggles his legs. Works his face into a frown.

"Good," Simon says. "Now, why are you angry? What's the backstory in your mind? Our playwright can only tell us so much, which is why one actor will play a character one way and another actor will play the same character differently. They've both considered the text, and what may be beneath the text.

"Why are you so angry in the chair, not-Jeremy?" Simon's voice is soft.

The stage is very quiet, like we're all holding our breath. It feels kind of magical to me, this anticipation. Like when you're reading a really good book and your fingers can't wait to turn the page. That breathlessness of not knowing what's next. But I'm nervous, too.

Jeremy's forehead creases. His legs jiggle faster. "I'm waiting for someone to come see me. He's late. He's *always* been late. And I know when he finally comes out of that gray door, he's not even *going* to be happy to see me. He'll call me names, make fun of me, because that's what he always does, and why do I keep trying? I took a bus two hours to get here because no one else will see him and I had to read this stupid book for homework and everything sucks."

Jeremy throws the book across the stage. It lands with a thwack in the darkness of the left wing. His face is flaming red. People are quiet.

Then we applaud.

Simon touches his chin thoughtfully. "Good, Jeremy. You came up with a very compelling backstory right then. Thank you."

Jeremy gets out of the chair and lumbers over to me.

"That sucked," he whispers glumly. "I don't really like being in front of people. I prefer making sets. Background stuff."

"It was good," I say softly. "It was brave. I couldn't do it."

Simon looks around. "Liza?"

Liza pops right over to the chair, smoothing the legs of her overalls. "Oh, cool. Can I be, like, a really prim person from the 1950s who has to read this book for a college class? And a churchgoer. That sounds good. And I secretly like the book, but I feel guilty about it?"

Simon waves his hand. "Sally forth, Liza. Sally forth."

Liza fusses about, arranging herself in the chair. She clutches the paperback to her denimed chest, crosses her feet at the ankles, angles her head just so. When she starts speaking, her voice is high and sweet.

She always did like playacting. That was one of the things she liked to do when we were friends. Make up stories, act them out. We could do that for hours and hours.

After a few minutes, Jeremy whispers, "Luther *was* late, though. I finally took the bus and he only came out with five minutes of visiting hour left."

His eyes are so sad.

"I can't even make up a decent backstory. Real life just gets in the way." He crosses his arms and puts his head down while Liza spins her world.

The outpatient clinic smells like strong coffee and cigarette smoke on people's clothes. We had to cut through a cluster of smokers to get to the front doors of the building.

"Mom's going to think we smoked now," Joey says, sniffing his jacket.

"Pee day," someone against the wall mutters to him. "FYI."

"No worries if you're clean," someone else says.

The yellowy-nailed boy isn't here this time. Joey walks up to the counter to check in. He comes back with a cup.

"I had to do it all the time at Blue Spruce," he says. "It's no big deal."

"How often do they check?"

He shrugs. "Whenever they want, I guess. I mean, they can't *tell* you in advance or that would ruin the purpose."

The blue-shirt person comes out and calls the group to start.

"See you in a bit," Joey says, walking away with his cup.

The skinny guy against the wall says, "You could cheat easy, you know."

"How?" I say.

"People trade pee. Like, you could have a clean person pee in a baggie and keep it in your pocket and then pour it in when you go to the bathroom. They aren't real strict here. Some places search you first, but not here."

"That's a little gross," I say. "Keeping a baggie of pee in your pocket."

"Better than the alternative." He picks at his chin.

175

"Nah, man." A girl leans forward in a chair. "You have to be careful with that. I loaned my pee to a dude and they figured it out real quick because it turned out I was pregnant and he got sent back to jail for it."

The skinny guy frowns. "Where's your baby?"

The girl shrugs.

My phone buzzes in my purse and I pull it out. The security guard shakes his head and points to the NO CELL PHONES sign on the wall. "Outside," he says sternly.

I get up and go outside, making sure to stand away from the smokers.

I need help with this book sorry this PLAY

Gage. My face flushes.

I look around the parking lot, at the smokers, the run-down cars, except for ours, shiny and new. The bent straws and fast-food bags strewn on the pavement. Such a dirty and dismal place. Maybe if the place was cleaner, people here would feel better about things. About getting help. It makes even me feel low, like there's no hope. I look down at my phone. But . . . there is a way to feel better, at least for me.

Okay, I type back.

**Maybe u could help me later I have a paper
to write**

I'm with my brother right now,
then I have to go to work with him

. . .

Why do you have to go to work with him?

It's complicated. My mom
likes me to kind of watch him.

. . .

Oh right. Because of the accident?

Well, he OD'ed. He was in rehab,
remember? We're at outpatient now.

Right

. . .

Come over after

What? That'll be late. It's a school night
**I see the light in your window I know you
stay up late Just tell your mom you're helping me**

. . .

**Mothers love me, Emmy
It'll be warmer than the pool house**

I breathe in the smoky air, which burns my lungs a little, so
I move farther from the smokers. The lights in the parking lot
blink on, casting a hazy glow over the lot. Going over to Gage's
would mean what? His bedroom?

. . .

You there

See you around 9:30, I type.
Simon said we are made up of all our experiences.
I'm just filling in my backstory.

A half hour. That's all. Ok?

Ok

21

LATER, AT HANK'S HOAGIES, Joey shuffles out from behind the counter, his arms loaded with packets of napkins, bundles of condiments, and a damp rag. Under the harsh ceiling light, he looks tired and pale.

I close my iPad. "Let me help you," I say.

"No, you don't have to. Keep studying."

"If I don't help you, we'll get out of here later, and you need to study, too," I say. "Go get the mop." I want to make sure we get home in time for me to go over to Gage's.

Joey's closing duties are stocking the lobby tables and mopping the floor. Hank does the register count. His wife and a sallow-faced girl take care of cleaning the kitchen and prep area. I've done this a few times already, and I have the drill down. Hank never seems to care that I help.

I wipe the red-checkered tablecloths and stuff the holders with napkins, slide forks into plastic containers. Joey wheels out the yellow mop bucket and dunks the mop inside. He squeezes out the mop and slaps it on the floor, twirling it across sticky spilled soda stains and droplets of dried mustard.

I carefully count out ten each of the condiments for the bins on the tables. Headlights of passing cars flash by the large window facing Main Street. There are tiny lights in the trees on the avenue that make them look starry, pretty.

I grab my things and step out of the way so Joey can finish.

Hank comes out behind the register, drying his hands on a towel.

"Good kids," he says to me. He punches some buttons on the register and the cashbox pops out. He cradles it in his arms.

"Your mother made a decision yet?" he asks me.

"I'm sorry?" Hank is a perfectly round being. Round eyes, round body, and a round, balding head underneath the orange sub shop hat with the dancing hoagie.

"The Mill. Coupla offers to buy the building. Can't sit empty forever. Shouldn't, at least."

"She doesn't really talk to me about those things," I say slowly, wondering why he's asking me.

"Sure hope she decides to do the right thing. Those condos go in, we'll get a whole lot of people from the city who want to live out here with trees and woods and the river. People who spend money."

His wife turns around, her face sweaty. "Or, if they turn the Mill into condos, we'll see chain shops," she says. "Subway will show up, drive us out of business. Kaminski's Hardware will be replaced by Walmart or Home Depot."

"I don't know anything," I say carefully. Joey passes by me, wheeling the mop bucket into the back.

"Some rinky-dink group wants to buy that big old building for nothing. Your mom tell you that? Turn it into housing and services for the deadbeats down on Frost River." Hank shakes his head. "That happens and we'll get the *wrong* kind of traffic from the city. More of those deadbeats coming here for a hand-out. We've already got too many, if you ask me."

"But I mean, those people need help, too, right?" I think of the security guard at Joey's outpatient center, who called the people at the center junkies.

And Joey. Joey could be—sort of *is*—one of those people. Or might be, if not for my family's money propping him up.

"You say that," Hank says. "Because you can. You aren't hurting. Your brother isn't hurting. Every morning when I open up, I have to kick out a bunch of lazies in the alley who've been picking through my dumpster. Only a matter of time before I get jumped or robbed. Had to put in security cameras, just in case."

The girl in the kitchen says, "I like Walmart. They have everything under one roof. I'd like not to have to go to three different places in town, if you want to know the truth. Or take the bus to the city to the mall."

Hank's wife says, "Be quiet, Caroline."

Caroline goes back to scrubbing the grill.

"Anyway," Hank says, shutting the register. "I do hope your mother makes the right call. I did her a favor, maybe she can do me a favor. Do the town a favor."

The look in his eyes says *Your family owes Mill Haven.*

It makes me feel queasy.

Joey comes out in his hoodie.

"Bye, Hank," he says. "Bye, Marie. Bye, Caroline."

"Good boy," Hank says. "I'll see you on Friday."

On the way to the car, Joey says, "Hank won't let me count the register at the end of the night, you know. He thinks I'll steal the money. What a joy working in this town is."

Joey slumps into the dining room chair, pulling two subs from his backpack and plopping them on the table. "I got you a sandwich," he says.

He lifts his iPad and notebooks from his backpack and takes

off his hoodie. His orange Hank's Hoagies shirt is crinkled and stained.

I look at my phone. Nine-fifteen. Fifteen minutes to go over to Gage's. I walk upstairs and peek into our mother's room. The lights are off. She's a lump under the covers.

In my bathroom, I brush my teeth, run a comb through my hair.

I look at myself in the mirror.

Plain.

Maddie would be in here dusting her face, contouring, lining her eyes, arranging her hair, and would emerge flawless, perfect.

But I'm not Maddie.

Downstairs, Joey is munching his sandwich, spilling daintily sliced strands of lettuce on his lap.

"Hey," he says. "Can you help?"

"Um . . ." I hesitate. "What's up?" I don't want to be late to get to Gage's, so I'm speaking fast.

"I don't get these problems in Nicholson's class. I just don't . . . like, the problems are confusing."

"I'm kind of going somewhere."

Joey puts his sandwich down. He frowns. "Where? It's a school night."

I take a deep breath. "Over to Gage's. He wanted help on a paper."

Joey's eyes widen. "Gage? Like, next door Gage?"

"Yes." I hold my breath, watching his face.

"Why would he ask you for help?"

"What?"

"He has an academic tutor. All the athletes do. So they can stay on the team. He doesn't need you."

"W-well," I stammer. "I mean, we were talking and he asked, is all."

"Emmy, he's *Gage Galt*. It's just weird that he would ask *you*."

There's a tiny sliver of suspicion in my brother's voice and it hurts me. I knew it. Even though he said anyone would be lucky to have me, he doesn't think it's possible "anyone" would include someone like Gage.

"What's that supposed to mean?" I ask him slowly.

"Nothing. Sorry."

Joey pushes the bread of his hoagie with a finger. "I just really need your help, Emmy. I wouldn't ask, I know I'm supposed to be doing it all myself, but I'm so tired. You got to do your homework at Hank's. It's almost nine-thirty and I'm just starting mine."

His shoulders sag. He drops his head in his hands. I think back to when he first got home from Blue Spruce, how his head was high.

It seems to have been dropping lower and lower the longer he's been back.

"Can't you . . . can't you text your tutor or something?"

"I can't text her this late," he says softly. "Just forget it. It's fine."

My phone pings.

U coming

I look at my brother, hunched over the table, his sandwich forgotten, the circles under his eyes prominent from working late and studying late. My mom is working him too hard, and it isn't fair. And here I am trying to get away from him so I can go kiss a boy in his bedroom.

I take a deep breath. "It's okay, Joey. It's all right."

My heart deflating, I take off my sweater, hang it on the back of the dining room chair, and sit down.

"Show me," I say. "Show me where you're having problems."

Joey pushes his iPad to me.

My phone lights up, but I turn it off.

"Here," Joey says quietly. "This stuff. It makes no sense to me."

My brother smells of oil and onions, and he's so tired, he can't even finish his sandwich and his eyelids are drooping.

"Let me," I say. "I'll do it. Just go up to bed, okay? I'll finish."

"I can't let you do that, Em. I won't learn it. I have to learn it for the test." He's whispering.

"You can ask Amber about it tomorrow. She can talk you through it."

"Emmy."

"Go, Joey. Just *go*."

I finally get to bed at midnight after finishing Joey's math and then the flashing of my phone wakes me up. It's 2:14 in the morning and my eyes struggle to read the text.

Come to the window

Why

Just do it

I get out of bed and limp to my window, parting the drapes. Fuzzy snuffles and rearranges herself on my bed.

Gage is in his own window, looking back, wearing a white T-shirt and gray pajama pants.

I missed you tonight

You did?

Yeah

I missed you, too

He holds up his phone and takes a photograph of me, the flash pinging like a star.

Hey! What was that for? I type.

Because I missed you. You look cute all sleepy like that

Okay then. I smile.

I hold up my phone, take a picture of him.

How do you like it!

He's looking at his phone.

Raise your shirt a little

What

I stare at him. Take a step back.

Like with your hand, so I can see your skin

No

I've seen it before. It's just a picture. I have to go to a pitching camp this weekend. Need something to remember you with. For . . . you know.

I stare at the words of his text.

Just raise it a little

There's a warmth spreading through me that's kind of confusing but also feels good. I put my phone on the windowsill, take a fistful of my T-shirt, and raise it along my belly.

That's nice maybe a little higher

I raise it a little higher.

From his window, he motions for me to raise it even higher.

I shake my head, *No.*

He watches me for a minute and then hooks his fingers in the waistband of his pajama pants and pushes them down one hip. He motions for me to do the same.

You promise you won't show anyone?

I would never do that, Emmy

I push one side of my pants down and hold it there, keeping my eyes on his face.

He holds up his phone. The flash brightens like a tiny star again.

Beautiful, he says. *Perfect.*

Mis_Educated

Today was a good day
Sometimes you win:
Go forth, Watsoners, and create
Your own list of classic reads.
We've been released.
No more Lolita, no more Hester Prynne,
No more West Egg, East Egg
Bring forth your hobbits and faeries
Bring forth girl queens with swords
Bring forth the damn pig and spider
Your Whartons and Riordans
Your Lewises and Woolfs
Your Baldwins and Morrisons
And you can even read Proust
(what a boring old gas bag, tho).
What shall we take on next
The extremely sad practice
Of dismembering frogs in bio?
How about woodshop? I mean,
Who puts kids in charge of heavy machinery?
What about Kramer's visual art
Is it all white people?
I was today-years-old when I learned
Those marble statues *turned* white
Over time
They were as colorful as sunsets
Just like people
On to other things:
Fall Fest is coming up
What sort of drama is going to happen?
Young hearts, a dance, some
Thumpin bass and a little something
Snuck into the punch bowl
Should do the trick.
Who's getting ready for the dance?

233 likes

#heywoodhaulers #heywoodhigh #heywoodhypocrisy
#revolutionnow #heywoodfallfestival #millhaven

NatetheGreat nobody ever dances with me

WoodyB i'm picking The Wimpy Kid books, jk

GentleBen I don't want to cut those frogs poor little froggies

MandyMandy I love Edith Wharton! Detention was totally worth our book boycott, btw

LzySusan I can't believe you guys got to Watson like that

BlakeMars Did you hear about the mill? Might get sold so richy riches can have nice apartments and meanwhile me and my mom are stomping on roaches every hour

MrPoppersPenguins Anyone seen a little blond girl named Carly? She's my sister. Been missing from Dover since last May. DM me

LucyK Candy loved dances. She was on the dance team, remember? She taught me how to dance in eighth grade. She was so beautiful when she was dancing.

TashaJack Anybody want to do anything about Helen Hoover the History Teacher from Hell telling us slavery was a necessary evil? I'll wait.

22

MAX DEVOS STARES AT the paper in his hand like he's never actually seen a paper product before. "So, like, you're saying I can read any book I want? Any book?"

Mr. Watson is fiddling with a pen. He looks at us all sternly. "Yes. Any book. A minimum of two hundred pages. It must be fiction. And you must write a thirty-page paper on why you think this is a piece of classic literature that should be read by students of your age. You'll need to use at least ten of the literary terms that I'll discuss during the remainder of our classes and you must use them correctly. You must cite your sources of support for your arguments. Typed, titled, double-spaced. You may not use illustrations. That means *drawing*, Max."

"I know that, I'm not *stupid*," Max says huffily.

You can just tell Mr. Watson wants to say *Are you sure?* by the flicker of his mouth, but somehow, he reins it in.

Someone says meekly, "Thirty pages? Don't you think that's a—"

Mr. Watson holds up one long, wrinkly finger. "I'm asking you to read one book. One. You can write the paper. I'll have no more discussion on this. This is what you wanted, this is what you get. No tests, but a paper. Your one goal is to make me want to read the book. Are we in agreement?"

Daniel Wankel gives me a sidelong glance. *Not bad,* he mouths.

He's wearing a really soft-looking gray scarf today. I wonder what his scar must look like, how long it is, if it's thick or thin. If it hurts, or itches, like the one on my knee, which is bumpy and raised and red.

"What are you going to read?' he whispers as Watson starts writing things on the board. The whiteboard marker makes a pleasant squeak, like a tiny bird singing.

"I don't know," I whisper back. "Maybe *The Portrait of a Lady*. I read it last year for another class and then again after I got home from the hospital over the summer. I just really like it for some reason, you know?" I liked it, Isabel Archer figuring things out in such a quiet way, even as she kept getting bumped around. Some parts were very dense, like a lot was happening under the surface that I didn't quite understand, which is actually how I often feel about my own life, to be honest, but reading it also made me feel a weird sense of comfort, like someone had wrapped me in a giant blanket. Isabel wasn't quite sure what direction her life was going to go in, either.

I wait for Daniel to maybe say something like "Oh, I was in the hospital, too," or "The hospital, I know what that's like," but all he says is "That's cool."

"Thirty pages." Max deVos grins. "Thirty pages of hobbits. I can do that."

Liza Hernandez pumps her fist. "Yes," she says softly. *"Yes."*

In Drama Club, Simon Stanley paces the stage with a giant piece of chalk. He talks about *staging* and *blocking*. "Actors are like chess pieces on the stage. Wherever the director decides they need to be in a particular scene, it's designed for maximum emotional effect." He points to the ceiling and to the sides of the stage. "Lighting helps, too. Lighting can highlight a particular moment. It's a subtle signal to the audience that something is important, an emotion is heightened, things are changing, or ending. Make sense?"

Everyone nods.

"A *role* is the part you play in a production. Characters are the moving parts to keep the story evolving, keep all your chess pieces in play, keep the emotions alive. Actors for the stage learn how to use their presence, their voice, their physicality, to convey the meaning of the story. The play. 'The play's the thing,' as we've all heard."

Simon marks an X in the middle of the stage. "You," he says, pointing to me. "Stand here, please."

"What?" The blood drains from my face. Everyone is looking at me. Lucy Kerr whispers to the girl next to her and glares at me.

Jeremy nudges my shoulder with his. "Go on," he whispers.

Simon points to Priscilla. "Pris, you go out into the seats, the middle row."

Priscilla jumps off the stage, lean and lithe as a colt, and runs to a seat. I look beyond her to the seats in the back, where Joey usually sits if he doesn't have tutoring. I wish he was here now. That might make me less nervous.

Simon says, "Come now, Emory, dear. The lovely thing about theater is that we simply have no *time* for shyness. The audience can't wait forever." He smiles gently.

I walk hesitantly to the X, all eyes on me.

"Now, repeat after me," Simon says.

"For sweetest things turn sourest by their deeds;
Lilies that fester smell far worse than weeds."

I repeat it, but softly.

"Now, what do you think that means?" Simon asks.

I blink. Sweet, getting sour by something done, or something someone has done? Beautiful things that die are worse than ugly things we expect to die?

I say that, but quietly. Simon says, "Wrong! Just kidding. Maybe. Maybe that's your interpretation of it. That's fine. You have to try to interpret your character's emotions and motivations from what the playwright has given you on the page, and from what the director asks you to do. Bring them to life. Now, who is speaking?"

"A girl?"

"Okay, that's a good start. Where is she?"

I imagine a girl walking in a field of flowers.

"In a field of flowers?"

"Okay. We can start there. Do you think she's sad, wistful, mad?"

"She sounds . . . maybe wistful, like she's sad that lilies die. I don't know, this is a weird quote."

"Shakespearean sonnet, child. Nothing weird about that. If we don't have the Bard, we don't have half of our language. Now, your character is a wistful girl in a field of flowers. Let the audience know that. Start by thinking about whom she might be talking to. Is she addressing herself or someone else?"

I look out at Priscilla, my heart beating in my ears. She looks back at me, her face half shadowed. I can feel everyone's eyes on me and my stomach clenches. I freeze, my blood pounding in my ears. Are they whispering about me? Time seems to stretch before me, like elastic. I think I might faint.

Simon Stanley whispers in my ear, "In this moment, you are not you, Emory, dear. Someone else has written your story for you. They've made you a wistful girl in a field of flowers, sorry that beautiful lilies die. No one is looking or listening to *you,* they're looking and listening to that girl. They don't see you, they see *her.* You aren't here, you're invisible. You're invincible inside the skin of someone else's story."

Priscilla leans forward, her face smooth and glowing, her long hair shining. She's so easily pretty and confident. She's like one of the lilies in the quote. So beautiful, but when she dies, she'll reek terribly, just like the rest of us.

A kind of wave drops over me then. *No one can see me,* the meek mouse, the invisible girl, the girl in the car with Candy, Joey's sister, the girl who hardly speaks and floats through life.

No one knows that *that* girl kisses the most popular boy in school. That *that* girl stood in a window across the way from that boy and arched and lifted her shirt and let him photograph her and felt wild and perfect and strong when he wrote *Perfect.*

My blood is pulsing, remembering that from last night. And what I watched him do, after.

Perfect.

I feel protected, someone else's words in my mouth. I swallow and at that moment Simon Stanley whispers, "What if the girl isn't wistful, but full of darkness and revenge?"

Priscilla in the auditorium seats, lithe and perfect in her own way, the way everyone wants girls to be perfect, and she wants a boy that is already had, by me, and she doesn't even know it.

A weird thrum happens in me then. I step forward, a deeper, clearer voice rising up in me, as the girl in the field watches the pretty girl on the horizon, thinks of her hand on the arm of a handsome boy, feels all the hot jealousy swirling.

"For sweetest things turn sourest by their deeds; lilies that *fester* smell far worse than *weeds.*"

A few kids clap. Mr. Stanley says, "Well done! Very nice emphasis. I *felt* that."

I breathe hard through my nose. I want more lines, I can feel that want in my mouth, for someone to tell me what to say, figure out how I feel and give me the words. It's so much easier than figuring out what to say on my own.

Simon Stanley pats me on the back, his hand warm. "Courage. Acting is courage. A trust in the words, in the story, in the role you're playing. Now, you, your turn." He points to the short red-haired girl. "Your turn."

As I walk back to Jeremy and Liza, I can feel Priscilla's eyes on me, curious and searching.

My mother is chopping scallions in the kitchen when we get home. Joey and I put our backpacks down. He heads to the refrigerator.

"I'm making dinner," she tells him. "You can wait."

He closes the refrigerator door with a sigh and slides onto the stool next to mine, pulling out his phone so he can check his texts. There's a mound of paper on the island, unusual for my mom, who likes to keep things neat. A paper with letterhead that says *NewDay* catches my eye and I pick it up. I scan the page. *An innovative, empathy-centered approach to recovery, healing, and housing.*

"Mom," I say. "What is this? I thought you said condo developers wanted the Mill? Who are these people?"

I keep reading. Recovery center and services. Assistance living. Job training. For the people Joey's boss called deadbeats.

My mother lays her knife down. "Give that to me," she says, lifting the paper away from my hands. "It's nothing."

Joey glances up. "Hoagie Hank is very interested in what you're going to do, Mom. He can't stop bugging me about it."

She folds the letter up and slides it back into an envelope. "He shouldn't be discussing that with you, Joe. In any case, I've had offers. It's not in good shape and the city wants me to do something."

"What do they want you to do?" I ask. "Hank said you should sell it to the condo developers."

"Hank has a big mouth and big dreams," my mother says.

She looks tired today, gray smudges underneath her eyes. Her makeup is usually perfect. "These people, NewDay, are a nonprofit. They want to buy the entire thing, even the old worker houses, and turn them into a recovery center and shelter. It's possible the auxiliary buildings could be other things. All for a dollar. Can you imagine that? Offering me a dollar?"

"Recovery center?" Joey says.

My mother gives him a steady look. "Yes. The whole shebang. Addiction services. Meetings. Needle exchange. Living space to help people get back on their feet, job training, skill assistance. Everything in the city is strained to the gills and we've got space out here. The river, the woods. The Mill is on an enormous amount of land."

I think of the outpatient center that Joey goes to, how it seems more crowded every time we go. If that's the only place in Mill Haven for people to get help and it's already overcrowded, I can't imagine what it's like in the city.

"But that sounds good," Joey says. "That sounds like an awesome thing."

She ponders the scallions on her cutting board. "Maybe. But maybe condos would be a good thing, too. People would move from the city, pay good rents, buy things in town, bring new businesses. And I would get a hell of a lot more money selling to developers than a lousy dollar from a nonprofit."

"But the nonprofit," I say tentatively. "That would help people, like even local people? The bridge people. The ghosties. People at Joey's outpatient center. Right?"

"I wish people would stop using that word. *Ghosties.*" My mother sighs. She picks up her knife and starts dicing a red onion. "It's uncouth."

"You should sell," Joey says. "Sell it for something good."

"Good means different things to different people in this town, Joe, and it's complicated for me. It's my legacy. That's a family building, a family history. That building is older than this house. That building is responsible for this town. Or was. It deserves respect."

She shakes her head. "One dollar, can you imagine?"

"Mom," Joey says. "The Mill put a lot of people to work but it also put a lot of people out of work when it closed. Wouldn't it be better to sell it to people who need it for a good purpose, rather than just build fancy apartments for people who don't actually need help?"

"Joseph." My mother sounds exasperated. "Don't talk to me like our family ruined this town. We built this town. We built the schools, the library, the hospital. We're not responsible for what happened after the Mill closed. That's just . . . history. And economics. Mills close. Jobs go overseas. Plants close. Things change."

"We did kill the river."

I look at Joey, surprised he said that out loud. My mother doesn't like to talk about that, all the textile dyes and chemicals the Mill used getting dumped in the river.

"Excuse me?" she says.

I touch Joey's elbow with my own. My mother is getting the Look. He should ease up a little. Things seemed like they were going well, for once.

"The river. Remember? It used to be called Salmon River way back when, in those good old days. Plenty of healthy salmon, flipping around, swimming upstream, living the sweet life, until they started dying and everyone figured out the Mill was dumping chemicals there. And now we call it Frost River, like the salmon were never there in the first place."

"No one knew, Joe, that the chemicals would do that. Who could know such a thing all those years ago? My god, am I responsible for every bad thing that's ever happened in this town? Is it all on *my* shoulders?"

"Maybe," Joey says, and I can tell he immediately regrets it.

My mother slams the knife on the cutting board, sending up a spray of red onion bits. Joey and I lean back in shock.

I pick some out of my hair.

"That's lovely, Joe. Just lovely," Mom says bitterly.

She gathers the papers together and holds them to her chest. "I'm not quite hungry anymore, thank you. You two can make dinner. Make sure to leave some for your father."

She walks out of the kitchen and we listen to her go up the stairs. In a few minutes, the door to her bedroom closes.

"That was kind of harsh," I say.

"It is what it is." He reaches out and grabs some scallions, popping them into his mouth. "But think about it, Emmy. See the bigger picture. Mom's money paid for me to go to a fancy rehab where I dug holes for my shit. But what about our groundskeeper? Remember him? Jim Tolford? He literally busted his back making our lawn pretty, year after year, and where is he now? Living under a bridge, because those painkillers he had to take to keep his job making our lawn pretty also got him fired, because he got addicted. He had to take those pills because he literally did backbreaking work for us. Why didn't Mom get him help? Was he not a person to her? How am I any different from him?"

He stands up.

"He taught me to ride a bike, Emmy. Not Mom, and not Dad, because they weren't around. And you know who wraps our Christmas presents in all that lovely paper? Goldie, the woman who washes our dirty underwear. Mom pays her extra for Christmas chores. If she suddenly passes out in the laundry room, is she gone, too? Just like that? Like she never mattered? She's worked in this house for fifteen years. That matters."

He rubs his face.

"I'm sorry. I'm tired. I'm really tired. I'm busting my ass, too, to do all the things she requires, and if I fail, I'm out. That's what Mom does. If you fail her, you disappear."

"Joey." I'm sorry I even started the conversation about the Mill with Mom now.

"I'm going upstairs," he says. "I have homework, remember? And I don't want to be disappeared for failing to follow Mom's rules."

I toss and turn in bed, thinking about what Joey said. Disappearing. Like Candy. Like our groundskeeper. I kick at the sheets and comforter.

You up, I text.

It's late

Come to the window

Hold on

Gage appears in his window, rubbing his eyes.

Show me, I text. *And I'll show you.*

He looks at me for a long time.

Takes his shirt off.

You now, he texts.

My heart pounds, but I do it. Slip off my T-shirt. I hold arms across my breasts at first, and then I lower them.

It's a weird feeling in me then, to be open, in the window, separated by just glass and air, my body protected and unprotected at the same time. It feels scary, but also exciting. To see the expression on his face change, soften. To watch him see me.

I pick up my phone.

Start, I text.

You do it too

And that's what we do, in the window, together but separate, until we are panting and spent.

I put my shirt on, lie back in bed, warm and electric, but I feel sad, too.

I have to find some words. I have to be someone other than me, always waiting.

I would like to be someone else. The kind of person who reaches out to take what she wants, where everyone can see, rather than in secret, like the velvet hatbox on the shelf in my closet.

I think I was just that girl in the window, but I need her more than just every once in a while.

> Do you think maybe we could
> do something else sometime?

Like what

I don't know. A movie or something

We aren't in the pool house now, so he can't kiss my words away.

Show me, I want to say. *Show me to the world, don't disappear me.*

It's just our thing, remember. I like this,
not all that other stuff.

. . .

If that's not cool anymore it's okay,
but you have to say so

I stare at the ceiling, my heart dropping. I don't want to be disappeared by Gage. He's my *one* thing.

No, I type, *it's fine. It's fine.*

Good night, Em.

. . .

But you never know

In the dark, I smile.
You never know.

23

I SLIDE ALONG THE CAFETERIA wall to the far back, my usual place by Jeremy Leonard nowadays. Liza always comes, and I'm careful not to talk too much and make her angry, because I have nowhere else to eat lunch. They've closed the library for lunch hours now, to encourage "social interaction."

Jeremy moves his backpack to his other side and slides over a little.

"Thanks," I say.

"No worries," he says, moving his notebook and pens out of the way.

He goes back to drawing. I open my Tupperware and he glances at my food. "Very healthy," he says.

I look down at the carrots, pita bread, and celery. "My mom packs it. I can't believe my mom is still packing my lunch." Once, she said, *If you start gaining weight, you'll never take it off. Every diet ends up adding ten pounds.* Then I think about how Joey told me I've been trained to always go along with whatever Mom tells me.

"Well, what would you eat if you packed your own lunch?" Jeremy asks.

I look at his lunch. "Doritos."

He pushes the crinkly bag to me. I push the Tupperware to him.

He crunches on a carrot. "God, that's loud. Sorry." His face flushes.

I crunch a Dorito chip in solidarity and we laugh.

Liza slides in on the other side of Jeremy. "Hey," she says to him.

She looks at me. "Hey."

I look up, mid–Dorito crunch, surprised.

"Hi," I say tentatively.

She pulls out her peanut butter and jelly sandwich from the wax paper. "What did you decide to read for Watson's class, now that he changed the syllabus?"

I actually look around the table, like she's talking to someone else, before I realize that yes, Liza Hernandez is really talking to *me*.

"*The Portrait of a Lady*," I answer. "You?"

"Nice," she says mildly. "If a little boring. I'm doing *Invisible Man*."

"Hey, I brought you something, Liza." Jeremy reaches into his backpack and pulls out a comic.

"Excellent!" Liza thumbs through it. "I don't have this one. Thanks."

They start talking about comics and characters and artists and I start arranging leftover Doritos into triangle houses, one by one. This is not as easy as it is with baby carrots.

"Very creative," a voice says. "Using foodstuffs as art. Mind if I sit?"

"Daniel W.," Liza says. "Always a pleasure. Of course."

Daniel slides onto the bench across from us, slipping a Dorito from one of my houses and examining it.

"If you aren't going to eat that, give it back," I say. "I'm hungry."

He grins and gives it back to me.

I take the Dorito back and eat it. As I do, Gage passes by

the table with some of his baseball friends. His eyes light on me briefly before slipping away and I look down, concentrating on my lunch.

"Oh, wow. Interesting," Daniel says, watching me and looking over at Gage. "Very interesting."

My cheeks start to burn.

"What?" Jeremy says. "What's interesting?"

"Nothing," Daniel says softly. "And everything."

I look up, meeting his eyes. I've never noticed how blue they are.

I look back at my pile of Doritos. Go back to making triangular orange houses. Anything to forget about the warmth spreading in my veins from looking too long at Daniel Wankel's blue eyes.

Then Daniel says, "So, it's the season of love. The first dance at Heywood Hell. Who's headed to Fall Festival on Friday? My calendar must have been full last year, as I don't remember attending, and perhaps I don't want to miss it again."

"Well," I say. "I think you were a little busy with, uh, other things."

"Cancer, Emory. You can say it out loud, and also, the dance?" Liza says. "Ugh. Typical high school bullshit. No thank you."

"I certainly was busy, Emory," Daniel says. "Not dying, which is quite an adventure, to tell you the truth."

He meets my eyes.

If Daniel had died, he'd be a photograph in the memorial cabinet in the hallway, and not here across from me, stealing Doritos, or in Watson's class, murmuring about West Egg, East Egg, why so many eggs.

He looks away from me then and grins at Liza.

202

"Come on, Liza," Daniel says in a teasing voice. "Don't you just want to see what it's like? How the other half lives? I'm kind of interested in observing, aren't you? As a purely cultural experiment, of course."

"Well," Liza answers. "When you put it that way. Maybe you can jam the toilets like you did on the fifth-grade field trip to the natural history museum. Remember that?"

Daniel laughs. "My first act of civic rebellion. How could I forget?"

I remember that. The anticipation on the early-morning ride on the bus to the city, all of us sleepy but excited to be not in school, to be going somewhere. Sack lunches. The bouncing of the wheels. Liza sharing the blue-gray seat with me. And then Daniel, that's right, skinny Daniel with the always-messy hair leading a bunch of kids into the men's room at the museum to rip toilet paper from the rolls and stuff it into the water until the bowls were full and then flush them, all at the same time.

I didn't do any of the stuffing or flushing, but I was with Liza, so I was part of things, even if it was at a distance. I felt swept up in their laughter and danger.

"How about it, Emory? You feel like dancing?" Daniel nudges me with his elbow.

I can feel Liza watching us carefully.

"I can't," I say. "I have to hang out with my brother. He's in recovery, you know?" It feels a little weird, saying it out loud.

"Bring him," Daniel says.

"You should go," Jeremy says to me. "You don't have to watch out for him. He needs to watch out for himself."

"I know," I say, "but he's pretty lonely right now and it doesn't feel right to—"

Liza interrupts me. "Jeremy's right. You can't put your life on hold for somebody else, you know? Sometimes you just have to do what you have to do to make yourself happy. And if you're not, like, solid with *yourself*, how can you help somebody else?"

When I look at her, she busies herself folding her wax paper into a small, smooth square.

"I'll even drive. I'll pick everybody up. How's that?" Daniel says.

"I'm in," Liza says.

"Me too," Jeremy says.

They all look at me.

"I'll think about it," I say.

Liza changes the subject. "So, Daniel. What are you reading for Watson's class now? Something suitably white-boy intellectual? *Infinite Jest*? *Cloud Atlas*?"

"Actually," Daniel says, "I was thinking of doing *Charlotte's Web*."

Liza and I burst out laughing at the same time, which feels . . . surprising and nice.

"I can't help it." Daniel shrugs. "I just really like that tender little pig."

Simon Stanley is walking around the stage, writing down what everyone will do for the variety show.

Jeremy says, "You should go to the dance. Joe has to take care of himself. You shouldn't feel like you can't have a life, you know?"

"But I do have to take care of him," I say. "He's my brother. You get that, right? I feel protective. I don't want him to relapse."

Jeremy looks at his shoes. "You wouldn't be using him as a shield, would you? I mean, so you don't *have* to do things?"

Simon Stanley appears before us. "Jeremy, you're off the hook since you're a third-year and have done it before, unless you're dying to again. Otherwise, we can use you on sets."

"Sets," Jeremy says.

"Emory?"

"I really don't want to," I say hesitantly. "I'm just not comfortable doing that sort of thing." I've already put myself in front of people during two years of dance team. That was enough public exposure for a lifetime. And what I did with Gage in the window, that was still private, just the two of us. This . . . would be just me, alone, on a wide stage, staring back at many, many people. Just the thought makes my stomach tighten.

Simon tucks his yellow legal pad under his arm. "You've been doing a lovely job during our exercises, Emory. You could choose something short, like one of Ophelia's monologues from *Hamlet*. You might surprise yourself."

"I don't know."

"Here." He passes me a packet of monologues. "Take a look, let me know your thoughts. I really do think you'd be wonderful. And . . ."

He looks around the stage. He waves Liza over.

She ambles over to us, hands in the pockets of her overalls.

"Liza," he says. "You are now Emory's partner in crime. Emory is feeling nervous and shy about performing in the fall variety show and you've been doing this for two years. I want you to be her person."

"Excuse me?" Liza asks.

"No, really, that's okay," I say quickly. "I can do it myself."

"Her person," Simon Stanley repeats. "She needs to choose

a monologue. You can help her. And she'll need some coaching and practice. You're very good at this. You helped Thad so much last year."

Liza and I look at each other.

"If I must," she says.

"Well, don't put yourself out or anything," I say tersely.

"Perfect!" Simon Stanley claps his hands, ignoring our snark.

Liza pulls her phone from the back pocket of her overalls. "Give me your number. We might need to get together outside of school."

"It's the same," I tell her. "It never changed."

"Ah," she answers. "Like so many things."

I wait for Joey in the hallway outside the library until he's done with his tutoring session. When he and Amber come out, they're all smiles. She gives him a little wave goodbye before heading down the hallway.

"Did you tell her you're in recovery yet?" I ask.

"No. You don't have to be so pushy. She's really nice."

"Sorry," I mumble. "I'm just looking out for you."

"Well, you don't have to look out so *hard*." He sighs. "Dad texted. He wants us to stop and see Nana on the way home. She's back from Aunt Dory's and I don't have work or outpatient today."

"That actually means he wants us to rake Nana's leaves, you know."

"I know." He smiles. "I miss her."

"Me too, but she's going to yell at you," I warn him.

"I know," he sighs.

* * *

Our nana is sitting in her small yard on a lawn chair, a blanket on her lap and a cup of coffee in her hands.

She starts to put the coffee down on the leaves and stand when she sees us coming up her walk, but Joey waves her down. "Don't get up," he says. "Here I am."

He leans over and gives her a big hug.

"Joseph," she says, beaming. "I've missed my handsome boy."

Then she slaps his head.

"Ow," he says, rubbing his ear. "Nana!"

"That's for being a stupid boy. I trust you're done with all this . . . whatever it is. It's done, yes?"

"Nana," I say. "It's kind of a long process."

"You be quiet. Am I talking to you? No, not yet. I might have words for *you* later, but right now all my words are for Joseph."

Our nana is not mean. She's just blunt. Joey kicks some leaves.

"I'm working on it."

"The young should not die before the old," she says. "How dare you waste a life you haven't even lived yet."

She sips her coffee.

"So, stop being stupid, Joseph."

"Wow, Nana, you really know how to greet a guy."

She gives a hard nod. "I love you. Now go get the rake in the shed and do something about this yard while I talk to your sister."

She looks me up and down. "Sit."

I look at the ground, thick with leaves, and think of my

knee. "Maybe not right now. My leg. Remember? It's hard to bend that way right now."

"Of course I remember. I'm not addled. Do you think I'm addled? I think your father thinks I'm addled."

"He does not."

"Well, your mother does, then. Always trying to get me to move into that room. I live *here*, in my house, the one I have lived in since I was born, and I'll die here, surrounded by my trees and my leaves and that awful man who lives next door with the sickly cat."

Joey starts raking leaves into crisp piles.

"You look different," Nana says. "Something in your face. What's changed?"

"Nothing. Just school and stuff. You know." I kick some leaves out of the way. I don't know how to tell her that everything has changed. Gage. Candy. Joey.

She studies me. "It's a boy. Or a girl. Don't look so shocked. I watch TV. I know how the world is now. It's all okay with me, whatever you want. Live your life, don't waste it, like I told Joseph. Oh, look, your face is red. I'm right. I'm always right."

"Nana," I say, embarrassed. *"Stop."*

"Nana," Joey calls. "You are exhausting, you know that, right?"

"Well, I have to say everything now. Who knows how much time I have left?"

"Nana," I say. "Don't say that! That's sad!"

"Pfft," she says, setting her coffee cup on the ground. "Death happens. We need to accept that and look around and appreciate what we have and change what we don't like. Am I right?"

"You should really come live with us, Nana. The room is

really pretty and we'd love to have you," I say. "And you could harass Joey whenever you wanted." It *would* be nice, having her there. Mom and Dad are gone so much, it would be comforting to have Nana there to talk to.

"Hey," Joey says. "Not fair."

"Work harder," she tells him. "Look, the leaves are falling just as fast as you are raking. More raking, less talk. And make one bigger pile, not so many tiny ones."

"Why?" He stops raking.

"How dare you question an old woman."

She turns back to me. "So who is this boy or girl?"

"Nana." The last thing I need is to try to describe what's happening with Gage to Nana. I'm not sure how one would phrase that to a grandmother.

She shrugs. "You don't want to tell me, don't tell me, but I'll tell you one thing: they should hold your hand when you go out together, no matter what. And they should never walk in front of you. They should walk next to you, because you walk through life together, do you understand?"

"Nana." Her words hit me suddenly and I tear up, because I do want to walk next to Gage, in front of everyone. I don't want to stand in front of a window forever, or hide in a pool house.

"Don't cry. That's silly. Don't be a silly girl like that. It's good advice. Joseph!"

"What?" He walks over to us, wipes a gleam of sweat from his forehead. It's cool outside, but he raked a giant pile of leaves in his hoodie and now he's panting.

"Go." Nana points to the pile.

"Um, what?" Joey says.

"Run through them. Dive into them. That was your favorite

thing as a little boy, do you remember? Your father would bring you over, he'd rake leaves, and you'd run pell-mell through them. I loved the sound of your laughter. Do it now. Remember what that felt like, when you had no worries. For me."

Joey hesitates and then takes off running, a gray-hooded blur. He flares out and then lands, hard, in the mound of leaves.

And just lies there.

"Joey?" I say hesitantly, wondering if he's hurt.

There's no sound from the pile of leaves.

"Oops," Nana says. "Perhaps I've hurt him."

I run over to the pile, pushing leaves out of the way. "Joey, are you okay?"

But my brother isn't hurt. He's crying, his face encrusted with dried leaves.

"She was right," he says. "It was glorious. And I'm going to do it again."

After dinner I sit in my closet, the tips of my clothes tickling my nose, as I text Maddie.

I've been thinking about the dance, about Gage. And Nana saying someone should take your hand and walk next to you. The whole Liza telling me to grow a spine thing.

Hey

Hi! What's up? How's Joe?

He's good

How's dear old Heywood High?

It's ok

You ok

210

I take a deep breath.

I might have a sex problem.

Immediately, she video calls. I debate not picking up, but finally, I do. I turn on the tiny lamp I have in the closet. I spot my old blue bear and cradle it in my arms, like it can protect me. I haven't been in my closet in a long time. I missed it.

Fuzzy walks in and nestles at my feet.

Maddie says, "What. Is. Going. On. Are you in your closet?"

"Yes."

In the background, I can see the walls of her dorm room: band posters, pictures of yoga poses. Filmy scarves hung up everywhere. Bunk beds.

"Are you actually *having* sex? Is that the problem?"

"I'm not sure. I mean, I don't think it's sex. Maybe. This is kind of embarrassing." My face flushes.

"This is very confusing, sister."

"We do things, but, like, there hasn't been . . . penetration." I whisper that word.

"If you can't say that word in a normal voice, you shouldn't be doing whatever it is you're doing, that's rule number one."

I hold my breath. I really have no idea how to phrase, out loud, to my sister, that I've been making out in a pool house with the town baseball star and that sometimes we masturbate together in front of our windows.

There really isn't a good way to say that.

"Emmy."

"What."

"*You* texted me. You have to talk, or I can't help you."

"We don't take off our underwear. We make out, mostly. *Things* happen."

"They call that dry-humping. You're welcome. But you can still get pregnant that way, because sperm can travel through underwear. Unless we're talking about a girl. Wait, let me correct myself. Does this person have a penis?"

"Yes."

"Who is it?"

I hesitate. "No one you know."

"How long have you been dating?"

"We aren't technically dating."

Her face changes. She gives me a stern look.

"So, you're just hooking up?"

"I . . . guess. Yes. Yes, I think so."

"Well, that's sex, Emmy. Sex is sexual activity. Virginity is different. Virginity is an idea, a construct. A level of purity created to make girls not get too lusty, frankly. To make them prizes. Congratulations, you're a sexual person. When I come home for Thanksgiving, I'm taking you to the clinic in Dover for the pill. Do you know about Plan B? Do you have cond—"

"I'm kind of sorry I asked now," I interrupt. "This is kind of overwhelming." My head is spinning. This is a lot to take in all at once.

"How long have you been hooking up with Mr. No-Name?"

Tears spring to my eyes. "Last spring."

Maddie says, "Oh, dear."

She pauses. "I'm just trying to get to the heart of this, so bear with me. This is all consensual, right? Like, you like this, he's not pressuring you? Emotionally?"

"I don't think so. I like what we do."

"Then what's the problem?"

I start to cry.

"Oh, honey, what is it?"

"I don't . . . I think . . . I might like him more than he likes me. Maybe. I'm not sure. But we agreed to keep it a secret, but I'm thinking . . . I mean, it would be nice, right, to go somewhere together, where people could see us."

"That's called a date."

I wipe my face with the hem of a dress. I'm pretty sure my sister has never had to deal with anyone who wanted to keep her a secret.

"Usually, people have a few dates and then get busy, not the other way around, but you can do it that way, too. I'm uncomfortable with the secretive aspect, to be honest. Are you sure he doesn't have a girlfriend or something? That he's not just practicing on you? You don't want to be a practice girl."

"He doesn't. I don't think he does. He just says this is easier, and less of a distraction."

"Uh-huh." She turns away for a minute and whispers to someone, then comes back. "Sorry, that's my roommate. She's making a vending machine run."

She sighs. "This . . . is not an optimal situation. I mean, the longer you do this, the more you miss out on, while you're with Mr. No-Name, who doesn't want to have an actual relationship with you. Do you know what I mean?"

"Not really. I've never *done* this before. Ever."

"Well, what if someone else asked you out? Would you say no because you and Mr. No-Name are getting it on god knows where? That person might be really nice and treat you really well and take you places and the whole glitzy flowers and roses and kisses and dances thing or whatever you want . . . and you'd miss out. And you shouldn't miss out. Does that make sense?"

"So what should I do?"

"Well, unless you want to spend high school getting dry-humped by a person who doesn't want to pick you up and take you to a movie, I'd ask them: Do you want to go out? And if they say no, get out of it."

"How do you even ask that? And if he says no, I mean, then I probably won't even have him anymore."

"You deserve better than to be a secret, Emmy. You don't have to take scraps. You can have the whole damn thing if you want it."

Maddie's voice softens. "In ten years, how do you think you'll feel about this? Honestly? Good? Bad? Lonely?"

"I don't know." That seems very far off, ten years. Unfathomable. I would be out of college. Doing something my mother deemed respectable. My stomach ties in a little knot as I remember I have to register for the PSAT and study and study and study and help Joey and all of it. Everything suddenly seems too large to carry and my head clouds.

"Emory, you've been in a little shell your whole life. Your whole life has been *Mom* and Joey, basically. You should find out what it feels like to have someone like you. Love you, even if it hurts, in the end. Sad as that sounds."

I remember Maddie crying over Thornton Cooper. They dated for two years. She broke up with him when she went to college and he went into the army. Thornton was nice. He had long, lovely fingers and played checkers with me while Maddie was getting ready. It always took Maddie a long time to get ready and when she finally appeared, Thornton's whole face would change, become brighter somehow. The thing that I want. To be seen. Make somebody's face light up, get bright. Like I matter. Instead of just, Oh. There's Emmy.

Maddie turns and whispers again and then her face comes back. "I have to go. My roommate needs to study. But when I get there on break, off to Dover we go and don't do anything more than what you're doing, do you promise me?"

"Okay."

"Are you crying?" Her voice is gentle.

"No," I lie.

"Oh, honey," she says.

"I'm fine," I say. "It's fine."

She sighs. "Okay, I have to go for real. But listen, don't send him naked pictures. That shit lasts forever."

"Wait, what?" I say, but her face is already gone.

I stare at my phone, my heart sinking. Before I can stop myself, I'm messaging Gage.

Hey

. . .

Hey what's up

I'm just wondering something

What

Those pictures. Can you maybe delete them?

I love those pictures

It would make me feel better if you deleted them

Ok, I can do that. Are you mad?

No, I just want you to get rid of them

K

. . .

Gage

Yeah

Are you going to Fall Festival?

I might make an appearance, sure

215

I type and retype words until I finally settle on something.
Not too forceful, nothing to scare him away.

> Maybe we could go together, no
> pressure, not like a big deal
>
> . . .

That would be a thing, Em

> It doesn't have to be. Just friends.

I don't know

> . . .

Maybe we could hang out a little while we're there, he types.
I hold my breath. This is like a baby step, but it's a step.
K, I type back.

24

M Y MOTHER AND JOEY are in the kitchen the next morning when I walk in. I steel myself for what I'm about to say. The baby step *I'm* about to take. My mother hasn't been in a great mood lately, and the conversation about the Mill the other night only made her touchier.

"I'm going to go to the Fall Festival," I announce. "It's Friday."

My mother puts her phone down on the island and stares at me. "Excuse me? With whom?"

"Some friends. They asked me. Kids from school." I keep my voice neutral but firm. Like it's no big deal.

"*What* kids?"

"Liza and a boy named Daniel," I say. I leave out Jeremy, because the Luther aspect might freak her out.

Joey raises his eyebrows. "You and Liza patch it up? That was quick." He drinks orange juice from the carton until my mother takes it from him with an annoyed look.

"She's my partner in Drama Club. And we eat lunch together. We've kind of been forced together, but it's not so bad."

My mother looks at me steadily, sipping her coffee.

I wait to see if her face is going to morph into the Look. If it heads in that direction, I'm in trouble. I hide my hands under the lip of the kitchen island so she can't see them shaking.

She's stays quiet.

"I've never been to a dance, Mom. This shouldn't be . . . hard."

"Jesus, Mom, just let her go. She never goes *anywhere*." Joey shakes his head.

"All right then, Emmy." She sets her coffee cup on the counter. "You can go with Joe. He doesn't have to work that night and it will do him good to get out, too."

Beside me, Joey does a double take. "Uh, did anyone ask me if I wanted to go to some stupid school dance? Which I don't. And if we all recall, the last time I went to a party with my sister, it didn't turn out very well."

"Joey," I say. "It won't be like that. It doesn't have to be."

"Joe." My mother's voice is hard and sad at the same time.

I look at Joey and mouth, *Please.*

He takes a long breath. "Okay. *Okay.*"

"Thank you," I say. "*Thank* you."

I look over at Daniel in Watson's class. Everyone is reading quietly. Mr. Watson is busy at his desk.

"I'm going to the dance," I whisper. "My brother's coming with me, so I don't need a ride."

"Nice," Daniel whispers back. "Very cool. Mr. Baseball can't pick you up?"

"Stop it," I say. "It's not like that. You don't know anything."

Daniel shrugs. "I probably don't. But you know what I do know?"

"What?"

He holds up his copy of *Charlotte's Web.* "I think the case can be made that this pig has some sort of anxiety disorder due to early piglet abandonment. I might have to add that to my paper."

I can't help myself. I laugh.

* * *

On Friday night, my mother hands Joey the car keys. "Rules," she says. "Back by midnight. No drinking, no drugs."

"I'll be with him, Mom," I say. "Don't worry."

"Rules," he answers. "Tattooed on my brain." He taps his head.

My mother's eyes look watery.

"I'm so pleased," she says. "Look at the both of you. So lovely."

"We need to go," Joey says, nudging my shoulder. "Before the waterworks start."

The gymnasium is an explosion of pumpkins and gourds and orange-and-yellow streamers. White and royal blue lights, the Heywood High colors, hanging from the rafters, dangling among the sports championship banners. Some kids are really decked out in dresses and heels, hair pinned prettily up. Most kids are casually dressed. I'm wearing a gray cotton dress over leggings, with a long pink sweater, glittery gray butterfly barrettes I stole from the thrift store on Rose Street in my hair. My stomach feels flippy and excited. I'm looking around for Gage, but I don't see him yet.

"Well," I say to Joey. "What now? I've never been to one of these."

"Stay away from the punch. Probably not spiked, but you never know. Just drink water. Find your people, I guess. I've only been to one, freshman year, and I was stoned, so I don't remember much." He winces. "Maybe this wasn't a good idea."

"I'm not sure about that," I say, pointing but trying not to be too obvious. "Over there."

Joey's tutor, Amber, is leaning against a wall, checking her phone. Her hair is up, pretty tendrils hanging down the sides of her face. She's wearing jeans and a tank with a shrug. She looks around the gym. I can tell Amber is nervous, like me. She's tapping one foot and keeps blowing tendrils of hair away from her cheeks.

Joey seems frozen, just staring at her.

"Go," I say. "Talk to her. It's not like you don't even know her."

"Right. But usually we talk about homework. It was built in. I can't really go over there and talk about *math* at a *dance.* Like before, with a girl, I'd be high, and so would she, and so . . . you know, you just talked shit. I don't want to mess this up."

He pulls his hood over his head. His protective mechanism. I reach up and pull it down. If I'm about to do what I think I'm about to do, he can damn well go over there and talk to a girl he already knows is into him.

"Stop hiding," I say. "Just go."

He nods and takes a deep breath. "Text me," he says. "If we get separated, let's meet back in this spot at nine, just to check in."

"Okay."

He squeezes my hand gently before he starts walking toward Amber.

Then I'm alone. The music is loud, vibrating through the soles of my shoes. I pull my sweater a little tighter. I feel exposed all of a sudden.

Maybe my dress is too snug. Maybe this was a bad idea. I don't see Gage at all. What was I thinking? It's not like I can

220

dance-dance, anyway, not with my knee. Maybe I can't do this after all. I start to feel panicky. Look at all these kids. They all seem like they know what to do, how to act, and here's me, wrapping my sweater tighter around myself and hoping I disappear.

"Hey, you came." Daniel Wankel appears next me in his ubiquitous sport coat and wool scarf. He grins. "Cool. Now I don't have to stand by myself. We can stand alone together."

"I thought Liza and Jeremy were coming with you?" A wave of relief floods through me, just looking at him.

"They did. Over there," he says, pointing to the snack table. "We took the bus. My car's dead."

Liza and Jeremy are delicately picking up tortilla chips one by one, not bothering with plates. Liza did not dress up; she's still in her overalls.

"Your dress is cool," Daniel says.

"I feel stupid," I say. "Do you ever feel that way, like you don't fit? Or everybody else seems to know exactly what to do all the time?"

Daniel gives me a curious look. "Nobody knows what to do at any time. That's the great lie of high school, that everyone but you knows how to live."

"That's very profound," I say, teasing him. He's easy to talk to. Not like with Gage, where I'm always preplanning what I should say to him and then stuttering over the few words I *do* use with him.

He shrugs. "It's what my dad says. I'll be sure and tell him you found his wisdom profound. It's just one of the many life lessons he teaches me while I mow the lawn and he drinks beer."

Jeremy and Liza come over to us. In the corner, Amber and Joey are laughing. She pushes some hair away from her face.

It makes me feel happy, just then, to see Joey smiling. Maybe tonight will turn out all right for everyone.

"You made it," Liza says. "And wow, you went all out. Look at you."

Is she smirking? It's hard to tell with Liza sometimes.

I wrap my arms tighter around myself.

Jeremy says, "You look nice."

It looks like he's brushed his hair and put on a clean T-shirt. He looks softer in this light, less lonely.

"You too," I say.

Daniel says, "It's not a dance if there's not dancing. Does anyone want to dance?" He looks at Liza. "You, Ms. Liza?"

"Well . . ." Liza draws out the word. "I think I promised the first dance to Jeremy."

And then, for a split second, Jeremy looks at me, which Liza notices. Hurt flashes across her face. But it's gone before Jeremy sees it, and Liza grabs his arm. "Let's go embarrass ourselves. Second one's yours, Daniel."

She and Jeremy walk out onto the floor, melt into the sea of bodies.

"That was weird," Daniel says. "You and Jeremy have a thing, or something? I could have sworn you were smitten with Mr. Baseball."

I shake my head quickly. "No, Liza likes Jeremy. I don't know much about relationships, but I know I'm not going to get in her way."

"Good plan," he says. "Oh. Look. Speak of the devil."

I follow his eyes across the gymnasium.

Gage Galt is standing in a crowd of his baseball buddies. They're all neatly dressed: expensive polos, good jeans, the right sneakers. His hair is clean and perfect. *He* looks clean and perfect.

"Mr. Baseball," Daniel says lightly.

My hands are shaking.

Be someone else, I tell myself. Be anyone else, any other girl who would walk up and ask someone to dance.

It's like Gage and I skipped to step fourteen, so I never learned steps one through thirteen, the beginnings of a relationship. What Maddie was talking about.

"Listen, from what little I've gleaned from you so far," Daniel says, "you have a thing for Mr. Baseball, but as your friend, I have to tell you, that situation is beginning to look complicated, so you need to tell me your plan. I can advise you."

Some girls have joined the group, floating around the crowd of boys like colorful, confident flowers.

"I was going to ask him to dance." Just saying that out loud makes my face flush.

"Hmm. Let me think about the best way to accomplish that. It's a little crowded over there at the moment, so you may want to hold back until there are less people, in case you get shot do—"

But his words don't touch me, because whoever the girl I need to be is, she's coming out, right now, just like Simon Stanley said. I fall back into myself, make the old me recede, and even though my heart is beating so loud I can barely hear myself think, I'm walking, this new girl in my old shoes, ignoring the painful twinges in her knee, carrying me across the gym to Gage and his group.

"Abort the mission," Daniel whispers behind me. "Abort the mission!"

But I can't. I'm halfway there and I can't stop now.

I stand at the edge of Gage's group, looking in.

No one notices me, but they notice this new, effortless girl, because she says, in this same voice she used in Drama Club to tell a girl on the horizon that she would fester, "Hey, Gage. You want to dance?"

The group parts, everyone looking at me. It gets quiet.

One girl covers a smile with her hand and ducks her head.

Gage turns around, looks at me. Blinks. Once, twice.

He hesitates for a second, but then he grins and holds up his hands. Says, "You know, I'm not much of a dancer. I might need to sit this one out. Thanks for the offer, though."

His eyes tell a different story. *What did I tell you.*

The braver girl who's overtaken me says, "Oh, come on. It's a dance."

Gage's mouth opens. "Yeah, I'm just not—"

"Oh, *you!*"

Priscilla appears, dressed in a swingy teal dress, her hair blown out, eyes smoky and beautiful. "Oh, you!" she cries again. "Come on. Don't be shy."

Touches his arm, pulls him away from the group, even as he pretends to protest.

The braver girl watches them go.

Then she disappears, replaced by me.

A tall brunette says, "I'm sorry, honey." Like a mom. A coo.

I turn around quickly, my body on fire with shame.

Behind me, one of the guys says, "Isn't that Maddie Ward's sister? Man, Maddie was *hot*. That apple fell far, far from the tree."

Maddie is hot. Maddie is beautiful. Maddie makes people's eyes light up when she walks into a room.

One of the girls says, "Oh my god, she's crying."

I let him do things to me. We did things together. I'm like a giant flame, hot and ashamed.

I have to get out of here. Desperately, I look around for Joey. He's still there, with Amber, but Lucy Kerr is with them, and Joey's face looks weird. Amber is hanging back from them, her face confused. Lucy is right up in Joey's face, jabbing his chest with a finger.

He walks away from Lucy quickly, two hands banging open the exit door by the snack and punch table. I hear Daniel call my name. I follow Joey, my heart racing.

I just want to get out of here now, like Candy at the party.

So, so stupid, why was I so stupid. Invisible was better. Invisible is *always* better.

That way, things hurt less.

Outside, it's cool and dark, grass stiff from the chill. Heavy clouds hang in the sky. I call Joey's name. I don't see him anywhere. Where could he go so fast?

I text him. *Where are you?* Nothing. Laughter and music vibrate from the building. I have to hide. Why couldn't he just dance with me? Why am I good enough for one thing and not the other? Practice girl. That's what Maddie said. I feel sick.

I keep walking, fast, until I almost run into the chain-link fence that surrounds the practice field.

It's dark, no lights. The stars are hidden behind the clouds. *A star is mighty good company.*

The bleacher bench is cold and hard, but I don't care. Tears splash down my face and I wipe them away as fast as they come. I want to vomit. I want to scream. I want to keep crying. I want to rip all of my skin off because all the places that Gage ever touched me, ever turned me electric, are burning now.

I cover my face with my hands, choking on my own sobs.

"Hey."

I keep my hands on my face. Just what I need. A witness to my stupid weeping.

"That was brutal," Daniel says. "I'm sorry."

"Can you just go away?" I say. "I really don't need anyone watching my breakdown, if you know what I mean."

"I can't," he says. "It's in the high school handbook. You never let someone cry alone on the bleachers."

"That page must have been missing from my handbook," I say, sniffling.

God, I'm so stupid.

Daniel pulls a handkerchief from his pocket and hands it to me.

"What are you, like, ninety? Who has handkerchiefs?"

"I do. It's environmentally friendly. Don't worry, there's no nose debris. It's fresh."

I unfold it and cover my whole face. I just sit there, everything blacked out, and then Daniel starts talking.

"These *are* the best years of our lives," he says finally. "It's just going to get way worse from here, so this is nothing. Maybe tomorrow the zombies will come. Eat our faces. Or an apocalyptic rain will wash us all into green pulp. Or maybe we're in an alternate universe, and in two seconds, when you look at me and our eyes meet, we'll both be transported instantly and come awake in a different world, one where I'm a hard-hearted detective in a trench coat and you're a brilliant but maligned scientist, and somehow, all this pain, as they say, will be useful to us."

There's a pause.

"It could happen," he says. "Sometimes I wish it would happen."

I pull the handkerchief down, wipe under my eyes, and sigh, looking at him. He's staring at the sky, like he's seeing something I can't behind all the clouds.

"Car accidents, cancer, addiction, broken hearts? That will be useful to us?" I say.

"Maybe."

I don't know why I say it, but I do. "Why don't you just let people see your scar?"

He gently takes the handkerchief from me and folds it up, sliding it into the pocket of his coat.

"Because they wouldn't believe me. Because they'd think it was from something else. Like trying to hang myself, or cut my throat, because this place is just one big rumor factory, and really, no one wants to hear it was just run-of-the-mill cancer, a thousand cells working silently for a long time, in ways I don't understand, while I was doing dumb stuff, like playing *Minecraft*. I don't understand it. And it scares me. And every time I have to look at the scar, I'm afraid those cells might be working again, while I'm reading *The Scarlet Letter* for the umpteenth time or buying Max deVos chocolate from the wobbly vending machine. Or even now, talking to a crying girl at a crappy high school dance. I prefer to pretend it doesn't exist. Because *I* have to keep existing. And I can't keep existing if I'm constantly thinking that I'm dying inside and I don't even know it."

I sniffle. "Is that more profound wisdom from your dad?"

"Funny. You're very funny. No, that's all me."

He peers at me. "Your eyeliner is a little smeared. You look like a very sad lounge singer. It's a good look for you."

I sigh. "I have a scar. On my knee. From the wreck. It itches."

"Mine, too."

"I think about it all the time. The accident," I say. "Candy. I dream about her."

He nods. "I liked her. She was kind. I remember that. Not many people are, really, when it comes right down to it."

We are quiet. Then he says, "You could do better than Gage Galt. Or I should say, differently. I mean, he's *benign*. Does he even talk about anything but baseball?"

"We never talk. He prefers to do other things." It's out of my mouth before I realize what I'm saying.

Daniel says, "Wait, what do you mean, 'other things'?"

Just then, a group of kids, Gage among them, tumble onto the practice field, Gage complaining, *Nah, I'm tired. Not right now.*

Yeah, man, just a few. Let's have some fun.

Roly Martin, Gage's catcher, squats at one end of the field. He holds his bare hands like a mitt. Weaves a little on his haunches. He seems drunk. *Here, buddy, right here.* He thumps the inside of his palm.

"Emory, are you hooking up with Gage Galt?" Daniel says.

"Please." I touch his arm. "Don't tell anyone. It just . . . kind of happened."

It feels like a huge weight has lifted off me, saying it out loud.

"Emmy?" Joey is suddenly here, standing in front of the bleachers, staring at us.

My brother's voice is . . . thick. And his face looks droopy, somehow. Like the muscles are too relaxed.

Fear floods through me. I know that face.

He's high.

My stomach sinks.

"Oh," Daniel says. "Hey, Joe."

228

"Joey," I say. "Oh, no. No."

A couple of girls walking onto the field slip, catch each other's elbows. *Whoops.* Someone tosses Gage a ball.

I can't see for shit, he says. The practice field is unlit, the stars above us blunted by the clouds.

Come on! everyone shouts.

Gage's foot paws at the mound. *I don't know.*

Galt, Galt, Galt.

Joey's eyes are red and soft as he squints at me. "Did I hear that right? Is that why you're out here crying? Why's your makeup all messed up? Did Gage Galt mess with you?"

"Joey, let's just go home. Now. Let's leave. Give me the keys."

I stand up, teetering a little on the bleachers.

"What did he do to you?"

Joey's voice is uneven. He looks over at Gage, on the pitching mound.

Galt, Galt, Galt. Gage tosses the ball lightly in his hand.

"Let's just take a step back," Daniel says, getting up. "No biggie. She was rebuffed on the dance floor by Stud Muffin out there, but I think we're handling it. High school, am I right? You know what Tim Burton once said? 'The only things that scare me are high school and my relatives,' and—"

My brother turns and takes off onto the field.

"Oh, god," Daniel says. "Uh, I'm not really the fighting type and these guys . . . oh, hell."

He takes off, too, and I run after him, flashes of pain shooting up my knee.

Joey is high and I have to stop him.

Gage is in his windup when Joey shouts something like *Hurt my little sister.* Gage, startled, whips his head toward Joey.

"Joey, no, man. No, I'm sorry—" Gage cries, but his foot slips, his arm still poised midair behind him.

Gage falls backward on his arm. There's a sickening snap.

Everything stops.

Someone screams. It isn't me.

It's Gage.

TWO

25

"**H**E'LL BE OKAY." DANIEL is nervous, tugging at the seat belt across his chest. "I'm sure it's not bad. Oh, turn here."

I turn right. I'm driving, being extra careful because of my knee and since I haven't driven a car since the accident. Joey is in the backseat, his face a mixture of dread and sickness. He's rocking back and forth.

I can't believe it's happening again: my brother in the backseat of a car, fucked up. And that again, I had a role in disaster. If I hadn't had beers at the party, I could have driven us home. If I hadn't asked Gage to dance, Joey wouldn't have tried to attack him.

And I can't stop the tiny voice in my brain, either, whispering: But nobody makes your brother get high, do they? He keeps doing that all by himself.

"Are you okay?" Daniel asks.

"No!" I yell. "No, I'm not. Nothing is okay. Nothing is *ever* going to be okay. I just keep messing everything up!"

Daniel touches my arm. I shrug him off. I need to concentrate on the road, catch my breath, think. *Think.* Because my parents, my *mother,* are going to be ballistic.

We all heard the snap. Heard Gage scream, watched him writhe on the ground. There's no way this isn't bad.

Roly Martin ran to him first, pushing Joey away. Priscilla and the other girls ran to get help. One boy called 911. "Should

I?" he kept asking, holding his phone up. "I'm not sure? Yes? No? Somebody help me!"

Daniel yelled, "Call!"

We stood on the field, watching as the crowd grew bigger: the teacher-chaperones, including Simon Stanley, running from the gym, panic in their eyes, kids taking pictures, filming, because it never really happens if you don't post it somewhere, right?

The more kids who came, the farther back we receded, until we were on the very edge of the crowd. Joey's shoulders were hunched, his eyes sloppy.

"Oh, god, what did I do?" he mumbled.

"Nothing," Daniel said. His voice was firm. "He slipped, is all, when you yelled. He might've slipped without you yelling. The grass is very sketchy right now. It's dark. He couldn't see to get his footing properly." He tried to mimic Gage in his windup and release and just looked awkward and uncomfortable.

"Joey," I whispered. "Why did you get high?"

How many days did he have that are gone now? I can't understand why he would do this. I don't care about Gage, I just care about Joey right now. And this is bad.

"You're mad at me. I know you should be mad at me. It's okay."

Okayokayokayokay, just like he used to say.

"I'm not mad at you." I grabbed his arm, but he shook me off. "Just tell me what happened."

"Lucy Kerr happened. I was having a cool time with Amber. Thought we might dance and then Lucy came up and was all, 'Just thought you should know your new friend is a loser and a druggie and oh, let me tell you about my friend Candy. You don't want to get in a car with this guy.'"

"Oh, god," I said. "Joey, no."

Daniel winced.

Joey said, "So I left. Found Noah out by the trailers in back, you know, where they do overflow history and stuff. It just . . . I just needed my feelings to *stop*. I feel sick. I gotta get out of here . . ."

He started stumbling toward the parking lot and the car. I caught up to him, Daniel behind me, and I stuck my hand in Joey's back jean pocket, dug the keys out.

Joey didn't even bother protesting.

Daniel lives in a small brick house not far from Polish Town, where our nana's house is. The housing stock is good here, my father said, because the houses were built by immigrants and they were frugal with money and needed the home to last forever, so they built carefully and solidly, no fancy flourishes. My dad grew up in Polish Town, with four brothers and a sister, Dory. She's the only one who lives near us. Everyone else moved far away.

I stop the car too quickly and we all lurch forward. I can hardly breathe. I have to get Joey home, hide him from our parents somehow until his high wears off.

Before they find out what happened to Gage.

"Well," I say to Daniel, trying to keep my voice from shaking. "That alternate universe is looking better by the minute. How soon can we get there and what should we bring?"

"I have an excellent supply of stylish trench coats, so I'm fully prepared. Listen, it's going to suck, and then it won't, okay? Then it will just be *after,* and you can deal with that."

"I can't."

"You *can*."

He gets out of the car.

I lean my forehead against the steering wheel.

"I'm sorry," Joey mumbles from the backseat.

There's a rap on the passenger-side window and I look up.

Daniel is back. I press the button. The window rolls down.

"Emory," he says.

"What?" I'm impatient to go. I need to figure this out.

"Gage Galt is a blip in the cosmos. There are tons of guys who would die to dance with you." He looks like he's about to say more, but my phone flashes and I have to look away from him.

"Oh, god. It's my mom," I say, my heart sinking. "I have to answer her."

He gives me a rueful smile and turns back up the walk.

Where are you?

On way home, I type.

Come home quickly.

She knows. Our mother knows.

"Mom knows," I say. "She says get home quick."

"I'm so sorry, Emmy. I'm so sorry," Joey says.

My mother knows. Joey keeps saying he's sorry. Gage is hurt. I humiliated myself in front of a group of kids I'd otherwise care nothing about and for what? To end up in a car, taking care of my brother. *Again.*

And suddenly, I'm screaming at him.

"Fuck Lucy Kerr, Joe. Liza told me to grow a spine, but maybe *you* should. Why didn't you just tell her to go to hell? Why was your answer to her . . . her . . . shittiness to go get high? You spent three months in rehab and you learned *nothing*?"

I stop, because he's crying. The silent kind. I can see the tears sliding down his face in the rearview mirror and a wave of shame so powerful it makes me almost feel numb washes over me.

On the way home, I stop at 7-Eleven. Buy him a Coke to wake him up. Something sugary and sweet. Buy a bag of potato chips and a wrinkled, overcooked hot dog. I don't know if this is going to help. I don't know what I'm doing. I don't know anything.

He follows me around the store like a whipped dog.

Back in the car, he sits in the front seat, sucking the Coke back in three gulps. Crams the food in his mouth.

Then he climbs past me and lies down in the backseat.

"Emmy. I have outpatient tomorrow. They might test me."

"Great, Joey. That's just great."

He covers his face with his hands. His voice is muffled. I can't understand what he's saying.

I take deep breaths to calm down. I back the car out of the lot, start driving toward home.

"Stop the car," Joey mumbles. "Stop it, stop it."

I pull over. Oh, god, did he take too much of whatever he took?

Joey opens the backseat passenger door and the hot dog, the chips, the soda, splash onto the ground. Don't choke, I think, please don't let him choke.

When he's done, he closes the door, leans back against the seat. Wipes his mouth. I pass him a mint from my purse and pull back onto the road.

In the rearview mirror now, he's smiling now. Peaceful.

"I remember this feeling," he murmurs. "I don't care what happens."

"Oh, my god, Joey, *please*," I beg him. "Please, just maintain."

I have to stop freaking out. I need to think.

"Emory," he says. Then he starts to laugh.

To *laugh*.

"Jesus Christ, Joey, *what*?"

"What were you *doing* with Gage Galt? I mean, Gage. *You*."

I listen to my brother, high, laughing and rolling in our backseat, slopping around like human Jell-O.

I pull into the driveway. Our garage door rises to reveal our bikes, skis, lawn mower, and the rows and rows of Christmas decorations in boxes and big plastic tubs, the locked cabinet with all the things Joey could steal, hidden safely away by my mother.

Still in the car, I ask him, in a hollow voice, because I'm not sure if it even matters now, but somehow, I need to know, what he took with Noah by the trailers.

He's not laughing anymore.

He swallows thickly. "O. I did O. Oxy. Crushed a couple. Oh, god, I haven't felt like this in so long."

He sounds relieved. Like he's somewhere comfortable and safe.

I look at the locked cabinet against the wall, full of everything my mother thought would hurt him.

But she can't lock away what's in the world outside this

house. No one can. This is a battle without a plan, without armor, without logic.

"I have to get you in the house without Mom seeing how messed up you are right now. If they see you like this, flopping around like a sack, they will know. They will *know*."

Joey sits up and leans forward, his breath hot in my ear. "It won't happen again. I *promise*. Just help me. Please."

The garage door whines down behind us. The side door to the kitchen opens.

My father peers out.

Maybe I should just tell them. Maybe this is it. Maybe Joey is like the girl at the outpatient center. Margaret, on her ninth try. Maybe this is all just the beginning for Joey. Maybe this is the beginning for all of us, and I'll never be free.

"Please don't tell them, Emmy. I . . . it won't happen again, I promise. I *promise*."

I close my eyes.

Please, Emmy. His words bash around my brain, my heart. If I tell, they'll send him to military school. They'll send him away.

I open my eyes. My dad is beckoning to us to come into the house.

My whole body trembles as we walk in the door to the kitchen. Joey's not stumbling so much anymore. Maybe he remembers how to maintain out of sheer panic.

My dad gives us a resigned look. "A lot's happened tonight," he says. "I texted you, Joe. Why didn't you answer?"

"I was—"

I cut Joey off. "Dad, let me explain."

Our dad gestures toward the hall. "Nana's here. She had a fall earlier. They brought her into the hospital. They wanted to keep her for observation, but she refused. I think she's okay, just a little shocked, but she's going to stay with us for a while. I think that's best. How was the dance?"

Joey and I stand in silence until I nudge him with my elbow. He weaves slightly at my touch and I hold my breath, watching my father's face.

"Good," Joey says finally.

"Break some hearts, did you?" My dad grins. He didn't notice Joey wavering. I wonder if he's already had his nightcap, or two.

"Not really," I say, relieved. He doesn't know about Gage yet, which is good. But I know it's coming. I just can't figure out how to tell him first, head it off.

"Mom will be home soon. She went over to Nana's to get some things for her. Why don't you go in and say hello?"

Nana is in the downstairs guest room. There's a walker next to the bed. She looks very tiny, tucked in among all the fluffy pillows.

Her face breaks out into a smile as soon as she sees my brother. "Joseph, my goodness. How handsome." She's half propped on pillows, her foot up on a pillow. "You must have been the prince of the dance."

"Hey, Nana." Joey bends down, hesitating slightly before giving her a kiss on the cheek. "Are you okay?"

"Oof, your breath." She waves a hand in front of her face.

She frowns at us. "Your father has been trying for years to get me into this cell and now I guess he's finally succeeded. At least for a bit. What's a turned ankle? I raised six children. I'm tough as nails."

She looks at me. "Why is your makeup smudged? I suppose it isn't a dance without a little crying, but you need to fix your face, dear."

I lean down to hug her. She smells like oatmeal cookies and liniment oil.

She pats the space next to her on the bed. "Sit with me. I'm lonely in here. I miss my house already. Who will get my mail? Feed that strange orange cat who comes around?"

"Mom will have someone do that, Nana," I say. "She'll take care of it."

There's a buzzing and Nana looks around, finally pulling her cell out of the pocket of her robe. "What is this? What's happening? What does this mean? I don't understand these things." She holds the phone up to us.

Joey takes it from her. "It's Maddie, Nana. She's video calling you."

"What? Where? Like television? This is a phone, dammit."

"Let me show you," Joey says.

I go into Nana's bathroom, close the door. I look at my phone. It was buzzing nonstop in the car. There are tons of texts, all from Liza.

Uhhh

I don't really know where to start

I started this night thinking you liked Jeremy

I like Jeremy

And I was mad

And now all hell has broken loose

What happened???

Gage hurt his arm really bad

I don't know what the injury is exactly

But somebody told somebody told somebody else

That he was mumbling when the EMTs showed

Something about you and the pool house

And I gotta know, E, because it's blowing up

Were you hooking up with Gage Galt

Em

Talk to me

Oh, god. Everyone knows. Me and Gage.

All I wanted was to put on a dress and go to a dance and be normal for one night and now the world has gone to hell.

My thumbs hover over my phone.

I could tell her, but what would that help? It would just cause more trouble.

Can't deal right now, I text.

There's a sharp knock on the bathroom door. I open it to find my mother standing there, her phone gripped tightly in her hand.

"Why," she says, "is Beth Galt ranting at me on my voice mail about a fight you and your brother had with Gage Galt at the dance?"

"Um." That's the only thing I can muster.

"Emory." My mother gives me the Look. "You're going to have to do a lot better than that."

26

I'M PRESSED AGAINST THE wall in the hallway, outside my parents' room, Fuzzy at my feet, listening to the sound of my parents' voices through their door.

After Nana went to sleep, my dad found Joey in the kitchen, guzzling water. My father said, "We need to talk," and Joey put down his glass and followed him into the den. When he came out he went straight up to Maddie's room. When I passed by and whispered his name, he didn't answer. He was buried under Maddie's quilt. I went in and put my hand on his back, just in case, to make sure he was still breathing.

I always think of my dad living downstairs and my mother living upstairs, and to have them both in their bedroom at once now, on the same floor, after so long, is an eerie sensation.

Poor boy is hurt, I understand, but I don't know how that's our fault.

Beth Galt says Gage said something about turning Emory down for a dance and Joe got mad.

It's hardly Joey's fault if he defends his sister. The boy slipped and fell, that's what Joey told me. Isn't that what the other kids said?

It's no one's fault.

That woman is insufferable. My mother's voice is bitter.

Abigail.

Half drunk all the time.

Abigail.

What is going on with Emory? I had no idea she liked Gage. She's such a sweet girl! Why not just dance with her?

You know, it's high school, unrequited love, hurt feelings everywhere, who knows.

Silence.

My father says, *I always wondered what would have happened if we'd met here, in high school. If you hadn't been away at boarding school. Would you have liked the Gage Galt of Heywood High or just me, the kid from Polish Town?*

Pause.

Instead, I had to go halfway around the world, all the way to Japan, to fall in love with a girl from my own hometown. The girl who lived in the big, mysterious house on the hill. And now I live here.

Imagine that. My mother's voice is softer now.

Imagine that.

I don't think I've ever heard this story before, of them in Japan. I wonder what else is in my parents' backstory that they haven't told us?

My father comes out of their bedroom. He doesn't notice me as he goes down the stairs and I wonder how many more years it will be until they are in the same room again, talking to each other instead of at each other.

I go to my room, close the door, peel off my gray dress, the black leggings, my cardigan with the small white buttons. Put everything away neatly. Put my pajamas on. Wash my bleary, stained face in my bathroom. Wipe it clean, like I wish I could wipe everything clean.

I pause before my bedroom window.

Gage's house is dark, except for the porch light. They're still at the hospital. If it wasn't serious, they might be home by now. My stomach feels sick. This is not good.

On my bed, my phone is flashing.

Liza.

I know we haven't talked in years, really talked, and I'm sorry about that, but really, it was my due to be a bitch, you know? Because I'm the one who got cut out of your life in the worst way. But I think this might turn out bad and if you need help, I can help you. Okay? I just want you to know that.

Thank you, I type, grateful. I put the phone down beside me on the bed. Fuzzy jumps into my lap and I hold her close.

People know about me and Gage, everything we tried to keep secret. Joey got high again. Relapsed, like the Blue Spruce handbook said he might. And I'm not going to tell my parents. How much worse can things get than that?

Oh god. Joey's outpatient. He has a group meeting. What if they test him? My stomach squeezes.

I reach for my laptop and start typing. I'm in it now, lie after lie, to save my brother.

Can Oxy be found in a pee test
How long does Oxy stay in the body
Is there a difference between male urine and female urine

The next morning my mother is stirring eggs in the pan and turns around as I creep softly into the kitchen. "There you are. I was wondering when you would make an appearance."

She pushes a glass of juice toward me. I wrap my hands around it, avoiding her eyes. I know what's coming and it's not going to be good.

"Why don't you tell me what happened, Emory? Why Gage Galt is now undergoing some surgery I can't even pronounce."

"Are you going to yell at me?" I ask.

"I can't make any promises."

I swallow hard and look her straight in the face. "I asked him to dance and he said no. And I was outside, on the practice field, on the bleachers, and Joey found me, and I was upset, and so Joey ran over to Gage. But he didn't touch him, I swear. Gage slipped."

"Was your brother high? Drunk? Answer me honestly, Emory."

She's giving me the Look, so I do everything in my power not to let my eyes veer from hers, to appear steady and calm, because whatever else is going to happen, her finding out Joey was high would be worse than that.

And I know I shouldn't lie for my brother, but it was one time, and she will annihilate him even for this one time. I can help him make it back from this one time.

"No. I had my eyes on him the whole time. He was talking to Amber, his tutor, and then he ran after me when I ran outside."

My mother drops a sugar cube in her teacup.

"And what happened with you and Gage? His mother seems to think something more was going on."

That's right. Liza said Gage was mumbling about me and the pool house as they took him away from the practice field. I can't let my mother know about that, either.

I shake my head. "Nothing. A stupid crush."

"A crush?"

"Yes. One-sided, all me. I asked him to dance. He said no. I freaked out. End of story."

"You understand it all looks bad. The optics are bad."

I nod.

"I know we don't always connect," she says. "I'm sorry for that. I never really felt like my mother and I saw eye to eye, either, and I always wanted it to be different with me and my daughters. You can tell me anything, but the one thing you can't do is lie, especially where Joey is concerned. Do you understand? He can't learn to take responsibility for his sobriety if we enable him."

"I'm not lying."

The words feel heavy and bitter in my mouth.

"All right, Emory," she says, turning back to the eggs in the pan. "You've always been my good girl, so I believe you."

The juice is harsh on my tongue and I gently, quietly, spit it back into the cup.

Later, Joey and I drive down Main Street on the way to his outpatient meeting, past all the cozy, rustic-looking shops: the Bean There, Done That Café, Merkel's Fine Books, the Quiltery, where my mother likes to buy hand-stitched napkins and frothy doilies for presents for out-of-town relatives. Main Street in Mill Haven is postcard-perfect, giving everything an innocent, gleaming shimmer, so unlike how my life feels right now.

I think about all the things I want to say to Joey at this moment. How mad I am. How scared I am, for him. None of them seem right. None of them seem like they will change a thing, except make him more ashamed.

When we get to the outpatient clinic, Joey parks the car in the lot and we sit, for what seems like forever, until he finally speaks.

"They're going to test me, I know it," he says. "I can feel it. Oh my god."

He's breathing heavily. Panicking.

"I had one hundred and thirty-one days clean and I messed it up." His face is paler than usual.

My god. He had so many days and because Lucy Kerr is grieving and I wanted a boy to dance with me, that's gone. But a little voice in my head murmurs, Was it *all* me? Why didn't Joey . . .

"Joey." I keep my voice calm. I don't want to make him ashamed. Accuse him. "Why didn't you just find me? I was *right* there."

Joey whispers, "Everything just . . . came down on me. I know you're here, but I'm alone in this. No one gets that. I wish you could get that."

We are noise for Joey, just like he said. The world is noise for Joey. A constant beating down, like rain on rooftops.

Hands shaking, I unzip my backpack.

I lied for Joey and now I'm going to cheat for Joey. Because I don't want him to get sent away to a military school, or another rehab. Not right now.

"Mom is going to kick me out when the test turns positive. I'm so sorry, Em. I don't know what to do."

I pull out the baggie filled with my pee and hold it out to Joey.

"What *is* that?" He looks horrified.

"For your test. It's mine. Some people were talking about it one time when we were here. Take it," I say. "You can use it. I'm definitely not pregnant or on drugs, so you're clear there. Some tests can tell the difference between male and female pee. Those ones are expensive, though. I don't know what kind this place uses, but this is your only choice if you want to save yourself right now."

There is a part of me, a really large part, that wants him to say no. That is aching for him to say no.

That wants him to say *I shouldn't have gotten high under any circumstances and I should take my chances, I messed up and now I have to deal with what that means.*

But he doesn't. Just like I didn't make the choice to tell our parents.

We're just two liars, sitting in a car.

He carefully takes the baggie from me and tucks it under his hoodie and shirt, in the waistband of his store-bought holey jeans.

After his outpatient, when we are in the parking lot heading to the car, he says, "They didn't test me. I dumped it down the sink."

He looks relieved, but I'm not. Maybe part of me hoped he would get tested, and the test would somehow pick it up, or see that it was female urine, and then everything that probably should happen would happen, but without me betraying Joey to his face.

In the car, I tell him to drive me to the hospital so I can see Gage. I just want to see him. And I want him to tell everyone that he just slipped, that Joey didn't attack him. I want to chip away at all the bad things being hurled at Joey right now, so it can be a manageable mess instead of a hurricane.

"I don't know if that's such a good idea," Joey says slowly.

"Then stay in the car," I tell him.

*　　*　　*

When I walk in, Ryleigh is sitting next to Gage's bed, holding his hand. His other arm is suspended in the air, in a heavy brace that's wrapped all the way around his shoulder. His eyes are closed.

I wonder if he's feeling the same ocean I felt when I was in the hospital. The endless waves of morphine ocean.

Looking at him makes me feel weak, too. His perfect mouth, his soft skin. Everything I wanted so much, and I feel guilty and queasy for thinking that, while he's here in this bed, hurt. Just like I was in the summer.

Here I am, visiting him, but he never came to see me.

"Ryleigh," I say quietly.

She turns. She looks happy to see me at first, and then her smile dies.

"Emmy. My mom's in the cafeteria." Her lips tremble. "She's really mad at you."

"I know."

Gage's eyes flutter open.

He looks like Joey looked the night of the accident: heavy-lidded, dulled down.

"Ry," he mumbles. "Go outside. Just for a sec, okay? Keep . . . keep Mom busy if you see her."

She gets up and squeezes my hand as she passes.

"You," he says when she's gone. His voice is thick. "I didn't think you'd come here."

I step closer to the bed.

"I'm sorry," I say. "It was an accident. Joey didn't mean it, Gage."

"You told your brother." His lips are dry. "We had a deal."

"I thought . . . You said maybe we could hang out a little at the dance. I thought maybe things were changing, just a bit."

Slowly, it comes to me, how wrong I was: Gage was only appeasing me. To keep me quiet, keep me his. He didn't think I'd really go through with it. The truth sits inside me, a cold stone, as cold as his eyes looking at me from the hospital bed.

"I don't think I'm going to pitch again." He's blinking fast. "I can't understand what they're telling me, but nobody's smiling, so it isn't good."

"You will. You'll have therapy, you'll be fine. My dad says—"

"Your dad doesn't know anything about baseball. I'm done. I'm meat. I'm nothing now."

"Gage, no." Tears are running down my face. "No, that's not true. I'm *sorry*."

"This must be what your brother felt like, huh? All these drugs in me. Can't feel anything. Maybe that's my story now. Maybe I'll end up under the bridge, just another ghostie. This was all I had, Em. I'm not smart, like you."

I touch his good hand. I want to tell him that I'm not as smart as he thinks, that everything I'm doing right now is downright stupid, but I can't seem to stop myself.

"Gage, I'm sorry about what happened. But it wasn't Joey's fault. You slipped. The ground was slippery and cold. He didn't *push* you. You need to tell people that."

Gage stares at the ceiling. He pulls his good hand away from me.

And as I watch it slide across the blanket to rest on his lap, I know, right then, that I will never kiss Gage again, that everything we did is over. That it was over the moment I showed up at the edge of his friend circle at the dance, the moment I decided to make him see me in the light, instead of the dark.

"I just wanted you to like me," I whisper. "Was that so bad?"

I'm ashamed of the need in my voice.

His head rolls toward me. "I did like you, Emmy. Just not the way you wanted. But forgive me if I don't feel very sorry for you right now. Your whole life isn't smashed to hell at the moment."

He closes his eyes, presses the button with his good hand. To get those good waves. To wash me away.

"I want you to leave," he says hoarsely. "I just need you to leave. You and your brother, whatever you touch, you ruin."

I struggle with the car door. My hands feel flimsy and weak and I'm still crying.

Joey pushes it open from the inside. "Jesus, what happened in there? What did he say to you?"

"Why?" I snap, sliding into the seat. "Do you want to ruin his other arm?"

Joey's face turns bone white.

"I'm sorry," he says.

"Stop *saying* that!" I yell.

He starts the car, his face grim and hurt.

"*I'm* sorry, Joey," I say, trying to catch my breath, calm myself. "I'm sorry I raised my voice."

We're driving out of the lot, his hands tight on the wheel.

"Joey."

He doesn't speak to me for the rest of the ride, and when we get home, he goes straight to his room, gets dressed for his shift at Hank's Hoagies, and leaves without taking me with him or saying goodbye.

27

M Y PHONE VIBRATES AGAINST my thigh. I'm staring at the ceiling in my room.

I pick it up.

Maddie.

What the hell happened?
Talk to me
What happened to Gage?
Was Gage Mr. No-Name?
You have to talk to me or I'll call Mom.

I punch out the message as hard as I can, not caring if I break the screen.

Please. Just leave me alone. I just need
to be ALONE.

But I scoop up Fuzzy and go downstairs to Nana's room and lie in bed with her, watching television, and she's quiet, just like I wanted her to be.

I fall asleep beside Nana, and when I wake up, I'm still there, and my mother is standing above me, telling me it's time to get ready for dinner.

Joey's jaw is clenched in the car as we sit in the school parking lot on Monday morning. We were quiet the whole drive here. He's not wearing his fancy store-bought holey jeans today or the nice Gap hoodie. He's back in his old, messy, wrinkly clothes. The ones I put in a plastic tub and shoved in the back of Maddie's closet. He must have really wanted them to go digging for them, wanted the safety of their comfort. Something that makes him feel like himself. His old self.

"I'm sorry," he says. "I know you didn't mean what you said on Saturday. But we have to be a unit now. This might be bad. It looks like I broke a very popular guy's arm, and I'm not well liked anyway."

He pauses. "And it might be bad for you, too."

My stomach is in knots. "Okay," I say softly, pulling the hood of my jacket over my head. "But maybe we can just sit here for a little bit, until the lot clears out."

"All right."

It's starting to rain. The last stragglers are moving quick to get inside.

Rain is slipping down the windshield, gradually erasing the world outside, and I wish, wish, wish we could stay inside this car forever.

I feel my phone vibrating in my back pocket as I'm walking down the hall, but I don't take it out. Instead, I turn right, toward first period. I'm already late.

"Ms. Ward," says Mr. Hoolihan. "Earth science waits for no one. You're lucky I didn't mark you absent."

Every single kid in class is staring at me as I make my way to my seat in the back. I slide onto my chair and put my backpack on the floor.

Then I see it.

Whore.

Scrawled on my desk in black marker. The letters are big enough to be seen, but just small enough for a teacher not to notice right away.

I freeze, my blood running cold. Mr. Hoolihan starts talking at the front of the room. I rub the sleeve of my hoodie across the word, but it doesn't budge. I lick my fingers and wipe them on the desk, but that doesn't work, either. This wasn't on my desk last Friday and I always sit here. It's assigned in Hoolihan's class.

Kids are snickering. When I look up, they quickly look away, hands over their mouths.

I pull my copy of *The Portrait of a Lady* out of my bag and lay it horizontally over the word so I don't have to see it.

My phone vibrates in my lap.

"Ms. Ward, would you please turn your phone off?" Mr. Hoolihan is exasperated.

"Sorry," I mutter. I grab my phone and jam it off, put it back in my backpack.

The whole class period, I can feel that word crawling up at me through the pages of the book.

It can't be meant for me. It can't.

Hallway.

More stares and snickers.

I think: this will pass. No one knows. It's just Gage and his broken arm. Or maybe they heard Joey got high.

Think of ocean fish, like Joey once told me, so I do. Dotty-back. Barracuda. Seahorse.

I make it through my other classes, but it's weird, the stares I'm getting. I don't think I can make it through lunch, so I hide in a bathroom stall until it's time for Lit.

In Watson's class, there's a piece of paper on my desk when I sit down. There have been stares and whispers all day. I hid in the bathroom during lunch. I turn the paper over, stomach clenching.

Let me know when you reopen the pool house for business

The paper is snatched out of my hands by Daniel Wankel.

Daniel glances at it and then tears it up. "You jerks!" he shouts. "You think this is funny? Huh? You proud of yourselves? Look at yourselves. I see you, Mary Mitford. I know stories about you, you want me to share them with everybody?"

Mary Mitford flushes bright red. She turns back around in her seat.

"I thought so," Daniel says. He lets the pieces of paper flutter to the floor.

"Are you okay?" he asks.

My face is frozen. I can only nod, even though I'm not. I just don't get who would even care about me and Gage and the pool house, in the real scheme of things. Why should it matter? People hook up all the time.

Liza rushes into the room, worry creasing her face. She shakes her head.

I'm so sorry. I texted you, she mouths.

Mr. Watson rushes in, coffee cup in hand. "My apologies for being late." He laughs and looks around at all of us.

No one joins in.

When the bell pings to signal the end of class, Mary Mitford turns around.

"You can run, but you can't hide. Slut."

"Shut your mouth, Mary Mitford, or I'll shut it for you." Liza is standing with her fists balled.

Mary Mitford scuttles away.

"I texted you," Liza says. "I'm so sorry."

"We should leave," Daniel says. "I'll get my car, meet you by the side door. That's the quickest way out."

"I don't understand," I say, my voice trembling. "I can't just leave."

"It's just going to get worse," Daniel says. "You should go home. Come back in a few days, when it dies down."

"Actually, I don't think she should go home," Liza says.

"Are you *crazy*?" Daniel says. "Look what people are doing!"

They give each other a look I don't understand.

Kids are starting to file into Watson's room for the next class. Liza grabs my arm and hustles me out the door. Daniel follows.

In the hallway, she pulls me into an alcove. "I don't get it," I say. "What's going on? Who the hell cares if I hooked up with Gage in the pool house? We didn't . . . it was hardly *anything*. No worse than what other people have done. I'm a *no one*."

Liza bites her lip. "Listen, Emmy, remember when I told you you were going to have to get a spine if you wanted to survive the year? Well, now is the time."

She turns to Daniel. "She shouldn't have to leave. She didn't *do* anything wrong. She hooked up with a guy. Are you telling me she should be ashamed and driven out of school for that?"

Daniel says, "Well, no, but the——"

"There isn't any 'but,' Daniel. If she leaves, it'll get ten times worse when she comes back."

She turns back to me. "Emmy, if you want to go home, go home. But you if you want to stay, I'm with you."

The warning bell for next period blurts through the hallway, making me jump.

I don't want to stay, because this is the worst thing that could happen to me, having everyone notice me all at once, and not in the most positive way.

"He didn't make me, you know," I say softly to Liza. "I wanted to."

"I get it," she says. "It's just words. That's all it is right now, words. But . . ."

The way she tightens her face worries me.

"Liza, what? What aren't you telling me?"

"There's . . . there's something else."

But the bell rings then, the last one before class starts. The warning bell, and we all scatter like mice.

But even as I sit in my next class, snickers around me, I keep thinking of what she said.

There's something else.

Liza is waiting for me in the hallway after class. She grabs my arm.

"Tell me," I say. "Just tell me."

"There are pictures," she says slowly, walking me down the hall, her arm crooked in mine. She's keeping me on the inside, by the lockers we never use, protecting me from the crush of hallway kids.

"No," I say. Oh, god, no. He said he *deleted* them. "They weren't . . . it was just . . . he said he got rid of them. I *asked*."

She pulls me into the bathroom no one likes, the one at the end of the hall by the science labs. The sinks are always dirty. It smells.

"It will blow over," she says firmly. "I haven't seen them. You don't even have to tell me what they are. It doesn't *matter*. But they'll feed on this. And you have to be ready."

I slide down the wall to the dirty floor, tears crashing down my face.

"I can't do this," I mumble. "I just can't. I can't take any more."

I should just leave. I should just go home.

"It will be okay," Liza murmurs, patting my hair.

"J-Joey . . . ," I stammer. "Joey got high on Friday. Everything is a mess."

"Oh, god," Liza says, sitting down next to me. "Oh, god, I am so sorry, I am so sorry, Emmy."

We sit like that the whole free period, in the dirty bathroom.

I'm exhausted by the time Liza and I get to Drama Club. Simon Stanley is showing kids how to work the lights when Lucy Kerr appears beside me.

I stiffen, try to prepare myself for more words. Liza dried my face in the bathroom, fixed my eyeliner, and told me to suffer through it. *It will pass,* she promised. *It will pass.*

If I can just get through this, then I can go home. I can go home and have some peace. Everything will die down. Me and Gage in the pool house will be old news. The photos might be another thing, but how long can that last, really? Then I shudder, looking around.

How many of these kids have seen me now? Naked, in a window? I cross my arms across my chest.

"Wow, so you and your brother, everything you touch, you hurt or kill," Lucy whispers.

Liza and Jeremy are practicing with the lights across the stage. One swings high over my head, momentarily blinding me.

"Just go away," I whisper back harshly. "Leave me alone."

"Did you really think Gage Galt was going to be into you? I mean, come on. Look at yourself. Dirty pictures in a window. You're like, *nothing*. Just like your loser brother."

I don't know what does it. Maybe that she said he wouldn't be into me. Maybe that she called me nothing, which is what I always think I am in this world anyway, but to hear it, actually hear it out loud, from someone else, it rips through me.

"You know, Lucy, you blame me for Candy, for giving her a ride home. That's fine. I get it. But did you ever once think how I felt about it? How I felt, listening to her in the car? I was the very last one to hear Candy MontClair alive in this world. Do you think I don't think about that every day? Because I *do*."

I'm walking toward her so forcefully she has to walk backward, and she stumbles a little.

"You don't need to remind me of it. I *live* it. And I don't care what you say about Gage, because you know nothing, and I mean *nothing*, about me and him. But don't bring my brother into it, and you know why? He had one hundred and thirty-one days clean before that dance, Lucy. One hundred and thirty-one days. And in one fell swoop, you ruined that. Did you know that? He had all those days and after you, he didn't. Who's the dick now?"

Simon Stanley is calling my name, but I don't care. I poke Lucy in the chest, hard.

"And *you* have to live with that now, Lucy. That was your cruelty. You didn't need to do that, and you did. You put *that* into motion, and if you can't forgive me for Candy, fine, but I will never forgive you for doing that to Joey, ever. You didn't even give him a chance. You have to give people a decent *chance.*"

"Emory Ward." My name again, sharper now.

"What!" I yell.

I turn around, breathing hard. Lucy runs over to Simon Stanley.

But it wasn't Simon who called my name.

It was Principal Patterson.

28

PRINCIPAL PATTERSON SIGHS.

"It's been a long weekend," she says. "I'm sorry for what happened at the Fall Festival. From what I understand, your brother got into an altercation with Gage Galt?"

"No. Yes. S-sort of." I can't help but stammer. "He didn't actually hit him or anything. Gage slipped. I swear, he slipped on the grass before Joey got to him."

She folds her hands. "I understand. There are some differing stories, but I'm sure the truth will come out. I'm a little concerned about something else right now."

I brace myself. I think I know what's coming. But what are they going to do, expel me? Maybe that wouldn't be so bad. I'd have to go away to boarding school, probably, but at least I'd be far from here.

She reaches into her desk drawer and pulls out a phone.

"This is Mr. Galt's phone. Someone found it on the practice field and turned it in this morning. It wasn't locked, and in an attempt to determine whose it was, we looked through it."

She presses the phone and turns it toward me.

There I am, in my window.

Fingers pushing the side of my pajama pants down. A hand pushing one side of my shirt up.

My blood runs cold at the same time my face gets very, very

hot. This is not something I wanted anyone to ever see, least of all my principal.

He said he deleted them. And he didn't. He lied to me. He *lied.*

"I don't—"

"This wasn't taken on school property, but both of you are minors—and of course I'm not trying to shame you. But it has come to my attention that this photo, and others on the phone, may have been shared before the phone was turned in."

She hands me a tissue. I wipe my eyes. I do not want to sob in front of her, so I try to be very quiet with my crying.

"I know that high school can be very rough, and that you've had a hard time this year. With the accident. Your brother. I know what's been happening with your peers today and I think, just for a day or two, that you should think about staying home. Let things simmer a bit."

"Am I getting suspended? Expelled? I didn't do anything wrong."

"Not a suspension. Not at all. I just think you should stay home. I've called your father to come get you. He's on his way."

"You called my *dad*?" Oh my god.

I'm going to have to talk to my dad in the car about sexy window photos with my not-boyfriend. Photos that my *dad* has probably seen by now.

I thought things couldn't get worse, but evidently, they can.

"Your mother was in court, so yes, we had to call your father."

Oh, god. My *mother*. Boarding school is looking better and better.

The phone on her desk lights up. "Yes," she says, picking up the receiver. "I'll send her out."

She puts the phone down. "Your father is here, Emory."

My dad is waiting by Mrs. Tisby's desk. He gives me that specific grimace parents have when they're boiling with emotion but don't want to show it in public.

The silence between us lasts through the hallway and until we're out in the parking lot.

I steel myself, waiting for him to yell at me for interrupting his work, or for the photos, but he doesn't.

Instead, he just turns to me and shakes his head.

"Oh, Emory," he says sadly. "How did we end up here?"

And I don't know what to say to that, because it's all too much to put into words.

Then he's hugging me, something he hasn't done in a long, long time, and I'm crying against his jacket.

We're walking to the car when I hear my name. I turn around.

It's Amber, Joey's tutor. She runs up to us.

"Hey," she says.

"Hey," I say back. "Uh, Dad, this is Amber, Joey's tutor."

"Hello," he says.

"Hi." She turns to me. "Listen, if you see Joey, will you tell him that what happened . . . on Friday? What that girl said. It doesn't matter to me. Will you tell him that?"

"Why can't you just tell him yourself?" I say. "Aren't you supposed to be tutoring him right now?"

She shakes her head. "No, he didn't show up. I've been wait-ing, and I texted him, but he hasn't answered."

My dad and I sit in his car in the visitors' parking lot. We're both texting Joey, the photos of me forgotten for now, but getting no replies.

"Where do you think he could be?" my dad asks.

I shake my head. "Should we call the police? What if some-thing happened to him?"

I'm nervous, thinking about the dance, and the Oxy, and that maybe, just maybe, he's doing something like that right now.

Joey you have to answer, I text.

My dad drives around Mill Haven. "Maybe he's parked some-where," he says. "I don't know. I'm at a loss, frankly. With everything."

He sounds exhausted.

"I know you're mad," I say slowly. "And I'm sorry."

My dad sighs. "I'm not mad at you, Emory. I might be a bit disappointed, but I'm not mad. And if I am mad, it's more at myself than you."

"Why?" I ask. "Why would you be mad at yourself?"

He drives along Frost River. The rain is still coming down, giving the world outside the car a smeary, dreamy look.

"What kind of father am I if my daughter can't come to me and tell me she's having trouble with a boy? Or if I ignore my son, hoping his problems will fix themselves? Your mother likes to manage things. She's good at it. But I let her do it alone for too long. And for that, I'm sorry."

"I wish you were home more," I say. "I miss you. I never see you."

He glances over at me. "I'm going to try to do better."

He looks away from me, his face deepening into a frown. I follow his gaze to the river.

"Dad? You okay?"

"I usually don't get out this way very much," he says. He pulls into the Frost River parking area, just a dirt patch, really. It overlooks the river and the beach.

We both look farther down, by the bridge.

The sea of people has grown. There are mountains of trash. People sleeping in piles, close together.

"What," my dad says slowly, "in god's name is going on down there?"

Before I can answer him, Joey texts me.

I'm home.

29

JOEY IS SITTING AT the kitchen island with Nana, a baggie of ice against his face.

"Roly Martin," he says, pulling the baggie away. My dad presses Joey's swollen cheekbone with his fingers.

"Nothing's broken," my dad says.

"Thank goodness," Nana clucks, nibbling a cookie.

"How did this happen? Where were you? We've been texting all afternoon." My dad takes off his jacket and hangs it on the chair.

Joey hands him his phone. "I was here. You can check the tracker. Roly jumped me on my way out of the locker room after PE. Mad about Gage, still. I'm not much of a fighter. I took off when I got loose and I drove around for a while. Just needed some time alone."

Time alone. I try not to be obvious about it, but I sneak a look at his eyes, to see if they're red, or slidey, like they were the night of the dance. He's not Jell-O-ey and sloppy, though. He's sitting up straight on the kitchen island stool.

He looks at me and Dad. "I'm not high. You can give me a test. I'm telling the truth."

My dad shakes his head. "I believe you. Are you in a lot of pain?"

"No, but . . . Emmy, you should go upstairs. Mom's up there, and it's . . . not good."

*   *   *

The door to my room is open. I stop short, my heart beating in my ears.

Clothes, blankets, jewelry, books, everywhere, littering the floor. The drawers of my dresser are pulled out, socks and underwear a mess.

My mother is sitting on my bed, the vintage black velvet hatbox on her lap, the lid off, dropped on the floor.

"This is mine," she says softly, petting the velvet. "This was passed down to me. You . . . stole it from me."

I've never heard her voice so low and it chills me.

"Mom," I say weakly. "I can explain."

"I got a call from Principal Patterson after I got out of court and I was so confused. The things she was saying to me. I didn't understand them."

She raises her eyes to me.

"And then I got the most horrible photos on my phone. I don't know from who. Of you. In that window, there. For everyone to see. And I thought, That can't be true. That's not my daughter. My daughter wouldn't do that."

"Mommy." I don't know what else to say.

All my secrets are out now.

She runs her fingers through the stolen items in the hatbox, sifting them through her fingers, letting them fall and clatter back into the hatbox.

"And I came in here. I thought, Maybe she's on drugs. Maybe she's like her brother. And I found this. And these."

She holds up the glamorous, expensive watch. It gleams in the palm of her hand.

"This isn't yours. Where did this come from? All of this? Where? This money? These . . . things?"

"Mommy, please," I say.

"You've been lying to me this whole time. A thief and a liar and . . ."

She looks at the window, the one I stood in, where Gage took the photographs.

When she looks back at me, her eyes are lost.

I think I've broken my mother in a way that Joey didn't. A way that's maybe worse because she never saw it coming.

"Mom," I say. "Mom, please."

"I don't even know you. I don't even know my own daughter. Why did you do this? Why on earth would you do all these things?"

My mouth trembles. "I . . . I felt lost."

"Lost?"

"You don't even see me. You've never seen me." My voice is shaking. "You see Maddie, and you see Joey, but you don't . . . see me. You never have."

"You're not making any sense. Of *course* I see you, you're my daughter."

I bend down and start picking things up randomly, throwing them on my overstuffed pink recliner chair. Suddenly I hate that chair.

"I don't even like that chair, Mom. You picked it out. You never asked me what kind of chair I wanted or if I even *wanted* a chair in my room. You pick out my clothes. You tell me what classes to take. You tell me to take dance. You wouldn't even let me take my pain pills and I was in pain. I'm *still* in pain. You got rid of my friend. My only friend."

I'm rambling now, kicking clothes out of my way. I rip down the Polaroids of me and the girls on the dance team that I carefully clothes-pinned to a fairy light in my room. Throw them to the floor. I put them up because that sort of thing went with a girl with an overstuffed pink chair in her room. That sort of thing belongs to the daughter my mother wants.

"And I go along with it. Because I don't want to cause you any more trouble. Joey is *trouble.* I just keep quiet, waiting for you to notice me. And look, now you only notice me when you see a picture of me literally naked in a window. That's what it took."

I wipe the tears from my face. It feels good to tell her this but scary, too.

She's just staring at me, her eyes wide and her mouth open.

"And I stole stuff. And it felt *good.* That I could take things for myself and have something that *I* chose. And maybe that was wrong, what I did with Gage, but that felt good, too, like somebody was paying attention to me, finally. Do you think I want to spend time in a smelly hoagie shop on a Saturday night? I deserved to be kissed after that, that's the way I see it. I love Joey, and I love you, but I shouldn't have to . . . have to . . . with you it's like it was with Gage, and wanting him to dance with me, where people could see. I shouldn't have to *ask.* I shouldn't have to wait for the *scraps* of whatever you have left after dealing with Maddie and Joey."

I can't say any more, I'm crying too hard.

My dad is standing in the doorway, his eyes surveying the mess.

"Abigail? Emory?" His voice is worried.

My mother puts the hatbox on the bed very carefully and

stands up. She passes by me, brushes by my father, and then I hear the door to their room closing.

"Emmy?" my dad says.

"Can you just leave me alone, please? Please?"

"Emmy, talk to me."

"Dad, *no*, not right now."

He closes my door.

I climb onto my bed. I feel empty. Tears just pour down the sides of my face onto the pillow and I let them.

My phone pings several times, one after the other. I lift it up. Check the messages.

Let me know when the pool house opens

It's always the quiet ones

You doing another window peep show 2-night

I turn my phone off and throw it across the room so it lands on the stupid overstuffed recliner I never liked.

Then I bury my head under a pillow and cry myself to sleep.

If I was Joey, I'd be pawing through the house looking for anything, something to dull all this down. Forget I'm even *me*.

I get it now. I really get it.

At some point in the night, I open my eyes to Joey setting Fuzzy next to me.

I blink. "Stay?" I say.

He hesitates, then nods. He curls up next to me, his cheek swollen, the bruising starting to pop out.

We don't say anything.

We just fall asleep together.

I dream that Joey is standing far away from me, on the beach in San Diego, telling me he's sorry, that he always lets everyone down and it won't ever happen again. The sound of the waves carry his voice to me and I try to call back to him, tell him it's okay, that everything will be okay, but the waves drown me out.

When I wake up, he's gone.

30

I WAKE UP TO THE sound of shouting. My mother's voice, something about grades and disappointment, and then Nana chiming in, "Easy, now. Everyone take a breath."

And then Joey's voice, "I'm never enough, am I?"

I scramble out of bed, but before I can get to the door to go downstairs and see what's up, it flies open.

I brace myself for my mother, but it's Liza who is standing there.

"Whew," she says. "Your brother just took off in a hurry. I could hear yelling all the way outside on the sidewalk."

I sigh. "I guess they were fighting."

Liza takes one look at the floor and sits right down and begins folding my clothes and straightening up the things my mother threw out of my drawers. She glances briefly at the crumpled Polaroids, smooths them out, stacks them in a pile.

"What are you doing here?" I ask, rubbing my eyes. "You should be in school."

She shrugs. "My grandmother called in for me. I can miss a day. I haven't been in your room in so long. When did you become such a slob?"

I sigh. "My mom kind of freaked out and tore my room apart. Somebody sent her . . . the photos."

"Oh, wow," Liza says. "Aye. That's . . . not good. I'm kind of impressed, by the way. I didn't tell you that yesterday. You're famous. That's really why I'm here."

"What do you mean?"

"Damage control. I know how these things work. Where's your phone?"

I point to the recliner. Liza leans over and picks it up, scrolls through it.

"Wow, a lot of our classmates actually *can* spell," she says mildly. "Color me surprised."

I giggle.

"Did you see all of these?" she asks.

"No. I just kind of went to bed after yelling at my mother about how unloved I felt. It was that kind of night."

Liza puts the phone down. "You know, Emmy, I was mad at your mom, and you, for a long time. More your mom. If she hadn't butted in, my parents would still be with me. That's what I thought, anyway."

She picks at the cream-colored throw rug on the hardwood floor.

"But if they were still with me, where would *I* be right now? Would I be getting straight As? Would I still be hiding food from them so they wouldn't trade it for drugs? Did you know I did that?"

I shake my head. "No, I didn't know it was that bad. We were kids."

"Well, there was a lot I couldn't tell you because I didn't know how. The truth is, your mom kind of did me a favor, if I look at it in a certain way. By trying to protect you, she might have saved me."

She folds up a pink cardigan, lays two white socks on top of each other.

"My parents got freaked out by her and left. A neighbor finally called the police. My grandmother came to take care of us, and she does a good job, and I love her. I didn't know how nice it was to have someone kiss you good night before bed and not just yell at you to go to bed, or even remember you *should* be in bed. Your mom isn't all bad. Her execution may be faulty, but her intentions are good."

She pauses. "I think, anyway."

She cocks her head at me. "Don't you have to pee or something? I always have to pee right when I get up. Go pee. Then we'll get to work."

In my bathroom, I pee, wash my face, and brush my teeth. My face looks pale and tired in the mirror. From my room, I hear my phone ping again and again and Liza murmurs, *Shut up, you. I'll deal with you miscreants in a minute.*

I'm glad she's here. I'm glad to have her back.

"Okay," she says when I come back out. "The first rule of Slut Club is to create a diversion."

"Slut Club?"

"*Slut* is basically what everyone is calling you. Among other things."

"Oh." I sit on the bed and hold a pillow against my stomach, like it's going to protect me from whatever Liza is about to say.

"But you didn't do anything wrong." She pauses. "I wouldn't have placed bets on you hooking up with Gage Galt, of all people, but the heart wants what it wants. Kudos on the window photography, but it was consensual, yes?"

I nod. "Yeah, but I did ask him to delete them and he didn't."

"Do you . . . do you think he was the one who shared them?"

I think for a long time about that. "No, I don't. I don't think he would do that. Principal Patterson said someone turned the phone in to the office and that it was unlocked. Whoever found it probably saw the pictures and shared them."

"How great it must feel that our principal has seen you naked."

"Not exactly something I ever thought would happen, no."

She picks up her backpack and digs out a notebook and pen. "Well, anyway. Teenagers are creatures of the moment. They like to pile on. Half of them don't even care what happened between you and Gage, or even that his arm is messed up. They just want any excuse to join the crowd if it means they can bring somebody down and feel better about themselves. Not slagging our colleagues, that's just the way it is. So we have to give them something new to think about."

"I don't see where you're going with this," I say. "I'm kind of confused."

"The way I see it, we give too much leeway to boys. Why isn't anyone calling Gage a slut for hooking up with *you*? Why was Patty Bailey harassed out of school last year because she got pregnant and decided to keep the baby, but Rick Braverman got to stay? What was all that business about his life being ruined by her poor decision? Remember that?"

I shake my head. "I was kind of busy last year. Trying to keep Joey afloat. I didn't really keep up with a lot of stuff."

Liza regards me. "You can't fix him, you know."

"I know."

"You can't fix him because he isn't broken. He's just Joey. He has a disease. It's management and care, like cancer. You hope for the best. But, for the record, you should tell your parents he got high and then let whatever happens, happen."

She gives me a long look.

I tear up a little. "Can we get back to the thing you're planning? I don't feel up to talking about Joey right now."

"Okay. But we're going to talk about Joey at some point, all right?" She tosses me my phone. "Read out the names or numbers of the people who texted you."

I hold the pink phone in my lap. "Why?"

"I'm going to find out who they are. I worked in the office last year a few hours a week with Mrs. Tisby as part of communications work-study. I still have access to the student directory with names and phone numbers because Mrs. Tisby isn't smart enough to change the password. And then I'm going to use the power of social media."

"You? How?"

"It's better you don't know. That way you can claim total innocence. And when you come back to school Thursday, try to look as sad as possible, okay?"

"Well," I say. "That won't be hard."

"Start reading. And then delete and block."

31

WHEN LIZA AND I go downstairs after finishing her mysterious list, my mother and Nana are in the kitchen, making lunch.

"Would you girls like something to eat?" my mother asks. I notice that she doesn't look at me, just busies herself with pulling out bread and slicing tomatoes.

Liza slides onto an island stool. "I would," she says.

I slip onto a stool next to Liza. I wonder how long it will take my mother to acknowledge me directly.

"You have grown so much," Nana tells Liza. "You were just a little thing the last time I saw you."

"I think I'm taller than you now," Liza says.

Nana smiles.

"Well," Liza says, her voice awkward. I can tell she notices that my mom is freezing me out. "We cleaned up Emory's room."

Her voice trails off.

My mother hands her a plate with a tomato and cheese sandwich.

"Thank you," Liza says. She bites into her sandwich delicately, chewing slowly.

My mother slides a plate over to me.

"Thank you," I say.

My mother sips a cup of tea. "Quarter grades are up," she says lightly.

I stop eating my sandwich. "Oh?"

"Yes." She finally looks at me. "You did well. All As, except for American Classics. There's no grade posted for that."

Liza swallows. "That's because we only have one assignment. A paper. Thirty pages at the end of the semester. There was a bit of a rebellion in class about the reading list."

"Interesting," my mother says.

She gazes at me. "Your brother's grades were not what I'd hoped."

My heart sinks. "What . . . what were they?"

"They were Cs and one D."

"Well, that's . . . not bad. Is it?"

"He needed to get at least a B-minus in each class." She tilts her head to the Rules for Joey under the magnet on the refrigerator. "He had a tutor. I don't understand what happened."

Nana shakes her head. "You work him too hard. A job, school, his therapy. How can he do well when he's tired?"

My mother doesn't answer her. She just keeps staring at me.

"I was disappointed. And I think he was, too. He left for school this morning a little upset."

"I heard that," I say. "I heard you fighting. Did you make him feel bad? He's trying! I sat with him while he did his work and he was trying. It's just hard for him, Mom. He's not me. He's not Maddie."

I'm very aware of how quiet Liza is, and what she said upstairs, about telling my parents Joey got high. But I can't. I just can't.

"I understand that, Emory. I'm not trying to pick a fight

with you. Maybe Nana's right. Maybe things were too stringent. I'll have to sit with your father and perhaps we can work out a better plan."

"Maybe you could ask *Joey* what he needs," I say.

"Your brother isn't very good at articulating his needs, Emory. That's one of the issues. If he needed help, he needed to ask for it."

"Maybe he's *afraid* to ask for it, Mom."

Liza gets up and pointedly puts her plate in the sink.

"I should probably get going. Thanks for lunch, Mrs. Ward. It was nice to see you again. You too, Nana Ward."

Nana gives Liza a hug. My mother gives her the faintest of smiles.

"Walk me to the door?" Liza asks me.

I follow her out to the living room, and as she opens the front door, she says casually, "I meant to ask upstairs, but I forgot. How did you and Gage, like, even start this whole weird process?"

I look at the floor. Remembering it makes me feel sad, all of a sudden, because it was so small, and unexpected.

"A poem," I tell Liza. "It started because of a poem. That Anne Sexton one from eighth grade, remember that? The warning the stars one. He remembered it."

I look at the floor, almost ashamed. "He told me I was beautiful. Perfect."

"You are," Liza says. "You absolutely are, in the messiest, best way."

I try to smile.

Liza shakes her head. "Poetry always causes trouble, you know."

She pats my shoulder.

"See you," she says, closing the front door behind her.

Back in the kitchen, I take a deep breath. "Mom. Joey is trying. But he needs some room to breathe. And to maybe . . . fail a little. Is that so bad?"

"Well," my mother says. "I did mention military school again this morning. Really, it might be his best option. Away from here. From his memories. A fixed schedule. But he wasn't happy with that suggestion."

"You *didn't*." I stare at her. This is the worst thing she could have said to him. It was the last thing he wanted, to be sent away. To be disappeared.

"I was frustrated." she says. "I'm very frustrated right now. I have the town council on my back about the damn Mill, I've agreed to pay for the Galt boy's hospital and rehabilitation therapy in exchange for them not pressing assault charges. There's *you*."

I wince. "You're paying for Gage?" This is all too much.

"I have to live next door to these people, Emory. I have to throw them an olive branch. I hope you're done with that boy, though."

I push my sandwich around my plate. "I'm done," I say softly.

"I mean, for goodness' sake, I'm not stupid. I read the *paper*. I *hear* things. I know what kids do these days. The photo thing. Sexting." It's like that word burns the inside of her mouth, because she takes a long sip of her tea. "But I never thought *you* would do it. We have to hold ourselves to a standard, Emory. These things can follow you for the rest of your—"

"I said I was *done*. I said I was *sorry*."

"Abigail, please," Nana says. "No more today."

My mother sighs.

"Fine. Now, what are you going to do with the rest of your accidental day off? You don't even have to go to Hank's Hoagies with Joey today. You're free."

"I guess . . . I guess I'll read my book for American Classics and make some notes for my paper. And I have to look at the monologue packet for Drama Club. The performance is in two weeks." Great. Now I have that to go through. Standing up in front of god knows how many people, blaming me for Gage, maybe having seen the photos. My head spins. It's too much. I wish I could just go upstairs and sleep forever.

Nana claps her hands. "Oh, a play! How nice!"

"No, Nana, it's just short pieces all night. Like a kind of variety show."

My mother nods in approval. "That's very nice. Make sure you tell me when it is and what time, so we can all be there. I'll put it in my calendar."

When she turns around to rinse the dishes, I pull out my phone and text Joey.

> Don't stress about your grades.
> It's going to be okay. It will.

Mis_Educated

I see you. All of you.
Reposting and snickering and sharpening your high school
blades.
I know each and every one of you.
I've known you for years.
You didn't much notice me, though. You often don't notice
girls like me.
Smart (boring). Doesn't dress sexy (boring). Too opinionated
(boring bitch).
I could go on and on but while you were busy not noticing me,
I was taking notes on you. I know more than you think I do.
And if you think writing nasty notes on her desk
Leaving them on her voice mail
Texting them
Whispering in the hallway
Sharing pictures of her again and again
Is funny. Or payback. Or justice. (For what, even?)
I'm going to show you how wrong you are.
I want to talk about addiction.
My parents are gone. Poof. One day there,
One day not. But when they were there,
I propped them up. Made dinner. Took care
Of my brothers. Shopped. Counted pennies.
Hid what I could so they wouldn't sell it.
They sold all our shoes once.
I mowed four lawns to earn enough money
To buy us more at the Salvation Army thrift store.
Mowed those lawns in bare feet.
That's the thing about loving an addict.
You don't want to lose them.
You'll do anything to keep them with you.
Keep them alive.
You'll lie, beg, cheat, steal.
But you start to feel invisible.
Because everything is about them.
Never about you. You can't even think about you,
You're so busy taking care of them
Because you don't want to lose them.
But it's hard to be invisible.

You just want someone, sometime
To see you. Look at me, you beg
Inside your head. Notice me.
Love me.
Love me.
You'll make up your own minds.
The wrongheaded often do.
But remember this:
What would you do to be seen?
How would you feel if a boy asked you
To recite poetry and didn't snicker at you?
What if he called you Perfect
And Beautiful
And was nice to you in all those ways but one:
No one could know.
But you felt loved, so you went on.
People will do anything for love.
I know I would.
It's an addiction.
I would do anything
If it would bring my parents back to me.
I'm guessing this girl isn't the only one
With a story like this. Or a version of it.
The story of a boy and girl and kisses
And hookups and secrets and lies.
So why are we shaming her?
Tell me. Tell me your stories.
Tell me who wronged you.
Boys don't get to make the rules
About what girls can be
And if you're tired of being shamed
And tired of shaming others
Meet me in the shitty science lab bathroom
Tomorrow before first bell.
Let's give them something to talk about.

324 comments

3.1k likes

+ for more

#heywoodhigh #heywoodhaulers #heywoodhypocrisy #metoo #gagegalt #millhaven

SZ1789 Nate Rabinowitz

GiGi Carl Granger

FrancesP Tucker Michaels

MandyMandy Allan Jefferson

PristTine Roly Martin

LzySusan That janitor fall of 2019. The handsy one.

HelenOfJoy Allan Jefferson, Chris Munoz

32

I'M SITTING WITH NANA on the couch and deleting messages on my phone. Most came in earlier, when I was doing homework, but they seemed to trickle off. I can't believe kids are still messaging me nasty stuff, but they are. I don't even read what they say, I just delete and block. I almost miss Joey's text in the flood of mean messages. He sent it an hour ago.

I am truly sorry
I never meant to hurt you or cause everyone
so much pain
I let you down
I know you tried
It's just too hard

It's okay, I text back.

He doesn't answer. I call and leave a voice mail and wait a few minutes, but he doesn't call back.

"Joey sent a weird text," I say to Nana, my voice tentative. "He sounds strange. And he's not texting or calling me back."

"He's probably feeling ashamed," she says. "Call him at work. He should be there now, yes? He can't not take a call at the hoagie shop. He's the one who answers the phone!"

But it's Hank who answers, his voice clipped and professional. "Hank's Hoagies, here to help with your hunger needs."

"Hi, Hank, it's Emory, Joey's sister."

"Oh, hello there, Emory. I hope Joey's feeling better. He wasn't looking too good."

"Wait, is he there?"

"No, he said he felt sick. I sent him home."

"When?"

"About two hours ago. Is everything all right?"

"I'm at home, but he's not here."

A pause. "Well, I sent him home because he said he felt sick. He looked sick."

My brain is moving slow and fast all at once. "Sick like what?"

"Oh, a little sweaty. Dazed. Fluish, or something. Moving slow. Lots of people getting sick this time of year. Always happens."

I click off.

It's just too hard, Joey texted.

Nana turns the television down. "What? What is it?"

"Joey left work early two hours ago. He said he was coming home.

"Mom!" I yell, jumping up from the couch and running into the kitchen. "Mom!"

My mother's hands are clutched together as the police take notes in our living room. Nana has called my dad and he's on his way back from the hospital.

My mom is giving them Joey's work outfit description, his height and weight, hair color. They ask if he's been having any problems lately, something that would make him stay away from the house. "Teenagers, am I right, Mrs. Ward? It's always something. Maybe he'll cool off, come back tomorrow. You might want to try contacting his friends. See if they've heard anything."

"He's in recovery for opioid addiction, Ted," my mother says. Sometimes I forget she knows everyone in this town, practically. "I think that should be an issue here. We did have an argument earlier today."

She told him she was disappointed in him, I think. *I let you down,* he said.

I'm standing off to the side, by the front picture window. I want to be right here in case he drives up.

"I understand. We can make the rounds of some places. Make some inquiries. Is there anyone who might know where he went? Someone familiar with his patterns?"

"He kept a low profile," my mother says. "We tried to keep him busy. We didn't want him associating with those people anymore. We did put a tracker on his phone."

The two cops look at each other. "That's good. We can work with that," says Ted.

"Maybe someone from his past? A close friend he might turn to?" That's the shorter policeman.

No one knew Joey like Luther Leonard. I get up and walk into the den and text Jeremy.

Jeremy

Oh my god are you ok? It's been a crazy day.

I know. Listen, Joey's missing. Can you call Luther?
Is that a thing? And ask him where Joey might have
gone? He might have an idea. The cops want to know.

. . .

Emory, I'm sorry. I can't.

Why???

. . .

**Because Luther got out last week. He turned
eighteen. He got his release packet and we haven't
heard from him. At all.**

Oh, god. Oh, no. Not Luther Leonard. Joey wouldn't.
Would he?

"Mom," I say, coming back into the room.

"Emory"—she holds up her hand—"I'm speaking with the
officers."

"Mom."

"*What,* Emory?"

"Luther Leonard got out of juvie last week. He turned eighteen. And he's the only one who might know where Joey is,
only no one knows where Luther is."

Ted, the tall cop, rubs his neck. "The Leonard kid? I should
think he'd be long gone. Boy made some pretty big enemies
last June."

The bag of drugs he never delivered. I wanted him to turn
right, he wanted to turn left, and instead, we flew into the air.

"I have to tell you, ma'am, these things can sometimes drag
out, especially at this age. And kids, they tend to protect their
friends, at least for a while. We'll head down to Hank's and see
if we can suss anything out and ask around town and we'll let
you know."

My mother gets up and walks them to the front door.

289

"There's nothing we can do but wait," she says when she comes back in.

"We can drive around," I say. "Go to Frost Bridge, the river, ask around. Anything. We don't have to just sit here."

"Emory, this has been an exhausting day and I think we should stay put. He's seventeen. He's probably . . ."

I know what she wants to say. That he's getting high.

And that's what we should be worried about, but I don't think she wants to say it out loud.

"Blowing off steam," she finishes. "After our fight. I'm sorry I said what I said. Sometimes we don't say exactly the right things. And I don't want you traipsing around town after what happened. It might not be safe for you, either."

Nana takes my arm. "She's right, Emmy. We'll want to be here when he comes back. He'll come back."

I text Max deVos.

> Have you seen Joey?

He texts right back.

Nah, what's up I heard Roly sucker punched him

> We can't find him

Oh no, that's bad, I'm sorry

> . . .

I'll let you know Emory if I see him or anything

> . . .

I just wanted to be his friend again

I'm helping Nana get ready for bed when my dad calls. My stomach is in knots and I've been shaking all day, wondering if Joey is okay, where he is, if he's high or hurt.

"Emmy," Dad says. "I need you and your mother to come down to the hoagie shop. The police found . . . something."

"Dad, what? Did they find Joey? Is it bad?" I hold my breath. Please let him be okay. Please let him be okay.

There's a silence.

"Just come down, please. Right away."

My dad is waiting for us in the brightly lit entryway of Hank's Hoagies.

"Abigail, it's not good. I just want to warn you."

"Neil." My mother's face turns gray. She looks like she might vomit. I take her arm.

"He's not dead," my dad says, "it's just not . . . good."

He turns the CLOSED sign around on the door and leads us behind the counter to an office in the back. Hank and his wife are in there with the police.

"I remembered," Hank says sadly, wringing his fingers. "The surveillance cameras. I have them trained on the back alley and the front register."

He presses a button and we watch the tiny television.

The camera is wavery at first and then shifts into focus.

"I had him in the back at first, making sandwiches, because of his face. Did he get in a fight? Horrible bruise," Hank says.

"But I moved him to the front, just for a little while, so I could take a break."

There's Joey at the front counter, taking orders, his orange cap askew, his shirt untucked. Handing out sacks of hoagies, wiping the counter down. Staring off into space. He looks . . . resigned.

Like all the energy has been drained out of him.

And then he stands up straighter. Holds his head a little back, like he's afraid of what he sees. Looks back toward the kitchen. Turns back to the counter.

A figure approaches the counter, dressed all in black. Black knit cap, black hoodie, black jeans. A familiar, loping walk.

Something dark on his face.

An eye patch.

"That's Luther," I say softly. "Luther Leonard."

Joey backs away from the counter, but Luther leans across it, on his elbows, like he has all day. Like he came in to shoot the breeze.

I can barely breathe, watching this.

"I'm very sorry," Hank tells us. "There's no sound."

We watch as Luther leans on the counter, talking. Joey keeps looking around, shaking his head.

But Luther stays. And gradually, Joey steps closer to the counter. His face is down. I can't read his expression.

Luther glances around casually and reaches into his pocket.

Slides something across the counter to Joey.

The cops sigh. "Yeah," Ted says matter-of-factly. "There you go."

The little baggie sits on the orange counter between Joey and Luther.

Luther holds his hands up, backs away, disappears from the camera's view.

Then it's just Joey, alone with the baggie of drugs.

I feel like all of us have stopped breathing. I feel like my heart is in my throat.

Don't do it, I think. Don't do it. Make us wrong.

My mother starts to cry. "I can't," she says. "I just can't."

She leaves the office.

Slowly, Joey reaches out and places his hand over the baggie. Puts it into his pocket. Turns around and disappears into the back of the hoagie shop.

No. No. *No.*

"He went on a restroom break," Hank says. "So I came back and covered the register."

In the video, Hank is at the counter now, wiping it down, tidying up the napkin dispenser.

How many minutes are passing between the moment Joey stops being the Joey we know now and becomes the Joey we knew last year? I can't tell.

I think of what he told me. Feeling wings spreading inside himself. Like he was loved, but also didn't care if he was loved.

That he's probably thinking since he already slipped once, why would it matter now?

I let you down.

Joey appears back on camera. Hank stays for a minute.

"I was asking if he was okay. He looked paler. He said he was all right. I'm sorry." Hank is twisting his orange Hank's Hoagies cap in his hands.

Hank leaves the register and Joey restocks napkins, takes orders, and slowly, I begin to see it.

We can all see it.

The way his movements get slower. Each punch of the register keys takes longer than the one before. He starts weaving back and forth. He slumps forward, his head drifting to the counter. A customer waves his hands and Hank comes out, pats Joey on the back.

"He looked very sick, like I said. The flu. A stomach thing. I told him to go home."

"I'm a doctor," my dad says softly. "It's probably heroin. He's about to throw up. And after that, he'll either be very, very high, or very, very dead. Oh, Joey."

My dad's voice cracks. He reaches for my hand, holds it hard.

"And then he left," Hank says. "You can see from the alley view, right here, that he gets in his car and drives away."

One of the policemen is taking notes. "We'll track his cell, but he probably ditched it after texting his sister. And we can keep a lookout for the car, but in my experience, he's probably going to sell it for parts for quick money. Chop shop or something. Whatever he can get."

"How would he even know how to do that?" my father asks.

Ted the tall cop shrugs. "You'd be surprised. People and drugs . . . it's like living a double life."

Caroline shakes her head. "This is so very sad. So many people like this now. Here, in Mill Haven, of all places."

"Did you check the register, Hank? Any money missing?"

"He's not a *thief*," my father says.

"It's not him, sir," says Ted. "It's his addiction. People do what they have to."

Hank says, "The money is fine. It's already been counted. I do hope you find him soon, though. It's his birthday in four days. See, I have the employee birthday calendar right here. We buy a cake, sing a song."

"It's a real nice time," Caroline adds.

He shows us a tiny desk calendar. Someone has drawn a birthday cake and written *Joey* on the date.

My dad sucks in his breath, hard.

"What?" I say. "What?"

"He turns eighteen," my father says, his voice barely a whisper. "And then it's no longer a priority to look for him. He's an adult. He can do as he pleases. Isn't that right?"

I squeeze my dad's hand.

If we don't find Joey soon, we'll lose him forever.

The policemen look at each other and then my dad.

"That's correct," Ted says kindly. "He wouldn't be a priority. He's eighteen and he can go wherever he likes."

My mother sits in silence in the backseat as we drive home. The not-talking is killing me. I want them to say something, do something, anything, so we don't have to sit in the silence anymore.

"Dad," I say suddenly. "Turn here."

"Why?"

"It's the bridge. Where the ghosties are. Let me check. Maybe he's there."

"Emory," my mother says sharply. "That's dangerous. I can't have you going down there. That's for the police."

"Dad," I say, ignoring her, my voice hard. "Turn, let me look."

My dad puts the turn signal on.

"Neil!"

"He's our *son*, Abigail."

He parks in the dirt lot that overlooks Frost Bridge and the river.

You can see them from there. Tarps and tents, shopping carts and sleeping bags. A few fires in metal trash cans, flickering in the light rain.

"We'll be right back," my dad tells my mom. "Text Nana. Let her know what's happening."

My father and I get out of the car and pick our way down the wet, worn path in the dark, stepping over crushed soda cups. Condoms. Needles.

"Be careful," he says.

But I don't care. I just want to get down to the site, to see if Joey is there.

"Emmy," my father says. "Don't just go barreling in there."

I turn around. "Dad, I want to find Joey. Don't *you*?"

"I do, Emory." He takes a deep breath. "But this is their *home*. It's not just something you barge into. You wouldn't like it if someone just broke down our door, would you? You can show respect."

Some of them are looking at us.

"Excuse me," my dad says, stepping in front of me protectively. "I'm sorry to bother you. I'm looking for my son. Tall kid named Joey. Wearing an orange shirt? From the hoagie shop on Main? Short hair, kind of messy. Got in a fight, has a bruised cheek."

Spent needles gleam around the edges of my dad's shoes. I shrink a little behind him.

There must be fifty people down here. It's hard to tell in the dark, and some of them are sleeping huddled together. All of them are wet from spending the day in the rain.

A woman stands up. "I haven't seen anyone like that today. I've been here since around noon."

Her face is dirty.

"Can you, maybe, if you do see him, ask him to come home, please?" I say.

"I sure will," the woman says. Her voice is pleasant, like we're talking about the weather and not some messed-up missing kid.

My father nods. "Thank you. Thank you so much."

"You think you could help out a bit?" the woman says.

My father looks startled. "Yes, of course."

He peels some bills out of his wallet and hands them to the woman.

"Bless you," she says. She takes the bills, counts them, tucks them inside her jacket.

My father hesitates, looking around at all the people. The flickering fire. The empty soup cans. Rolls of toilet paper, right out in the open, next to sleeping bags and blankets.

A couple of people get up and stand next to the woman.

There are so many people down here. Like my dad said, this is their *home*. In the cold rain. Freezing and huddling together for warmth.

My father makes a little sound in his throat, looking at all of them.

Then he takes the rest of the money from his wallet and clears some of the needles aside with his sneaker. He spreads out his handkerchief on the ground and lays the money on it carefully, so it's not dirty from the ground when they pick it up.

"Thank you," he says. "For your help."

*　　*　　*

Back in the car, he sits for a long time, watching them.

He turns around to face my mother. Her face is frightened, which scares me, because she's never frightened. Or at least, she doesn't show it.

"Look at these people, Abigail. This is our *town*. *Your* town."

My mother's voice is soft. "I don't understand what you expect me to *do*, Neil."

My dad's voice falters as he turns back around.

"Well, I'm not sure, Abigail," he says tightly. "But those people need help, or this is the place they will die."

Then he starts the car and takes us home.

I pace in my room, Fuzzy nervously darting in between my legs. I feel weird, like I can't get a fix on myself. Like I'm floating away from myself. Not real.

When my phone flashes, I'm so startled I almost drop it. It's Maddie, video calling.

"What the hell happened?" she asks. "Mom texted me and then suddenly the police are calling me, asking me if I've heard from Joey."

I sit down on my bed. "He's gone. He and Mom had a fight and . . . we went to Hank's Hoagies and watched the surveillance video. Maddie, Luther was there."

My sister's face crumples. "Oh, shit, no."

"He handed him drugs over the counter and Joey took them and then . . . he left. He disappeared."

"Well, where the fuck is Luther? He's probably with him. Tell the police to find him."

"I think they'll try, but who knows where he might be. He could be anywhere."

"I'm not sure what to do. I should probably stay here, right? In case he, I don't know, heads out here? I mean, shit, what should I do?"

"I don't know. I guess? I mean, he might go anywhere."

"Maddie." I hate the way my voice sounds so small.

"What?"

"I . . . Joey got high the night of the dance. I didn't tell Mom and Dad."

She's quiet. "I get that. You probably thought you could fix it."

"Should I tell them now?"

Maddie blows air slowly. "I don't know. Maybe. Maybe not. I mean, what's it going to solve at this point?"

"I don't know." I say. "I don't know what to do. About anything."

"It's okay, Emmy. Just sit tight. And take care of Mom. She's going to put on a tough act or she's going to go quiet. Either way, take it easy on her."

"Okay."

"Love you, Emmy-bear," she says.

"Love you, too."

As soon as Maddie hangs up, I start texting Joey, over and over. The police said he'd ditch his phone, but maybe he hasn't yet. There's always a chance. That I can reach him.

> Come back
> Please come home
> I love you
> We'll help you
> We saw the tape with Luther and we just want
> you to come home

Please Joey
Answer me
Come home
Answer me
Answer me
Answer me

I'm startled awake on the couch by my phone. I slept down here last night. Upstairs felt too empty, without Joey. I wanted to be by the front door again, too, in case he drove up the driveway or walked up the stoop.

It's Daniel.

"Things are very weird here at Heywood High," he says. He sounds out of breath.

"Joey's missing," I tell him. "He . . . it's a long story, but he relapsed. Again."

"What? Oh, god, I'm sorry. What can I do?"

"I don't know. Maybe ask around school. See if anyone has seen him or knows where he is?"

"Okay, I'll try. I'm sorry. That's bad, Emmy."

"I know." I try to keep my voice from breaking.

He sighs. "Hey, I don't know how she knew what to do, but she knew. She really did it. This place is going batshit."

"What? Who?"

"Liza. She organized this whole Hester Prynne thing. Instagram callout or something. There's, like, so many girls walking around with giant red, well, I guess I should say, *scarlet,* letters on their shirts. And flyers on the lockers with guys' names on them. Guys who . . . you know . . . did stuff, or talked about it, spread stuff, about girls. And now everybody's ganging up on

Roly Martin. I guess it was him who found Gage's phone and posted the pictures of you."

I don't know if I should feel weird or proud, listening to this. Mostly, I can't feel anything because I'm too scared about Joey. All of this, the photos, Gage, it seems very far away now.

"That's wild," I say slowly. "I guess *The Scarlet Letter* came in handy after all."

"I know," he says. "And whenever teachers take attendance, people, even some guys, are answering 'No shame' instead of 'here.' Nobody's talking about you anymore. Well, sort of, but in a different way."

No shame. "I don't know what to say," I tell Daniel.

"It's a little overwhelming," he answers. "I just hope you're okay."

But I don't know how I can be okay, with Joey out there, somewhere.

"Daniel, Joey's friend, Luther . . . you know, Jeremy's brother? Went to Joey's work and gave him drugs. That's how I know he relapsed. We saw the video," I say. "That's what happened. He's gone."

It hurts to say it, about the drugs.

"I'm sorry, Emory."

"I'm going to look for him."

"How?" he asks. "Where?"

"I don't know, Daniel. I just don't know. But I'll figure it out somehow."

I hang up with Daniel and look out our front window, at the sloping streets and fine houses and pretty lawns. Joey could be anywhere out there, and I have to find a way to bring him back.

33

M Y MOM IS IN her bedroom with an ice pack on her head and my dad is at the hospital. I'm scrolling through my phone, looking for more people, anyone, that I can message that might know where Joey is, or where he would go.

Then I see it. Shadow's number.

Joey's Blue Spruce counselor.

"Pick up, pick up," I mutter, listening to the phone ring on his end.

"Shadow Glenn." His voice is casual, like it's an ordinary day for him out in Colorado, while my world is upside down.

"Hi," I say hesitantly. "This is . . . this is Joey Ward's sister, Emory. I don't . . . I don't know if you remember him? He was there this past summer. We talked on the phone. You and me."

Please remember me.

There's a pause. "Yes, Emory, hello. It's so nice to hear from you. Is everything all right?"

"No," I say, my voice cracking. "No, everything isn't all right. At all."

I hear him breathe in deeply. There's a murmuring in the background where he is. People talking, dishes clanking.

"What's happened?" he asks.

"Joey's missing," I tell him. "Two days. Um . . . has he called you?"

"The last time I heard from him was a few weeks ago. We

chatted. He was having a bit of a hard time and I think our talk helped."

My heart sinks. Joey talked to him a few weeks ago. He must have been hurting more than he could let me know.

Shadow pauses.

"I was afraid something like this might happen," he says. "I'm sorry to say that."

"What?" I say. "Why?"

"He sounded a bit hesitant and lost. That's not unusual in itself, but he was remote in a way that worried me."

"Okay, well, now we can't find him and . . . I don't . . . I'm not sure what to do. We called the police, we did all that, but he turns eighteen in two days and if he isn't found, they won't look for him anymore."

I take a breath. "He did some Oxy. A couple of days ago. And the place he was at when he disappeared, his work . . . they had a video camera and it showed one of his old friends coming in and giving him something in a baggie over the counter. Joey took it."

"Emory. I'm so sorry. I really am. I know how hard this is." Shadow sighs. "Relapse is very, very common, especially in the first year. Recovery isn't an exact science and it's not one size fits all."

"But what . . . what should we do? You have to help me." My voice sounds desperate. I *am* desperate.

"Joey will come home when he's ready," Shadow says. "I can't advise you to go looking for him. I wouldn't want you to put yourself in harm's way."

"But I have to get him back. I have to help him. Tell me what to *do*," I beg.

"Hope."

"What?" I say, unsure if I heard him right.

"Hope. Keep hoping. If you pray, keep him in your prayers. If you have the means, make flyers and put them up around town. Make a social media account. Post his picture and messages to him. You never know when he might try to look you up. You never know who might see it and contact you and give you information about where he is. You just don't know."

"But that's not . . . I need something definite," I say, choking back tears.

"There are no definites in recovery, Emory. You have to throw that way of thinking out the window. I've seen people come in here and they leave and they don't use for twenty years and one day they wake up and go buy a hit on the street corner and they're right back where they started. I've seen people go through recovery several times over. I've had kids come in here in the worst shape and they leave and five years later, they're still in recovery, still sober, taking it day by day. You just never know. The only thing you know is to never stop hoping."

"So I just . . . wait?"

"What time is it there?" he asks. "It's a school day, right?"

"Yeah, but I'm at home. I want to be here in case he comes back."

"I would go to school. I would do the best I could, do my homework. But I would go to school. He might go there, looking for you. And if you aren't there, he might leave. Do what you normally do. And hope. But you can't stop living while you wait. You have to learn how to do both at the same time, or you'll be in no shape to help him when he asks for help."

"I just can't . . . I can't believe he took the baggie. From his friend."

"It happens, Emory. He's not a failure. He's wired differently than you are."

"What does that mean?"

"From what I understand, Joe was put on some behavioral drugs pretty early on, and then he suffered an injury, which led to painkillers. What was he, eleven? It's not really a great idea to push pharmaceuticals on young kids. Brains are in development until our midtwenties. When you add drugs to a developing brain, we don't learn how to read our own signals naturally. We follow the signal of the drug. And sometimes addiction is genetic."

I think back to when Joey told me he had a broken receptor in his brain.

"I know this is complicated and painful," Shadow says. "I can talk to some counselors here and some of Joey's team members from his group. I'll let them know to be on the lookout. And you can call me anytime you want."

"That's it?" I say. I feel deflated and lost.

"I'm afraid that's it, Emory. It's all about waiting now. And hope."

I hold the phone in my lap.

Then I open up Instagram. The last time I posted was last Christmas, just a silly photo. Maddie and Joey in the matching red pajamas our mom still likes to buy for us every year at Christmas. Like we're her little kids forever.

They're in front of the tree, sticking out their tongues, surrounded by piles of prettily wrapped packages. It was a rare good day. My dad was home. We were all home.

I upload a picture of Joey, from that day at Nana's, with the leaves, when he looked happy.

This is my brother, Joey Ward. He's seventeen, almost eighteen. He's missing. If you see him, please let me know. His hair has been longer. He was wearing an orange Hank's Hoagies shirt. He lives in Mill Haven. Joey if you see this, please come home. #missingkids #millhaven #joeyward

I post it.
I do the same thing on Twitter and Facebook.
Please come home.

34

M Y DAD DROPS ME off at school the next morning. He has
a stack of flyers with Joey's photo that he's going to post
around town.

I walk through the parking lot in a daze. Nobody is calling
me names now.

When I walk into school, I see Joey's friend Noah, the one he
did Oxy with at the dance. When he sees me coming, he walks
faster, but I catch up with him, force him against the lockers.

"Have you seen Joey?" I ask. "Tell me the truth. I know you
guys got high together. I know what you gave him."

He's a skinny kid with dark circles under his eyes. He holds
his hands up. "Don't blame me, I didn't force him. And I don't
know where he is. The cops were already here yesterday and I
got pulled into the office to talk to them. A bunch of us did.
Nobody knows, I swear."

I search his face. He looks scared.

I believe him.

I push away from him.

There are a bunch of kids staring at me.

"If anybody knows where Joey is, please tell me," I say. "He's
my *brother.*"

Heads shake, people back away.

So awful, someone murmurs as I walk away. *So horrible.*

Like Joey is already dead.

I sit in my classes like a ghost. The teachers give me sad looks. Daniel and Liza and Jeremy are quiet with me at lunch. They repost Joey's photo on their own social feeds.

In Drama Club, Simon Stanley touches my shoulder in a kind way. "I'll keep my eyes peeled," he says.

"I don't know if I can do the variety show," I say.

"I understand. If you change your mind, let me know."

The gentleness in his eyes makes me want to cry.

When my dad comes to pick me up, I ask him if we can wait awhile before driving home.

"Why?"

I twist my fingers together. "Please don't get mad, but I called his counselor at Blue Spruce. There was this day, after Joey came home from rehab, and he was having a hard time and he called him, the counselor. Shadow. That's his name. And Shadow wanted to talk to me. He said I could call him anytime."

My dad shakes his head. "I'm not mad. I hadn't thought of that. Of calling them. That was a good decision, Emmy."

"Anyway, he said to just keep coming to school and stuff, because maybe Joey would show up here. So maybe we should sit here for a little bit. In case he comes here. He'd know I'd be getting out of Drama Club right about now, you know?"

My dad turns off the car.

"Yes, we can wait, Emmy. We can wait for a little bit."

We sit in the car until it's dark out and the lot lights pop on, yellowy and harsh, but Joey doesn't come.

Then my father starts the car and we drive home.

35

M Y DAD SITS IN his den, making more flyers. My mom has
gone to sleep and Nana is nodding off on the couch, Fuzzy
in her lap. I'm awake. I haven't done any homework or eaten
and I don't care. I'm just sitting with my phone, endlessly typing words.

Texting Joey.

Please come home
I miss you
I love you
Come back
Please come back home

36

WHEN I GET THE mail the next afternoon, there's a letter addressed to me from Arizona, but no name. I'm so excited to open it because it might be Joey, of course it could be, maybe it's *possible* he drove all the way there, right? Anything could be possible.

I almost rip the letter in half opening it.

But the letter isn't from Joey.

Dear Emory,

I know you probably don't want to hear from me, but I needed to write this letter. First, I want you to know that I didn't share those pictures. I never showed them to anyone else. I forgot to delete them. I should have done that right away when you asked, but I forgot. I just forgot. I'm sorry for that. Roly Martin found my phone on the field and he is the one who shared the photos. I am really sorry for the embarrassment and trouble that caused.

I'm in Arizona at the physical rehabilitation center. I'm not sure how long I'll be here or even whether it will work. I'm not mad about it, even though my parents and the whole thing about your mom paying for this might make it seem that way. I hope everything works out, but I have to face that it might not.

I don't really want to talk about myself here. I just wanted to tell you that I'm sorry for what happened with us. I'm not sorry for knowing you and how we were together, but I'm sorry for leading you on. I did things the wrong way. I didn't ever want to hurt you. I just want you to know that.

Your friend, Gage

Your friend.

I keep staring at those words. His handwriting is shaky. I guess he used his left hand, since his right arm is messed up. Maybe it hurts him too much to write with it.

I think of the way his hands felt on me, soft and sometimes tentative and sometimes sure, and the way I felt all sorts of things: electric and seen and full of pleasure. How I would have done anything for that feeling, and did.

I wish I could feel that way now, to make all the awfulness inside me go away.

But I can't. I just have to sit here, and feel all of it. Every last horrible thing.

37

LIZA MUNCHES HER SLICE of pizza. "I'm just not feeling it," she says. "You seem wooden."

"You *think*?" I answer.

Daniel leans back in the recliner in my room. "I have to say I agree. No offense, but your presentation needs work."

"No," Jeremy says, looking up from his comic book. "She'll be fine. The right lighting and costume, that can all help. I can do that part. That's my specialty. The little touches."

I throw the Ophelia monologue on my bed. "I can't do this."

"You can," says Liza.

"I can't. For one thing, I'm not good at public speaking, and two, I kind of have other things on my mind at the moment, if you haven't forgotten."

They all look at each other.

"Think of it as a respite," Daniel says. "Something to do to let your mind rest a little. You could read from *The Portrait of a Lady*."

"I don't think I'm compelling enough to pull off the density of Henry James onstage, Daniel."

"Oh, I think you're compelling enough." He grins.

I look at Jeremy. "Have you . . ."

He shakes his head. "No, I haven't heard from Luther. I'm not going to, Emmy. I'm sorry."

I check my feeds to see if anyone has commented on my posts about Joey.

Nothing. A few people responded when I first posted, about seeing someone who maybe looked like him down by Frost Bridge, or by Hank's Hoagies, and my dad and I drove around, but we didn't see him. Some people just make rude comments, but I delete them. Joey's eighteenth birthday has come and gone. My mother and father haven't mentioned it, and I don't want to tell my friends, because they're trying to be supportive, but it's a hole inside of me, this feeling that Joey has slipped far, far away from us.

I lay my phone carefully back on the bed, make sure the volume is up, so I can hear it in case he calls or texts.

"You should do something," Liza says. "Anything. You used to play piano. Play something."

"I haven't played in a long, long time," I tell her. "I'm not near ready enough for that."

"Simon said you could write something yourself, didn't he?" Daniel scratches Fuzzy's head. Fuzzy has a thing for Daniel, I think.

"Yeah."

"Well, what would you write about?" Liza asks.

"I don't know."

"Well, what are you feeling?" She picks some pepperoni off her slice and pops it into her mouth.

"I've never understood that," Daniel says. "You're literally eating a slice of pepperoni pizza, which has the pepperoni on it, yet you take *off* the pepperoni and eat that separately."

"You eat your pizza your way and I'll eat my pizza my way," Liza tells him. "Emmy, what are you *feeling*?"

"I'm feeling . . . a lot. Too many things. I miss Joey. I'm worried about Joey. I want Joey to come home. I'm worried about my parents and I'm mad at my parents. I'm mad at myself for messing up with Joey. Not doing better. I miss Gage, in a weird way, not because of liking him, but because I miss . . . I miss being touched. Everything was messed up about that situation, but I needed it. And I think that makes me like Joey, that I let it go on, even though it wasn't healthy, because I just wanted to feel *better*. And I'm mad that I got called a slut for that, but I'm also weirdly happy you came up with the idea of Hester Prynning the school, because I feel less alone. I'm mad that Lucy Kerr called Joey a druggie and a loser."

Liza puts down her pizza slice.

"Then write that."

"What? No."

"No," says Daniel. "She's right. Write something like that. A monologue. A poem."

"People will think I'm a freak," I protest.

"Trust me, you don't really have anything to lose at Heywood High at this point," Jeremy says. "People have seen you naked."

I give him a look.

"I mean, not me," he says quickly. "I would never."

"I looked," Daniel says.

"Are you kidding?" I ask him.

"Sort of," he laughs. "I deleted it before I got a good look. I promise. It's all a blur, really. A very pleasing blur."

"Enough," Liza says. "Write it. You like poetry. Do it like that."

"I like poetry," I say. "I don't *write* it."

"I might be able to help you with that." Liza smiles.

This is my brother Joey Ward. He's been missing
for ten days. He was last seen at Hank's Hoagies on
Main Street in Mill Haven. He was wearing an orange
shirt. His hair has been longer. He may be confused
or disoriented because of drug use. If you have seen
him, please let me know. Joey, if you are reading this,
please come home. I miss you. I love you. I am going
to be at Heywood High tomorrow night at 8 p.m. if you
want to come there. Please let me help you.

I CAN'T SLEEP AFTER POSTING. I lie awake, looking at the ceiling, all sorts of images of Joey running through my head. Joey
lying in the woods, high or hurt. Joey wandering in the streets
somewhere, shivering in the cold. Did he have his hoodie when
he went to Hank's for his shift? What if he's not warm enough?
What if . . .

I don't want to think that last thought. That one makes my
stomach twist into a ball of fire. I jump out of bed and make my
way downstairs.

My dad is in his den, standing by his printer. Flyer after flyer
shoots out with Joey's face and HAVE YOU SEEN ME?

"Dad?"

He turns to me. "Emory. It's late, honey."

"I could say the same for you."

He takes off his glasses and rubs his eyes. "I'm just printing some more of these up. I might take a drive tomorrow and post some in other towns. It might be time to think about Joey not being in Mill Haven anymore."

He hesitates. "I talked to the police a little while ago," he admits. "They found his car in Franklin Township. Stripped of parts. His phone was in the car. I won't tell your mother until the morning. She needs to rest."

Franklin Township is about thirty miles away from Mill Haven. And his phone. All my texts . . . disappearing into the ether. I cover my face with my hands, holding my tears in.

"It could be anything," my dad says quickly. "Maybe he sold the car here or traded it to someone and they left it out there. Who knows?"

I uncover my face, sit down in the leather chair across from him. It's a beautiful den. Built-in bookshelves with his medical textbooks and my mother's law books. We have such a beautiful life on paper.

"I don't know how Mom can sleep," I say. "I feel like I'm splitting apart."

"Don't be hard on her, Emory. She spends the days calling hospitals to see if he'd been admitted. She's splitting apart, too. He's our *child*. That's . . . I don't even know how to explain it. It's just . . . a very raw kind of *missing*, what we feel right now."

The printer chugs to a stop and he takes the flyers, fitting them into a neat stack.

"I'm going to watch my baking show now," he says. "Do you want to sit with me, since you can't sleep? You have your show tomorrow night. You need to rest, just a little."

"Okay," I say.

I follow him into the living room and he flicks on the flat-screen and sits on the leather sofa, pats the seat next to him and dims the lights.

"Don't you . . . don't you want your drink?" I ask tentatively. "You usually have a drink when you watch your shows."

My father shakes his head. "No, no, I don't think so, Emory. I don't think I want that."

He opens his arm and I fit myself in. His body is warm.

"Dad," I say. "Just in case, is your phone charged? Do you have it?" I hold up my phone.

"Yes," he says. "Yes. I have it, just in case."

39

I 'M WATCHING LUCY KERR sing a song from *Hamilton* in honor of Candy MontClair. She's wearing a light blue period costume and her hair is up and gleams in the lights that Jeremy Leonard so expertly controls. When she's done, there is thunderous applause.

"I can't do this," I whisper to Simon Stanley in the wings. "I can't go out there."

"You *can,*" he says. "I know you can. Breathe in, relax, remember that they aren't seeing you, they are seeing the person on the stage reading the poem. They aren't looking at you. They're listening to the words."

"But the words are *about* me."

"Emory," he says. "Sometimes you just have to speak up."

Liza is onstage. She's the emcee. She's saying my name.

Polite applause.

Simon Stanley nudges me ever so slightly, and then a bit harder, and then there isn't any turning back, because I'm already out there, under the lights, walking slowly to my mark.

I swallow hard. It's actually a little difficult to see the people in the audience. They just seem like so many floating heads staring at me, probably thinking of the photos, laughing silently at me, but it's too late now. I scan for Joey anyway, especially along the sides of the auditorium and in the back, by the doors. He might be there, in the shadows. He might have seen my post, somewhere, on someone's phone or laptop. He might have come.

My mom and dad are here, but I'm not sure where. Nana is at home, her phone by her side, watching television. Waiting.

I don't see him. My heart is like a drum.

I adjust the microphone. It squeaks. Someone in the audience says, "Yeesh."

"I don't have a title for this poem," I say softly. In the wings, I can see Liza in the corner of my eye, motioning me to step closer to the mike, so I do. Above me, the lights dim until it's just me in a spotlight, exposed and alone.

The paper is shaking in my hands.

I take a deep breath.

> *A girl walks onto the stage and you are thinking*
> *She will deliver you poetry, some rare beauty*
> *That will sink inside your heart and live there*
> *And help you live your days.*
> *You'll fashion a story for her sad eyes*
> *That fits how you need to see her.*

> *I am a girl on a stage and I have nothing beautiful for you.*
> *I am a girl on a stage and you think you know my story*
> *But how can you know my story when*
> *I haven't even written it yet*
> *When I haven't had a chance to live it yet*
> *How can you know my story*
> *When you don't even know me*

I stood in a window and looked at a boy
And felt pleasure and you wrote the story
Of slut and whore

My family built a mill that built this town
And you wrote the story of
Rich bitch and conceited

A girl had a headache at a party
And I offered her a ride home on a rainy night
In a car driving too fast and you wrote
The story of murderer

You've never asked how it felt
To listen to her breathing in the backseat
To say her name and receive no answer
And to know an act of kindness
Would be taken and twisted by the universe

I am your pleasure, your sport
Because you think I have everything
And can lose nothing

But I have lost the one thing I never wanted to
I have lost my brother
And people call that story

Addict and junkie and loser
And you close the book on me, and him.
You have read us the way you wanted to
And put us back on the shelf

But I'm not done with that story yet
I would walk naked down Main Street
In front of a thousand people
If it would bring my brother back
Let you shout murderer and slut and whore and rich bitch
Until my eyes bleed and my ears shatter
If it would bring him home to me
I would do all of those things
All of my days
With all of my heart
Because it would matter
I will do all of these things
Because I am not ready to say The End
Because I don't want to die
With a question burning in my heart:
Did I try as hard as I could to live
In service of the poets and saints
Who ask us
To live with our whole hearts
Who ask us to believe in impossible things
Who ask us to never stop loving the stars
Who ask us to never stop writing our stories

Then the spotlight goes dark.

40

I HAVE TO WADE THROUGH throngs of parents and students in the hallway after the show to find my parents. Part of me is searching for Joey, too, just in case. But he's not there.

People sneak looks at me. Murmur. I know they think we've gotten what we deserved. They're like Hank, thinking we owed this town, and now we know what it's like, to have lost something too.

My mom gives me a hug, almost too tight, and I want to wiggle away, but then I remember what Dad said last night about how parents feel a special kind of missing for their children.

She finally pulls away. "That was lovely, Emory. Hard, but lovely. I'm very proud of you."

I'm not sure she's ever said that to me in my life, and my eyes well up.

My dad rubs my shoulder. "Well done."

"We should probably go," I say.

"Isn't there a cast party or something, after? Or you have to strike the set? Isn't that what usually happens after something like this?" my mother asks. "It would be all right, if you wanted to go to that."

"No. I'm good," I say. "I'm good."

*   *   *

In the parking lot, we're getting into the car when I hear my name. I whip around. Joey?

But it's not Joey. It's Daniel, jogging toward me.

"Hey," he says, smiling. "That was really great. Much better than Ophelia. And the curse words . . . chef's kiss. Betty from the Café was next to me and I thought she was going to lose it."

"Her coffee is always lukewarm," I say.

"Like her heart," Daniel answers.

I smile, and then I don't, because it feels both right and wrong to do this, to think I'm possibly flirting with someone in a parking lot when my brother is missing. I didn't know you could feel both sad and hopeful all at once, and how much the mingling of those two things would hurt.

"It was mostly Liza, you know. The poem," I say.

"But it was your feelings. It was you," he says. "It was cool."

"Thanks." I hesitate. "I thought . . . when I first heard my name out here, that it might be Joey. But it was you and I was not . . . disappointed at that."

Daniel kind of ducks his head. "Is that a good thing?"

"Yes," I say slowly. "I think it is, but it's also confusing. Do you know what I mean?"

"I do."

We stand there, in the harsh yellow light of the parking lot, our breath coming out in white puffs in the cold. In any universe but this one, we would probably kiss.

But our universe is not that one. Not right now.

Daniel takes a breath. "I'll be here a little while longer. I'll keep an eye out. I look for him, too, you know. When I go into town. Take the dog for a walk."

"You do?" A feeling of warmth spreads through me. "That's . . . amazing."

"I do. Remember when I told you I always think about a thousand different things happening at once in my body, like when I'm doing something mundane, and I don't even know it?"

"Yes. I liked that. It was an interesting thing to say, the way the world might be working against us, inside us or out."

I could probably talk to Daniel Wankel for hours.

It's like what Joey said. You should just feel comfortable talking to someone. It should come easy, not hard.

"A thousand different things could be happening right now, to get Joey back, and you don't even realize it. Things you aren't even thinking about. So, yeah, I could get up and get my dog's leash and take her to the park, and maybe he'd be there. On a bench. Walking. I don't know. But he'd be there. He'd be found. And if my dog hadn't whined at me to take her out, I never would have known. You know? Millions of infinite things that add up to a whole."

He takes my mittened hand in his. I look down at his fingerless gloves, his slightly chapped knuckles.

"That's kind of a comforting thought," I answer. "Maybe it means right now, something is happening that I don't even know that will bring Joey back, or me to him."

"I'm a comfort kind of person."

He's smiling at me in a way that makes me feel warm. A different way than with Gage. It feels nice inside me, a little piece of light inside all the darkness that is me missing Joey.

"Emory," my dad calls from the car.

"I have to go," I say.

"If you need anything, let me know, okay? I'm here," Daniel says. He lets go of my hand, turns.

"Daniel," I say. "Wait."

He turns back around, his eyes bright and wide.

"I . . ." I take a breath. "I like you. But things are also weird right now and I'm . . ."

"Emmy, I know," he says. "I'm not going anywhere. I've been here all along."

I watch him jog back to the school before I turn to get into the car.

"Who was that?" my dad asks when I get in.

"A friend," I say, my heart in my throat, but in a good way. "He does not live next door, so I promise no window pictures."

He and my mother look at each other in the front seat.

"Well, he has wonderful taste in scarves," my mother murmurs.

We're almost home when my dad makes a sharp U-turn. My mom braces her hands on the dashboard and cries out, "Neil, what are you doing?"

I'm thrown against the passenger door and have to right myself. "Dad, please. I've had enough accidents for one life-time."

"I'm not ready to go home yet," he says. "I'm not ready to just go back and sit in the house and wait and wait. I want to do *something*."

"Dad," I say. *"What?"*

"If I can't save my son tonight, I'm damn well going to save somebody, even it's just a small thing."

In the convenience store, my dad is shoving rolls of toilet paper, cans of beans, hand sanitizer, soap, and Gatorade into his basket. My mom and I can see him from the car through the big glass windows of the bright store as he moves around. At the counter, the clerk hands him a carton of cigarettes and some pints of alcohol.

"What's he doing?" she asks.

"I don't know," I say, but actually, I do. I just don't want to say, because it will scare her.

We sit, waiting, not talking about the fact that a HAVE YOU SEEN ME? flyer with Joey's face is taped to the inside of the convenience store door.

My dad comes out of the store laden with plastic bags. He opens the trunk and tosses them in.

When he gets in the car, he says, "We're going to Frost Bridge."

My mother sighs heavily. "Neil."

"Abigail."

"Don't fight," I say. "Please, not now."

At the lot to Frost Bridge, my mother says, "No, Neil, absolutely not. It's cold outside and I have on good shoes." She's huddled in the front seat.

"You have hundreds of shoes, Abigail. I'm doing what Emmy said in her poem. I'm trying to live with my whole heart here. And if I can't help Joey right now, I can help some people and so can you. Fuck your shoes and get out of the car."

I can't believe my dad just said that to my mom, so I get out of the car quickly and help with the bags from the trunk.

"Go, Dad," I say softly. "That was a *lot*."

"Some things just have to be said aloud, Emmy. Maybe none of us have been saying what we need to say."

My mother gets out of the car, drawing her coat up to her chin.

"I can't go down there," she says hesitantly. "It's steep. I'll fall."

My dad angles out his elbow. "Then I'll help you."

"They'll rob us," she whispers.

"No, they won't, Mom," I say quietly. "They're just people. They *live* here."

"Hush," my father says kindly.

I'm behind them, watching as my mother's heels sink into the dirt path. She's holding on to my dad for dear life. There's something very tender about the way he's supporting her so she doesn't stumble. He's walking with her, not in front, just like Nana said you should do.

There aren't as many people at Frost Bridge as last time and I wonder where some of them went. I don't see the same lady who was here before, who said she'd keep an eye out for Joey. I put the bags on the ground and look carefully around for a charcoal-gray hoodie, an orange Hank's Hoagies shirt, but I don't see them.

"Neil," my mother says in a low voice. "I don't like this."

"I don't care if you don't like it, Abigail. But you should see it. Don't you understand? Any one of these people could be Joey and I sure as hell hope wherever he is, somebody is bringing him food. Or water."

One by one, people are getting up, walking over to my father slowly. I help him hand out the cans of beans, the rolls of toilet paper. Everyone says thank you. Some say *God bless.* My dad lines up the hand sanitizer and water bottles, the pints of alcohol and cigarettes. He brings out a new handkerchief, lays his money down.

"Has anybody seen a boy named Joey?" I call out. "Orange shirt?"

"No, sorry, ma'am," one man says. "I haven't seen anyone like that today."

I can feel my mom deflate behind me.

"Well, if you do," my dad says, "please tell him to come home."

"Yes, sir." Murmurs from the crowd.

In the car, my mom is quiet. Finally, she says, "I don't understand why you got them cigarettes, though. Or the gin. How does that help? That just seems like exacerbating the problem."

"People go through withdrawal, Abigail. You can't expect them to do it cold turkey, in bad weather under a bridge. How does that help anything? They could get sick doing that on their own. Choke on their vomit and freeze to death. Same with cigarettes. I've got a patch on right now to help me. What do they have? Restricting addictive substances to be punitive or pious . . . that doesn't solve anything."

"Dad, you're quitting smoking?" I say. "That's really, really good."

"I am," he says grimly. "It's quite painful, but I'm determined."

"Drive slower, Neil," my mom says softly.

"Why?" my dad asks.

"I can't see the sidewalks clearly," my mom says. "I need to see the sidewalks."

"What for?" my father asks.

"Because," I say quietly from the backseat. "Because of Joey. We're looking for Joey. Just in case."

My dad nods and slows the car down.

41

Emory_Ward

Joey I didn't see you tonight
I miss you, I wish you'd come home
I wish I could say people applauded like demons
Or fiends when I was done with my poem at the show
But they didn't
I think Mom cried, but it was hard to see
But she was there with Dad
Everyone misses you
I thought maybe you would be there
I thought maybe, wherever you are
You could hear the words I was sending to you
Hear the fact of my missing you
And walk and walk and walk
Through cold nights
Back to me
So I could tell you
That all of the pieces of you
Are beautiful
And not wrong
And not shameful
I wish I didn't have to write these words
I wish I didn't have all this missing
I keep thinking how much I love you
I keep wanting love to be enough
Because if it was
You'd be home now

#missing #joeyward #millhaven #findjoey

I'M ALMOST ASLEEP WHEN I hear my door open. I look up blearily. I'm tired and drained after the show, and visiting Frost Bridge, and writing a post to Joey on Instagram that I feel like he'll never see. "Mom?" I say.

She lifts up the covers and slides in next to me, her shoulder against mine.

"Your father was trying to teach me a lesson," she says.

"Maybe," I say. "I don't know. I don't really understand adults half the time."

It feels nice, her being next to me, in the dark. Safe.

"I was thinking about what you read tonight. Do you . . . do you feel like I closed the book on your brother?"

In the dark, it's a little easier to talk to her. In the light, you can see the Look, which I'm always afraid of. "Kind of," I answer. "You just expected him to . . . be better. Right away. Like it was a thing you put on one of your lists. *Get sober.* Something to check off."

"It's the way I was raised," she says. "Work hard, don't let your problems stand in your way. Figure out how to fix them and do it." She pauses. "I loved my father, but he was a stern man."

"But Joey's not a problem to be fixed," I say softly. "He's a *person.*"

"I know that," she says. "Don't you think I know that? I just want him back. I would do anything to have him *back.*"

She's shaking next to me, her body jiggling like she's outside without a jacket in zero-degree weather.

I have never seen my mom cry like this and I think of what my dad said, the *missing* part inside her. I wrap my arms around her and hold her as tight as I can.

42

I T'S SNOWING. IT'S BEEN thirteen days since Joey disappeared.
The flakes fall slowly at first and then quickly, turning
the world outside the front window white.

My father brings wood inside from the shed, begins stacking
the logs in the fireplace. Rolls up old newspapers from a stack
next to the fireplace. Slides wooden matches against the box.
Scrape, crunch, crackle, flare. All noises seem amplified to me
because we are so quiet all the time now, waiting.

Waiting for Joey to be found. Waiting for Joey to come home.
That's our new life.

"A fire," Nana says, settling on the couch. "A fire is always
nice."

Nana is better now, more agile, and she could go home, but
she doesn't. She wants to be here, with us, and I think we need
that.

Flashes of color among the white flakes through the window. Orange, black, green. Small children in costumes and
masks, plastic pumpkins hanging from their hands. I blink,
peering harder through the glass.

How could I have forgotten?

"It's Halloween," I say. "We don't have any candy."

"We'll turn the porch lights off," my father says. "They
won't come to the door if the porch lights are off."

He dusts off his hands. "I have to go to the hospital for a

bit and then I'll be back. I'll call the police again and see if they have any updates."

He checks his watch. "Your mother should be home from the airport with Maddie in a few hours. If the snow keeps coming down, they might be delayed, but don't worry. We have enough to worry about right now."

Maddie stayed longer at school, but she's finally coming home for a few days.

"Early in the year for snow," Nana says. "Maybe a hard winter ahead."

I think of Joey out in the world. In the cold. Shivering and high. Unsafe, far from me.

I make popcorn in the kitchen. Every time my phone flashes, I pick it up, because it might be him, but it isn't. It's Daniel, or Liza, or Jeremy, but I don't answer, because I'm tired of talking, of texting.

Hopeless. Empty. Like nothing I do to make things better will matter anyway.

It's a burning feeling, living with a missing person inside you. A ghost hole, a nefarious, sharp pain.

Nana flips through the channels. Sports, a cooking show. Enthusiastic people renovating homes, ripping out perfectly good cabinets. What is good enough for one person is not good enough for another.

I stoke the fire. The heat feels nice, making me drowsy. I'm so very tired.

I must have fallen asleep, because Nana is shaking me.

"Your phone," she says. "Your phone."

I sit up, rubbing my eyes. It's not a number I recognize, but I answer anyway.

"Hello? Joey?"

"Hey, Em. It's been a long time."

I feel like all the blood has drained from my body. The familiar, silky voice.

It's Luther Leonard.

"Hey, do me a favor and if you're with anyone, go into another room, okay? This is a private conversation."

Nana is looking at me. *Is it him?* she mouths.

"I'm serious, Em. I have something you want, so pay attention."

I look down at Nana, shake my head, point to the kitchen.

"Okay," I say softly into the phone as I walk. "I'm alone."

I open the door to the garage, flip on the light, close the door behind me.

"I've missed you, Em."

"Do you have him, Luther? Do you know where he is?"

"I do and I do, but I want something in return. You cost me a lot of money, you know? If only you'd let me make that stop. If only you'd done that, so many things might be different right now."

"I'm sorry, Luther. I am. Just tell me where he is."

"I lost an eye because of you, Emmy. And time. I lost time. And money. You *owe* me."

"I don't have any money," I say. "You're a few years too early. My trust fund doesn't happen until I'm twenty-five."

"Funny. Your parents do. You think I don't know about the safe? I spent a lot of time in that house, Emmy. Remember? I spent years in that house, playing with your brother. I know about the safe because we used to pretend to be safecrackers. Tried to figure out the code. It was fun. Things at your house were always fun. Not like at my house."

"We were nice to you," I say. "We were always nice to you."

"I didn't say you weren't. You and me were friends. We played Angry Birds together. But listen, we have to get this show on the road, because honestly? If I have to read one more of your sad-sack posts about your brother on Insta? I will *die.*"

I swallow. Luther saw my posts, which means . . . maybe Joey did, too.

"What is it you want me to do, Luther?"

"I want you to go to the safe, get everything that means money in it, put it in your backpack, and bring it to me. And then you can have Joey back. He's ready to go, I think. He's not cut out for life on the run, you know?"

"I don't . . . I don't know the combination to the safe. I might be able to get some mo—"

"I guess you better figure it out real quick, then," he says, cutting me off. "I know you can figure it out. It's always some stupid thing like a kid's birthday or something. Parents are basic like that. Think of what your dad likes and think hard. They always like special corny shit. And then get in the car and I'll call you back in one hour and tell you where to meet me."

"How do I even know he's with you? Did you hurt him? Lu—"

But the voice that comes through the phone isn't Luther's. It's scratchy and low and sick-sounding, but it's my brother.

"Just get him the stuff, Emmy."

Slow, like he can barely breathe.

"Joey, did he hurt you? Are you okay?" Relief floods through me. He's *alive.*

"Just bring it, and I'll come home."

"Joey—"

"Emmy!" It's Luther again. "Don't even think about calling the cops, either. I'll know. It's just you bringing the stuff. Nobody else."

"I don't have a car. My parents are—"

"Then you better figure out how to get one, Emmy. And ticktock, ticktock, time's wasting."

The phone goes dead.

Nana glances up as I walk back into the room. "Is everything all right, Emory? You look pale as a ghost. Come sit."

Don't let her see me shaking. Don't let her hear my voice trembling.

"It's nothing, Nana. Just my friend. He's . . . having a problem. I might go out for a little while with him, talk it out. Okay?"

Normal voice. Normal face. Pretend like nothing is wrong. Don't make her suspicious. Don't mess this up like I've messed everything else up.

"Well, all right, if you have to. I'll be fine here."

"I'm just going to go change."

Nana turns back to the cooking show and I cross the room like I'm going upstairs, but go to my father's den instead.

In the den, I stand in front of the safe. Basic, Luther said. *Parents are basic.*

This isn't a safe like in old movies, the round combination kind. It's digital. What if there's a mechanism, like if I fail too many times and it sets off an alert to the police or something? I try my birthday, my fingers trembling as they punch the keys. A little screen flashes ERROR.

I can get Joey back, if only I do this. He'll be *home*.

I close my eyes.

Basic.

My father was happy once. I remember. He played with us. Read to us. Built Legos and splashed in the pool. It was only later, after Joey started having problems, that he stayed away more and more. Started smoking in the car after a shift. Made the hospital his home when we needed him here.

But he was still there for me sometimes, late at night, when I had nightmares, when I called out from my bedroom; he sang to me, my head against his chest, his heart thrumming in my heart, just us in the dark.

What would my father choose?

Special corny shit, Luther Leonard said.

My mother said, "That silly song, Neil. My god, I can't believe you sing that to her."

He would laugh. "I can't help it. I love it. It's from my childhood. First song I knew by heart."

My eyes fly open.

Jenny I got your number

Jenny don't change your number

867-5309

There's a beep and a click and I pull the door open.

There are rolls of cash, a watch case, accordion folders full of paper, and the boxes of jewelry my mother stashed in here before Joey came home from Blue Spruce. Because he might be a thief.

It turns out, the thief is me.

*   *   *

"Nana."

She swivels around on the couch.

"I'm leaving now. I'm going to wait for my friend on the porch. Watch the trick-or-treaters."

"Okay, dear. It's nice you're helping your friend."

I say bye and head out the door.

At the end of the front stoop, I pull out my phone. Daniel answers on the first ring.

"Hello, you. Are we going out with pillowcases to score some candy? I might have a funny fake mustache around here somewhere."

"I need you," I say urgently. "I need your car. Like, right now. I can't explain. I don't have time. I just need you to come get me right now."

"Emory, what's going on?" he asks, suddenly serious.

"Just come *right now*." My voice cracks. *"Please."*

When he pulls up, I walk around to the driver's seat and open the door. "Move over," I say. "I'm driving."

"Such attitude," Daniel says. "I like it." He scooches over the gearshift, landing awkwardly in the passenger seat. I throw my backpack on his lap.

"Ow," he says. "What's in here? It's heavy."

"Buckle up," I tell him. I toss him my phone. "And when this rings, put it on speaker, but do not speak, do you understand?"

"Emory, what's happening? You're acting like we're about to rob a bank or something." His voice wavers a little. "I mean, are we? I would have worn my best scarf."

337

"Actually," I say, turning the ignition, "I kind of already did."

I start driving.

"Emory, tell me what this is, right now. I didn't give up a night of candy for weird espionage. I mean, that's cool and all, but you're kind of freaking me out."

"We're going to get Joey," I say.

"What?"

"Luther Leonard. He's with him. He said . . . he said if I brought him stuff, he'd give me Joey. He said he's ready to come home and this is the deal. So here we are." I laugh nervously, glancing over at him.

His face is grim.

"Emory," Daniel says slowly. "We should call the police. This sounds sketchy."

"No," I say sharply. "He said not to do that, or it was off. I *talked* to Joey. He's ready to come back."

"I'm calling the police," Daniel says. "This isn't right. It's not safe. It's . . . it's *weird.*"

"Daniel, if you call the police, I will literally push you out of this car while I'm driving and leave you to die on the side of the road."

"That's a little . . . violent. And here I thought you were just a nice quiet girl with excellent taste in cardigans who likes to gaze out the windows of classrooms with her chin in her hand."

"Daniel." I glance at him, then back at the road. "If you were me, and you had a chance to help somebody you loved, wouldn't you do anything? *Anything* you could?"

"If you don't stop crying, you're going to crash," he offers. "Blurry vision."

I wipe my face with one hand. I didn't even realize I was

crying. I can barely feel anything with all the adrenaline running through my veins.

"And yes," Daniel says quietly. "Yes, I *would* do anything."

"Then shut up and help me."

"What's in the backpack?"

"Money. Jewelry."

Daniel laughs, sharply and high, like a small child. "Oh my god, this really is a heist. I'm going to have a panic attack, right here and now—"

My phone rings. Daniel looks down at his lap, stricken.

"Answer it," I hiss. "But don't say anything. Just put it on speaker."

From the corner of my eye, I can see his hands fumbling, fingers trembling. He holds it up and out for me.

"Hello," I say.

"Emmy," Luther says. "Were you a good kid? You have what I need?"

"Yes," I tell him.

"Excellent. Drive north out of town. Get on Wolf Creek Road. When you see me, you'll see me."

I'm on Main Street. I take a left.

"Wait." I pause. "Wolf Creek Road?"

"That's right, Emmy. Where this whole shitshow started."

He clicks off. Daniel puts the phone back on his lap. "Wolf Creek Road? That's way out there."

"I know," I say, my body flooding with fear.

Snow is coating the windshield, just like rain smeared it that night, making everything hard to see. I turn on the wipers, take a deep breath.

"He's taking me back to where it happened. The accident."

43

THE PINE TREES ARE dusted with snow, the branches hanging out over the road like white hands. I'm not sure exactly what I'm supposed to be looking for. A car? Luther and Joey, standing by the side of the road? What I *do* know, though, is that I'm not supposed to have Daniel because Luther said not to bring anyone.

"You have to get down," I tell Daniel. "Scrunch down there. Take off your jacket and put it over you. I wasn't supposed to bring anybody."

He turns and looks at me. "Oh, well, now is a good time to tell me that, Emory," he says, and I flash him a weak smile. "Thanks so very much for that. As Adam Sandler so succinctly put it in *The Wedding Singer:* 'I could have used that information yesterday!'"

"In a better universe, I would laugh very hard at that, Daniel Wankel."

He thunks the backpack into the backseat and wriggles out of his blazer. "You know, while you've been sitting there stone-faced, yet also weeping, which is weird, and we can talk about that later, I've been having a lot of thoughts. Like, what if he has a *gun*? What if he's not alone? What if I end up hog-tied at the bottom of Wolf Creek? What if—"

"Just get *down*," I snap. I'm starting to get more scared. It's so dark on this road and I'm remembering how twisty it was, and how the rain that night obscured everything. How it sounded like Candy was drowning in her own blood.

We are driving through sheets of white snow and I can barely see anything.

Daniel pushes the passenger seat back a little and squats on the floor, awkwardly trying to throw his jacket over his head. I reach down carefully, keeping my eye on the white road, and try to fix it so it covers him.

I don't think Luther would have a gun. We played Angry Birds together. He was never mean to me at school.

But the thought makes me quiver anyway. People can change. They're onions, like Simon Stanley said. One layer might reveal one thing, but go farther and you might discover another, one that stinks worse than what came before.

I drive slower so I can make sure to spot something in all this white, anything, on the side of the road, in the thickets of trees.

Then I see it. A little kernel of orange light to the right, off a clearing. A cigarette.

And a car farther down the clearing. A figure steps out from under a cape of snowy pine branches, holding the orange glow.

It's Luther. He motions for me to stop. "Over there," he calls. "Park over there."

I move the car. On the passenger seat, my phone buzzes. My dad. *Shit.*

"I can't get that," Daniel whispers under his jacket.

I ignore him, and the phone, and reach back for the backpack. I hold it in my lap for a second, staring at the parked car. It's about twenty feet away, snow layering the trunk, the roof.

He's in there. He has to be in there.

I open the door to Daniel's car slowly. Close it slowly. Walk toward Luther slowly. My sneakers slip in the snow.

He has a black knit cap pulled down low over his forehead. And an eye patch.

"You like it?" he asks. "Makes me look pretty villainous, right? Wanna see?" He makes a show, like he's going to lift up the patch. There are scars crisscrossing his face from where his head went through the windshield.

"Jeremy told me about it," I tell him.

"How is my little brother, anyway?" He takes a drag on his cigarette.

"He misses you."

Luther flicks his cigarette into the snow, shrugs. "Hand it over."

"No," I say, standing my ground, "not until I see Joey."

Luther looks back at the car and whistles.

The door opens and slowly, Joey steps out. Gingerly, like he's sore or sick. He's not wearing the orange Hank's Hoagies shirt anymore, but he has the charcoal-gray hoodie on. I can't see him very well in the darkness.

"Joey," I call, my heart beating fast. "Come here. Come by me."

But he stays where he is, his head down.

"Not until I get the stuff," Luther says.

I hold the backpack tight. It's the only thing I have to do to get Joey back, just hand it over, and then I can take him home, get him help. Do it better this time. I know we'll all do it better this time.

"Emmy, I don't have a lot of time here," Luther says.

He reaches out his hands, and like I'm dreaming, like I'm weightless, I hand it to him. He kneels down and unzips it, starts pawing through it. "Nice, nice," he murmurs. "What was it, anyway?"

"Joey!" I shout. I start walking, but Luther reaches out and grabs my leg with his hand. It's my bad leg and, still kneeling, I slip in the snow, falling next to him.

"What was the combination to the safe? I'm curious."

"It was a song. Just a stupid song my dad sang to me when I was little." I try to wrench my leg out of his grasp, but he tightens his grip.

"Basic. I knew it."

"Joey, get in the car!" I shout. He starts shuffling toward me, but then he stops.

"What's wrong with him?" I ask. "What did you do to him?"

"He's high, Emmy. What do you think?"

I struggle to get up, but he's still holding my leg. "Why did you do it, Luther? He was trying to get clean and then you . . . you just walked in and gave it to him. How could you? He was supposed to be your *friend*."

Luther gazes at me, snow frosting his knit cap. "I did it *because* he's my friend, Emmy. He's the only friend I ever had, you understand? We got each other. I *get* him. You guys never got him. Told him he was stupid and lazy. Broke him down, piece by piece. But I always picked those pieces back up. That's what friends do. I missed him. Weird, right?"

He zips the backpack up with one hand while holding my leg. "I spent a lot of time thinking in juvie, Emmy. A *lot*. In between trying not to get my ass kicked. And you know what? Parents are fucked up. They never really see their kid for who they are. Everything a kid does different, a parent tells them they're *wrong* for it. They have this idea of what a kid *should* be rather than what the kid *is*."

He lets go of my leg and I scramble up, toward Joey. I'll drag him to the car if I have to.

Luther catches my arm. "Not so fast. Not yet. I'm gonna walk back to my car and drive away, okay? He'll stay here. Don't follow me. Don't call the police. I know you have someone in your car, too, but I'll forgive you. Dark woods, a girl alone with a bad guy, I get it. We're even."

He lets go of me, holding out one hand for a second, like I'm a deer that might sprint, like he'll block me if he has to.

"Stay," he warns.

I can feel Joey so much my skin burns. My heart burns. He's still just standing there, not looking at me.

Luther says, "I have to ask, Emmy. Does it freak you out to be here? Because of . . . you know." His voice is eerie.

"It was just over there, remember? Do you think her blood is still in the creek water, with my eye?"

I feel like I might throw up.

Luther laughs.

He walks backward toward his car, watching me. He opens the car door, slings the backpack inside, slides in. Starts the engine. Slowly drives forward, turns, and then drives around my brother, still rooted to his spot.

I start walking, quick. I want to shout Joey's name, but I'm so full of fear and hope that I don't even have room for words.

Luther stops the car.

Joey lifts his head.

Even in the dark, I can see how shadowed his eyes are, how thin his face has gotten in such a short time. Something has morphed inside him. Whatever he did before the accident, whatever he was, he's not even that anymore.

He's something else. He's gone far, into a place I'm not sure I can reach.

"Joey, please."

"It was my idea," he says, so low I can barely hear it over the hum of Luther's engine. "I'm sorry, Emmy. Just go home now."

And then he gets into the car and Luther peels out of the clearing and down Wolf Creek Road, me screaming in the snow after them.

44

M Y FACE IS BURIED in Daniel Wankel's coat and snow covers our heads, our jackets. Last summer I listened to a girl die in these woods, right across the road, as our twisted car lay half in and half out of Wolf Creek, the water burbling around us. I listened to my brother breathing raggedly. The sound of sirens filled my ears and my world was upside down and changed forever. These woods keep taking things from me.

I say that to Daniel.

His arms are around me. "We should go now," he says. "We need to get you home."

I tried as hard as I could to bring my brother home.

And he didn't want to come back.

My dad flings the front door open as soon as we walk up onto the porch.

"My god, where have you been? We've been out of our minds, Emory."

I walk straight past him, past my mother, wringing her hands next to Nana on the couch, and Maddie, still in her puffy winter coat from her flight. They're all shouting at me, but I don't hear them. I grab the key from the file cabinet in the mudroom off the kitchen.

In the garage, I stab the key into the cabinet lock.

Where my mother hid everything. Everything that could hurt Joey, tempt him, break him.

But it was always outside this house, waiting for him to falter.

In the living room, Daniel is murmuring to my dad. They all get quiet when they see me, just standing there.

I hold up the bottle of Vicodin. "I'm going to take some of this now, okay? Because my knee hurts like shit. It has for months. But I'm not going to take three, or four, or twenty. Just two. Because I hurt, and I need something, and because Joey isn't coming back. I saw him. He's not coming back."

I pop two pills and swallow them, dry, and let the bottle fall to the floor.

It is beautiful, like wings, like Joey said. On my bed in my dark room, staring at the ceiling. I feel like warm air. I feel like ocean water on the most beautiful of days, soft and drifting and perfect. Untouchable. I get it now, I do.

How glorious it is to drown.

When I wake up, Maddie is next to me, stroking my cheek.

"Daniel told us everything," she says. "Listen, Mom and Dad don't care. The jewelry, all that. The Oxy at the dance. They're just glad you're safe, okay?"

Her fingers feel nice on my skin.

"That little shit. Luther Leonard," she says. "I could kill him. I might."

I shake my head. "Maddie."

"What?"

"It was Joey's idea. For me to take the jewelry. Not Luther's. He said so."

"*What?*"

"Don't tell Mom and Dad. That would kill them, I think. Right now."

"That was a ballsy move, sister. Robbing your own parents to get your brother back."

I roll away from her. Joey's shadowed face swims before my eyes, so I close them. I just want to sleep.

I don't dream of Candy. I don't dream of Joey. I dream of the ghosties, on the rocky river beach. The way their empty soup cans rattle against pebbles and stones. The way they stack spent cigarettes in small piles and clench together when they sleep, a human mass of sadness trying to stay warm. The way my father and I visit them with offerings, like you do with the dead. Flowers here, a candle there, a can of beans here, a pint of gin there.

My mother holds my forehead. "You aren't warm."

"I don't feel well," I lie. "I feel sick."

I'm still in my clothes from Halloween night, even my jacket. I'm too hot and I'm starting to smell, but I don't care.

"You've missed three days of school, Emory."

I shrug, rolling over and pulling the covers over my head.

"Emory, please."

Emory. Emory. Emory.

Her voice is like knives in my ears.

45

"**G**ET UP." SHARP FINGERS, poking my shoulder through my duvet.

"Get up, or I will stand here and sing 'Seventy-Six Trombones' until your ears bleed, Emory Ward."

Simon Stanley is in my bedroom. Simon Stanley is trying to pull my duvet off me.

I peek up at him. I live in a weird world now, a world where brothers go missing and drama teachers show up in your bedroom.

"That's better. Now, up, up. We're going for a drive. And I'm not taking no for an answer. Also, I'm your teacher, and I will fail you. Wait, we don't have grades. Drama Club is voluntary. Shit. Just get *up*, Emory Ward."

He drives us to the Mill Haven Cemetery in his crappy little Honda ("courtesy of my illustrious teacher's salary, enjoy," he told me when I got in), spread out on the high hill. The pathways are slippery, and he holds on to my elbow as we walk. "Aging is not the most fun thing in the world," he says. "In fact, it downright sucks."

"I don't understand why we're here," I say tiredly. "I really just want to go home."

"We'll just be a little bit. To say hello. To say goodbye," he answers. "I come here quite often to see my mother. She's over here." He points where we should walk.

He bends down, groaning a little, and brushes leaves from her gravestone. He sighs.

"My mother was a pained woman," he says. "My father was an alcoholic. A charming one, like something you'd see in some old black-and-white movie. Always jolly, laughing, a joke when you needed it. But a terrible sadness inside that he tried to drown out. But we loved him. We cleaned up after him, we put him to bed. We called his work when he wouldn't wake up and said he wasn't feeling well. And then he died. One day, he just didn't want to be alive anymore."

"Oh," I say. It kind of sounds like what I've been doing for Joey for years, except for the dying part, but after what I saw in the woods, maybe that's not far off. I breathe in deeply, trying to stuff down the hurt that thought brings me.

Simon Stanley blows on his hands in the cold air.

"My mother was never quite the same. A suicide, especially, does that to you. It was a long, long time ago, and back then, when that happened, people liked to shame you. Said she should have been a better wife, a better woman. This town didn't treat her very well and she changed. Closed herself off from everything. From me. I couldn't wait to get out of here, to tell you the truth. The day after I turned eighteen, I took the first bus to New York City, thirty-seven dollars in my pocket and a suitcase full of dreams, as they say. That's the beauty of youth. You don't need much if you just have a dream."

"I'm getting really cold," I say, wrapping my arms around myself. "And I feel like you're about to break out into song." It's also a little scary, what he's saying about his mom and dad. I like to think of Simon Stanley as permanently cheerful, even though he told us that thing about people being full of layers, like onions, and that you have to peel them back to truly get to know them.

He laughs. "Well, I do teach theater, so that might happen. But shut up and listen anyway.

"I wanted to find my people," he goes on. "Bright lights, big city, dreamers like me. Gay, like me, because that was not a thing in Mill Haven back then, at least not openly. And I had the time of my life, to tell you the truth. I fell in love, I was in plays, I lived in a disgusting walk-up with four other people and we lived on bags of rice and bottles of wine and grew our hair long and fell in and out of love and were broken and alive all at the same time and it was glorious. But then my mother got sick and I came home. To take care of her. She was difficult to the very end, but that's what you do. You get up every day and try to love your people, even if they make it hard. Because what else do you have, in the end."

He tugs on the sleeve of my coat. "Come, let's walk."

We make our way up the path, surrounded by gray stones and marble crypts. Tiny little plaques in the ground, flat, for babies. The air is sharp and cold and part of me wishes I'd brought a scarf. I pull up the collar and hood on my coat.

"Here," Simon says.

I look down.

Candace Pauline MontClair
2002–2020
Our beloved angel, taken too soon
"Who lives, who dies, who tells your story?"

There's a lump in my throat. I wish we hadn't come now. I haven't dreamed of Candy in a while and I don't want to start again. That's part of why I took the Vicodin after seeing Joey at Wolf Creek. Being back there, I felt her in a way I haven't in a while, and I just wanted to make sure that that night, of all nights, I did not have to see her.

"It's from *Hamilton*," Simon tells me. "A song Eliza sings at the end. Candy had a lovely voice."

Simon points across the cemetery. "Shannon Roe is over there, and Wilder Wicks, he's down that little incline. I have a lot of students here. Too many. But I try to visit them often because even though they're gone, they remind me."

"Of what?" I ask.

"To appreciate what I have, in the here and now. To not miss it. Because it might be gone, at any moment. And we can't control that, no matter how hard we try. Whatever the universe is, it's always got the upper hand and we only have this one chance."

He pauses. "What are you going to do with your one wild and precious life?"

"What?"

"It's a line from a poem by Mary Oliver. One of my favorites. I chose New York and shiny lights and rice and heartbreak and then I chose here, and teaching. I made those choices for myself. The thing about adults is, we're always trying to keep kids safe. That's our job. We want you to have a good life and get a good education and be a good person and do good things and sometimes, frankly, we fuck it up. Your childhood is like one long rehearsal, performing a script we wrote for you in the middle of the night that makes no sense to you but seems perfectly coherent to us."

Simon turns to me. "I'm sorry, I get very long-winded sometimes. I just want to say, Emory, that you can't give up.

This is life. It's basic. It's struggle and joy. Sometimes you have one and not the other. My life here was awful. I went away and had joy. And then I came back and had struggle, but I also had some joy from the past to sustain me."

"I don't really understand what you're trying to tell me," I say slowly. "We're surrounded by dead people and I've just heard your life story. It was really cool, don't get me wrong, but I'm kind of feeling empty and alone now and I'm not sure what any of this means."

"Emory Ward, look around you. This is it. This is what everything is going to come to, for everyone, in the end. Do you really want to sit in that bed for the rest of your life doing nothing, only to end up here?"

"No," I say. "I guess not."

"Struggle and joy, Emory," he says. "The most important thing is never to *give up*. And you're giving up before you've even had a chance to begin. I don't care if you come back to school. Do what you want. Spend the rest of your life reading books and working in a doughnut shop, I don't care. But don't give up on yourself. And don't give up on your brother. He's the struggle. He will be for a long time. But somewhere, too, you are going to find joy. And it's not going to happen if you keep hiding under your fifteen-hundred-dollar duvet cover."

46

LIZA SHAKES ME AWAKE roughly.

"Hey," she says loudly. "Up. Now."

I roll over, rubbing my eyes. "What? Why are you here?"

"Are you, just, like, ever coming back to school?"

"Did Simon Stanley send you here?"

"No, but he did tell me he gave you a very inspirational speech. He's pretty proud of it, and yet here you still are," she says. "You kind of look like a zombie. When was the last time you showered?"

I shrug. Everything just . . . aches inside me. Like I've been stripped clean.

"Well, was it all bull?" she asks.

"Was what all bull?"

"What you said in your poem. Remember? Walking down Main Street naked to get Joey back. All that. That stuff that broke my heart."

"It should have. You wrote most of it."

She sighs. "Yes, but you felt it. I could tell when you read it. You really feel it. I'm sorry about the woods. Daniel told me."

"He's gone," I say. "He doesn't want to come back."

"But he might. Sometime. When he's ready. You can't stop hoping."

I put a pillow over my head, but Liza pulls it off.

"Get dressed," she says. "And shower. I'll be waiting outside."

*   *   *

"What if they have guns?" Liza whispers from the backseat.

"I feel like I've been down this road before," Daniel says. He drums his fingers on the steering wheel. "And I still don't like it."

"Sorry," I say.

"This isn't quite as exciting as the Great Jewelry Heist, Emory, but it might get close," he answers, smiling nervously.

We stare at the house, half hidden by evergreen branches. A dirty pink sneaker dangles from a low branch, swaying in the wind.

"I don't have a good feeling about this," Jeremy says. He's huddled in the backseat with Liza.

We're silent.

Then I get out of the car. Because if I don't do this, I am full of bull, like Liza said. And if I don't do this, who will? Joey is me, and I'm Joey. I have to fit us back together somehow. Daniel follows me.

"Do you have a plan," he whispers. "Maybe we should have had a plan."

My heart is beating in my ears. "My plan is to ask where my brother is. That's it. That's all I've got in my toolbox, Daniel."

Really, it looks like any other house you might find set off in the woods. A tricycle half buried in the snow. A rusted swing set off to the side of the house. Smoke puffing from the chimney.

I knock on the door.

"Oh, god," Daniel says. "We're going to die. A tattooed man named Mick is going to open this door and force us into a life of drug servitude and defilement and I didn't survive cancer for this—"

355

A middle-aged woman opens the door.

"Can I help you?" she says. Her voice is pleasant. Her hair is gray. She's plump and wearing a green robe.

I pull out the folded flyer from my pocket. "I'm looking for my brother. This is him. Have you seen him? Maybe he comes here sometimes?"

She looks at me, then Daniel, then around us to the car. "Who said?"

"A boy. Luther Leonard." The lie rolls easily from my mouth.

She's studying my face.

"That little shit cost me a lot of money back in the summer," she says finally. "You know where *he* is?"

"No," I say nervously. "I sure don't."

"Let me see." She slips the flyer with Joey's face from my hand. I can smell the remnants of cooked bacon in the house.

"I know him. Nice kid. Not like some."

"Has he been around recently?"

"A few weeks ago, maybe. I get a lot of traffic. I can't really help more than that. People are in and out."

I fold the flyer back up, my heart sinking.

"You try Frost Bridge?" she asks.

"He's never there," I say.

She nods. "It's getting real cold out. You have to think where they go when it's too cold to be outside. You know, where they won't be bothered. Empty places, stuff like that. I have to get back to work now."

She starts to shut the door.

"Wait," I say.

The door opens again. She puts her hand on her hip.

"If you see him, Joey, the nice kid, could you tell him to please come home?"

"Maybe," she says.

It's out before I can stop it.

"How can you do this?" I whisper. "I mean, all *this,* all these people's lives? *Kids'* lives?"

She looks at me for a long time.

"You do what you have to do," she says finally. "And you live with it. Like I said, I have work to do."

She shuts the door.

Daniel whispers, "The drug dealer in the green bathrobe has to get back to work now. My god, what have you done to my life, Emory Ward?"

We're driving back down Wolf Creek Road when Liza says, "She said empty places?"

"Yeah."

I meet her eyes in the rearview mirror.

She nods.

"The Mill," I say.

Daniel presses the gas.

It isn't hard to get into the Mill. They've cut the chain-link fencing and spread the holes wide. It's easy enough to crawl through. Daniel helps me. Liza helps Jeremy. They've broken the padlocks on the front doors of the main building with bolt cutters. Most of the lower windows are covered in particle-board or are broken, the glass jagged and sharp.

Inside, it's half dark, some morning light peeping through the dusty, high windows.

Daniel whistles.

They are scattered everywhere. Playing cards, holding their hands over small fires in old cans. Someone has strung up a makeshift laundry line. Tents are everywhere.

There are Pup Pop cups from Ziggy's EZ Mart, chewed straws, wads of dirty toilet paper, dirty clothes. Used needles. Just like Frost Bridge. Somewhere, far off in a corner, a baby is crying, and the sound makes my heart hurt.

Jeremy nudges a blanket out of his way.

"Careful," I say. "People live here. This is their home. We have to be respectful."

"Fan out," Liza says. "There are like a hundred people here. He could be anywhere."

I remember the boy at the outpatient center, the one with the holes up and down his arms.

How he said people were weak and drugs filled the holes in their souls. There are a lot of holes in my family's mill right now. Too many to be filled.

The needles are everywhere, mixed in with the garbage on the floor, dirty clothes. People go to the bathroom everywhere.

I walk along rows of people sleeping, peering down at each face. I have the flyer and hold it out, but I don't have much hope. It seems like some people can't even comprehend what I'm asking. Or they don't care, because why should they? I'm no one to them.

Each body I pass, my heart sinks lower and lower. Each time I hold out my flyer and get a shake of the head or an impassive stare, I try not to lose hope.

And then I think about what Simon Stanley said. About the

struggle and the joy. I'm surrounded by all this struggle right now. Joey is going to be a struggle, a long puzzle of a struggle that might take a lifetime to complete, but maybe, just maybe, I can try to turn what I'm seeing right now into the joy part.

I pull out my phone and call my dad, keeping my voice low.

"Emory," my dad says, relieved. "I went to your room, but you weren't there. I'm glad you're out of bed, but could you tell me where you are, please? I don't need two missing children."

"I'm at the Mill," I tell him. "And you should bring Mom."

It's hard to read exactly what's going through my mother's mind as she walks slowly through the Mill. She's gingerly stepping over sleeping bags, stuffed trash bags being used as pillows. The baby is still crying somewhere, an eerie sound that hangs in the air.

"I used to come here all the time when I was little," she says. "It was always so busy and loud and important-sounding in here. So many people, working."

"Mom," I say gently. "We don't need condos in Mill Haven. Someone else can do that."

Daniel and Liza are next to me. Jeremy is off to the side, helping a woman unroll her sleeping bag.

My dad appears, a baby in his arms and a gray-faced teenage girl by his side. The baby. The one who was crying.

"Abigail," he says. "This is Carly. I met her a few months ago when she came into the ER. She ended up having an emergency C-section."

"They cut you open," Carly says matter-of-factly. "It's a bitch."

"The thing is," my dad continues, "Carly was on methadone

while she was pregnant, trying to get better, but when you get a C-section, a doctor prescribes you painkillers. Vicodin. Oxycodone. The very thing Carly was trying to wean herself from. Doctors can't not prescribe that for a patient who's just had major surgery. So recovering mothers are sent back out into the world with the very thing they're addicted to. With very little support at home, and very few skills to cope."

"I came here," Carly says. "It seems okay. Better than where I was. My mom stole my Percocet and said the baby was bothering her."

My mother reaches out and touches the baby's cheek softly.

"Abigail," my dad says. "I don't know where our son is. I'll never stop hoping he comes home and gets help, but right here, right now, we can *do* something. You can build something else that matters in this town. Look around you. These are all versions of Joey. Think of that."

My mother looks at Carly. "I'm sorry about your mother. A girl needs her mother when she has a new baby."

"Mom, you can do this," I say. "Fuck your shoes. Remember?"

My mom is quiet, her face sad as she gazes at the baby, as she looks around at what the history of her family has become.

"I need some time to think," she says slowly. "I just need a little time."

"Okay," I say, grateful. "We can do that."

My father has taken a leave of absence from the hospital. Every few days, three of us, me and my father and Liza, take boxes of canned beans, bags of apples, toilet paper, baby wipes, bottled water, to Frost Bridge and the Mill. I sit to the side while my father talks to the people, taking their histories and temperatures, checking their injuries and illnesses. He cleans up the old needles and gives them new ones. Delivers strips of Suboxone, hands out flyers for the outpatient center.

Because, he tells me, they can't stop doing what hurts them. They can't control it, but he can try to keep them safe while they do what they need to do. Each time we go, there are more of them, but there is never Joey.

At night, after everyone is asleep, I'm still texting him, even though his phone is dead and gone. Even though my words will drift into darkness and silence, they still matter. It still matters to say them, each and every time. Maybe in that alternate universe Daniel talks about, one word, somehow, some way, will reach Joey, wherever he is. A slight murmur in his ear that causes him to look around and think about us. Me.

Come home, I type.

> Please answer me
> Answer me
> Answer me

Joey has been missing for thirty-four days.

47

"THIS IS VERY FESTIVE," Daniel says, surveying Simon Stanley's living room. It's decorated with red-and-green streamers, Christmas lights, and a tiny green tree with silver ornaments in one corner, by the piano. Simon Stanley is plunking out a jazzy song, singing in a wavery voice. It's the end-of-semester party he holds for the Drama Club.

Everything is bright and lovely in this house, but I can't feel it, at least not all of it. Always, now, I feel the fact of Joey's absence inside me, somewhere deep and painful. I shake my head, try to clear my thoughts. Concentrate on Daniel.

"Thanks for coming with me," I say. "I felt like I needed to get out of the house for a bit."

"I wouldn't have missed this for anything," Daniel says. "Theater people are so much more fun than regular people, in my opinion. Maybe I should join Drama Club in the spring."

"I could see you, onstage, *emoting*," I say, smiling at him.

"You look pretty," he says. "The gray cardigan. It suits your eyes."

And there they are, small butterflies in my stomach, flitting around. I don't think I had butterflies with Gage so much as what I now feel like was anxiousness, always afraid I would say the wrong thing and drive him away.

This feels better than that.

"Daniel," I say suddenly.

That girl, the one who came out before at the dance, she's back. I can feel her, and this time what she's going to do is right.

"Do you want to go outside? Get some air?"

"Anything," he says. "Sure."

I grab our coats from the rack by the door and we slip out, Simon still singing. *Nothin' but bluebirds, all day long.*

Daniel hooks his arm in mine as we go down the front steps.

"Cold," he says, looking up at the sky.

"Daniel," I ask. "Can I kiss you?"

His eyes drift to mine.

I hold my breath. Maybe I was wrong. Maybe this isn't what I thought it was. What it might be.

"I've been waiting four months to hear you say that, Emory," he says quietly. "But I've never kissed anyone before. I've only seen it in the movies. And in the hallways at school. I'll do my best, but—"

I pull him to me.

And it doesn't feel like it was with Gage, urgent and scary. Instead, it feels like sinking, very slowly, into a pool of warm light. Soft and perfect.

"Wow," Daniel says slowly. "That . . . damn. The poets were right."

"I think I felt the earth move under my feet," I say.

"The stars are exploding in the sky," he answers. "I'd like to do that again, as soon as possible, like right now."

He's bending his head to mine when my phone pings in my coat pocket.

"Sheesh," Daniel says. "Technology is supposed to make things more convenient, but I'm kind of hating it right now."

I pull out my phone, my hands shaking in the cold, my lips still tingling from the kiss.

Em
It's me Max
I'm at a house in Franklin Township, 3722 Bolton
He's here
Out of it but here
I don't know for how long tho

"Oh my god," I say to Daniel. "It's Max deVos. He knows where Joey is."

My fingers tremble as I text back.

Max, stay there, please please
don't let him leave please

I'll try but get here quick

Daniel takes my phone from me. "Let's go. You can call your parents in the car."

We run, slipping down the icy sidewalk to Daniel's car. We have to sit for a minute, waiting for it to heat up. I call my dad. He picks up on the first ring.

"Emory? Are you all right?"

"Dad, Joey is at a house in Franklin Township. I'm driving there now with Daniel. You and Mom meet us there."

"Your mother got delayed in the city. She was meeting with NewDay to hear their proposal about the Mill. The snow is heavier there. She's waiting it out. Text me the address. And Emory, please drive carefully. The weather."

I hang up, text him the address.

"This could go either way," Daniel says softly, starting the car.

"I know," I say, steeling myself.

Struggle and joy, I tell myself. Like Simon Stanley said. There's struggle and there's joy.

3722 Bolton is a beat-up house at the end of a dead-end street. Max has been texting me the whole drive, letting me know Joey is still there.

Daniel and I sit in the car, looking at the house. My dad isn't here yet.

Here, I text Max.

"Well," Daniel says. "What do you want to do? Should we just . . . walk in?"

Before I can answer, there's a tap at my window. Daniel and I both jump.

It's Max deVos, blowing on his bare hands to keep them warm.

I open the door and get out.

"I was looking for him," he says. "You know, all this time. Different places."

"Thank you," I say. "Max, *thank you.*"

"He doesn't look good, Emmy. He's kind of . . . gone. It's hard to explain. He's in a room in the back with some guys. Don't . . . like, don't make a big deal when you come in, okay? Just act like you came to, you know . . ."

"What?"

"Like, get high. I mean, I'm *not.* I haven't, for a while. But I know how this stuff works, in places like this."

I nod and follow him up the walk to the front door, Daniel behind me.

It's musty inside from cigarette smoke. There are a bunch

of people on a couch in the front room, smoking bowls and watching a movie. A couple of people are sitting on the floor, backs against the wall, zoned out. Daniel holds the back of my coat with his fingers, gently.

Max nods to the people he passes.

I don't know if this is going to be like the movies, where a seedy-looking person jumps out at us and asks us what we want in a threatening voice, but I also know that I've done a lot of things I was scared of lately, and I can handle this. I can handle this because Joey is down this long hallway in a room, very close to me, and I need to get to him, whatever happens.

Max opens the door.

What did I think? That I would walk into a room with people shoving needles in their arms? Vomiting? Guzzling from liters of vodka? Maybe.

But it's just a room with a couch and a huge flat-screen and a couple of guys playing *Apex Legends,* silently, blinking slowly, my brother on the floor, watching.

He doesn't have the gray hoodie anymore and now his hair has grown out so much it covers his large ears. He's got his hands stuffed in the pockets of a worn wool suit coat, the kind old men wear to play chess in the park on a cool day. He's sniffling. He looks drowsy, like at any moment he might fall into a restful, deep sleep.

Max sits on the couch with the other guys, picks up a controller. Daniel hangs back, by the door.

"Hey, Joey," I say softly. My knee aches a little as I bend to sit next to him.

His face drifts to mine. "Emmy. *Emmy.* Oh, no, why are you here? No, *no.*"

He shakes his head back and forth.

"Joey," I say. I slide my hand into his jacket pocket, curl my fingers around his. "It's okay. It's all right."

"I didn't want you to see me like this. Never," he says.

"I don't mind."

"I let you down."

"No," I say firmly. "No. Never."

His fingers, ever so slightly, tighten around mine in his pocket.

"I'm tired," he says.

"Me too."

"I read . . . your stuff. I just want you to know that. Luther showed me."

He starts to cry, his head falling against my shoulder. Inside my jacket pocket, I feel my phone ping. It has to be Dad. He should probably not come into the house. I angle my head to Daniel and then to my pocket. He comes over and bends down, slides the phone out, very easy, like Joey is something that shouldn't be startled. *My dad,* I mouth, shake my head.

Daniel nods, starts texting as he moves back to the doorway.

Joey lifts his head and looks at the flat-screen. "Crypto," he says. "I used to love playing as Crypto, with Luther."

"I remember," I say gently.

There's a long silence.

"I don't know what's *wrong* with me," Joey whispers, his voice ragged. "I just can't stop."

"There's nothing wrong with you," I say. "You . . . need some help, is all."

"I don't . . . I don't know how to live." He sighs deeply, his breath troubled. "Emmy, help me. Oh, god, help me."

"Okay, Joey," I say. "I can do that. I can do that."

I stand up, pulling him gently to his feet, lacing my arm through his. Max gets up from the couch and follows us down the hallway. Joey is heavy against my body. Daniel takes his other arm.

Outside, Dad is waiting at the end of the walkway, in the freezing air, on his phone. He shoves it in his pocket when he sees us.

All the air goes out of Joey when he sees our dad. Daniel and I catch him before he falls.

Dad rushes up to us. "It's all right, son. It's all right now," he says. "I'm here, and I'm not mad. I'm not mad at you, Joe. *I love you.* But let me see if you're all right, okay?"

My dad is crying silently, squinting back his tears as he opens the back door to his car, helps me set Joey inside. He picks up his medical bag from the car floor and starts checking Joey's eyes, his blood pressure. He's talking to him in a smooth, gentle voice. *Do you want help, Joey? Let us help you.* Joey keeps his eyes on my face as he nods slowly.

I feel like I don't want to breathe, because at any moment, any noise, anything at all, could suddenly make Joey come to, run, leave us again.

Daniel is squeezing my hand.

My dad stands up and walks over to us. "He doesn't need the hospital. His vitals are slow but steady. I made some calls before I came. There's an open bed in a facility about three hours from here. Your mother will meet us there."

He takes a deep breath. "Emory, anything could happen on the drive, even when we get there. He may change his mind. And he can. He's an adult. Do you understand that?"

I nod.

"It means if while we're driving and he changes his mind, we might have to let him go. It means even if he agrees to sign himself into the facility, he can still leave at any time, because he's an adult. We just . . ."

He falters. "This isn't a thing we can control, Emory. All we can do is try to help, do you understand?"

I think about when Shadow told me that sometimes it's just the beginning and it will happen again and again. Relapsing. And sometimes it works for a long time, until it doesn't.

It's a very long road without an end. I can see it stretching out before me.

Slowly, I nod again. "I get it, Dad. I get it."

My dad turns back to the car and tucks Joey's legs in, shuts the door, and goes around to the driver's seat. He turns the car on.

Daniel faces me.

"This is good," he says. "Text me what happens. I'll think good thoughts. Good god, you're shaking like a leaf."

He unwraps his scarf and carefully winds it around my neck, tucking the ends into my jacket.

The scar around his neck is long and pinkish, like someone drew a very thin necklace across his skin. I touch it gently. Daniel doesn't flinch.

"It's okay to be afraid," he says. "I have your back."

He kisses me softly, and I walk around the car and open the door.

I fasten my brother's seat belt and then my own. My father turns the car around and drives down Bolton, away from the beat-up house.

"I let you down," Joey says quietly.

My father glances in the rearview.

"I let *you* down, Joey," he says. "I won't do that again."

I think he's sleeping because his eyes have drifted closed, the lights from the highway grainy as they flash by the windows, and I almost don't hear him when he speaks, his voice is so soft.

"I knew, Emmy," he says. "When I saw Max, I knew."

"Knew what, Joey?"

"That he would call you. And I felt grateful. And that's why I stayed. I knew you would come for me. I just wish . . . you didn't have to see me like this, but there's no other way."

"I'll always come for you, Joey."

And I will, forever and ever. I take his hand.

"I wouldn't do this if I wasn't high. I'd never be brave enough if I wasn't fucked up. That's so fucked up and shitty, but it's true. I have to be messed up just to be brave enough to go get better."

He heaves a sigh so large I'm afraid it will break his body apart.

"I don't want to live this life anymore," my brother says.

I pull the scarf up over my mouth so he can't hear me cry.

There's a wheelchair waiting outside Ridgecrest and what looks like a nurse and two counselor-type people in front of huge glass doors. The light from inside is so bright it hurts my eyes to look at it.

My mother is with them. She starts to cry when she sees us pull up.

She doesn't say anything when my dad helps Joey out of the car. She just wraps him in her arms, tightly.

When she's done, one of the counselors, a gentle-looking old man, says, "I'm Barry. Are you ready to go inside, Joe?"

My brother doesn't say anything for a long time. I'm afraid he's going to do what my dad said. Change his mind. Run. Walk away.

"What's going to happen?" he asks.

"We'll get you rested," the counselor says. "In detox for a week or so, then general, and then we'll see. We'll go very slowly, Joe. Does that sound all right to you?"

We wait, my mother gripping my arm.

"Yes," my brother says finally. "But I don't need that." He gestures to the wheelchair.

He begins walking.

We follow my brother into the bright light.

Emory Ward
American Classics
December 21, 2020
The Portrait of a Lady

Dear Mr. Watson,

First, let me start by saying that I understand this is not the paper you wanted me to write. I know what grade I will receive and I'm fine with that. Wait, I don't want to use the word "fine." I've been thinking about that word so much for the past year and a half. How we say we are "fine" when we really aren't. How we use it to accept a situation we don't know how to deal with. "It's fine." When really, in our heads, if you could see, would be these words, scrawled in giant permanent marker: "Help me." I don't want a poor grade, but I also realize that I don't have a lot left in me at this moment in my life and that this paper, as my brother Joey might say, "is what it is."

I first read *The Portrait of a Lady* by Henry James last year, for another class. (Is that cheating if I reread something I read for another class? It can't be, can it, since teachers assign us some of the same books for years on end; remember, I've been reading *The Scarlet Letter* for about four years now. Maybe it's not that we don't want to read it, but that by now, we're *bored* of it. Something for you to think about when you plan the book list for the future.)

Now, as then, I don't know if I fully understand what happens in the novel, but I loved it anyway. Isn't that strange? To love something you can't fully grasp? It isn't even something I can attach one of your required literary terms to. I just felt a sensation while reading it—I felt swept up, transported, enveloped, comforted, even. I *sank* into the book. Isabel Archer is batted about not necessarily by any choice of her own, but by what is expected of her: to conform, to belong, to be married, to take her place as a woman of privilege and intelligence, regardless of her own dreams and wishes. Forces that shaped her life long before she was even born. I guess I identified with that because of who I am in my family, in this town, even this high school. I don't feel like I get to make many choices on my own. They were set out for me before I was even a thought to my parents, polished and gleaming. They were set out for me the moment the first brick was laid for the Mill.

Do you want me to talk about the Mill? I'm sure you've heard that my mother is going to sell the buildings and the land to a nonprofit, instead of a ritzy condo developer. There's going to be a big fight, probably. Zoning things I don't quite understand. It took my mother some time to make this decision and I hope Mill Haven, as a whole, accepts what she's trying to do. Did you know, long ago, that the whole idea behind the Mill, besides money, was also one of benevolence? I think that's a fantastic word, by the way. Build the Mill, the foundry, and fan out, across the town, with dormitories for the workers (who were, in the beginning, farm girls), and then, because the workers needed it, build the school, give them a hospital, a library, houses, and on and on. And when the Mill closed, a part of the town died. The river was dead. It just sat there, for years and years, a ghost at the end of town. If I stand in my brother's attic room, on our hill off Aster Avenue, did you know I can see practically the whole town? All the big houses on our hill, and then down to Main Street, and to the east Polish Town, where the houses are smaller, and the west, where they are smaller still. From my hill, I see everything, and at the very end of it, always, is my beginning: the Mill. I think my mother is grappling with that. How to be benevolent again. But you can't push her; I've learned that. I might be getting ahead of myself, here. But I'm thinking of that word, *benevolence,* a lot. We could all probably be a little more benevolent in life. We all live here, after all. We all share the same mighty good company of the stars at night, and everyone deserves kindness, and survival. Everyone deserves to be seen.

You know who I am. Or you think you do, much like people think they know Isabel in the book. Presumptions based on her appearance, her background. I'm quiet, I like to read, my family has a lot of money, my life will be safe. I am a good and safe girl, is what you probably think, and your job is to guide me through my intellectual development. But (and no offense intended here), as Isabel says in the book, "I don't need the aid of a clever man to teach me how to live. I can find it out for myself." And for better or worse, that's what I'm doing right now.

I think that might have been one of the problems with your book list. You chose that list because those are the books that *you* loved, that *you* know, that *you* think we should read (and also, *Lolita* is completely inappropriate for high school; I don't know why you thought you could sneak it in there. Plus, do not under-estimate Liza Hernandez; if anyone from Mill Haven is going to make their mark in the outside world, it's Liza). You didn't really look at us as individuals when you made that list. You just probably saw us as one seething mass of hormones and cell phones and memes and sighs and boredom that could be whipped into shape with a healthy dose of symbolism, allegory, and foreshadowing, just to name a few of the literary terms you asked us to use in this paper.

Someone I used to know said that's the problem with adults. They just see kids as they *want* them to be, what they *aren't*, and not as they *are*. I think about that all the time. Like, how much time and pain and suf-fering could be eliminated if you just accepted the kid in front of you and stopped trying to fix them. Maybe there is no "fixing." Maybe there is just heartbreak and love and trying to help them stay alive, whatever it takes.

You don't really understand that sometimes we need to see *ourselves* in the books you assign, in all our messiness and confusion. And in case you think I haven't learned anything literary all semester, I can tell you that foreshadowing happened at my kitchen island in August, after my brother Joey returned from rehab and was presented with a list of rules he had to follow if he wanted to stay in our house. He came into the house with his head held high. He left the table with his head down, after reading all he would need to do to be loved. If I'd spoken up then, maybe what happened

375

wouldn't have happened. If I'd told my parents he relapsed, maybe what happened later wouldn't have happened. I don't know for sure. A smart person once told me that life is working against us all the time, inside and outside us, in a thousand different and silent ways that are invisible to us, and there is nothing we can do about it. You just have to do the best you can and go on, and hope for the best.

This is not going to be the thirty-page paper you wanted. I have to get up early in the morning and drive to see my brother at his new rehab center and that is my priority at the moment, not a school assignment. I think that in the grand scheme of things, you should be able to understand this. My brother not dying is my priority at the moment. And other things, too, like me figuring myself out a little (because I am a mess). And I know you are probably rolling your eyes at this moment and thinking that I could have "managed my time" better and that the due date has been on the portal forever, but I really couldn't. I was busy being a liar, a wanton girl, a jewel thief, an enabler, a safecracker, a sister, and a daughter. Someday, I would like to read a book about *that* girl, to be honest. Find it and put it on your future book list, please.

The last thing I will say about *The Portrait of a Lady* is this: yes, it was written by a bespectacled old white man who, of course, controlled everything about Isabel and her interior thoughts, but there's a lot he got right. And I think the thing he got most right is what I really hold dear about this book, and why I will probably read it several times over the course of my life.

It doesn't give you a happy ending, because, well, life doesn't. Not always. Sometimes it might make you wait a long, long time for it, and even then, it might not look like what you'd imagined.

Isabel has an earth-shattering kiss (I have recently had one of these, by the way, but we don't have to go into that right now) with Caspar Goodwood and yes, how nice it would have been for her to go off with Caspar and not go back to Rome and to wrap the book up and give her great love and all that stuff. But she didn't. She went back to Osmond, and to Pansy, and Henry James doesn't really tell us why.

That, to me, is an honest and good way to end a book, because that's exactly what real life is. It can't be summed up tidily and neatly. You don't know what is going to happen, or how things are going to end, and we probably get into way too much trouble trying to plan for and predict these things. But in the end, you just don't know. My brother might come out of rehab and be okay for years and years, or maybe just a day, and then one of those thousand things working against him might win. And then we will be back to a place that's kind of like when Caspar Goodwood says, "You must save what you can of your life," and begin to rebuild, again.

I prefer to think of when Isabel is comforting Ralph as he is dying. Isabel says that pain is not the deepest thing and Ralph agrees, saying that pain always passes (I'm still torn on this, but I'm young, so we'll see).

That's how this book spoke to me. Sometimes your life falls to ash and you sift through, waiting for the pain to pass, looking for the remnants in the debris, something to save, when really all you need is right there, inside you. And next to you, hopefully, in the form of a person. Have you read this book? Do you remember what Ralph says to Isabel as he lies dying?

Love remains.

And that's really all you can hope for, in the end. I have to believe that. I have to hold on to that.

AUTHOR'S NOTE

As Ryleigh notes early in *You'd Be Home Now,* more than twenty million people in the United States struggle with substance abuse each year. If you think that's only adults, think again: that statistic begins with users at age twelve.

Twelve. And that's only what has been documented. Because substance abuse care hasn't been fully integrated into our health care system, the number of kids and adults currently struggling is probably much, much higher.

Right now, a family member or a friend is probably struggling with substance abuse. You might know it. You might not. You may be struggling, and keeping it a secret, because you don't know who to tell, or how, or where to get help. Maybe you feel ashamed, like you've let people down. Maybe you feel, like Joey does in this book, that you're unworthy, or a loser.

You are not any of those things. Not one bit.

Addiction is a disease, plain and simple, and should be treated as such: with care, management, and empathy. It requires hourly, daily, and lifetime diligence. I have been in recovery for nearly thirteen years at this point. It's painful and lonely and there are days when I feel like I can't go on anymore. But I do. I keep walking toward the future, whatever it may be. I have friends and family and a group that I trust who walk this road with me.

When we think about the twenty million people facing

substance abuse disorders, we also have to think about the people not included in that number who are touched by it in some way. Family members. Friends. Schools. Communities. And when you add those people, the number of people affected by addiction rises exponentially. This is not an invisible crisis. It's a public health crisis. It's in your house, your town, your school. It's sitting next to you on the bus. It's in the face of the person who asks you for spare change outside the store. It's the person who does your taxes, polishes your nails, takes your ticket at the movies, or tells you it's time to register for the SATs.

The face of addiction is you and me and everyone.

I chose to write this book not from the point of view of Joey but from that of his sister, Emory. She's watching from the outside as her brother wrestles with addiction. When I visit schools to talk about my books, I often give a writing exercise called "My Biggest Secret." I ask students to write down the biggest secret they've never told anyone on a piece of paper. I don't ask them to read it aloud, because it's a *secret,* after all. When they've written their secret, we talk about using that as the first line of a book and how to answer the questions the secret raises, at which point the secret is no longer a secret: it belongs to fiction, and thus, a story is born.

One afternoon after students had left the school library, I was helping put chairs back into place when I saw a yellow sticky note on the floor. I picked it up.

I love my sister but I hate my sister because she is on drugs. That is all my parents care about, not me. It's like I'm invisible.

I pinned that sticky note to my laptop when writing Emory's story of invisibility. Because when we talk about addiction, we have to talk about collateral damage: the mental health of the kids and adults surrounding the addict. How do you live when your life has been upended by someone else's health crisis? When you feel guilty about wanting to go to a dance, or be kissed, or go away to college, because right next to you, someone else is suffering?

Emory's feeling of invisibility leads her to make some faulty choices, but in the end, it also awakens her to something larger: you have to make a choice to fight to help those you love survive, but you have to fight to let yourself live, too. After all, as Liza tells Emory, "And if you're not, like, solid with *yourself*, how can you help somebody else?"

We need to get solid with ourselves and change the conversation surrounding addiction and mental health from a punitive one of "You did this to yourself" and "You're weak" and "That's not my problem" to one of empathy, compassion, and care. We need to demand full access to care for everyone, not just those lucky enough to have insurance (which is pretty meager for most people here in the US, let's be honest).

Because you know what? There are millions and millions of Joeys and Emorys out there, and they should not be invisible.

They live here, too.

RESOURCES

Al-Anon and Alateen
al-anonuk.org.uk

Alcoholics Anonymous (AA)
alcoholics-anonymous.org.uk

FRANK
talktofrank.com

Narcotics Anonymous (NA)
ukna.org

We Are With You
wearewithyou.org.uk

**The National Association for People Abused
in Childhood (NAPAC)**
napac.org.uk

Smart Recovery: Self-Management and Recovery Training

smartrecovery.org.uk

Families Anonymous

famanon.org.uk

Stonewall

stonewall.org.uk

ACKNOWLEDGMENTS

I had a writing teacher once who told my class that you never really know how to write a book until you reach your eighth book. Gasps and despair filled the small seminar room. After all, most of us were struggling with finishing a draft of what we hoped would be our *first* book. An *eighth* book? That seemed distant and unlikely.

I'm not even close to an eighth book, but I can say *You'd Be Home Now,* my third book, the very one you are holding in your hands right now, was the most difficult for me to figure out how to write (and this is coming from a writer whose previous two books tackled self-harm and grief). It started as the seed of an idea gifted to me by Delacorte publisher Beverly Horowitz: "Why don't you write a contemporary *Our Town* and focus on the opioid epidemic?"

Maybe you've seen a production of *Our Town,* Thornton Wilder's 1938 play about small-town life in Grover's Corners, or perhaps you've seen the 1940 film version. It's a grand and touching story about life and appreciating it while you have it (that's the short version).

I spent a lot of time thinking about the play and the characters and taking notes and musing and wondering how to fold the opioid crisis into this story of what was, in the beginning, a story about a girl, Emory, and a boy, Gage, and the small town of Mill Haven. I tend to overwrite everything in the beginning (Big pharma! A house fire! Robbery!), and it's only with the help of my magnificent editor, Krista Marino, and my agent, Julie Stevenson, that I was able to rein things in and realize the story was really about Emory and her brother, Joey.

So I wrote the story of a quiet girl, the "good one" in her family, who experiences addiction through the struggles of her wild brother, Joey. And I owe all the gratitude in the world to Krista Marino, Lydia Gregovic, and Julie Stevenson for shepherding this book and helping me fine-tune the story of a girl and her brother and the long path they'll walk together. Extra thanks to this trio for agreeing to do virtual meetings with me during a pandemic, when I often couldn't leave the house for days and desperately needed to talk to someone other than my dogs and cats.

As always, I am extremely grateful to everyone at Delacorte Press and Penguin Random House for giving my stories a home: Beverly Horowitz, Barbara Marcus, Judith Haut, Monica Jean, Mary McCue, Kristin Schulz, Kelly McGauley, Mary McCue, Neil Swaab, Elizabeth Ward, and Jenn Inzetta. Thank you for the care you've given to Emory and Joey's story.

Writing is solitary and lonely even at the best of times, so I have enormous gratitude for friends like Janet McNally, Karen McManus, Lygia Day Peñaflor, Shannon Parker, Bonnie-Sue Hitchcock, and Liz Lawson for keeping me on track with gossip, encouragement, tales of yurt life, trapeze adventures, and endless GIFs. And big thanks to my friend Beth, who let me borrow her last name for a character in this book and also went on many a dog walk with me where we talked about everything *but* writing.

And in the interest of full disclosure, I'd also like to thank coffee and *Grey's Anatomy* for being my constant companions while writing *You'd Be Home Now*. (Every writer's process is different!)

ABOUT THE AUTHOR

Kathleen Glasgow is the author of the internationally bestselling novel *Girl in Pieces*, *How to Make Friends with the Dark*, and *You'd Be Home Now*. She is also the co-author of the *New York Times* bestselling teen mystery *The Agathas*. Kathleen lives and writes in Tucson, Arizona.

kathleenglasgowbooks.com
🐦 @kathglasgow
📷 @misskathleenglasgow
♪ @ kathleenglasgow

A heartbreaking, triumphant,
and hopeful story about one girl's battle with self-harm.

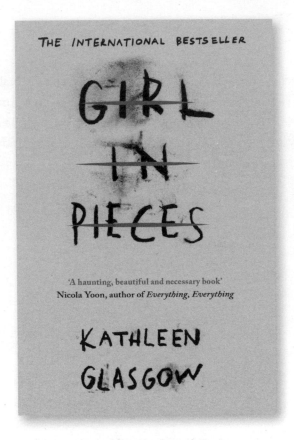

An International Bestseller

"A haunting, beautiful, and necessary book."
Nicola Yoon, author of *Everything, Everything*

"*Girl, Interrupted* meets *Speak*."
Refinery29

The story of an awful, universe-gone-mad-mistake, and one
girl's emotional battle for clarity and forgiveness.

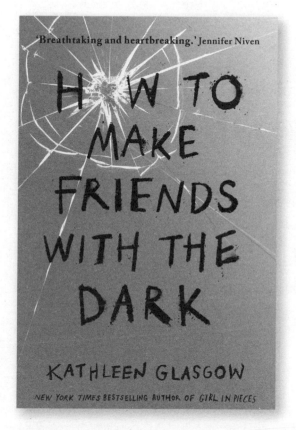

"Breathtaking and heartbreaking, and I loved it with all my heart."
Jennifer Niven, author of *All the Bright Places*

"A rare and powerful novel, *How to Make Friends with the Dark*
dives deep into the heart of grief and healing with honesty,
empathy, and grace."
Karen M. McManus, author of *One of Us Is Lying*

It's the biggest mystery of the summer. The most popular girl in school is dead and everyone's blaming the wrong guy.

"Part Agatha Christie, part Veronica Mars, and completely entertaining."
Karen M. McManus, author of *One of Us Is Lying*

"Full of twists, mysteries, and so much heart, *The Agathas* will keep you up late guessing who-exactly-dunit. Perfect for readers who like their thrillers with an extra dose of fun!"
Erin A. Craig, author of *House of Salt and Sorrows*